"We are friends, a

Reese nodded. "We are.

"Wouldn't you also agree that friends help friends?"

He ran a hand along his jaw. "I would."

"I don't mind if this puts us in close proximity." Callie's bow-shaped lips curved upward. "I enjoy your company."

"I enjoy yours, too." A little too much. And therein lay the problem. Reese really liked Callie. He especially liked this new Callie, the one who dressed in rich, bold colors that made her skin glow and her eyes sparkle.

Her transformation awed him. Her beauty stole his breath.

"If you will give me a chance—" she pulled her hand away from his arm "—I believe I can be of great assistance in your search."

Hadn't he already arrived at that same conclusion? "That is not the point."

"What is the point?"

He couldn't remember.

"I need a day or two to think this through," he said, grasping for any reason to make his exit before he said or did something he couldn't take back.

Renee Ryan
and
Clari Dees

His Most Suitable Bride
&
The Marshal
Meets His Match

LOVE INSPIRED
INSPIRATIONAL ROMANCE

LOVE INSPIRED®

INSPIRATIONAL ROMANCE

ISBN-13: 978-1-335-47439-1

His Most Suitable Bride & The Marshal Meets His Match

Copyright © 2020 by Harlequin Books S.A.

His Most Suitable Bride
First published in 2014. This edition published in 2020.
Copyright © 2014 by Renee Halverson

The Marshal Meets His Match
First published in 2013. This edition published in 2020.
Copyright © 2013 by Clari Dees

This edition published by arrangement with Harlequin Books S.A.

For questions and comments about the quality of this book, please contact us at CustomerService@Harlequin.com.

Love Inspired
22 Adelaide St. West, 40th Floor
Toronto, Ontario M5H 4E3, Canada
www.Harlequin.com

Printed in U.S.A.

CONTENTS

Renee Ryan grew up in a Florida beach town where she learned to surf, sort of. With a degree from FSU, she explored career opportunities at a Florida theme park and a modeling agency and even taught high school economics. She currently lives with her husband in Nebraska, and many have mistaken their overweight cat for a small bear. You may contact Renee at reneeryan.com, on Facebook or on Twitter, @reneeryanbooks.

HIS MOST SUITABLE BRIDE

Renee Ryan

For the Lord does not see as man sees;
for man looks at the outward appearance,
but the Lord looks at the heart.
—*1 Samuel* 16:7

To my amazing, handsome, fabulous husband, Mark.
Because of the love and grace you show me
on a daily basis, writing romance is easy for me.
I just have to look at you and know happily-ever-after
is real. Love you, always and forever.

Chapter One

Denver, Colorado—1895
The Tabor Grand Opera House

Tonight should have ranked among the finest of Callie Mitchell's life. Certainly all the elements were in place. She sat in a box seat, on a plush velvet chair, watching a world-class performance of *Roméo et Juliette*.

Based on William Shakespeare's play, the popular opera consisted of five drama-filled acts with four— *four!*—duets between the main characters.

Callie was supposed be happy.

She *was* happy. Almost. But not quite.

Stifling a sigh, she took her gaze off the drama unfolding on the stage and glanced around. Horace A. W. Tabor had spared no expense in the construction of his opera house. The expert woodwork, elaborate chandelier and vibrant frescos made for a luxurious decor unrivaled by any other theater in Denver.

Perhaps therein lay the problem. Too many sights assaulted Callie, begging her to gawk in openmouthed wonder.

She was entirely too sensible for such a vulgar re-action. After all, she was the more levelheaded of the two Mitchell sisters, the boring one. Everyone said so.

Another sigh worked its way up her throat. Callie only had herself to blame for what people thought of her. She'd deliberately cultivated her uninteresting persona after her shameless act all those years ago when she'd attended school in Boston.

Fortunately, no one in Denver knew just how close she'd come to ruin. God may have forgiven her sin. Callie could not. Nor could she forget and thereby risk repeating the same mistake twice.

She closed her eyes for a moment—just one—and lost herself in the music. The heart-wrenching melody washed over her, each note more superb than the last. An urge to hum told her she was inches away from losing control.

She whipped open her eyes and focused on the woman perched on the chair beside her. A renowned beauty in her day, Beatrix Singletary's golden brown hair held not a speck of gray. And her face barely showed that nearly two decades had passed since Mr. Singletary, now deceased, had won her hand in marriage.

Serving as the widow's companion had come at a time in Callie's life when she'd needed a change and a reason to focus on someone other than herself.

The music hit a crescendo.

Callie turned her attention back to the stage. This time, she did give into a sigh. The doomed Juliette had no idea the pain she would soon suffer because of love.

Callie knew. Oh, how she knew. Not only because of the incident in Boston, but also because of...*him*.

She didn't dare glance in his direction, though he sat directly across the theater, in a box seat mirroring Mrs. Singletary's. *Don't look,* Callie ordered herself.

Do. Not. Look.

She looked.

The breath clogged in her throat. Her heart slammed against her ribs. Reese Bennett Jr. She knew every facet of that strong, handsome face. The full breadth of those wide, muscular shoulders. The dark, intense eyes that were the same rich color as his hair, a shade nearly as black as a raven's feather.

He sat with his father and seemed a little too content for a man recently jilted. Not by Callie. She would never reject an offer of marriage from him. He'd proposed to someone else, and would have married that someone else had the stubborn girl not left town.

The fact that the person in question was Callie's younger, prettier sister was a source of intense distress. Fanny had made a terrible mistake. And the longer she stayed away the harder it would be to rectify her rash decision.

Reese would not stay single for long. Not only was he a successful attorney, but he was also very masculine, so utterly appealing. Any number of women would happily take Fanny's place.

Callie could not allow that to happen. He must remain free of any entanglement until Fanny came to her senses.

Stubborn, headstrong girl. How could she have rejected Reese? He was…so very…wonderful. Callie swallowed. Restrained another sigh. Felt her eyelashes flutter.

As if sensing her watching him, Reese turned his head in her direction.

Their gazes met. Held.

Callie nearly choked on her own breath.

Floodgates of emotion burst open, giving her no time to brace for impact. Sensation after sensation rolled over her. There was something else in the storm of feelings running through her, something truly terrible, a scorching pain in her heart. *He can never be mine.*

The thought itself was beyond inappropriate, perhaps even a betrayal to the sister she adored.

Pressing her lips tightly together, Callie set her hands in her lap and willed away the emotion threatening to take hold of her. A quick, sharp gasp slipped out, anyway.

"Something troubling you, my dear?"

"No, Mrs. Singletary." Callie dragged her gaze away from Reese. Keeping her voice low enough for only the widow to hear, she added, "I… I was simply caught up in the music."

"Ah, yes." The widow swept a glance over the auditorium, stopping a shade too long on the box directly across from them. "Perfectly understandable."

Callie gave her employer a faint smile, praying they were talking about the opera. Surely, she hadn't given herself away.

Thankfully, the widow turned her head back toward the stage and studied the drama unfolding before them. After only a moment, though, she leaned back toward Callie. "I find the music quite lovely, I'd even suggest inspiring. What say you?"

Lovely? Inspiring? Were they watching the same

opera? "Not really. The music is haunting and the story is…so very—" she took a quick, hitching breath of air "—tragic."

"My dear, dear girl." The widow patted her arm in a way that made Callie feel both young and ridiculously naive. At twenty-three, and with *the incident* in her past, she was neither. "One must never focus on the ending when the story has yet to fully begin."

Had the widow not been paying attention? "Mrs. Singletary, we have come to the final moments of the third act. Tybalt is dead. Romeo has been banished for murder. Nothing but misfortune and heartache lies ahead."

"Oh, Callie, you are missing my point entirely. No matter the outcome, we must enjoy each moment of every journey as it comes."

The words were entirely too profound for an evening at the opera, alerting Callie that the widow, in her non-too-subtle way, was encouraging her to relax her serious nature.

It wasn't the first time she'd let Callie know her opinion on the matter. Arguing now would be useless.

"Yes, Mrs. Singletary." Callie inclined her head in a polite nod. "I shall try my best to heed your advice."

"That is all I ask." The widow settled back in her chair, but not before Callie caught a speculative gleam in her eyes.

Oh, this was bad. Very, very bad.

As if to confirm her suspicions, Mrs. Singletary ignored the performance and turned her attention back to the box across the auditorium. She held steady for one beat, two, then continued circling her gaze around the auditorium, stopping at seemingly random spots along the way.

Or, perhaps not so random.

If Callie wasn't mistaken, the widow only paused to consider single, unattached men around Callie's own age before moving on to search out the next section of seats.

Callie wanted to smack her hand over her eyes and groan aloud. Mrs. Singletary was hunting out suitable young men to court her.

Oh, Lord, please, no.

It was no secret the widow considered herself a skilled matchmaker. And why not? She'd made several high-profile matches in the past two years. Her most recent success had been her former companion, Molly Taylor Scott. Callie's closest, dearest friend, Molly was now married to one of Callie's older brothers. And—

No. Oh, no.

Mrs. Singletary *was* attempting to find Callie's one true soul mate. It didn't seem to matter that she'd made it abundantly clear she wanted no part in the widow's matchmaking schemes, either as an accomplice or the object of a pairing.

Callie hadn't made this declaration because she didn't believe in love, or want to be happily settled. She did. So very much. But the one man—the only man—she wanted could never be hers.

If only he hadn't asked another woman to marry him. If only that woman hadn't been Callie's sister, a woman who would come to her senses any day now and ask Reese to take her back.

The third act came to an abrupt, dismal close.

Mrs. Singletary enthusiastically applauded the performance. Callie very much doubted that look of joy on the widow's face had anything to do with the spectacular singing and superior acting.

As soon as the lights came up, Mrs. Singletary rose regally to her feet. "Come along, Callie." A cagey smile played across her lips. "It's time we indulge ourselves in conversation and refreshment."

Callie would rather stay behind. Unfortunately, that particular activity was not in her job description.

Giving in as graciously as possible, she squared her shoulders and followed the widow to the curtained exit of their box seating. Against her better judgment, she glanced over her shoulder and allowed her gaze to find Reese once again.

If only...

Reese remained in his seat during intermission, while his father left to work the crowd in the atrium. He knew he was ignoring his duty. As the new managing senior partner of his family's law firm, Reese should be circulating among the other opera patrons, engaging in small talk with current clients and scouting out potential new ones.

At the very least he should make a point to speak with the firm's most important client, Beatrix Singletary.

Reese couldn't drum up the enthusiasm.

He'd already endured three acts of the ghastly *Roméo et Juliette*. He needed this moment alone to gather the fortitude he would need to suffer through the remaining two acts. He didn't especially dislike opera, not in general, just this particular one. The main characters' senseless behavior struck an unpleasant chord.

The impulsive, reckless actions of youth, the unchecked passion that overwhelmed all common sense and eventually led to needless death, it was all so… familiar.

Reese battled against the fourteen-year-old memories always lurking at the edges of his calm nature. They came stronger tonight, momentarily bringing back the fear. The helplessness. The searing pain of grief he'd vowed never to experience again.

Love was a costly proposition best avoided.

Poised between the pull of the past and a need to push toward a predictable, steady future, he looked out over the nearly empty seating below.

The din of conversation and high-pitched laughter grated on him. He kept his reaction hidden behind a blank stare.

To the outside observer he probably appeared to be enjoying this moment alone. If anyone looked closer, would they sense the dark mood beneath? Would they falsely attribute it to his broken engagement with Fanny Mitchell?

He shifted in his seat, fought off a frown.

He regretted losing Fanny, as one might regret the loss of a good friend. Her erratic behavior had given him pause, though. He'd been so careful in his choice of brides, so meticulous. Fanny had seemed a good fit. Until her sudden change of heart had revealed an inconsistency in her character that Reese had missed originally.

Though unexpected, her actions had saved them both a lifetime of regret.

Enough. Enough thinking. Enough pretending he was enjoying himself. There was nothing keeping him from leaving. He would rather spend his time pouring over legal briefs, anyway. The dry, precise language always managed to restore his tranquility.

Decision made, he stood, turned to go and…

Froze midstep.

He was not alone in the box. Two women had joined him. But when? He hadn't heard them enter. How long had they been standing there, watching him?

The older of the two gave him a slow, significant smile, alerting him that he was staring.

He firmed his expression and opened his mouth to speak.

The widow cut him off before he could begin. "Why, Mr. Bennett, I believe we caught you on your way out."

"You did." He hooked his hands together behind his back. "That's not to say your arrival isn't a pleasant turn of events. Good evening, Mrs. Singletary." He inclined his head in the widow's direction. "You are a vision as always."

He didn't need to catalog her attire to know this to be true. She spared no expense when it came to her clothing and made sure her personal style rivaled any woman in Paris, New York or London. As a result, Beatrix Singletary was undoubtedly the best dressed in all of Denver.

"That is very kind of you to say." She swept her hand in a graceful arc. "I believe you know my companion."

"Of course." Reese continued to look into the widow's eyes another two seconds before turning his attention onto Callie Mitchell.

For a moment, they stared at one another with mutual discomfort. Reese felt the muscles in his back stiffen, and knew his reaction had nothing to do with Callie's personal connection with his former fiancée. He always had this disturbing visceral response to the woman, a woman most looked past in order to focus on her more glamorous sister.

Reese suspected that was exactly what Callie wished people to do.

"Miss Mitchell." Her name came out sounding oddly tortured, even to his own ears. He cleared his throat. "You are looking quite lovely this evening, as well."

"Thank you, Mr. Bennett." Her gaze didn't quite meet his, nor did she make a move to enter the box fully. Shadows still curtained most of her hair and face.

"Mrs. Singletary." He addressed the widow once again, wondering at her sudden arrival. "To what do I owe this honor?"

"The theater is far too full of people milling about, even on the landings between the tiers of box seats." She flicked a wrist in the direction of the curtain behind her. "We thought we might escape the maddening crush and sit with you a moment before the rest of the performance begins."

Odd. The *maddening crush* had never bothered her before. He'd seen her happily mingling amid the largest of crowds. He couldn't help but wonder again at her sudden presence.

"Please, come in and relax, partake in the desserts the Tabor has provided for my father and me tonight."

Gesturing to his right, Reese stepped aside to let the woman pass.

The widow went directly to the small buffet table and studied the offerings. After a moment, she released a weighty sigh. "There are too many choices. Come closer, Callie." She waved the girl forward. "I shall rely on you to fill my plate."

"Yes, Mrs. Singletary." Callie hesitated only a beat before moving, her steps surprisingly graceful for a woman of her height, a mere head shorter than his six feet two inches.

She floated along like a snowflake, slowly, smoothly and icily controlled. Eventually, she emerged from the shadows completely and Reese's heart kicked an extra hard beat.

His stomach knotted with tension.

Did Callie know the way she'd ruthlessly secured her pale blond hair off her face displayed her arresting features in startling detail?

His stomach rolled again.

This was not a new reaction for Reese, nor was it in any way a pleasant sensation. Callie Mitchell disturbed him.

He shook aside the thought, not wishing to dwell on how she made him...*feel.* Yet he could not look away from those sculpted cheekbones, the perfectly bowed lips and green, green eyes the color of summer-fresh leaves.

What a picture Callie Mitchell made. So pretty. So perfectly upright. Not a hair out of place. Not a wrinkle in her gown. An image that didn't completely ring true. The woman was too controlled, too perfectly put together.

Reese sensed she hid something a little wild beneath that measured calm. He'd sensed it from the start of their acquaintance and thus had made a point of avoiding her more often than not.

"Mr. Bennett, how are you enjoying this evening's performance so far?" Mrs. Singletary asked him the question as she sat on a chair beside him, settling her skirts around her with practiced ease. "Do you not find the music lovely?"

"Lovely, no. I find it extremely haunting."

A soft gasp came from Callie's direction.

He ignored the sound, and the woman. "The story itself is far too tragic to be considered enjoyable," he added.

"Isn't that interesting?" The widow reached out her hand and accepted the plate full of tea cakes and chocolates from her companion, who for some reason looked entirely disconcerted. "Callie made those exact observations not twenty minutes ago."

"Indeed." Uncomfortable hearing that he and Callie shared the same opinion, Reese adjusted his stance and deflected the conversation back to the widow. "I believe you were instrumental in bringing this particular troupe of performers to Denver. What do you think of their efforts so far?"

It was the perfect question to ask. The widow set about telling him her precise opinion. In great detail.

Listening with only half an ear, he nodded at all the appropriate places. Out of the corner of his eye, he watched as Callie returned to the buffet table. She contemplated the offerings once again. A delicate frown of concentration spread across her brow.

She huffed out a small frustrated breath. Though

it had taken her no time to decide what to pick out for her employer, she seemed at a loss when it came to filling her own plate.

Reese found himself oddly riveted.

Would she choose a soft, gooey confection? Or something with more substance? Maybe a mixture of both.

He had no idea why it would matter to him. What could her choices possibly mean in the grand scheme of the evening's events?

"Oh, my, Mr. Bennett, that is quite the fierce expression on your face." Mrs. Singletary's voice cut through his thoughts. "I take it you disagree with me."

He silently filed through the widow's last words. "In my opinion, four duets are three too many."

She let out a soft laugh. "You haven't enjoyed one moment of the tonight's production, have you?"

"No."

His brief response seemed to amuse her further. "I see even in matters of entertainment I can count on your candor."

It did not occur to him to be anything less than frank.

"But, truly, are you not pleased with any portion of tonight's performance?"

"Not in the least."

Watching Callie's attempt to make a decision, however, enthralled him to no end.

Mrs. Singletary made a disapproving sound in her throat. "Are you considering leaving the theater early, then?"

"I am."

"I cannot persuade you otherwise?"

He shook his head. "I'm afraid not."

He continued watching Callie hover over the buffet table. She was being so very, very careful and working so very, very hard to pick just the right confections to put on her plate. Her scrupulous process was oddly sweet and utterly adorable and Reese couldn't bear to watch another moment more.

"Pick one of each, Miss Mitchell."

Her responding flinch warned him his suggestion had come out harsher than he'd meant. He softened his voice. "There is no need to be particular. There is plenty to go around."

"I… Yes, thank you."

She began filling her plate with more enthusiasm. Halfway through, though, she looked up and stared briefly into his gaze.

Briefly was enough.

For that single moment, Reese caught a hint of something disturbingly familiar in her eyes, a willingness to push the boundaries when no one was looking. Dangerous, dangerous territory.

He knew he had a split second to make a decision before it was too late, before he forgot who this woman was and that he'd once been engaged to her sister. He could continue staring at Callie, attempting to fight off this unwanted fascination a few seconds more. Or he could turn his back on her.

He turned his back.

There. She was no longer riveting.

Reese was no longer enthralled.

Everything was back as it should be.

Chapter Two

The following morning, Callie woke early, with gritty eyes, a foggy brain and an uneasy heart. The bright August sunlight had yet to filter through the curtains' seams. Considering her gray mood, she preferred the muted dawn light. The events of the previous evening had left her feeling anxious and mildly out of sorts. It was as if her world had been tilted slightly off-kilter and she couldn't seem to regain her balance.

Whenever she found herself in need of comfort, she turned to her Bible. The Psalms especially had a way of putting matters into perspective, her favorite one reminding her to lean on the Lord and not on her own understanding.

Unfortunately, her mind kept wandering back to last night, to Reese. To the time they'd spent in his opera box.

Something had shifted between them, something new and utterly perplexing.

There'd been that awkward moment when he'd leaned forward and urged her to pick one of every dessert on display. His voice had held equal parts kindness and frustration, the odd mix of emotions confusing her even more. So she'd done as he suggested and filled her plate with sweets she had no intention of eating.

After that, he'd turned his back and avoided speaking to her directly for the rest of the intermission.

She'd been relieved. Then filled with despair.

Then relieved all over again.

Sighing, she curled her fingers around her Bible and pressed the book to her heart. Reese was so handsome, and in many ways so familiar, yet she hardly knew him. For all their interactions through the years, they'd never stepped beyond polite pleasantries.

Last night had been no different. Except…

Everything had been different. *Reese* had been different. The way he'd looked her directly in the eyes, as if she mattered, for herself, had left a peculiar feeling in the pit of her stomach.

Had anyone ever told her that she would one day be the center of Reese's attention, even for a few precious moments at the opera, she would have declared them quite mad. He'd barely spared her a glance before last night.

This was getting her nowhere. Callie was reading far too much into his behavior, looking for a hidden meaning where there was none. Now she was running late for breakfast.

She dressed quickly, choosing a basic gray dress and practical, low-heeled ankle boots. She secured her hair with extra pins this morning, smoothing and tugging until every stray curl had been ruthlessly tamed into submission.

Feeling more herself, she went in search of her employer.

She found Mrs. Singletary in the morning room, perusing the *Denver Chronicle,* which was laid out on the table in front of her. Her treasured cat, Lady Macbeth, slumbered in the bright sunbeam at her mistress's feet. A tray with pastries, coffee and two soft-boiled eggs in enameled cups sat untouched beside the newspaper.

"Good morning, Mrs. Singletary."

The widow looked up, frowned. "No, dear, absolutely not."

Callie's feet ground to a halt. "Pardon me?"

"That dress simply will not do." The words were spoken without meanness, but the censure was there all the same.

As if to punctuate her mistress's disapproval, Lady Macbeth cracked open an eye and studied Callie through the narrowed slit. A delicate sniff and she returned to her nap, chin resting lightly on her front paws.

Callie tried not to feel offended. But, really, dismissed by a cat? It was beyond humiliating.

Worse, Mrs. Singletary wasn't through inspecting Callie's attire. "That color is all wrong for you."

Perhaps the dull gray did clash with her skin tone. But no more than it had the other three times she'd worn the dress in Mrs. Singletary's company.

"The fit isn't right, either."

Callie resisted the urge to cinch the black ribbon around her waist tighter. Mrs. Singletary was correct on both points. The color was unflattering and the dress was, indeed, too large. That had rather been the point. Still, the widow's blunt appraisal stung. "I thought you didn't care what I wore."

"Now, see. That is where you went wrong. Of course I care. I care a great deal."

"You've said nothing before." Head down, Callie lowered herself into a chair facing her employer. "I don't understand."

"It's quite simple. You have been in my employ for precisely four weeks since I plucked you out of the Hotel Dupree kitchens where, I might add, your talents were completely underutilized." The widow leaned forward, trapping Callie in her gaze. "You are no longer underpaid kitchen help, but my trusted companion. It's high time you look the part."

Callie carefully placed a napkin in her lap. She should have known this was coming, should have prepared for this eventuality. Mrs. Singletary was the best dressed woman in Denver. Of course she would care what her companion wore.

"We will begin rethinking your wardrobe today."

So soon? "What's the hurry?"

"As I already mentioned, how you dress reflects directly back on me."

Well, yes. Yet Callie couldn't shake the notion that the widow had a different reason for wanting her to dress better.

"Besides—" she smoothed her hand over the newspaper, turned the page with a flick "—one must always be prepared for the unexpected visitor."

Something in the way the woman made this casual remark put Callie immediately on guard. "Are you expecting anyone in particular this morning?"

"No one out of the ordinary, dear." She picked up her spoon and tapped one of the eggs perched in its enameled cup. A perfect series of cracks webbed out in every direction. "Only my attorney."

Callie's heart lurched. "Reese? I mean… Mr. Bennett is coming here?" She swallowed back a gasp of dismay. "Today?"

She wasn't ready to see him again, not yet, not until she could process their odd interaction at the opera last night.

"He will be here this morning, and I should warn you." The widow turned another page of the newspaper. "Now that Mr. Bennett is once again overseeing my business affairs, he will be around quite often, perhaps even daily."

Callie breathed in sharply, the only outward sign of her discomfort. Her brother Garrett had handled the widow's business affairs until he'd married Molly and left town for a position in St. Louis. It stood to reason that Reese, as the senior partner in his firm, would take over in Garrett's absence.

If only her brother hadn't felt the need to strike out on his own, away from family and the prominent Mitchell name. Callie missed him so much. Molly too, nearly as much as she missed Fanny.

Oh, she was still angry at her sister, but this was the first they'd been apart for more than a few days at a time. With only a year separating them in age, they'd done everything together.

Now Fanny was living in Chicago. And Callie was here in Denver working for Mrs. Singletary. Not alone, precisely, but definitely more lonely than she'd ever been in her life.

"Did you hear what I said, dear?"

Callie started. "Er…no."

"I said I want you to change your dress before Mr. Bennett arrives."

Again, she wondered, *why the hurry?* Yet she didn't

feel comfortable enough to ask the question a second time. "Yes, Mrs. Singletary, I'll do so immediately following breakfast."

"Very good. Something in blue would be most preferable." The widow went back to reading the newspaper in silence.

Left alone with her thoughts, Callie picked up her spoon and gave the egg in front of her a good hard whack. The shell exploded into a hundred little pieces.

Pushing the ruined egg aside, she selected a pastry off the tray. As she ate, she silently reviewed the contents of her closet. She didn't own anything in blue. In truth, none of her dresses were any more exciting than what she currently wore.

The green one was the most modern in fit and style. However, the color was a sort of drab olive. Better, she supposed, than gray. Decision made, she brought the pastry to her mouth once again.

"Don't even think about putting on your green dress." The widow made this announcement without bothering to glance up. "The color is horrid on you."

Callie dropped the pastry back to her plate. "Surely, it's not…horrid."

"Horrid."

Trying not to feel insulted, Callie pulled her bottom lip between her teeth and thought a moment. "Perhaps the yellow one with the ivory lace collar?"

"No."

"The soft pink—"

"Not that one, either." At last, Mrs. Singletary removed her attention from the newspaper and looked up. Her unwavering gaze bore into Callie's. "You are far too pretty to hide behind pale, lifeless pastels and neutrals."

As those were the only colors in her closet, Callie frowned. "Which dress would you have me wear?"

"None in your current wardrobe." The widow placed her hand atop Callie's. "Those we will donate to charity."

She jerked upright, working for breath. "But if I give away all my dresses what, then, will I wear?"

A robust smile spread across the widow's lips. "Leave that to me."

"I find this conversation so very strange." She pulled her hand free from beneath Mrs. Singletary's and placed it in her lap. "You've never once said a word about the way I dress."

"We were still getting to know one another. Now we are friends."

Callie widened her eyes. Mrs. Singletary considered her a friend?

"And from one friend to another, you need to make smarter choices in your attire. If I didn't know better, I'd say you were deliberately trying to camouflage your natural beauty."

Callie pressed her hands together in her lap and fought off a strong desire to defend herself. Once she'd attracted the wrong man's attention and barely avoided disgrace. Better to be safe than put herself on display and risk another mistake.

"Finish your breakfast." Mrs. Singletary leaned back. "We have much work to do before Mr. Bennett arrives."

What did Reese have to do with—

Oh, no. Mrs. Singletary couldn't be thinking of making Callie more attractive for Reese. A match between them was… Why, it was impossible.

Tongues would wag all over town.

The potential for scandal made the very idea ridiculous. Reese's business would suffer, along with his reputation. And what about Fanny? Callie would never hurt her sister, not for anything in the world. And especially not over a man.

No, Callie wouldn't dare attract Reese's attention. Yet she couldn't allow anyone else to so, either, not before Fanny returned home and made things right with him.

While it wouldn't be easy seeing Reese and Fanny together again, it would be better than seeing him with someone else. Callie really hoped Fanny would come to her senses soon.

"If you are finished eating, we will begin."

"Begin?"

"Populating your wardrobe with more suitable gowns."

Callie could think of no good reason to refuse her employer. She set her napkin on the table and forced a smile. "I'm at your mercy, Mrs. Singletary."

Thirty minutes later, she stood in the widow's private dressing room, facing a full-length mirror. Two maids hustled about her, securing buttons, fluffing material in one spot, smoothing out wrinkles in another.

The dress was supposedly one of Mrs. Singletary's castoffs. Callie had her suspicions. Who could not want this gorgeous silk creation? The color was that of the Colorado sky, a deep, rich blue that somehow brought out the green in Callie's eyes. The fit was perfection. The silver buttons added just enough elegance without being too much for day wear.

Even with her severe hairstyle, Callie looked beautiful. She *felt* beautiful. But the woman staring back at her from the mirror was not Callie Mitchell. Not anymore.

Never, never again.

"Let's have a look at you." The widow paraded around her, considering her from various angles. "Much better." She nodded her head in approval. "You were born to wear jewel tones."

Once her closet had been filled with nothing but vibrant colors, Callie thought wistfully.

The housekeeper entered the room and announced, "Mr. Bennett has arrived for your meeting, Mrs. Singletary."

"Thank you, Jane. Tell Winston to show him to my office."

"Yes, ma'am." The housekeeper turned to go then caught sight of Callie. Her eyes rounded with shock. "Oh, miss. Look at you. Why, you're positively glowing."

Callie sighed at her reflection. She *was* glowing.

She'd never felt more miserable in her life.

Reese gathered up the contracts he'd brought with him and stuffed them in his leather briefcase. "I'll make the changes you requested and send over the revised versions before the end of business today."

"That will be fine." Mrs. Singletary sat back in her chair, eyeing him closely, her hands primly clasped in her lap.

He'd worked with the woman long enough to know she had more to say. Something he probably wasn't going to like.

When she remained silent, he braced himself and said, "Is there something else I can do for you, Mrs. Singletary?"

"On the contrary, it's something *I* can do for *you*."

He stifled a groan. Despite her unconventional reputation, the widow meant well. She had a kind heart. Her charity work spoke for itself. But she was also considered a matchmaker of the first order. A terrible thought occurred to him. Surely she wasn't thinking of making him her latest victim.

"I'm probably going to regret this, but tell me. What is it you believe I need?"

"A wife."

Reese pulled in a sharp breath and resisted the urge to snap back, to tell her he didn't need—or want—her input on such a personal matter.

She is your most important client, he reminded himself. One he knew well. Her meddling was never malicious and, more often than not, had a way of bringing about good rather than harm. Eventually.

Even if he suggested, oh-so-gently, that she mind her own business, all she would say was that he was her business.

From a certain angle, she would be correct. Everyone in town knew he was her personal attorney. His actions reflected on her.

Still. She was dangerously close to crossing a line. "There are many men my age still unattached."

She smiled at this, looking quite pleased with herself, as if his response was exactly what she'd expected from him. "True. But now that your father has stepped away from daily operations of your firm, it is up to you to ensure Bennett, Bennett and Brand remains the finest in town."

"Agreed."

"A wife will help you achieve that goal."

"I had a bride picked out," he said. "She begged off."

"A blessing in disguise. You and Fanny Mitchell did not suit one another in the least."

He gritted his teeth. "I disagree. We were an excellent match on many levels."

"Not on the most important point. You weren't in love."

No, he hadn't been in love with Fanny. And, as it turned out, she hadn't been in love with him, either. But they'd liked one another, found many things on which to converse. They would have had an amiable, comfortable life together. "Love is not a necessity in marriage."

"It is if you want a happy one."

Again, he disagreed. Happiness was fleeting, like a wave driven and tossed by the wind. Companionship. Friendship. Those were the things that lasted. The things Reese desired most. He also wanted children, a family of his own.

He needed a wife first.

"I am not opposed to getting married," he admitted.

"I'm glad to hear it, because your image needs improving."

He tilted his head, fought off a surge of irritation. "I always comport myself in a manner above reproach."

"Yes, yes." She waved this off with a graceful sweep of her hand. "You are the quintessential man of integrity."

"This is a good reputation to have."

"The very best. But, Mr. Bennett, may I speak plainly?"

He doubted he could stop her. "By all means."

"You are also considered stern and overly rigid."

He blinked. "People think I'm...rigid?"

"I'm afraid so."

He blinked again. Valuing lists and adhering to a tight schedule merely meant he knew how to plan ahead.

"I daresay a wife will soften your image."

"Yes, you alluded to that already. I don't have time to court a woman, especially now that Garrett Mitchell has left the firm."

"Ah, now we're getting somewhere. You see, my good boy—"

"Boy?" He let out a humorless laugh. He'd left his youth behind him a long time ago, the day Miranda had died in his arms. "I'm thirty-two years old and—"

"A very busy man." She beamed at him, as if announcing something he didn't already know. "That, Mr. Bennett, is where I come in. I will assist you in your search for a wife."

He didn't like the idea of this woman meddling in his life. But this was Beatrix Singletary, a determined matchmaker. Now that the notion was in her head, she would persist. Perhaps even go behind his back. He shuddered at the thought. "Define...assist."

"I will find your one true soul mate."

He'd already found her, when he was eighteen years old. "I'm not looking for a love match."

"Now, Mr. Bennett—"

"I am firm on this point."

She titled her head at an angle, her thoughts whirling in her gaze. She wasn't going to let the matter drop. "Perhaps if you explained why you don't wish to fall in love—"

"If I allow you to help me…" Was he really considering this? "I will expect you to adhere to my rules."

"That goes without saying."

Nevertheless, it needed to be said. "I mean it. Attempt to do things your way, or act on my behalf without my knowledge, and we're done."

"I understand completely."

Did she? Time would tell.

"I will draw up a list of the most important qualities I want in my future bride." Giving her specific requirements appeared the best way to retain control of the situation. "You will stick to the list."

"Mr. Bennett." She looked up at the ceiling and sighed dramatically. "Finding a suitable woman for you to marry cannot be approached with studied calculation."

He stood. "Then I will bid you good day."

"Now, now." The widow sprang to her feet with less grace than usual. "Let's not be hasty."

He paused, eyebrows lifted.

"Oh, very well." She puffed out her cheeks. "Draw up your list, if you must. I will look it over and see what I can do."

"Very good." He made his way to the door.

The widow joined him halfway across the room. "You will not regret putting me in charge of your bride hunt."

He offered a bland smile. "We shall see."

A tentative knock on the door had him turning at the sound.

"Come in," Mrs. Singletary called out in a cheerful voice.

The doorknob twisted. The hinges creaked. And then…

Callie Mitchell popped her head through the open slit, only her head, not any other part of her body. *Odd.* "You wanted me to let you know when it was noon."

"Yes. Thank you, Callie. But my dear, there is no cause for you to hover in the hallway. Join us."

Giving her no time to argue, the widow reached around the door and pulled her companion into the room. For several beats, the two women stared at one another. It was one of those silences far more eloquent than words. Clearly something had put them at odds.

Finally, Callie floated deeper into the room. She caught sight of him and froze. "G-good afternoon, Mr. Bennett."

He gave her a curt nod. "Miss Mitchell."

Breaking eye contact, she reached down to pick up the large tabby cat threading around her skirts like a black-and-white ribbon. Despite the added weight in her arms, she stood perfectly straight, her spine as unbending as a board, her lips pressed in a flat line.

While she held completely still, and silent, he took the opportunity to study her more closely. She'd pinned back her hair too tightly again. And the dull gray of her dress made her look almost sickly. All she needed was a pair of spectacles perched on the bridge of her nose to complete the masquerade of a spinster twice her age.

Reese's lips twisted in annoyance.

Callie Mitchell was deliberately masking her beauty. A gorgeous swan draped in ugly duckling's clothing. And she was doing so on purpose. But why?

Why did the woman wish to make herself unattractive?

What was she hiding?

Chapter Three

Callie held Lady Macbeth tightly against her for two equally important reasons. The first was so the cat could serve as a kind of furry shield between her and Reese. The other was a bit more practical. Holding the overweight animal gave Callie something to do with her hands.

Oh, but she desperately wanted to reach up and smooth her palm over her hair, to tuck away any stray curls. The gesture would only reveal her nervousness.

No one could know how anxious she felt in Reese's company, least of all the man himself.

But, really, why was he watching her so intently?

His unwavering focus made her beyond uncomfortable, slightly breathless. Perhaps a little afraid.

Not of him—never of him—but of herself. Of what she might do if he continued looking at her like…like *that*. His eyes practically bore into her, as though she was a puzzle that needed solving. That if he looked long enough and hard enough he could uncover her secrets.

She shivered at the prospect. He could never know the terrible mistake she'd made in Boston.

If only he wasn't standing so close, Callie might have a better chance of regaining her composure. She could smell his familiar scent, a pleasant mixture of books and leather and some woodsy spice all his own.

The man should not smell so good. The result left her poised in stunned immobility. And badly wanting to fidget.

At least he seemed equally uncomfortable. He was as self-possessed as ever, but also appeared wary. Of her? Possibly.

Probably.

No doubt her being Fanny's sister accounted for Reese's discomfort. But there was something else, too, something much more disquieting than their connection through his ex-fiancée.

"Mr. Bennett." Mrs. Singletary's voice broke through the tension hanging in the air. "Was there anything else you wished to discuss before you depart for your office?"

Jerking slightly at the question, he turned to face the widow directly. "No. Our business is sufficiently concluded."

"I assume I can expect your list by this afternoon."

He pinched the bridge of his nose. "I will work on it later today, as soon as I've revised the contracts."

"That will be acceptable."

Tucking his leather briefcase under his arm, he squared his shoulders. "Good day, Mrs. Singletary." He nodded in Callie's direction. "Miss Mitchell, always a pleasure."

His stilted tone said otherwise.

Callie didn't know whether to laugh or cry as she watched him leave the room. The moment he stepped into the hallway and shut the door behind him with a determined snap, she set Lady Macbeth back on the floor.

The cat waddled over to her mistress, pawing at the widow's skirt. Mrs. Singletary ignored the animal and fixed a scowl on Callie.

She winced. "Is something the matter, Mrs. Singletary?"

Fists jammed on her hips, the widow circled Callie, her gaze narrowing over the dress she wore. "I am waiting for an explanation."

Callie feigned ignorance. "I'm sure I don't know what you mean."

"You are an impertinent, headstrong young woman, Callie Mitchell." Although she attempted a stern tone, the widow's lips twitched, as if fighting back a smile. "If you didn't remind me so much of myself I would be seriously displeased with you right now."

"Your disappointment would be no less than I deserve."

The widow's smile came fully now. "Indeed."

"So you are not angry with me?"

"I should be, but no."

Best not to push the subject, Callie decided.

"Cook has several questions about the menu for Friday evening." Callie moved casually through the room, running her fingers along a stack of books on the shelving to her left. "She seems to be confused as to how many guests will be attending. I told her twelve. She thought it was only ten."

"Cook is right. You are wrong." The widow wagged

a finger at her. "And that was a wonderful attempt at distracting me, but it won't work."

"It was worth a try," she muttered.

"You changed back into that ugly gray dress, and I want to know why."

"It's not ugly. It's just—"

"Dismal, drab, *dreary*. All three apply equally."

Yes, she supposed they did. "I was going to say respectable."

"I thought I made myself clear." Mrs. Singletary circled her again, clicking her tongue as she made a second, slower pass. "You were supposed to remain in the blue dress all day."

"It needed several alterations."

"Not even one."

Callie pressed her lips together, but refrained from responding. What could she say, anyway? That she felt too pretty in the dress? That would only encourage the woman in her efforts to update her style.

"At the risk of being redundant, and I do so hate to be redundant, I will say it again. The way you dress reflects directly back on me."

"I know, Mrs. Singletary. But my goal is to blend in with the crowd, not stand out." She attempted a smile. "It would be unseemly of me to attract attention away from you."

"That's utter nonsense. With the right clothing and hairstyle you would, I think, be a great beauty, even more attractive than your sister."

Callie felt panic gnawing at her, tearing at her composure. No one was more beautiful than Fanny. "Please don't say such a thing."

After *the incident* in Boston, Callie had made sure

her sister outshone all others, including Callie. Especially Callie. She'd chosen Fanny's dresses and steered her toward the proper hairstyles to set off her unusual amber eyes and doll-like features.

How she missed her sister. As the only two girls in a house full of brothers they'd grown up with a special bond between them. They'd had their share of arguments through the years, the majority following Fanny's broken engagement. Nevertheless, Fanny was Callie's favorite person in the world. She missed her so much she thought she might weep.

As if sensing her fragile state, Mrs. Singletary pulled Callie to a chair and urged her to sit with gentle pressure on her shoulders. "Why do you insist on playing down your assets?" Her gaze softened, her tone warmed. "When there are so many to highlight?"

"Scripture teaches us that we are not to focus on external adornment." Callie lifted her chin. "The Lord doesn't look at outward appearances but what is in our heart."

Could she sound any more pompous, prudish and self-righteous? The moral high ground was a dangerous place for a woman like her...with her sordid past.

"I'll not deny God doesn't look at the things we humans look at. But Scripture also teaches that we are not to hide our light under a bushel. And, Callie, my dear, you are the very essence of light."

Simon had said something similar to Callie when they'd first met at a theater production of *As You Like It*. His leading-man good looks and smooth, practiced words had turned her head. Only when it was too late had she discovered his declarations of love held no substance. He'd been playing a role with her, merely acting a part as he did on the stage.

As a result, she carried the shame of her foolishness with her every minute of every day. "There's nothing special about me. I am a very ordinary woman."

"Now that's just false humility." Mrs. Singletary all but stomped her foot in outrage. "You are anything but ordinary. I never want to hear you say such a thing again."

Callie bristled.

Mrs. Singletary laid a gentle hand on Callie's shoulder, her gaze holding her eyes with deep sincerity. "You are a beautiful child of God, never think otherwise."

What a lovely thing to say. How she adored this woman. Mrs. Singletary had come into Callie's life when she'd been at her lowest, when the three most important people in her life had left her without a backward glance.

She could have returned to her family's ranch. But she couldn't see herself there anymore.

She couldn't see herself anywhere.

Where do I belong, Lord?

"Tell me, dear, why do you hide your true self from the world? What are you afraid of?"

If the widow knew what Callie had done, she would dismiss her on the spot. Mrs. Singletary may have a reputation for being unconventional in business matters. But she was an upright, faithful Christian woman who lived a blameless life. She would expect nothing less of her companion.

"I asked you a question." The words were spoken as gently as if she was speaking to a hurting child.

She knew Mrs. Singletary meant well. The widow only wanted to help, but Callie hesitated still, fearful of relaxing her guard and thereby spilling the entire story.

Her foolishness was not something she wanted to revisit, ever. The gullible belief that she was the most important woman in a man's eyes had nearly been her ruin. How foolish she'd been, falling for the famous actor's ploy. But Simon had only wanted her as a temporary substitute, until he could marry the woman he truly loved.

"I dress this way because it is respectable." *Too late,* an ugly voice in her head whispered. *It is far too late to regain respectability now.*

"What happened to you? What terrible trauma did you suffer that has made you afraid to embrace who you really are?"

"You…you wouldn't understand."

"You might be surprised." The widow closed her hand over Callie's. "I have my share of secrets and I've certainly made mistakes in my day. You'll find no judgment from me, no condemnation. You can tell me anything."

"I… I…wouldn't know where to start." That was certainly true. "It's complicated."

"Now I understand. The cause was a man."

"Yes." The cost of admitting that was so great tears welled in Callie's eyes. She stiffened her spine, refusing to allow even one to fall.

"However he betrayed you—"

"I didn't say he betrayed me."

"You didn't have to."

As if sensing her distress, Lady Macbeth hopped

on her lap. Callie hugged the animal close, burying her nose in the thick, silky fur.

In much the same way she would pet the cat, Mrs. Singletary ran a hand over Callie's hair. "Whoever he was, he didn't deserve you."

Callie lifted her head, felt the burn of tears in her throat and dropped her face back to the cat's neck.

"There is a man out there just for you," the widow said. "He will love you and care for you. Even the most mundane details of your life will matter to him. He is out there, Callie, and I will find him for you. I promise."

"No, Mrs. Singletary." Callie's voice hitched over the words. "Please, don't try to match me with anyone. I—" *Give her a reason. Any will do, even the truth.* "I... I'm not ready."

Crouching in front of her, the widow waited for her to look into her eyes. She studied Callie's face longer than was comfortable, her eyes searching, boring in as if she could read the very secrets of her soul. "No, perhaps you aren't ready," she decided at last. "Not yet. But you will be soon."

Reese went straight to his office after leaving Mrs. Singletary's home and shut the door behind him. He needed privacy, craved it as badly as air.

He laid out the contracts on his mahogany desk and began reviewing the changes he'd scribbled along the margins. He lost himself in the process, managing to focus for several hours before his mind wandered back to his morning meeting across town.

What had he been thinking? Agreeing to allow Beatrix Singletary to help him find a suitable bride?

He blamed the weak moment on the melancholy he'd been unable to shake since his disastrous evening at the opera.

Now he was stuck.

If he cried off from their agreement at this point, Mrs. Singletary would only continue her quest without his assistance. He'd seen her do it before. Several times, in fact. She wouldn't rest until she had him happily married off.

Reese wasn't opposed to getting married again. But he'd already had his chance at happiness. It had slipped away like water through splayed fingers. A split second had been all it took. One unseen root in the ground and Miranda's horse had gone down hard, landing on top of her after the initial tumble, crushing her delicate body.

Reese had spent the next three days at her bedside, holding her in his arms even as it tore at his heart to watch her life slip away one strangled breath at a time.

Shutting his eyes against the memory, Reese drew in a slow breath of air. He would never love again. Not because he didn't want to, but because he didn't know how to go at it half measure. He'd learned during his brief marriage to Miranda that he was a man who felt too much, gave too much, needed too much in return. Unspeakable pain accompanied such uninhibited emotion.

Thus, he would insist the widow keep to their agreement, and only suggest women who met his specific requirements.

With that in mind, he pulled out a fresh piece of paper and began constructing his list. He came up with seven items, the number of completion.

Fitting.

A familiar, rapid *knock, knock, knock* had him folding the list and setting it aside. "Enter."

The door swung open and his father's broad shoulders filled the gap. Other than the graying at the temples and the slightly leaner frame, it was like looking into a mirror and seeing himself twenty-five years from now.

As always, Reese Sr. got straight to the point. "I need to speak with you immediately."

Unsure what he heard in the other man's tone, Reese pushed away from his desk. "Of course."

He started to rise.

His father stopped him with a hand in the air. "Don't stand on my account."

Reese settled back in his chair.

Face pinched, his father strode through the room, then flattened his palms on Reese's desk and leaned forward. "I'm worried about you, son."

"There's no need to be."

"You left the theater abruptly last night." He searched Reese's face. "I need to assure myself you are well."

"I had contracts that required my final review."

"That wasn't the reason you left early." Pushing back, the older man stood tall. "I haven't seen that look on your face since…"

He hesitated, seeming to rethink what he'd been about to say.

"Since when?"

"Since Miranda's accident."

Reese's stomach took a hard roll. They never spoke of Miranda, or the accident that had taken her away from him. Now, after last night at the opera, Reese couldn't stop thinking of her, or how he'd sat at her bedside, willing her to stay alive, begging her to come back to him, praying for God to intervene.

She'd woken but briefly, said his name in a soft, wheezing whisper and then died in his arms.

She'd been eighteen years old. He the same age. They'd had only one month of happiness together. Thirty days.

Not enough.

And yet, far too much. He knew exactly what happiness looked like, felt like and, more important, how quickly it could be taken away.

"I don't wish to speak of Miranda."

"You can't run from the past."

He had every intention of trying. "Was there anything else you wanted to discuss with me? Something important?"

"This is important."

Reese said nothing.

His father came to stand next to him. "You need to get married again. I think it will help you."

Was the man in collusion with Beatrix Singletary? Impossible. Though they were polite with one another on most occasions, the two rarely saw eye-to-eye on most subjects. "I attempted to marry again, but—"

"You chose the wrong girl."

Although he'd come to realize that himself, his father's quick response gave Reese pause. "I believed you liked Fanny. You've been friends with her parents for years. If I remember correctly, which I do, you said you would welcome a match between myself and Cyrus Mitchell's daughter."

"I meant the other one. There is substance to Callie Mitchell, something far more interesting than most see when they first meet her. I thought you agreed."

His heart gave a few thick beats in his chest. Oh, Reese agreed there was much lurking beneath Callie's sensible exterior—a wild, perhaps even passionate streak that, if unleashed, could possibly lead to a life of recklessness.

He knew far too well how that ended.

A tap on the doorjamb heralded Reese's law clerk. A thin young man with regular features and an eager smile, Julian Summers was detail-oriented and thus invaluable to the firm. "Mrs. Singletary's companion is here to see you, Mr. Bennett."

His father lifted an ironic eyebrow.

Ignoring this, Reese stood and circled around his desk. "Send her in, Julian."

"Yes, sir."

A handful of seconds after the clerk disappeared in the hallway, Callie appeared, head high, spine ramrod-stiff, chin at a perfect ninety-degree angle with the floor. At the sight of her, Reese went hot all over, the inexplicable sensation similar to a burst of anger.

She was the same woman she'd always been. Yet, not. The past few hours had produced a remarkable transformation. Her cheeks had gained color. Her eyes sparkled.

Her skin glowed.

Simply because she no longer wore that gray shapeless garment from this morning but a blue silk dress that complemented her lean, lithe figure and brought out the green in her eyes.

The effect was devastating. Disconcerting.

Any words of greeting vanished from his mind.

There was something unreal about Callie now, something vulnerable and highly appealing. The impact of her beauty nearly flattened him.

Confounded by his reaction to a simple change of clothes, he blinked at her. "Miss Mitchell, I..." His brain emptied of all thought. Why was she here, looking like a fairy-tale princess? "That is, I wasn't expecting you."

She shifted from one foot to the other, then snapped her shoulders back. Ah, there she was. The Callie Mitchell he knew. "Mrs. Singletary sent me to pick up a package you were to have ready for her this afternoon."

He couldn't think of what package she meant. He remained silent so long his father cleared his throat.

Still, Reese couldn't make his mind work properly.

"Well, if it isn't Callie Mitchell." His father shoved around him. "How are you, my dear?"

"Mr. Bennett." She hurried to him, reaching out her hands to clasp his in greeting. "What a wonderful surprise to see you here today."

He smiled broadly. "You are utterly captivating."

Her face brightened at the compliment. "What a sweet thing to say."

"Only the truth, my dear. Only the truth."

Until this moment, Reese had forgotten how well his father and Callie got along. Watching the two interact so easily, their heads bent at similar angles, he found himself stewing in an unpleasant rush of...

Jealousy?

Absurd. Reese couldn't be jealous of his own father. And yet, he had to take slow, measured breaths to prevent himself from walking over to the pair, shoving his father aside and insisting Callie pay attention to him. Only him. As if he was some sort of spoiled, selfish child with no manners or common sense.

He managed to avoid stooping quite that low. "Callie." He barked out her name. "A word, please, in private."

One stilted sentence and Reese had crossed several unimaginable lines.

His father's responding grin spoke volumes. As did Callie's reaction. Had she stiffened at the familiar use of her name? Or because of the inappropriate request itself?

Reese wasn't sure he wanted to find out. But he made no attempt to retract his words. This conversation had been coming on for some time.

No turning back now.

Chapter Four

Years of practiced restraint kept Callie from gasping at Reese's request. But…but…*glory.* He'd just asked to speak with her. Alone.

She couldn't think why.

And that, Callie decided, was the primary source of her distress. Her shoulders wanted to bunch. Her knees threatened to give way beneath her. But she remained perfectly still.

Perfectly.

Still.

No easy task. Not with Reese looking at her with all that intensity. He was so focused on her she had a sudden, irrational urge to rush out of his office without a backward glance.

Callie had never been one to run from a difficult conversation. She would not start now.

Still, Reese's command, spoken so abruptly, was out of character. Why would he wish to speak with her, *alone?*

Seeking a clue—any would do—she slid a covert glance over his face. His chin jerked, very faintly, a sure sign that he'd shocked even himself with his words.

"Well, then." A corner of the elder Mr. Bennett's mouth curled upward. "I believe that's my cue to depart."

Callie started. She'd forgotten Reese's father still held her hands. Had he noticed the faint tremor in her fingers?

"There's no need to leave so soon," she said on an exhale. Even to her own ears, her voice sounded exceptionally calm, almost detached, with the emotional depth of a stone. *Perfect.* "I'm sure whatever your son has to say can be expressed in front of you."

She hoped.

"Perhaps. But alas, I have another appointment calling me away." With a fatherly smile, he gave her hands a quick squeeze before releasing her. "It was a pleasure running in to you, my dear. We must make this a more common occurrence."

The kindness in his voice, as much as the sentiment itself, calmed her nerves considerably.

"Oh, yes, Mr. Bennett." She managed to get both sides of her mouth to lift in a responding smile. "That would be lovely, indeed."

She'd always felt comfortable around this man, as though he was a second father. Callie desperately wanted him to stay but couldn't think of a reason why he should, other than to beg him to serve as a shield between her and his son.

Callie Mitchell was made of sterner stuff.

"Reese." Mr. Bennett gave his son a short nod. "We will continue our discussion another time."

A muscle knotted in Reese's jaw as he returned his father's nod with one of his own.

Another smile in Callie's direction and the elder Mr. Bennett quit the room.

She remained precisely where she stood, twisting the handle of her reticule between her fingers. She hated this anxious, almost panicky sensation spreading through her. Unfortunately, it couldn't be helped. Simply standing in the same room with Reese caused her anxiety.

She should not be here, alone with him.

She wanted to be nowhere else.

Time slowed. The moment grew thick with tension, the silence between them so heavy that Callie could hear their individual breathing.

"I don't think this is a wise idea, Mr. Bennett," she said, mostly to herself, and meaning it with all her heart.

"Callie." His lips flattened in a grim line. "At this juncture in our acquaintance, perhaps it's time you called me Reese."

She looked at him blankly, absently noting the way sunlight from the window emphasized the dark, rich brown of his eyes, the color of freshly brewed coffee. "Oh. But I—"

"I insist." His tone was both gentle and firm.

A dangerous pang snatched at her heart and the rebellious part of her thought, *Well, why not, we've known one another for years?*

"If you insist." She lifted her chin a fraction higher. "Then, yes, I should very much like to call you Reese."

His name came from low in her throat, and sounded really quite wonderful, as if she'd been meant to say his name, just that way, all her life.

She sighed. "Was that all you wished to say to me?"

"No." He rubbed a hand across his forehead. "Forgive me for not getting to the point sooner. I've spent the majority of the afternoon pouring over legal briefs and my mind is still half on the pages."

His confession softened her guard and Callie found herself feeling a moment of deep affection for this man. "My brother is much the same way," she said. "After a long day of pouring over contracts, Garrett is the worst conversationalist imaginable."

Reese visibly relaxed at this. "Then you understand my abruptness earlier."

"Indeed I do."

A shadow of a smile played across his lips.

Callie responded in kind.

For that one moment, everything felt right between them, comfortable even, a solidarity that went beyond words.

But then...

Reese's brow creased in thought. His brow often creased in thought, she realized, rather liking the result. The studious look made him appear half as stern as usual, twice as appealing. And so very, very handsome.

"You mentioned that Mrs. Singletary sent you over to retrieve a package from me." His brows pulled tighter together, making him appear more confused than thoughtful. "Do you know what package she meant?"

"She didn't give me any details." Callie tried to shrug off her own bafflement. "She merely said that you would be expecting me before the end of business today."

Frowning now, he glanced at his desk.

Callie followed the direction of his gaze, but saw no package, only several piles of papers, a cup of writing utensils, countless ledgers of assorted sizes and an ink pot.

"She must have meant the revised contracts." Making a sound deep in his throat, Reese moved around to the other side of his desk. Instead of reaching for one of the larger stacks, he placed his hand over a single piece of paper. Folded from top to bottom, it looked more like a letter than a legal brief.

Shaking his head, he muttered something under his breath. Callie didn't catch all of what he said, but she thought she might have heard something about *meddlesome, interfering woman*.

"Mr. Bennett… I mean, Reese," she amended when he looked up sharply. "Is something the matter?"

He drummed his fingers atop the letter. "No." He drew in a slow, careful breath. "Everything is in order."

His tone said otherwise.

"You are certain?"

For a span of three breaths, he said nothing, merely held her gaze. Then, he gave a single nod of his head. "Yes."

He looked back down at his desk, reached out and stuffed one of the smaller stacks into a leather satchel.

He started to flip over the lid then paused.

His gaze shifted to where the folded piece of paper still sat. A moment's hesitation and, with a swift move, he picked up the letter and placed that inside the satchel, as well.

His lips were twisted at a wry angle as he came back around his desk. "Here you are. The *package* Mrs. Singletary sent you to retrieve."

"Thank you."

Their fingers briefly touched as he transferred the satchel into her care. Callie smothered a gasp as her heartbeat picked up speed. Her mouth went dry.

Every muscle in her body tensed.

Her strong, inexplicable, tangible reaction over a light brush of their hands mortified her.

Hiding her reaction beneath lowered lashes, she turned to go.

Reese's voice stopped her at the threshold of his office. "Callie."

She paused, looked over her shoulder. "Yes?"

"I still have more to say to you."

Glory. That sounded ominous.

His footsteps struck the wood floor as he approached her from behind. Closer. Closer. He reached around her, grabbed the door as if to shut it, then quickly dropped his hand and stepped back.

Callie felt a cold rush of air sweep over her.

"I prefer not to speak to your back."

She turned around to face him.

He leaned toward her, a mere fraction closer. "I wanted to tell you…" His words trailed off as he considered her through slightly narrowed eyes. "That is, have a nice day."

Have a nice day? Reese had asked her to face him so he could tell her to *have a nice day?*

Perplexed, she gave up all pretense of control and gaped at the confounding man. If she was wise, she would turn around again and walk out the door. After, of course, she issued the same nonsensical platitude he'd just given her.

Or…

She could be a little more daring. She could tap in to the woman she'd been long ago, before a secret scandal had nearly ruined her.

"No, Reese." She took a step toward him. "I will not have a nice day."

A single, winged eyebrow lifted in surprise. "I beg your pardon?"

"I have five brothers," she said in way of explanation. "Three older and two younger."

Now both eyebrows rose.

It was a very intimidating look. Dark, brooding, slightly dangerous. Most women would be cowed. Callie was not. "I know precisely when a man is skirting around the truth."

"Did you just call me out for lying?"

At the sound of his masculine outrage, mutiny swept through her, making her bolder than she'd been in a very long time.

"Take it however you will. But I'm not leaving this office until you tell me exactly why you really asked to speak with me—" she closed the distance between them and pinned him with her gaze "—and why you requested to do so in private."

Reese's chest felt odd. His pulse quickened in his veins. His throat tightened. All because this woman, a woman he'd known for years, had morphed into a completely different creature than the docile, overly polite, levelheaded wallflower she presented to the world.

The transformation had nothing to do with the clothes she wore. And everything to do with the woman herself.

Proud and defiant now, her unwavering gaze locked with his. She was clearly waiting for him to explain himself, to tell her why he'd requested a private word with her.

He couldn't remember why. He could barely organize his thoughts beyond the shocked realization that the woman leaning toward him with a fierce scowl on her face was a total stranger.

Callie Mitchell usually drifted along the edges of most rooms, never drawing attention to herself, never making waves. At the moment, that woman was nowhere to be found.

On the surface, she'd changed nothing but her dress. Yet now, Reese saw the woman beneath the dull facade. A little wilder, a tad more dangerous, exciting and—

"Reese?"

He'd been staring too long.

He opened his mouth, then shut it again as several voices rang out from the hallway. Not wanting an audience, Reese reached to take Callie's arm. He dropped his hand before making contact. Touching her would be a terrible idea.

The worst of all terrible ideas.

He motioned her deeper into the office with a nod of his head. He did not, however, close the door behind her.

There was privacy. And then there was *privacy*.

"Please, Callie, take a seat." He indicated the set of chairs facing his desk.

She nodded, moving through the room with exaggerated dignity, her steps graceful yet carefully monitored.

Always so controlled, he thought, always hiding behind a veil of self-possession and restraint.

How well he understood.

The realization they had that in common left him vaguely disturbed.

Her posture perfectly precise, she lowered into the

burgundy wing-back chair facing his desk and placed the leather satchel upon her lap.

After a moment of consideration, Reese chose to sit in the empty chair beside her.

She twisted her hands together. With all emotion stripped from her face, she nearly fooled him into thinking she was completely self-possessed. But her gaze didn't quite meet his, landing instead on a spot just above his right eye.

She was nervous.

Good to know he wasn't the only one feeling uneasy.

Now that he had Callie alone—mostly—Reese wasn't sure how to broach the subject that had been nagging at him for some time now. The direct approach was always best. "We need to discuss the changing nature of our relationship."

Her gaze whipped to his and he noted, somewhat inappropriately, that her eyelashes were long, utterly enchanting and several shades darker than her blond hair.

"I wasn't aware we had a relationship."

He frowned at her stiff tone, oddly irritated. "Of course we do." It was awkward and uncomfortable, to be sure, but existed all the same. "Now that you are Mrs. Singletary's companion and I'm once again in charge of her business affairs, our paths will cross often."

"Mrs. Singletary said the same thing just this morning." She lowered her gaze. "My brother taking that job in St. Louis has brought changes to all our lives."

Before now, Reese hadn't considered what the attorney's departure meant to Callie. "You miss him."

"Very much." She worked her hands together in her lap. "I also miss his wife, Molly."

"You two were close?"

"Oh, yes, but not as close as—" She broke off, drew her bottom lip between her teeth, looked everywhere but at him.

"Not as close as you and Fanny," he finished for her.

She nodded. "I miss her most of all."

"That's understandable. You are sisters. And the only two girls in a large family of boys." As an only child he couldn't imagine what it was like to grow up with that many siblings.

"Fanny has always been my best friend." She met his gaze. "We are only eleven months apart in age."

Reese tried not to show his surprise, even as he did a mental calculation. He'd always thought Callie far older than her sister. Her maturity, her outer calm and, of course, her ability to control her emotions were qualities he attributed to a woman far older than twenty-three.

"Have you heard from your sister recently?"

"No." She shook her head. "She has not answered any of my letters."

"None of them?"

"Not one."

That didn't sound like Fanny. Then again, Reese was quickly discovering how little he knew the woman he'd once asked to marry him. How could she not respond to her only sister's letters?

No wonder Callie appeared upset.

For a shocking moment, he yearned to pull her to him and offer what comfort he could. The urge grew stronger when she wiped secretly at her eyes and snuffled a little. The sound was practically nonexistent, and all the more sorrowful because of the restraint.

"It must be difficult," he said, lowering his voice, "not hearing from your own sister."

"You have no idea." Her expression closed, but not before he'd seen the hint of misery in her eyes. "Have *you* heard from Fanny?"

"Of course not."

"I'm so sorry. Oh, Reese, truly I am." Her hand reached out and touched his forearm, as if she thought he needed comforting. "Do not despair. Fanny will come to her senses."

Surely, Callie didn't think he pined for her sister. For a long, tense moment, he watched her watching him with silent sympathy in her gaze.

This, he realized, was why he'd wanted to speak with her alone. They needed to sort a few things out between them. "I miss your sister, it's true. But not, perhaps, as you may think." He held her gaze, willing her to hear him. "I miss our friendship."

"Your...*friendship?*" She said the word as if tasting something foul. "Surely Fanny was more to you than a friend."

"At the time I issued my proposal I believed your sister and I were well suited." An error in judgment he didn't plan to repeat. Perhaps relying on Mrs. Singletary's help would turn out to be a wise move, after all. What better way to avoid pursuing the wrong woman again? "I'm not what your sister wants."

Callie flinched as though he'd slapped her. "Don't say that. Of course you are. Fanny is going to change her mind, I just know it. And then you and she can—"

"No, we can't."

"But—" she blinked at him "—if she came home, wouldn't you want to—"

"I would not." He touched her hand briefly, once again willing her to hear him. *Really* hear him. "Even if Fanny changed her mind tomorrow, I would not want her back."

Her eyes widened. Then narrowed. "Why are you telling me this?"

"Because I want you to understand that your sister and I will never marry." He waited for her to process his words, then added, "However, just because I'm not engaged to Fanny anymore doesn't mean you and I can't be…"

He paused, not sure how to continue. Even taking into account the personal nature of their discussion, this conversation shouldn't be so difficult. He was a trained lawyer, skilled at putting words together to make his case.

"I don't want there to be any more awkwardness between us," he said, finally coming to the crux of the matter.

Her shoulders relaxed, just a hair, but enough for Reese to know she agreed with him. "I don't want that, either," she said, her eyes shining bright with emotion.

Those eyes, he thought, they were unlike any he'd ever seen. How had he never noticed the various shades of green in them, or the way thin, gold flecks wove through the irises?

He cleared his throat, a gesture he seemed to repeat far too often in this woman's company.

"I believe you and I could be friends." He told himself this was a necessary step if they were going to be in daily contact. But, strangely, conversely, Reese actually wanted to be friends with this woman. "I'm willing to make the attempt."

Pulling her bottom lip between her teeth, she angled her head. "You used the same term to describe your relationship with Fanny. Are you not concerned what she will think when she comes home and discovers we have become…friends?"

"No."

Something flickered in Callie's eyes. A hint of rebellion? Reluctant interest, perhaps? Either way, he had her attention. And now that he did, he decided to change tactics. "Don't tell me you're afraid."

She abruptly straightened in her chair, her spine as stiff as a fire poker, her face free of expression. "What a ridiculous notion."

Oh, this woman was a true master of control.

Some long-remembered defiant streak of his own wanted to ruffle her calm. Just how far could he push this woman, Reese wondered?

He leaned in closer still. "Are you afraid of me, Callie?"

She sniffed with obvious disdain. *"Never."*

He'd known that would be her response. Somehow, he'd known. "Then we start anew, right now."

"You are very persistent."

She had no idea how persistent he could be when he wanted something. He wanted Callie's friendship. More than he should.

More than was wise.

"What do you say?" Feeling more alive than he had in years, he reached out his hand. "Shall we be friends?"

She took his hand, her smile bolder than before and far too appealing. "I'd like nothing better than to forge a friendship with you… *Reese.*"

The way she said his name, low and challenging, filled his chest with dread.

What have I just done?

Chapter Five

Callie exited Reese's office with purposeful strides. She could feel his gaze following her progress down the never-ending hallway that eventually spilled into the law firm's reception area. Was he watching her departure with a smile on his face?

Or did he wear that thoughtful expression she found so appealing? She desperately wanted to glance over her shoulder to discover what was in his eyes.

She kept walking, ensuring each step was precisely placed on the floor, one foot in front of the other. Heel, toe. Heel, toe. No doubt she appeared in complete control of herself.

Not true.

Her emotions, though carefully contained, were in tatters.

Why had she agreed to Reese's suggestion they become friends? It was true, she'd once wished to grow close to the man, perhaps even build something more than a friendship. But that had been before he'd asked Fanny to marry him.

Even if he hadn't offered for her sister's hand, Callie

was still, well, Callie. A staid, boring, sensible woman who took no missteps, crossed no lines and certainly never befriended a man outside her own family.

Feeling confused—and so very much alone—she attempted to pray for discernment as she exited Bennett, Bennett and Brand law offices. A cool, gentle breeze caressed her face yet the words wouldn't come, even in the privacy of her own mind. She hunched her shoulders forward and approached the waiting carriage.

"Ready to go, Miss Callie?"

"Yes, Horace." She smiled at Mrs. Singletary's coach driver. "I am more than ready to go home."

Home. Where was home for her now? Mrs. Singletary's massive house? The Mitchell family ranch?

Neither place called to her.

Another reason she felt so alone. *Lord, where do I belong?*

Heavyhearted, she climbed into the carriage. Once settled on the butter-soft calfskin seat, she rapped on the ceiling. The coach jerked into motion. Tightly coiled springs absorbed most of the dips and bumps along the twenty-minute journey across town. So smooth was the ride, in fact, that Callie relaxed her head against the plush squabs.

Her thoughts, however, continued to race.

Why—oh, why—had she reacted to Reese's obvious attempt to bait her? She may be many things, but afraid? Rarely. And yet…

She was afraid now. Afraid of what came next. Afraid of what a friendship between her and Reese really meant, especially with regard to Fanny.

A sob worked its way up her throat. For an instant,

just one beat of her heart, she wished her sister would stay away forever. In the most hidden part of Callie's soul the truth rang loud.

She resented Fanny.

The girl had callously walked away from a good man, the best of them all. And now, that same man claimed he wanted to be Callie's friend. *Her friend.*

No good would come from such an arrangement. Friendship often blossomed into something deeper. That was her greatest fear. Because, deep down, it was her greatest hope.

In fresh agony, she pressed her fingertips to her temples and squeezed her eyes closed. She knew the situation was hopeless—truly, she did—yet Callie yearned for something more. Something life-altering.

Something…she had no business wishing for herself.

The carriage drew to an abrupt halt, splintering the rest of her thoughts.

Thankful for the interruption, Callie gathered up the leather briefcase Reese had given her and exited the carriage.

Mrs. Singletary's butler met her just inside the front entryway. Thick threads of silver encroached on the few strands of red left in his hair, but his broad, welcoming smile erased at least ten years from his heavily lined face.

"Mrs. Singletary is waiting for you in her office, Miss Callie."

"Thank you, Winston." She smiled in return. "I'll head right up."

Leather satchel pressed against her heart, she hurried through the cavernous foyer with its mile-high ceiling and expensive chandelier hanging from the center. The sound of her heels striking the imported marble reverberated off the richly decorated walls, where several oil paintings had been strategically placed for optimal effect.

Callie paused at the foot of the winding stairwell to study a portrait of Mrs. Singletary and her now-deceased husband. The two looked beyond happy, yet Callie felt a wave of sadness as she stared into their smiling faces. They'd had so little time together, barely fifteen years.

It should have been a lifetime.

Sighing, she mounted the stairs. At the second-floor landing, she turned left and worked her way through the labyrinth of corridors that led to the back of the house.

As the butler had indicated, she found Mrs. Singletary in her office. The widow sat in an overstuffed chair, her head bent over a book, Lady Macbeth spread out on her lap.

Neither the widow nor the cat noticed Callie's arrival. She took the opportunity to glance around the room. Bold afternoon sunlight spread across the empty stone hearth. Bookshelves lined three of the other four walls. The scent of leather and old book bindings mingled with Mrs. Singletary's perfume, a pleasant mix of lavender and roses and…

Callie was stalling, though she couldn't think why.

Squaring her shoulders, she rapped lightly on the doorjamb to gain the widow's attention.

Mrs. Singletary lifted her head. "Ah, there you are." She closed her book and set it on the small, round table beside her. "I trust everything went according to plan."

What an odd choice of words.

Had Mrs. Singletary sent her to Bennett, Bennett and Brand with a purpose other than business in mind?

That would certainly explain Reese's initial confusion when she'd stepped into his office.

Then again…

He'd been buried in legal briefs prior to her arrival. He'd recovered quickly enough and had given Callie a stack of papers to deliver to her employer. Papers contained in the leather case she now held.

Papers his law clerk could have delivered, as was usually the case.

Realizing her steps had slowed to a halt Callie resumed moving through the room and addressed her suspicions directly. "I must say, Mr. Bennett appeared genuinely surprised to see me in his office this afternoon."

The words had barely left her lips when her foot caught on the fringe of an area rug and she momentarily lost her balance. In her attempt to right herself, the satchel flew from her hands.

Callie rushed forward. Unfortunately, she picked up the briefcase at the wrong end and the contents spilled out.

"Oh, oh, no." She dropped to her knees and began picking up the papers as quickly as possible. "I'm not usually so clumsy."

"Not to worry, dear." Mrs. Singletary set her cat on the ottoman in front of her chair and joined Callie on the floor. "These things happen."

Together, they retrieved the strewn papers, placing them in a neat pile between them.

Lady Macbeth, evidently sensing a new game afoot,

leaped on top of the stack and plopped her hindquarters down with regal feline arrogance.

The widow laughed. "Move aside, my lady." She playfully poked the cat in her ribs. "You are in the way."

The animal lowered to her belly, her challenging glint all but daring her mistress to protest.

Wrinkling her nose at the ornery animal, Callie carefully pulled papers out from beneath the furry belly. She managed to free the bulk of them when the cat gazed at the new pile with narrow-eyed intent.

"Oh, no, you don't." Callie snatched the papers off the floor and placed them on the table next to Mrs. Singletary's book.

Not to be deterred, Lady Macbeth went after a lone sheet of paper that had landed farther away than the rest.

Callie moved a shade quicker. "Ha."

Swishing her tail in hard, jerky movements, Lady Macbeth stalked off toward the fireplace and curled up on a rug near the grate.

Disaster averted, Callie glanced down at the paper in her hand. There was a crease in the center of the page, indicating it had once been folded in two. Written in a bold, masculine hand, it looked like a record of some kind, an inventory perhaps.

The third item from the top captured her notice. *Loves children, wants several, at least five but no more than seven.*

Beneath that odd statement, was another equally confusing entry. *Must come from a good family and value strong family ties.*

Callie frowned.

What sort of list had she stumbled upon?

Realizing it was none of her business, she pressed the paper into Mrs. Singletary's hand. "This is clearly meant for your eyes only."

The widow scanned the page in silence then clicked her tongue in obvious disapproval. "That man is going to be my greatest challenge yet."

At the genuine look of concern in the woman's eyes, Callie angled her head. "Is there anything I can do to help?"

"No, dear. Not just yet." The widow refolded the paper at the crease and stowed the list inside a pocket of her skirt. "Later, perhaps, once I consider my options I shall ask for your assistance."

Her tone invited no further questions.

Shrugging, Callie searched the floor around her. She found no more papers. "I think that's all of them." She sat back on her heels. "Would you like me to leave you alone to review the papers Mr. Bennett sent over?"

"Thank you, yes." The widow nodded distractedly. "I would."

"I'll be in my room if you need me." Callie rose to her feet and started for the door.

"Not so fast, dear."

She pivoted back around. "Yes, ma'am?"

"About the dinner party I have planned for Friday evening. I should like for you to attend as one of my guests."

Callie felt her eyes widen in surprise. In the entire month of her employment she'd attended precisely none of Mrs. Singletary's parties. "You wish for me to attend as…as…a guest?"

"Quite so." The widow moved back to her chair and

began spreading the legal papers across her lap. "Now that one of the ladies has declined her invitation there will be too many men at the table. Your presence will even out the numbers."

A hard ball of dread knotted in Callie's stomach. In the span of a single day, her perfectly ordered world was no longer so perfectly ordered. But aside from direct insubordination, Callie saw no other recourse than to agree to her employer's request.

"If you wish for me to attend your party then, of course, Mrs. Singletary, I am happy to oblige."

"Excellent. Most excellent, indeed."

Again, Callie turned to go.

Again, Mrs. Singletary called her back. "One final thing, dear."

Forcing a bright smile, she turned around a second time, preparing herself for the rest. Because, of course, there was more. With Mrs. Singletary, there was always more. "Yes?"

"When Jane and I were cleaning out my closet this afternoon we came across a lovely crimson gown that isn't at all the right color for my complexion. The garment would look far better on, say, a woman with—" the widow pinned Callie with a sly look "—flaxen hair."

Wasn't that convenient? Callie thought miserably, as she smoothed her hand over her light blond *flaxen* hair.

"I should like for you to wear the dress to the party."

Naturally.

Callie suppressed a sigh as yet another piece of her ordered life chipped away.

"Is there anything else?" she dared to ask.

"That is all for now." The widow waved a hand in dismissal. "You may go."

This time, when Callie stepped into the hallway, the widow did not protest her departure. A small victory, to be sure. But with the day she'd had, one she gladly claimed.

Despite a last-minute meeting with a new client, and the onset of a thundershower just as he left the office, Reese arrived at Mrs. Singletary's home a full minute before the designated time on the invitation. He stepped into the foyer at the precise moment a large grandfather clock began chiming the top of the hour.

As he shook off the rain, the widow's butler stepped forward and took his hat. "Good evening, Mr. Bennett."

"Good evening, Winston." Reese handed over his coat and gloves next. "Am I the first to arrive?"

"You are one of the last," the butler informed him. "The other guests are gathered in the blue sitting room."

"Has my father arrived yet?"

"Twenty minutes ago."

Twenty minutes? That seemed pointlessly early. Or had Reese read the invitation incorrectly? There was one way to find out. "Thank you, Winston. I'll see myself to the parlor."

"Very good, sir."

Reese spared a glance at the grandfather clock in the foyer as he passed through. One minute past seven. Certain he'd arrived on time, he nonetheless increased his pace.

Pausing at the threshold of the blue parlor, he took

in the scene. He counted eight people in the room already.

His father stood near the fireplace, where a small fire had been lit presumably to offset the damp air created by the rain. A woman in a red dress stood beside Reese Bennett Sr., her back to the entrance. The deep, rich color of her gown offset her pale blond hair. Twisted in one of those complicated modern styles with several tendrils hanging loose, the resulting effect was mesmerizing.

For reasons unknown, Reese could do nothing but stare in muted wonder. Then, the woman turned slightly, presenting her profile.

His stomach rolled in recognition.

His throat burned. His heart pounded. And still he continued staring, unable to look away. With the firelight brazing off her, Callie Mitchell reminded him of a lighthouse beacon calling to him, promising shelter, as if he was a floundering sailor in need of a safe haven.

Reese swallowed.

He should not be this aware of Callie. Nonetheless, a new alertness spread through him, a sublime shift from one state of being to another.

The sensation rocked him to the core.

He looked away, at last searching the large parlor.

Mrs. Singletary held court on the opposite end of the room, conversing with one of Denver's most prominent couples, Alexander and Polly Ferguson.

Their son Marshall, a man Reese considered a friend, was here tonight as well, as were two of his seven sisters. The young women were beautiful, with golden, light brown hair and cornflower-blue eyes. He was certain he'd met them previously but at the moment found it difficult to tell them apart. To further complicate matters, he recalled each of their names started with the letter *P.*

Both were in their early twenties and fit most of his requirements for a bride.

Were they here for his benefit?

If so, the widow had wasted no time in presenting viable candidates for his consideration.

One of the Ferguson daughters turned her big blue eyes in his direction. Reese shoved away from the door.

He'd barely taken two steps when Mrs. Singletary broke away from Mr. and Mrs. Ferguson. "Ah, Mr. Bennett, you have finally arrived."

At the hint of censure in her tone, he wondered again if he'd gotten the time of tonight's gathering wrong. "I hope I haven't kept everyone waiting."

"Not at all." Smiling now, the widow closed the distance between them and captured both of his hands. "There is still one more guest yet to arrive."

On cue, there was a movement in the doorway.

"And here he is now." The widow stepped away from Reese to greet her final guest. "Mr. Hawkins. I'm so glad you could join us this evening."

Jonathon Hawkins was back in town?

This was the first time the new owner of the Hotel Dupree had returned to Denver since he'd offered Fanny a job in his Chicago hotel.

By giving her the position, Hawkins had provided Reese's ex-fiancée a way to start over when the gossip over the broken engagement had become unbearable. Reese held no animosity toward the man. Fanny's departure had been good for everyone.

Callie seemed to have a differing opinion.

Her shoulders stiffened, her chin lifted at a haughty angle. When her gaze locked on Hawkins, the barely banked anger in her eyes gave Reese a moment of hesitation. He'd always sensed Callie had a large capacity for emotion hidden deep within her. But this…

He almost felt sorry for the hotelier.

Then he remembered his last conversation with Callie and her admission to missing her sister greatly.

With this new piece of information, he absorbed her reaction with a wave of sympathy. She and her sister had been close. He wanted to go to Callie, to offer his support, but her expression shuttered closed, as if she'd turned off a switch. A slow blink, a quick steadying breath and she wrenched her attention away from Hawkins.

Her wandering gaze landed on Reese.

A moment of silent understanding passed between them. Everything in him softened, relaxed, urging him to continue in her direction. His father said something and she turned to answer.

The moment was lost. And Reese immediately came to his senses.

Tonight wasn't about Callie Mitchell. The Ferguson daughters had likely been invited here for his benefit as the first candidates in his bride search. Reese would be remiss not to take this opportunity to know them better.

Chapter Six

Bracketed by Reese's father on her left and Marshall Ferguson on her right, Callie would be hard-pressed to find more pleasant dinner companions. Both men held a vast knowledge on a variety of topics and never let the conversation lag.

Under normal circumstances, she would consider tonight's dining experience a pleasant respite from what would have been a solitary supper tray in her room.

These were not normal circumstances.

As evidenced by the unexpected presence of the man sitting diagonally across the table from her.

Jonathon Hawkins.

Why had Mrs. Singletary invited the hotelier to this particular dinner party? True, the widow was in the process of expanding her business association with the man. Did she have to socialize with him, as well? On a night Callie was in attendance?

Swallowing a growl of frustration, she narrowed her gaze over Mr. Hawkins's face. In the flickering light of the wall sconces, his features took on a dark, turbulent, almost-frightening edge. A man with many secrets.

She supposed some women might find his mysterious aura appealing. Not Callie. She didn't like brooding, enigmatic types. Besides, with his glossy brown hair, steel-gray eyes and square jaw, he reminded her entirely too much of the man who'd deceived her and broken her heart.

In fact…

If she narrowed her eyes ever-so-slightly and angled her head a tad to the right, Jonathon Hawkins could pass for Simon.

Was the hotelier as equally duplicitous as the famous actor? Did he spout well-practiced lies to unsuspecting gullible women?

She knew the comparison was unfair, and based solely on her own prejudice, yet Callie felt her hands curl into tight fists. She briefly shut her eyes, battling the remembered shame of her own actions. Before her experience with Simon, she'd lived a life of unshakable faith. She'd lived with boldness, gifted by the Lord with utter confidence in her own worth.

But now, *now,* she had no such confidence. She felt lost, afraid and, worst of all, alone.

She had no one to blame but herself, of course. She'd made her choices and must forever live with the consequences.

Refusing to wallow over a situation of her own making, she willed Mr. Hawkins to look at her. He turned his head in the opposite direction and listened to something Mrs. Singletary said.

His rich laughter filled the air.

Callie battled a mild case of dejection.

How could the man be so blissfully unaware? Had he no shame? Did he not know—or care—about the pain his actions had caused? Were it not for his untimely job offer, Fanny would have stayed in Denver and worked things out with Reese.

Reese.

What must he be suffering? Surely, Jonathon Hawkins's presence here tonight had to be a physical reminder of the woman he'd lost.

Callie shifted her gaze to where Reese sat wedged between the Ferguson sisters. He skillfully divided his attention, speaking to both women at well-timed intervals, taking in every word of their high-pitched chatter. He didn't look upset. In fact, he was smiling. *Smiling!*

"Is the fish not to your liking, Miss Mitchell?"

She dragged her gaze away from Reese and focused on Marshall Ferguson.

"On the contrary," she said, picking up her fork. "It's quite wonderful."

"Such certainty, and yet…" Marshall dropped an amused gaze to her plate. "You haven't taken a single bite."

"Oh. Right." She filled her fork. "I sampled some in the kitchen before everyone arrived."

His mouth quirked up at one corner. "Ah, well, that explains it, then."

She took the bite on her fork, studied his handsome face as she chewed.

Still holding her gaze, Marshall sampled his own fish. Only when Reese's father said his name did he break eye contact and answer a question about railroad stock. Which soon segued into a lengthy discussion on water rights.

With nothing to add to either topic, Callie listened in silence. The brief interlude with Marshall had given her time to recover her equilibrium and she was grateful to the man.

She glanced at him from beneath her lashes.

In temperament and in looks, he reminded her of her brother Garrett. Marshall's tawny hair was a bit more unruly, and his brown eyes were several shades darker, but they could almost pass for brothers.

There was another glaring similarity between the two men. Marshall had once been engaged to Garrett's wife, Molly. Did he pine for his lost love? Callie wondered.

How did one ask such a question?

One *didn't* ask such a question.

Yet she'd practically done so with Reese the other day in his office.

Callie cut a glance across the table, noticed Reese was no longer engaged in conversation with either of the Ferguson sisters. Instead, he was watching her. Closely. Intently.

She looked down at her plate then just as quickly glanced back up. Reese was still watching her, just as closely, just as intently. She wished he would look away. Then, perversely, wished he would continue looking at her all night.

At least he wasn't conversing with either of the Ferguson sisters anymore.

Why not?

They were both very beautiful, educated, came from a good family and…

Callie suddenly remembered the words written in a bold, masculine hand she'd fished out from beneath

Lady Macbeth. *Loves children...must come from a good family and...value strong family ties.*

Qualities a man might look for in a wife.

Alarm filled her.

Was Reese actively seeking a woman to take Fanny's place in his heart? Had he enlisted Mrs. Singletary's assistance?

No. It was too soon. Fanny had barely left town.

"I understand your brother is practicing law in St. Louis," Marshall said, the gently spoken question sufficiently breaking through Callie's growing panic.

"Yes." She rummaged up a smile for her dinner companion. "I received a letter from his wife just today."

"You and Molly are still close, I presume?"

"Very. It was hard to say goodbye to her after the wedding, but the ever-faithful postal service keeps us in touch."

If only Fanny would write, as well. One letter. Callie yearned for nothing more than one, short letter from her sister.

"Is Molly..." Marshall hesitated, his smile dropping slightly. "Is she happy living in St. Louis with your brother?"

How best to answer such a loaded question? *The truth,* she told herself. *Stick with the truth.* "She has settled into her new life with Garrett rather nicely. She's even started her own millinery shop."

"I'm pleased for her." The relief in his eyes was more powerful than the words. "And your brother."

"I believe you truly mean that."

He turned thoughtful a moment, lifted a shoulder. "Though Molly is a generous, beautiful woman, she was not the woman for me. We would never have truly happy together. Content, perhaps. But not happy."

Something sad came and went in his eyes.

Wanting to soothe, she reached out and touched her fingers to his forearm. "I'm sorry, Mr. Ferguson."

He placed his hand atop hers and squeezed gently. "Molly and I parted ways amicably. We will always be friends."

Friends?

There was that awful word again, spoken by another man in reference to his former fiancée. Why would anyone propose to a woman he considered nothing more than a friend?

Oh, she knew many marriages were based on far less, and were entered into for a vast array of reasons. But in her family love was the most important foundation to marriage.

And now abide faith, hope, love, these three; but the greatest of these is love. The Bible verse was practically a family motto.

Realizing she'd been silent too long, Callie drew in a steadying breath. "I'm glad there are no hard feelings between you and Molly."

"You are different tonight, Miss Mitchell. More…" His words trailed off.

When several seconds passed and he didn't continue, she lifted a brow. "More?" she prompted.

"Charming," he said with a smile. "Engaging. Quite wonderful, really. Until tonight, I hadn't realized how…" His gaze fell over her face. "What I mean is, you are a very beautiful woman."

A rather inconvenient surge of pleasure surfaced at

the unexpected compliment. Callie had forgotten how lovely it felt to be called beautiful.

She shifted uneasily in her chair.

"I didn't mean to make you uncomfortable."

"You didn't," she assured him. "It's just—" she lifted her chin "—I'm not used to compliments."

"Then I shall make it my mission to pay you several more throughout the night."

"Please," she whispered, absently shoving at her hair, shifting in her seat again. "You really don't have to do that."

"I have made you uncomfortable again." He focused on his plate a moment, then turned back to her. "Did you notice how the rain earlier this evening brought a surprising chill to the night air?"

What a kind, sweet man, changing the subject to the universally innocuous topic of the weather.

For the rest of the meal, they spoke of nothing more substantial. Callie found Marshall Ferguson witty, amiable and handsome. She quite enjoyed his company. And decided to be glad for her position at the table.

As the servers began clearing away empty dishes and plates, one of the Ferguson sisters, in an overly loud voice, asked Reese if he'd heard from Fanny since she'd left town.

A full five seconds of silence met the question, whereby the girl's father cleared his throat.

"No, I haven't," Reese said without inflection. "Nor would I expect to hear from her since we are no longer engaged."

Though he didn't appear especially agitated, his icy tone said the conversation was over.

The girl missed the obvious cue. "Oh, but surely, after what you meant to one another you would wish to know how she's faring in Chicago?"

"She is faring very well" came a deep, masculine reply.

All heads turned toward Jonathon Hawkins and an expectant hush filled the air.

"You know Fanny?" the Ferguson sisters asked in unison.

He gave a brief nod. "Miss Mitchell is an invaluable member of my Chicago hotel operation, *our* operation," he amended with a nod in deference toward Mrs. Singletary. "With her attention to detail, she's all but running the place on her own."

"Isn't that lovely." Mrs. Singletary set her napkin on the table and stood. "Let us adjourn to the parlor for coffee and dessert."

And that, the widow's turned back communicated to the room, was the end of that.

The rest of the evening went by pleasantly for Callie. Until Jonathon Hawkins approached her.

"Miss Mitchell, it's a pleasure seeing you again."

Everything around her went still. Though she'd once worked at this man's hotel, she'd hardly interacted with him. Once, maybe twice, and only in passing, yet he acted as though they were old friends.

"Thank you, Mr. Hawkins." She gave him a brief nod and a forced smile. "It's nice to see you again, too."

"From what I understand," he continued, his gray eyes smiling, "your absence has left a considerable hole in the Hotel Dupree's kitchen operations."

Emotion threatened to overtake her. Now that she had his attention, there were many things Callie wanted to say to this man. A discussion of her former position in his hotel was not one of them.

"I'm sure you'll find a suitable replacement soon."

"Let us hope you are right." He fished inside the interior of his jacket. "Your sister asked that I give this to you."

Callie stared at him suspiciously. Then realized he was holding a letter in his hand from Fanny, folded in the special way they'd designed back in school. So happy to receive word from her sister, the annoyance she felt toward this man was nearly forgotten.

"Thank you." She plucked the letter from between his fingers and—feeling bold—asked the pressing question running through her mind. "Is Fanny truly well, Mr. Hawkins?"

"She's thriving." His eyes filled with pride and something else, something almost tender, a look that set Callie's teeth on edge.

"I recently promoted your sister to front desk manager."

Callie's heart dipped. No. No, no, no. Fanny would never come home now. She'd been reasonably happy working at the Hotel Dupree. But, Callie admitted to herself, Fanny hadn't *thrived*.

Sighing, she fingered the letter in her hand. She desperately wanted to read the words her sister had penned on the page. She didn't dare exit the party, though, not yet.

As if matters weren't already tense enough, Reese materialized by her side. "Callie? Are you unwell?"

She smiled thinly. "I'm fine."

Reese's eyebrows lifted in silent challenge.

Stuffing the letter from Fanny in her sleeve, she explained further. "Mr. Hawkins has promoted Fanny to front desk manager."

"Ah." Reese turned his attention to the other man. "So she's truly happy living and working in Chicago?"

"Quite."

"That's good to know."

Awkward silence fell over their tiny group.

"I see Mrs. Singletary motioning to me," Hawkins declared. "I should go see what she wants."

"I'll join you," Reese said, deserting Callie without a backward glance.

The two men fell into step with one another, their heads bent in conversation. Both were of an equal height and build, their hair nearly the same color. Callie hadn't noticed the similarities before and wasn't sure what to make of them now.

Were they discussing business as they made their way across the room? Callie would never know.

Soon the guests began to leave, Jonathon Hawkins first, the rest not long after him. Marshall Ferguson made a special effort to approach Callie and assure her he'd enjoyed sitting beside her at dinner.

"I had a lovely time, as well," she said, meaning every word.

"Perhaps we will do it again sometime soon."

"I'd like that."

She watched him depart with his family, wondering why she felt no sense of loss as he exited the room. Because, she realized, there'd been nothing special between them, at least not from her end. No spark, not one ounce of interest.

Had she learned her lesson with Simon? Was she

finally safe from making another, impetuous mistake where a man was concerned?

As if to test her theory, Reese came up beside her once again. Her heart skipped two full beats. Her throat tightened.

Her knees wobbled.

So much for *that* theory.

Before she could think how to break the silence between them, Reese's father joined them. "My dear, dear, girl, I have come to bid you good evening."

"Good night, Mr. Bennett." She lifted onto her toes and kissed his weathered cheek.

Smiling broadly, he nodded at Reese. "Son."

"Father."

With a strange, satisfied gleam in his eyes, the elder Mr. Bennett approached Mrs. Singletary. They spoke no longer than a minute and then he, too, quit the room.

The widow frowned after him, even as she worked her way over to where Callie and Reese still stood.

"It is my turn to say thank you, Mrs. Singletary." Reese took her hands. "The food was wonderful, the company—" he paused "—interesting and—"

"Before we say good-night, there is a matter of some importance we must discuss."

"Can it not wait until our Monday morning meeting?"

"It cannot."

He released her hands and took a step back. "Carry on, then. Say what you need to say."

"I have concerns about your list."

His eyes cut to Callie and filled with what could only be described as alarm, or perhaps cynicism, or perhaps he was simply looking at her as he always did and she was reading too much into the moment.

"What concerns?" he asked tensely.

Mrs. Singletary made an airy, circular gesture with her hand. "I believe several of your requirements need revising or, at the very least, expanding."

A muscle jerked in his jaw. "Those changes can be addressed on Monday."

By his stiff tone alone, Callie had a bad feeling about this alleged list. Then she caught sight of Reese's thunderous expression.

Oh, yes, a very bad feeling indeed.

Chapter Seven

Reese relaxed his jaw, inch by deliberate inch. All the evening needed was a discussion concerning his requirements for a bride. He'd already endured one of the Ferguson girl's intrusive questions, while fending off her sister's attempts to place her hand on his arm at inappropriate moments.

As if that hadn't been enough, he'd been forced to witness Callie share smiles with Marshall Ferguson. She'd blossomed under the man's attentiveness. Reese didn't fully understand why this bothered him, but it did. Massively. No matter how irrational, he didn't like knowing another man could make her smile.

She wasn't smiling now.

Her eyebrows were pulled together in a sweet, delicate frown. The same expression she'd worn at the opera when she'd agonized over her choice of dessert.

She looked equally adorable this evening, which inexplicably put Reese further on edge.

"This is not an appropriate time to revise my list." He spoke firmly, decisively, as he would in a courtroom, looking meaningfully at the widow in case she missed his meaning.

True to form, the contrary woman refused to give an inch of ground. "There is no better time than the present, while all three of us are together."

The *three* of them? "Callie has no cause to hear—"

"So, it's *Callie* now?"

Reese gritted his teeth.

"Oh, dear." Mrs. Singletary laughed softly. "You look quite put out. Perhaps we should sit down.

"Please, Mr. Bennett." Her tone took on an apologetic air, and her eyes filled with silent appeal. "All I ask is that you hear me out. I promise to be brief and—" her gaze shifted to her companion "—circumspect."

Had the widow continued wrestling for control of the situation, Reese would have left without another word. But she'd switched tactics. Short of being rude, which went against the grain, he was stuck.

He would prefer Callie not be nearby. But if Mrs. Singletary followed through with her promise and chose her words carefully, he had no cause for concern.

"Very well," he said. "I will hear you out."

He narrowed his eyes so the widow would understand that if she pushed too hard or revealed too much he would end the conversation immediately.

Her brief nod indicated she caught his silent warning.

Hands clasped behind his back, Reese waited for the women to choose their seats. Mrs. Singletary sat in a wing-back chair, while Callie lowered onto the brocade divan facing her.

After only a moment's consideration, he settled on the divan beside Callie.

He did not look at her. She did not look at him.

Awkwardness had returned to their relationship.

He started to push to his feet. Anticipating the move, Mrs. Singletary held up a hand to stop him.

"Callie." Lowering her hand, she smiled at the younger woman. "Would you be so kind as to retrieve a piece of paper off my desk?"

Callie blinked at her employer. "Which one do you mean?"

"You'll know it when you see it. It is a list of seven items penned in Mr. Bennett's handwriting."

"A list?" Callie's gaze whipped to Reese. "But—"

"Off you go, dear. The man doesn't have all night."

"Yes, Mrs. Singletary." Mouth pressed in a firm line, Callie marched to the door. At the threshold, she looked over her shoulder, sighed and then continued on her way.

The moment she disappeared into the hallway, the widow broke her silence. "I'm sorry to tell you, Mr. Bennett, but I will be unable to help with your bride search."

Reese blinked in stunned silence. This woman, who prided herself for being a consummate matchmaker, was relinquishing her duties? Before she'd even begun?

He should be relieved. He'd only cooperated with the widow's scheme to appease her and to maintain control of the situation.

Yet, now, as she attempted to step away from the project, Reese realized he wanted to find a suitable woman to marry. But with his schedule full and his time limited, Mrs. Singletary's assistance would have greatly expedited the process.

"Why are you begging off?" he asked.

"It's not that I don't wish to see you happily settled. I do, indeed." She picked up her cat and settled the overweight animal atop her voluminous skirt. "At the moment, I am overtaxed and am unable to give the matter my full attention."

It was a flimsy excuse at best. Reese had seen the widow orchestrate matches while simultaneously negotiating highly volatile business deals. Clearly, she was up to something.

"What other commitments are you referring to?"

"Oh, this and that, which will require me to go here and there."

The intentionally vague response had him reaching for a calm that didn't exist. "Perhaps you could be more specific."

"Of course." She nodded agreeably. "As you know, I am in the process of raising funds for a new wing on the hospital. If we are to break ground before winter, I must move my annual charity ball up by several months. Added to the expansion of my business partnership with Mr. Hawkins, well, my plate is full."

"I will put my search on hold."

"There's no need for such drastic measures." With the faintest trace of amusement shadowing her mouth, the widow leaned forward. "I have no plans to abandon you completely. I propose we put my companion in charge of your search."

"Callie?" Reese hauled in a sharp breath. "You are thinking of putting Callie in charge?"

"I understand your surprise, but if you would take a moment and view this from the proper perspective, you would see the value in my proposal."

He scowled at the ridiculous play on words. "What

you suggest is impractical, illogical and completely absurd."

"Now, now, do not give in to skepticism so early in the game." She made a tsking sound with her tongue. "My companion is acquainted with many young women in town. She will know their character personally, as well as their strengths and weakness, perhaps even their hidden shortcomings."

A valid argument, to be sure, but Reese couldn't imagine working with Callie on something as personal as the search for his future bride. Their friendship was still too new, too tentative.

There was another, more glaring concern that could not be ignored. "She is my former fiancée's sister. Her involvement in this could prove awkward."

"My dear Mr. Bennett, life is full of awkward moments." The widow spoke as if he was a slow-witted child. "How we deal with them ultimately reveals our character."

In the hushed silence of Mrs. Singletary's private office, Callie stared at the list in her hand. Now that she was finally alone, she desperately wanted to read Fanny's letter tucked inside her sleeve. But Callie sensed this piece of paper held equal importance, if not more.

There was no heading on the page, just seven items written in bold masculine strokes beside neatly spaced Roman numerals.

She scanned the list quickly, a hint of alarm crawling up her spine. When the sensation refused to desist, she read each item again, this time out loud.

"'Number one,'" she said, starting at the top of the page. "'Well-educated and articulate. Number two. Have a good moral compass. Number three. Loves children, wants several, at least five but no more than seven.'"

Callie stopped reading as the familiar line sunk in, twisting her insides into knots. What was Reese after?

Oh, but she knew. She knew.

Lord, please, no, let me be wrong.

Battling a wave of panic, she continued reading down the list. "'Must come from a good family and value strong family ties. Be an excellent hostess. A witty conversationalist. Conventional. Steady, absolutely no risk takers.'"

As Callie read the final entry her voice trailed into a hushed whisper. Her heartbeat thickened to a slow, painful thudding. Reese *was* looking for a wife, and he'd secured Mrs. Singletary's assistance in the matter.

The widow was the obvious person to turn to for help in such a matter. Reese was a logical cerebral man, it made sense that he would take the time to draw up a list of his preferred character traits to aid the widow in her search.

Callie couldn't allow her employer to succeed. She had to think of a way to keep Mrs. Singletary from finding Reese a suitable match or, at the very least, stall the process until Fanny returned home.

Again, Callie read the list, attempting objectivity on this third pass.

She sighed miserably.

What was the man thinking?

The qualities Reese had listed were so common, daresay ordinary. Any number of women in town could fit these characteristics.

With that thought came a surge of hope.

Perhaps there was another reason for this list.

Maybe Reese was looking for a housekeeper for himself and his father. Or an assistant in his law firm.

Even as the thought materialized, her gaze landed on the third entry from the top. *Loves children, wants several, at least five but no more than seven.*

No housekeeper or law clerk needed to desire children.

"What am I going to do?"

She needed a plan. But first, she must gather more information. She hurried back to the parlor.

At the same moment she entered, Reese strode across the room and returned to his seat on the divan facing Mrs. Singletary. The widow muttered something Callie couldn't quite make out and then patted his hand as if she was attempting to soothe his concerns.

That didn't bode well.

"Ah, Callie, there you are." The widow motioned her forward. "We were just discussing you."

That *really* didn't bode well, and sparked a kind of awful terror in her, even as excitement sang in her blood. Would Reese consider *her* a likely candidate?

Inappropriate thought. *Inappropriate.*

Reese belonged to Fanny.

Determined to protect her sister's interest, Callie led with the piece of paper outstretched in front of her. "Here you are, Mrs. Singletary. The list you requested."

She handed over the paper and, against her better judgment, glanced over at Reese. When their gazes connected, the floor seemed to shift beneath her feet. Why did he have to look at her like…*that?* The same way he'd looked at her in his private box at the Grand Tabor, as though she were a puzzle he needed to solve.

On ridiculously shaky legs, Callie moved to stand

by the hearth, steadying herself with a hand on the mantelpiece. The heat of the fire penetrated through the thin silk of her gown, yet did nothing to warm her. A cold sweep of foreboding ran through her veins.

She shifted, ever-so-slightly, and caught Reese still looking at her, his gaze tense and unwavering.

Oh, my.

As they stared at one another, silence fell over the room, very awkward and pulsing with all sorts of hidden meaning.

Mrs. Singletary's voice cut through the tension. "Now that you have returned, you will want to know what Mr. Bennett and I have discussed in your absence."

Callie nodded stiffly. "Yes, ma'am."

"Mr. Bennett is in need of your assistance."

"He wants my assistance?" She turned her gaze to meet his. "For what?"

His eyebrows pulled together in that thoughtful expression she found so attractive. For a long, stressful moment he looked undecided, obviously mulling over the best course of action.

Several heartbeats later, he let out a slow breath and reached out his open palm to Mrs. Singletary.

Nodding in satisfaction, the widow handed him the paper Callie had only just retrieved from her office.

He glanced down at the list. "Mrs. Singletary has recently pointed out that my image needs improving."

Callie gasped, a rusty sound that hurt her throat coming out. "That's ridiculous." She spoke without thinking, and straight from her heart. "Forgive me, Mrs. Singletary, but you are wrong."

"Am I, dear?"

"Absolutely." She felt a rush of frustration at her

employer's nonchalant response, angered on Reese's behalf. "Reese is a man of unquestionable integrity."

He chuckled softly. "Though I appreciate the sentiment, you don't need to defend me, Callie."

"I'm not defending you." She felt her shoulders bunch, forced herself to relax. "I'm speaking the truth. You are greatly admired throughout all of Denver."

He acknowledged this with a brief nod and a very small smile. "But as Mrs. Singletary pointed out, I am also considered stern and overly rigid."

"Nonsense."

"Nevertheless, Mrs. Singletary has presented a compelling argument. Now that I am the managing senior partner of Bennett, Bennett and Brand, my reputation matters. What I do, how I am perceived by others, reflects on my employees and my clients. Thus, the quickest route to softening my image is to find a suitable woman to marry, who will—"

"No." Callie's voice caught on the word. Oh, but this was terrible. Terrible. "You can't possibly be thinking of replacing Fanny with—" she glared at the list in his hand "—with, well, just anyone."

The smile he gave her was soft and full of silent understanding.

"Fanny is special," Callie declared when he returned his attention to the list. "There is no one like her in all of Denver."

Head bent over the paper, he nodded distractedly. "I don't disagree."

"My sister will be coming home soon." The words tumbled over one another in squeaking desperation. "You must wait for her return."

"Callie, you heard what Mr. Hawkins said." Reese

placed the paper face up on the cushions beside him. "Fanny is happy in Chicago. She is not coming home, at least not anytime soon."

"We don't know that for certain."

"Perhaps not, but you and I have had this discussion before. Even if Fanny returns to Denver tomorrow, I won't be renewing my suit."

Why did this proclamation send a surge of joy running through her? And where was her guilt for such a traitorous response? Callie loved her sister, and believed Fanny deserved only the best in life, including a second chance with this wonderful man.

"You won't truly know how you feel until you see her again." Who was she trying to convince? Reese? Or herself? "Please, Reese, just hold off on this until—"

"Fanny and I said everything we needed to say to one another the day she broke our engagement. It's past time I moved on with my life." He picked up the list again, scanned the page. "I want to find a bride, soon, no later than year's end."

His tone held such a lack of passion he could be speaking of any number of pursuits, all business-related. "Why?"

His head snapped up. "Pardon me?"

"*Why* do you want to get married?" She glanced at Mrs. Singletary. The widow gave her an encouraging nod, as if urging her to continue.

Callie drew in a tight breath and forged ahead. "Other than to enhance your image, why do you wish to marry by the end of the year?"

To his credit, Reese didn't answer right away. He considered her question silently, thoughtfully, then said, "I want to get married for the same reason I asked for your sister's hand."

She blinked at him, swallowed back a wave of trepidation and forced herself to say, "Because you want to fall in love again?"

He laughed, the sound abrupt, hard, almost bitter. "I am not seeking a love match."

Puzzled, she cocked her head. "Then what are you seeking?"

"Companionship, friendship and most of all children. I'd like a houseful of them."

He'd answered without hesitation, without even stopping to think about it, as far as she could tell. Admittedly, Callie couldn't fault his answer. Wanting children was a good reason to marry, almost as commendable as love. Almost.

"Now that we have the 'why' settled, let's move on." He passed her the list. "These are the specific qualities I'm looking for in a wife."

Callie pretended to read each entry as if for the first time. "They are terribly vague."

"Not in the least."

Throughout this interchange, Mrs. Singletary had remained silent. Callie looked at her now. Surely she had something to say, some advice to give. The widow ignored her completely as she paid avid attention to a loose thread in her skirt.

Sighing, Callie glanced back down at the list. "Any number of women could fit these requirements."

At last, Mrs. Singletary joined the conversation. "Well, then, your task will be all that much easier."

"*My* task?" Callie gasped. The list slipped from her fingers and fluttered to the floor.

"Yes, dear, I am putting you in charge of finding Mr. Bennett a wife."

Torn between frustration and sheer horror at the prospect, she rounded on Reese. "You have agreed to this?"

He lifted a shoulder. "Mrs. Singletary quite wisely spelled out the value in leaning on you for this particular task. I have weighed the pros and cons, and have decided I agree. You are the perfect choice."

Stunned by both his offhand attitude and his dry tone, Callie stared at him for an entire three seconds. "I don't understand."

"It's simple," he said. "You are acquainted with many eligible young women in town. And have cause to know them in ways neither I nor Mrs. Singletary could hope to achieve, especially considering my deadline."

The backs of Callie's eyes stung. Her breath clogged in her throat. Oh, this was awful, truly awful—a complete disaster in the making. She had to stop this madness.

Then again…

What if she agreed to Mrs. Singletary's scheme? Callie would then have the ability to control this terrible turn of events from a place of strength.

She could stall the process, delay the outcome or even mishandle her duties. If she scrutinized each candidate before introducing her to Reese, Callie could present only the ones he'd find unappealing.

In the meantime, she would contact Fanny and insist the stubborn girl return home. Before it was too late. Before Reese found another woman to marry.

"I'll do it," she declared, smiling sweetly. "I'll help you find a wife."

Chapter Eight

Reese watched in utter fascination as a complicated array of emotions spread across Callie's face. In less than two minutes, she'd gone from a state of shock to gaping outrage to panicked consideration, and ending, finally, with her features settling into a look of female resolve.

It was the resolve that put him immediately on guard.

He'd never seen a woman look quite that determined.

He hadn't misspoken when he'd claimed he'd carefully considered handing over his bride search to Callie. She came from a well-respected ranching family and had an unblemished character. Despite their personal connection through Fanny, Reese trusted Callie without reservation.

And, as the widow had graciously pointed out, Callie was personally acquainted with young women of equally high standing in the community. Relying on her to introduce him to suitable women made sense logically.

Yet Reese couldn't help but wonder. Had he been too hasty in agreeing to Mrs. Singletary's plan?

The widow, Reese could handle. He'd been doing so for years, tackling her business affairs with unprecedented success, regardless of her unconventional requests and thinly veiled personal agendas. That was business.

But Callie?

Callie, a woman he thought he knew, kept surprising him, making him reassess his preconceived notions of her character. Docile one moment, bold the next. Plain one day, jaw-droppingly beautiful the next.

Boring. Then exciting.

Demure and shy. Then confident and determined.

Which woman was the real Callie Mitchell?

The fact that he wanted to know the answer posed too many problems to sort through at the moment.

He'd made a mistake.

"I've changed my mind." He hauled himself to his feet, moving quickly, rolling his shoulders in order to maintain his balance. "I will select my own bride, in my own way."

He'd done so before. Of course, his previous efforts hadn't turned out well. But he knew what to avoid this time around.

"Now, now, Mr. Bennett, I believe you are getting ahead of yourself." With her lips set at an ironic angle, Mrs. Singletary placed her monstrous cat on the floor and pushed to her feet. "There is no need to make a snap decision merely because a few details have changed in our plan."

Technically, only one detail had changed. The sister of his ex-fiancée was now in charge of helping him find the woman to take her place. He'd almost find the situation humorous, if it wasn't so unspeakably bizarre.

"There has been nothing but haste in this entire process."

Reese only had himself to blame. He'd pursued the easiest route, pawning off the task of finding his future bride because he hadn't wanted to take the time to court another woman.

Yet, he didn't want to take another misstep, either, hence his original agreement to pass off the duty to the widow in the first place. Now, he was in a quandary. What to do?

Troubled by his indecision, he contemplated praying for guidance. Then he remembered he and the Lord weren't exactly on speaking terms.

"Reese." Callie gently touched his arm, a silent show of solidarity in the barely there gesture. "I would very much like to help you find a wife."

He studied her unwavering gaze and saw that the flicker of resolve was still there. Apparently, Callie had her own agenda in agreeing to the widow's scheme.

What could she possibly hope to gain by agreeing to help him? "You are aware this will put us in each other's company frequently."

"You object to my companion's company?"

"Of course not, that wasn't the point I was trying to make." And didn't that say it all? He, a trained attorney, a man used to applying words to great advantage, couldn't put together a decent argument.

"Reese." Callie gently squeezed his arm to regain his attention. "We are friends, are we not?"

He nodded. "We are."

"Wouldn't you also agree that friends help friends?"

He ran a hand along his jaw. "I would."

"I don't mind if this puts us in close proximity." Her bow-shaped lips curved upward. "I enjoy your company."

"I enjoy yours, too." A little too much. And that was the problem. Reese actually liked Callie. He especially liked this new Callie, the one who dressed in rich, bold colors that made her skin glow and her eyes sparkle.

Her transformation awed him. Her beauty stole his breath.

"If you will give me a chance—" she pulled her hand away from his arm "—I believe I can be of great assistance in your search."

Hadn't he already arrived at that same conclusion? "That is not the point."

"What *is* the point?"

He couldn't remember.

"I need a day or two to think this through," he said, grasping for any reason to make his exit before he said or did something he couldn't take back.

"By all means." Politeness itself, the widow stepped aside to let him pass. "In the meantime, Callie will draw up a list of suitable young women who meet your requirements."

Another list. As a man who lived his life by them, he was growing to dislike them immensely.

He cast a final glance in Callie's direction.

Smiling serenely, she twined her fingers together in front of her. The slight tremble in her clasped hands told its own story. Callie wasn't as confident as she appeared.

Good. He liked knowing he wasn't alone in his discomfort.

"I will be in touch in the next few days." He nodded to the widow. "I will see myself out."

"Oh, no, that simply won't do." Mrs. Singletary nudged her companion toward him. "Callie will escort you to the door."

After only a slight hesitation, Callie shifted to a spot beside him. "I'd like nothing better."

Beatrix Singletary watched the two young people exit the room. Both so erect in their posture, their shoulders rigid, their spines straight and unbending as their minds.

Her beloved companion. Her trusted attorney. Two wounded souls, refusing to live life to the fullest, tortured by secrets they kept hidden deep within themselves. It was really quite sad.

Neither would admit to needing the other.

Oh, but they did. They needed one another greatly, and would be far better together than apart.

Beatrix looked forward to watching them fall in love. She knew the exact dress that would look best on Callie at their wedding.

Satisfied she'd set them on the proper path, Beatrix knew better than to become complacent. Any number of complications could arise to foil her plan. Thus, she followed behind at a reasonable distance, her steps as silent as her cat's.

Stealth was hardly a necessity tonight.

Determined to show the world they were in control, neither Mr. Bennett nor Callie would look over their shoulders to see if she followed.

They kept a respectable distance from each other, looking neither right nor left *nor* at one another.

Beatrix narrowed her eyes in frustration.

Such discomfort in Mr. Bennett's strides, such awkwardness in the way Callie held her shoulders. Such a battle the two were going to put up to reach their happy ending.

Ah, but Beatrix Singletary refused to be disheartened, nor did she have any intention of giving up.

The good Lord had put Callie in her home for a reason. And that reason was walking stiffly beside the young woman, his chin in perfect parallel alignment with the floor.

When two people were meant to be together, as her dear companion and stern attorney were, they eventually found their way. Especially with a little nudge or two from an older, wiser matchmaker.

After seeing Reese out, Callie returned to her room instead of rejoining Mrs. Singletary in the parlor. Her nerves were too raw, her thoughts in too much turmoil to match wits with the clever woman.

Besides, Callie wanted to be alone while she read her sister's letter. Settling in an overstuffed chair, she carefully placed the pages on her lap. A mere half hour ago, she'd been eagerly anticipating this moment. She'd desperately wanted to read what her sister had to say.

So why wasn't she unfolding the pages?

Why was she hesitating?

Fear, she realized. She was afraid of what she would discover.

Sighing over her cowardice, she turned her head and looked out the window beside her. The Rocky Mountains stood guard, their mighty peaks clearly outlined in the deep purple sky. The rain had moved on. Now, pale moonlight cut shadows across the land while tree branches scratched eerily at the glass windowpanes.

Callie sighed again, pressed her lips tightly together and ignored the letter a moment longer. Something far more troubling weighed on her mind.

Why had she agreed to help Reese find his future bride?

Then again, how could she have not agreed? Mrs. Singletary would have taken over the task if she'd refused. And unlike Callie, the widow wouldn't stop presenting eligible women until Reese was happily settled.

Callie groaned. She didn't object to him getting married, as long as he married Fanny. Anyone else would be intolerable. But how was she to create a list of suitable woman who weren't actually suitable?

What a disaster.

The quickest, most expedient route to fixing this mess was to convince Fanny to return home immediately.

No easy task.

Not if Jonathon Hawkins was to be believed.

Did Fanny have any regret over leaving Reese behind? And if she did, would she put on a brave face, fearing she couldn't come home now that she'd made her initial, *hasty* decision to leave town?

There was one sure way to find out what was in her sister's head. Read the letter Mr. Hawkins had personally delivered.

Callie looked down at the folded paper in her lap.

What if her sister didn't regret leaving town?

What if she did? What if she wanted Reese back?

For a dangerous moment, Callie wished—oh, how

she wished—that Fanny was through with Reese once and for all.

Then Callie could… She could…

Find him someone else to marry.

The thought brought on such despair she nearly choked on her own breath.

No more stalling.

She unfolded Fanny's letter with fumbling fingers. She couldn't help but remember Jonathon Hawkins's expression right before he'd pressed the papers into her hand. He'd looked quite confident he was doing Callie a favor by giving her this missive from her sister.

Until tonight, she'd only thought of him as that odious man who'd given Fanny a reason to leave town. But as he'd stared into her eyes, she'd seen a man with nothing but good intentions.

Perhaps she'd misjudged him.

Callie coiled her fingers around the unread letter in her lap. The stiff feel of the paper reminded her that the answers to her dilemma could be right here, beneath her hand.

She lifted the letter until the moonlight illuminated the entire page. The beautiful looping scrawl definitely belonged to Fanny, but appeared much neater than usual, as if she'd taken great care with each word.

A sob worked its way up Callie's throat. How she missed her sister. Taking a deep breath, she smoothed out the pages and began reading.…

My Dearest Sister,
I scarcely know where to begin. If you are reading this letter, I can assume Mr. Hawkins has kept his promise and has delivered this to you

personally. I am so sorry I haven't answered any of your letters until now. I ask for your forgiveness. It seems a poor substitute to do so in writing, rather than speaking to you in person.

In answer to the question in your last letter, no, I do not regret leaving town. Nor do I regret breaking my engagement with Reese. I should have never agreed to marry him, at least not until I knew more about myself. Though not his fault, Reese proposed to an image I had created, not the woman I am, deep down, and that is solely my fault.

I have happily played a role all my life. The pretty, frivolous young woman. The adored sister. The treasured fiancée. But who is the woman beneath the various masks I wear?

I don't know. However, I am determined to find out. Until I do, I have no business marrying any man.

Please do not hold my departure against Mr. Hawkins. Had he not offered me this job, I would have found another way to leave town.

I close this letter with a single request. When next you see Reese, will you tell him I am doing well and wish him nothing but happiness for the future?

I love you, dearest Callie.
Yours most faithfully,
Fanny

Callie read the letter again and tossed it on the nightstand, only to pick it up and read it one more time. And then another.

Heart pounding, throat burning, she tried to remain detached, but she couldn't. Fanny didn't regret leaving town, but her reasoning for breaking her engagement with Reese was something Callie had never considered. Her sister had been hiding behind a mask, of sorts. No different than Callie herself.

While Callie had buried her true nature behind dull clothing and severe hairstyles, Fanny had been doing much the same with her fashionable dresses and sparkling personality. The difference, it seemed, was that Callie had always known who she was beneath the facade.

Apparently, Fanny did not.

Callie read her sister's letter once again.

Nowhere did Fanny mention she didn't still love Reese.

The battle wasn't over, then. Fanny could one day change her mind and want Reese back. Despite his assurance otherwise, how did he know he didn't want the same until he was actually faced with the choice?

Cold, hard resentment surged. For a treacherous moment, Callie allowed the dark sensation to fill her. After the pain Fanny had caused, she didn't deserve Reese.

Callie shoved the traitorous thought aside. It wasn't her place to judge her sister so harshly. The Lord's glorious, redemptive love called for mercy and forgiveness.

Besides, she'd agreed to help Reese find a wife, with the express purpose of keeping him from moving on until Fanny could make one final bid to win his heart. Her course was set.

Callie moved to her desk, dipped her pen in the inkwell and began the letter that would hopefully bring Fanny home.

She worked into the wee hours of the night, revising her words until she had them exactly as she wanted them.

The next morning, with very little sleep behind her, she woke groggy and out of sorts. Born on a ranch, she'd never been able to sleep past dawn. She rose with the sun and dressed for the day in her olive-green muslin gown. Thankfully, Mrs. Singletary hadn't raided her wardrobe completely.

Glancing down at herself, Callie admitted the color was drab, the fit unnecessarily large, and for the first time in years, she felt uncomfortable in her own clothes.

She missed wearing the bold colors the widow insisted she don, the ones that brought out the color in her skin.

This sense of dissatisfaction was the widow's doing, as was the wave of rebellion that urged Callie to dress in clothes that highlighted her assets.

Ah, but today was her day off. She planned to spend most of it in the kitchen at Charity House, the orphanage Marc and Laney Dupree had created for children of prostitutes. Boys and girls no other institution would take were welcomed into a loving, safe home and given a solid Christian upbringing, thereby breaking the cycle of sin in their lives.

Callie loved spending her free time with the orphans, many of whom weren't strictly orphans but rather children with mothers who worked in the local brothels. Though indirectly, Callie had a personal connection to Charity House. All three of her older brothers had married women either raised in the orphanage or formerly employed there. Megan, Annabeth and Molly were kind, God-loving women.

Her brothers had chosen well.

Exiting her room, she nearly toppled into Mrs. Singletary. "Oh."

Hands on hips, the widow lowered her gaze over Callie's dress. "You are determined to defy my superior sense of style."

Callie wasn't in the mood to defend her clothing choices this morning. She gave a tight, and slightly embarrassed, sigh. "It's my day off. What does it matter how I dress?"

Mrs. Singletary released her own aggravated puff of air. "You are proving most difficult, Callie Anne Mitchell."

"That is not my intent." With exaggerated dignity, she lifted her chin. "I'm helping out Laney Dupree in the Charity House kitchen today. We're teaching a few interested girls how to bake pies. It's a messy business and I don't mind getting wayward ingredients on this particular gown."

"That explanation is perfectly—" Mrs. Singletary shook her head in amused annoyance "—reasonable."

Callie swallowed a triumphant smile. "I know."

"I had hoped to discuss Mr. Bennett's requirements for a wife with you at some point today. Perhaps together we can make some sense out of his list," Mrs. Singletary continued. "I find his preferences are really rather—"

"Uninspired?" Callie suggested.

"Completely." The widow gave a little shake of her

head. "Why, any number of women in town could fit his requirements."

Callie nodded in agreement. If she thought this would end the discussion, she was wrong.

Mrs. Singletary seemed determined to say her piece. "Although the bulk of the task will fall on your shoulders I believe my input will increase your success. Especially as you design your initial list of suitable candidates for him to review."

"You have suggestions?"

"A few."

Callie remained silent for several seconds. If she refused the widow's input would Mrs. Singletary make a *few suggestions* to Reese on her own?

Perhaps. Perhaps not. Callie didn't dare take that risk. "We could discuss this when I return from my afternoon at Charity House."

"That will be fine." The widow started down the hall then quickly turned back around. "I am determined to see Mr. Bennett happily settled before Christmas."

"As am I." Finally, something they agreed upon, and probably the last for many days to come.

Chapter Nine

As he did most Saturday mornings, Reese exited the ridiculously large house he shared with his father and turned in the direction of Charity House. At this early hour the sun hung low, a big, fat orange ball against the blue, blue sky.

The sweet, lilting music of birds singing from their tree branches accompanied him on his short journey to the orphanage, a leisurely stroll that amounted to the equivalent of two city blocks in town.

Alone on the streets, Reese's mind wandered over several pressing concerns, eventually landing on last night's conversation with Mrs. Singletary and her companion. He'd meant what he said when Callie had pressed for a reason behind his bride search. He wanted children. As many as it would take to fill the house and turn the rambling old mansion into a home.

Growing up, Reese had secretly craved a large family. He would have settled for just one sibling, either a brother or a sister. Unfortunately, a week after his seventh birthday, his mother had succumbed to a fever and then died a week later.

His father had never remarried.

Looking back with the benefit of age, Reese wondered if he'd married young with the idea of filling his nursery as quickly as possible. Even at eighteen, he'd been ready to start a family. Miranda hadn't been quite so eager. The one time he'd brought up the subject, she'd laughed the idea away, claiming it was far too early in their marriage to talk about children.

Dark memories threatened to drag him into the past where only hopelessness and sorrow resided. He refused to surrender on this beautiful Saturday morning. The story of his life with Miranda, and the crippling grief he experienced after her death, belonged to his younger self. The man he was now had his entire future ahead of him.

Endless possibilities abounded.

The rewards of marrying again far outweighed the risks. Of course, he still needed to find a suitable woman to marry. A tiny, little, insignificant detail he'd put in Callie Mitchell's care.

He stopped at the street corner and inhaled slowly.

Had he made the right decision? Handing over such an important task to the sister of his former fiancée instead of relying on Mrs. Singletary's guidance?

The widow's arguments for the switch had certainly been sound. Though he didn't fully understand why Callie had agreed to help him find a bride, she *had* agreed. The deed was done.

The course set.

Instead of second-guessing his own actions—or Callie's—Reese crossed the street and focused on the moment, the here and now, prepared to enjoy his day at Charity House.

He passed through a sunbeam warming the cobblestones at his feet. The temperature was perfect for playing outside. Perhaps he would talk some of the children into an impromptu game of baseball, a favorite of the orphans.

One block later, he arrived at the orphanage. Charity House was an uncommonly grand structure, even for this posh neighborhood. Puffy white clouds moved rapidly through the sky above the sloping roof of angles and interesting turrets, the Colorado blue a perfect backdrop for the three-story structure.

With its stylish modern design and perfectly manicured lawns, Charity House looked nothing like an orphanage. Fitting, since many of the children weren't true orphans. Laney and Marc Dupree had created a safe, loving home for the abandoned boys and girls whose mothers often chose their unholy professions over their own offspring.

Did the children realize they lived in one of the most exclusive neighborhoods in Denver? That the gas lamps sitting atop poles at every street corner were of the highest quality? That the other mansions marching shoulder to shoulder in elegant formation along the lane housed some of the wealthiest families in the West?

What did it matter, as long as they were happy and safe?

Pleased he could play his part, small as it might be, Reese unlatched the wrought-iron gate and strode up the front walk.

Marc Dupree exited the house. Dark-haired and clean-shaven, the owner of Charity House wore a gold brocade vest and matching tie, the kind a banker or even Reese himself would wear for a day at the office.

Laney Dupree joined her husband a moment later. Petite and fine-boned, she was as beautiful as her home. She wore a simple pale blue dress with a high lace collar today. Her mahogany-colored hair hung loose, framing her stunning face with long wavy curls.

The couple clasped hands and approached Reese as a single unit. A gnawing ache twisted in his stomach. Reese and Miranda had never had that close, unspoken connection. He'd loved his wife desperately, with the unbridled passion of youth, but now, he wondered.

Would they have settled into a mature marriage, one full of contentment, comfort and peace? Or would they have continued living on the edge, all but laughing at danger and taking unnecessary risks with their lives?

He would never know.

The couple separated and Laney pushed slightly ahead of her husband, her smile radiant and full of welcome. "Good morning, Reese."

"Laney. Marc." He nodded to both individually, then dug into his coat pocket and produced the bank draft he'd brought with him. "For Charity House."

Laney reached out before her husband could and took the money. She looked down at the amount. "Oh, Reese, this is especially generous."

"It's from my father and me."

"Still…" She trailed off, her gaze full of silent gratitude.

"You do good work here, Laney, *important* work, work for the Lord." Reese didn't always understand God's ways, but he didn't deny that the Lord's hand was on Charity House. "I wish I could contribute more."

"You do plenty, not only with your money, but with your time." She folded the bank draft and handed it to her husband. "Thank you, Reese. And, please, pass on my gratitude to your father, as well."

"I will." Feeling slightly uncomfortable, he turned to Marc. "It's a beautiful day. What do you say we put together an impromptu baseball game?"

The other man's smile came quickly and easily. "Great minds think alike. I already sent most of the children outside. They're in the backyard picking teams as we speak."

On cue, Reese heard laughter floating on the light breeze.

"Come on." Marc gestured for Reese to follow him and Laney up the porch steps. "We'll take a shortcut through the house."

They entered through the main parlor. Everywhere Reese looked he saw order and charm, comfort and beauty. He found the attention to detail admirable. But it was the smells of home that tugged at his heart.

The tangy aroma of soot from the fireplace mingled with lemon wax from the floors and furniture. That sweet, homey bouquet, as well as the scent of baking pies, transported him back to his childhood, when his mother was still alive.

An unexpected bout of longing captured him, longing for a home and a family of his own, for a comfortable, settled life with a good woman by his side. The sensation came fast and hard, digging deep, slowing his steps. For a painful moment, the loneliness in his soul spilled into his heart.

His gut roiled.

Then he heard a familiar female voice, followed by a soft, throaty laugh.

The storm brewing in him calmed.

His senses unnaturally heightened, Reese became aware of additional chattering and giggles from young, girlish voices. *The sound of family.* He breathed in slowly, the scent of apples and cinnamon filling his nose.

The smell of home.

A sense of inevitability pushed him forward. When he stepped into the Charity House kitchen, his gaze sought and found Callie. He had one coherent thought—*her.*

She's the one.

He shoved the disturbing notion aside before it could take root.

The moment Reese's gaze locked with hers, Callie's lungs forgot how to breathe. The ability to communicate failed her, as well, though she couldn't think why. She knew Reese spent time at Charity House, she'd seen him here before.

Yet, somehow, his presence today felt different. New and special.

Life-altering.

There was so much emotion in his eyes, eyes still locked with hers. She recognized that haunted look, the hint of vulnerability in his stance.

How she wanted to go to him, to comfort and to soothe, as one kindred soul to another.

She didn't have that right.

Regardless of their budding friendship, they were

barely more than acquaintances. And as of last night, Callie was tasked with the job of finding him the perfect woman to marry. A woman who would have the sole honor of loving him into eternity, who would provide him with the children he wanted and create a home for them all.

The massive kitchen suddenly felt too small, too hot. Callie shoved a strand of hair off her face with the back of her hand.

Reese shifted to his left, splintering the tense moment, and their disturbing connection.

A moment later, Marc Dupree moved into view. Laney pushed past both men and moved to stand next to Callie. The other woman's presence gave her the strength to battle the rest of her control back into place.

She forced a smile. "Hello, Reese."

"Hello, Callie."

She could think of nothing more so say.

Reese wasn't exactly verbose himself. In the fractured silence that hung between them, he studied the chaos she and the half-dozen girls surrounding her had managed to create since she'd arrived.

"We are making pies," she said unnecessarily and perhaps a little defensively, as well. She'd always been a messy cook.

Until now, she hadn't realized just how messy.

"I enjoy pie." Reese sniffed the air. "Especially apple pie."

One of the girls giggled into her hand.

Reese winked at her, whereby her giggles turned into a fit of giddy laughter. This seemed to open the floodgates and the rest of the girls moved in around him, chattering over one another in an effort to gain his attention.

He was clearly a favorite among the assembled group. Callie understood why. With his wide smile and casual manner, he responded in a way that surely made each girl feel as though she were the most important person in the room.

Watching him now, in this setting, with the animated girls surrounding him, he was so easy to like.

He'd be just as easy to love.

Callie jerked back from the thought.

"All right, girls, that's enough." Laney nudged and pushed until she was in the center of the mayhem. "Let's give poor Mr. Bennett room to breathe, shall we?"

"We're heading outside to supervise a baseball game," Marc announced, dropping a glance over each girl. "Any of you want to join us?"

After sharing a brief glance with the others, the oldest spoke up for the rest. "We're making pies for supper tonight and are only halfway to our goal."

Callie smiled at the girl. At barely thirteen, Laurette Dupree was Marc and Laney's only natural child and already a beauty. With her mother's thick mahogany-colored hair and her father's steel-blue eyes, she was bound to break the hearts of many unsuspecting men one day.

"Since I'm also a fan of apple pie, we'll leave you to your work." Marc gestured for Reese to follow him out the back door.

The two men fell into step with one another.

Halfway through the kitchen, Reese stopped, turned back around and moved in beside Callie. He stood so close she could smell his spicy masculine scent over the baking pies.

Lowering his voice for her ears only, he voiced an odd request. "Don't leave until we have a chance to talk."

Though his words could be construed as a command, the tone he used was soft and engaging and made her stomach pitch.

"If that's what you want," she practically croaked. "I'll be sure to find you before I head back to Mrs. Singletary's."

"Splendid." He stepped back, smiled ruefully, then continued on his way.

Unable to take her eyes off his broad shoulders, she followed his progress as he retraced his steps. Confused and a little shaky, a sigh worked its way up her throat. The man made her feel things, things she'd never felt before, not even when she'd thought herself in love with Simon.

The moment he exited the house, several girlish sighs followed in his wake. Clearly, he had female admirers in this house.

Unable to censure herself a moment longer, her sigh joined the others. A mistake. She could practically feel Laney's gaze slide over her.

Callie kept her expression blank, tried to appear nonchalant. But she was hit with a wall of nerves. Had she just given herself away?

Far too perceptive for her own good, Laney leaned in close to Callie's ear. "*That* was certainly interesting."

Aware six pairs of eyes had swung in her direction, Callie busied herself with pouring another cup of flour into a large mixing bowl. "Don't read too much in to what you think you saw," she warned Laney, as well as herself. "Reese and I have agreed to become friends."

"Is that so?"

"Yes." She didn't expand, but rather attempted to change the subject. "How many pies are we short after that last batch?"

Laney eyed her for a long moment. "We need six more, seven if we want to bring one over to Pastor Beau and his family."

"Seven it is." Callie dug her fingers into the dough, giving her friend a meaningful stare before rolling her gaze over their wide-eyed, attentive audience. "Let's get started, shall we?"

Laney relented with a brief nod.

The next hour was spent mixing dough, rolling out pie shells and cutting apples into small wedges. The girls giggled and laughed their way through the process.

Not until the last pie was baking, and her helpers were cleaning up at the sink, did Laney pull Callie aside.

"You like him," she said without preamble, keeping her voice low. "Don't pretend you don't know who I mean."

Callie gave a weighty sigh. "Of course I like him. I like all my friends."

"Oh, really." Laney parked her hands on her hips. "So, you and Reese—"

"There is no *me and Reese*."

"Not from where I was standing. In fact—" Laney's lips curved upward "—you two looked very comfortable with one another."

"Reese and I are friends, Laney, nothing more."

"So you already said." Laney let out a soft chuckle. "And before you reiterate your point yet again, no man looks at a woman he considers a mere friend the way I saw Reese looking at you."

Callie swallowed, took a hard inhale. There was no excuse for feeling so dangerously moved by this observation. "You are reading far too much into this."

"Am I?"

"Have you forgotten?" Determined to keep this conversation between the two of them, she spoke the words in a hushed whisper. "He was once engaged to my sister."

"He's no longer engaged to Fanny."

"Not by choice."

That, Callie realized, was a critical detail she must always remember herself. The broken engagement between Reese and Fanny had not been Reese's idea. If he'd had his way, he'd be married to Fanny right now.

Depressing thought.

"Callie." Laney took both her hands. "Talk to me. Tell me what's so wrong with the possibility of you and Reese becoming more than—"

A spontaneous cheer burst through the opened window.

"Mother," Laurette called from the sink. "Is it all right if we went outside and watched the game?"

"By all means." Still holding Callie's hands, Laney smiled at her daughter. "Miss Callie and I will watch the pies."

As each girl hurried out the back door, Callie tried to think of a reason to abandon the kitchen, as well. None came to mind. She nearly despaired, but then rescue came in a tentative, barely there tug on her skirt.

"Miss Callie?"

"Yes, Gabriella?"

"I don't want to go outside." Big, sorrowful brown eyes met hers. "I want to stay here with you."

Moved by the request, Callie crouched down to make herself less intimidating. Somewhere between four and five years old, Gabriella Velasquez and her twin brother, Daniel, had only been at Charity House for a few weeks. According to Laney, their mother had recently died of consumption in a Cripple Creek brothel.

Callie smiled down at the sweet, precious child. She tried not to choose favorites. She tried to give of herself equally to all the children. But something about this reserved little girl, and her equally shy brother, had slipped beneath her guard.

Perhaps it was their unusual silence. Or the way they flinched when anyone, even other children, came near them.

"Oh, Gabriella, of course you can stay inside with me." She picked up the girl and set her on the counter. Callie adored this sweet child with the coal-black hair; sad, dark eyes and overly timid nature. "Want to help me count the pies?"

"I don't know how to count."

Callie brushed the child's hair away from her face, resisting the temptation to press a kiss to her forehead. "No time like the present to learn."

And so began Gabriella's first arithmetic lesson. *One plus one equals two. Two plus two equals four.* Basic, simple math equations every child should know. It was a shame Callie and Reese didn't add up that smoothly.

Chapter Ten

From his position facing home plate, Reese looked up at the darkening sky. Sometime in the past twenty minutes the weather had turned. Black ominous clouds boiled overhead, while a stiff wind carried the earthy scent of approaching rain.

Marc, in his self-appointed role as umpire, trotted out to where Reese stood on the makeshift pitcher's mound, which was nothing more than an empty flour bag. "What do you think? Should we call it?"

Distant thunder punctuated the question.

Reese looked back up at the sky, the children's safety foremost in his mind. "No lightning yet, and the first drops of rain haven't hit. I say we play on a little while longer."

"Agreed." Marc hustled back to his spot behind the catcher and made a circling motion with his hand. "Batter up."

A small, thin boy of about five years old approached the plate with slow, tentative steps. His wide, terrified gaze darted around the backyard, eventually landing on Reese. Taking pity on the apprehensive child, he moved forward several steps closer. Until today, Daniel Velasquez had kept himself separate from the other children, choosing to remain on the sidelines as an isolated spectator.

His willing participation this morning was monumental.

And deeply moving.

And Reese wasn't the only one who recognized the significance of the moment.

Daniel's entire team cheered him on, urging him to "swing for the back fence." Even kids on the opposing team shouted out words of encouragement.

Marc ruffled the boy's hair. "Remember how to hold the bat?"

Daniel nodded.

"Let's play ball." Marc settled in behind the catcher.

Bottom lip caught between his teeth, Daniel slung the wooden bat over his right shoulder then blinked up at Reese with eyes that had grown bigger and rounder.

Such courage in so tiny a package, Reese thought. Determined to honor this momentous occasion, he lobbed a slow, easy pitch over home plate.

Daniel swung with all his might. And missed.

Clearly dejected, his shoulders slumped forward and his eyes filled with tears.

"Ball one!" Marc called, then patted the boy on the back. "Try again, and remember to keep your eye on the ball."

Daniel's bottom lip quivered, but he heroically firmed it as he slung the bat over his shoulder a second time.

Reese tossed the next pitch a little lower and a bit slower. Daniel swung again. The very tip of the bat connected with the ball, sending it to a spot near Reese's feet. Not a magnificent hit, but a solid enough whack to qualify.

Cheers erupted from both teams.

"Head to first base!" Marc nudged the boy in the proper direction.

Reese made a grand show of fumbling the ball into his glove. He waited until Daniel had a solid head start before tossing the ball high over the head of the first baseman, who was too busy cheering on the little boy to notice.

Daniel's foot hit the pad and he headed for second base.

Wanting to give the boy a fighting chance, Reese hustled over and picked up the rolling ball before anyone else thought to do so.

With shouts of encouragement from the other children urging him on, Daniel flew over second base and continued on to third.

This time, Reese threw the ball short.

The little boy rounded for home, his mouth set in a determined line, his little legs pumping hard. His foot touched home plate seconds before Reese half-heartedly winged the ball into the catcher's glove.

Marc made a wide sweep of his arms. "Safe."

"You hit a home run." Caught up in the moment, Reese ran over, swooped Daniel into his arms and spun him around and around in the air.

The boy giggled and kicked his legs wildly. "I did it. I did it. I did it."

"Yeah, you did. It was a great hit, too." Heart overflowing with something akin to parental pride, Reese set the boy back on the ground and ruffled his hair.

His teammates immediately surrounded him.

Daniel soaked up the attention with a big happy smile.

Allowing his own smile free rein, Reese watched the celebration from a few feet away. He caught a movement out of the corner of his eye and swiveled his head toward the back porch. Callie stood behind the railing, watching Daniel with her heart in her eyes.

Ridiculously pleased that she understood the magnitude of Daniel's moment of triumph, Reese set out in her direction. Only as he drew close did he notice the little girl peering out from behind Callie's skirt. Reese recognized the child as Daniel's twin sister, Gabriella.

For reasons he couldn't understand, his heart lurched at the sight woman and child made, the very image of mother and daughter. His footsteps faltered. Where had that thought come from?

His pulse quickened, beating harder, faster than before, rushing thick and uneven through his veins.

Now that Callie no longer wore an apron covered in flour and pie dough, he was able to catalog her clothing in detail. Her dress was a drab, dull green, the color not particularly flattering. And yet, she radiated.

He couldn't seem to catch a decent breath.

Gabriella tugged on her skirt and whispered something Callie had to bend down to hear. She nodded and then scooted the little girl in the direction of the porch steps.

Hesitant at first, Gabriella descended at a snail's pace. Callie's face was calm as she watched the child's progress, but she clutched at the porch rail with a tight grip. The flicker of worry in her eyes told its own tale, as did the tightening of her lips, and the sigh that leaked out of her. A protective mother-hen leery over letting her chick branch out on its own.

"Gabriella." Bouncing from one foot to the other, Daniel called out to his sister. "Gabriella. Did you see me? Did you see me hit the ball?"

The little girl jumped off the last step, a smile splitting across her face. "You did really good, Daniel."

He beamed. "You have to try it next time."

"Okay." She paused. "Maybe." Another pause, then she sped over to her brother and joined in the merriment. One of the older girls tugged her close.

Charmed by the scene, and not wanting to miss a second of the festivities, Reese conquered the porch steps two at a time then took Gabriella's place beside Callie. He did a double take. Something had happened to her eyes, they'd turned greener, larger. Prettier. He could lose himself in their depths if he didn't take care.

"Hi," he said, pleased his voice sounded relatively normal.

"Oh, Reese." Callie reached up and brushed at his shoulder as if removing a speck of dust. The gesture was casually intimate and felt exactly right for the moment. "That was very kind of you, what you did for Daniel, ensuring he made it around all the bases."

Her words of praise made him feel strong, courageous, keen on conquering the world and slaying dragons with his bare hands.

Shrugging away the fanciful thought, he rolled back on his heels, came back down again. "It's what any man would have done in my position."

"No, Reese." She brushed at his other shoulder. "Not every man has it in him to be kind to children."

She sounded certain, and a little sad, as if she'd come across her share of bad characters.

Had someone hurt her?

A protective instinct shuddered through him and one thought rose above the others. *I want to fight this woman's battles.*

"You are a good man, Reese Bennett Junior."

Instant pleasure surged at the words that seemed to flow so easily off her lips. "Thank you, Callie."

Her eyes went soft with emotion. "You're welcome."

An odd sensation filled his chest, part confusion, part longing. He moved closer, a mere inch, no more.

The wind kicked up. The world paused, and then...

The swollen rain clouds unleashed their watery assault.

Chaos exploded in the backyard. Squeals and shrieks and giggles filled the air. Running feet. More laughter.

"Everybody inside," Marc shouted over the commotion.

One by one the children scrambled onto the porch. They crowded around Reese and Callie, laughing and tossing water in every direction. At the bottom of the steps, Marc hoisted Gabriella into his arms and set her down near Callie.

When Daniel stood in the rain, blinking up after his sister, looking forlorn and forgotten, Reese retrieved the boy in the same way Marc had rescued his sister.

Back on the porch, he had to shuffle his way through a maze of flaying arms and kicking legs to find a clear spot to set the boy down safely.

Marc took charge, Reese and Callie helping wherever they could. The three of them made quick work of gathering equipment in one pile, wet, muddy shoes in another, before herding the motley group of laughing, soaking wet children inside the house.

Retreating to her timid ways, Gabriella clung to Daniel, huddling close to him, her eyes wide and full of fear.

Callie approached the twins, crouched down to eye level. She spoke in a gentle voice, so soft Reese couldn't make out her words. Daniel nodded enthusiastically, pulling on his sister's arm. A blink of the eye later, the boy had his sister following behind the other children. The little girl didn't look especially overjoyed, and kept glancing back over her shoulder at Callie. But with her brother's encouragement, she obeyed.

Progress.

When the back door banged shut behind the twins, Reese realized he and Callie were alone on the porch. Just the two of them.

Fat raindrops pelted the ground. Thick clouds covered the sky. The muted gray light did nothing to conceal Callie's beauty, or hide the shades of caramel, gold and deep yellow in her hair.

And her eyes, those amazing, grass-green eyes, they stole his breath. *She* stole his breath.

Callie Mitchell was a beautiful woman. Reese realized with a sudden jolt that her appeal had nothing to do with her clothing, or how she chose to wear her hair, and everything to do with the woman herself. She was kind to frightened children, and he couldn't stop staring at her.

Nor could he deny the truth any longer. He was attracted to Callie Mitchell, captivated by a woman most considered unremarkable. Fools, all of them.

Reese knew he should feel awkward in her company, certainly alarmed at the direction of his thoughts. Instead, the sensation moving through him soothed his spirit. Calmed his soul. Urged him to let down his guard and relax, as if he'd finally come home after a long, endless journey.

Now, he was uncomfortable.

He took several steps back, away from Callie, and searched his mind for something innocuous to say. "Finished making pies?"

"Oh, yes." The smile she gave him sent his mind reeling. "All ten of them."

"Ten?"

"Apple pie is a favorite among the children."

He felt his smile return. "Kids with exceptional taste, I knew I liked them for a reason."

She laughed. "Apparently, the joy of apple pie knows no bounds."

"Or age limit," he said, laughing with her. He noticed a smudge on her cheek. Compelled, he reached up and brushed his fingertips across the spot.

Her eyes narrowed.

"Flour," he said, showing her the pads of his fingers.

"Oh." She let out a sweet, nervous laugh. "My secret is revealed. I'm a messy cook."

Affection enveloped him. Why had he never noticed just how striking and dramatic her features were? How had he missed the almond shape of her eyes, or how vivid and intense they were beneath finely arched brows?

Something deep and life-altering was gathering inside his heart. Reese wanted to pull Callie into his arms and kiss her.

He clasped his hands behind his back and cleared his throat. "Are you heading to Mrs. Singletary's anytime soon?"

"I am, once I say goodbye to the children."

"May I escort you home?"

"Yes, I…" A thousand questions leaped into her eyes. She voiced none of them. "Thank you, Reese, I would like that very much."

Thoughts scrambled around one another in Callie's mind, circling each another like a hawk swooping in for prey. She longed for so much, unable to define exactly what she wanted, yet knowing the man strolling beside her was at the heart of the sensation.

Despite her misgivings over the wisdom of allowing Reese to walk her home, her agreement had made perfect sense at the time. He lived in the same neighborhood as Mrs. Singletary, and would only have to alter his own route home by a mere block.

Callie lifted her gaze to the sky.

The rain had let up, but the air was still damp, the wind still raw. Much like her nerves.

The grind of wagon wheels sounded in the distance, along with the boom of a motor carriage firing into life. A baby wailed. A dog barked. "Do you hear that?"

Reese cut a glance in her direction. "Hear what?"

"The sounds of the neighborhood alive with activity." She swept her hand in a wide arc. "Listen."

He slowed his pace and did what she suggested. He listened.

"It's soothing, isn't it?" She smiled up at him.

"Knowing the world moves on around us no matter what's happening in our own lives?"

He stopped walking and turned to face her. "Callie Mitchell, you have the heart of a poet."

"Oh, I…" She thought of her love of the Psalms, especially the ones penned by King David. She enjoyed Shakespeare's sonnets, too, some of Byron's work, as well as Emily Dickenson's. "I suppose I do."

"You continually surprise me."

"Is that a good thing?"

"Exceptionally good." His eyes filled with quiet affection as he reached out and brought her hand to his lips.

The gesture was so unexpected, so sweet and gentle, her stomach dipped. She sighed, wanting this afternoon with Reese to last forever. Lovely conversation, lovely company, she couldn't ask for more. *Wouldn't* ask for more than this one perfect moment with a man she admired above all others.

Complicated emotions blazed to the surface. Forgotten hopes and dreams beckoned, and Callie forgot to wear her hard-earned, outward control.

Something had to be terribly wrong, because she and Reese were easy with one another. Comfortable.

Connected.

Still holding her hand, he guided her off the main path. Callie looked around, saw that they'd entered a small public park.

He led her toward a large leafy tree with several low-hanging branches. Their feet left indentions in the wet, muddy grass. Reese's were large and clearly defined, hers smaller, less pronounced, as if she was floating across the ground.

He let go of her hand, reached up and plucked a stem free from its branch. His gaze turned dark and turbulent as he fiddled with a green leaf, and then another.

Something was troubling him. "Reese? What's wrong?"

"It's Daniel and Gabriella." He wound the edge of the stem around his finger. "Although Daniel took a big step today, as did his sister, they're both uncommonly quiet and withdrawn."

Callie laid a hand on his arm, looked into his eyes. "They've only been at Charity House a few short weeks," she reminded him. "It's not unusual for new arrivals to hold themselves apart from the other children for months, sometimes longer."

"I know." The lines of worry around his eyes seemed to cut deeper. "But it seems unfair that they lost their mother so young and never even knew their father. I can only imagine what their lives were like before they came to Charity House."

"At least they're safe now, living in a loving home where they will be given the advantage of a Christian upbringing, renewed hope and unconditional love."

"I know. *I know.* But, Callie, they're too young to fear the world as they do." He tossed the branch to the ground with singular force. "The secret wounds they carry, it's unimaginable."

The intensity of his words highlighted his concern, a concern she shared. "That's not to say they won't one day find healing. Laney and Marc will take good care of them."

Reese nodded, but the tension in his shoulders didn't release. If anything, his shoulders bunched tighter. As she stared into his eyes, Callie saw the man beneath the stern exterior—a man of great feeling, with a hatred for injustice and the capacity to love deeply.

"I know what you say is true, Callie. Still, it's a pity the twins can't have a family of their own."

"They do have a family, at Charity House. Untraditional, to be sure, but one full of faith, hope and love."

He nodded. "It'll have to be enough."

His obvious concern for two precious children was endearing, and really sweet. Was it any wonder Callie found this man so attractive?

Sighing, she balled her hand into a fist and stared down at it. She wasn't supposed to find Reese attractive. She was supposed to find him a wife.

She'd nearly allowed herself to forget her duty, a duty she deeply regretted now. She'd only agreed to Mrs. Singletary's scheme in order to stall the process, at least until Fanny came home. Inserting herself into the equation was not part of the plan.

And yet, here she stood, hoping for something that could never be. Her assigned job was to ensure Reese stay unattached through the foreseeable future. An idea began to formulate in her mind. As the sister of five brothers, she had a clear understanding of what men found attractive in women. And, more importantly, what they found impossible to bear.

"Reese?"

"Yes, Callie?"

Oh, my. *Oh, my, oh, my, oh, my.* She really liked the way her name sounded on his lips.

He is not for you.

"It's time we discuss your bride hunt."

Chapter Eleven

At Callie's abrupt change of topic, Reese felt his mouth tighten around the edges. A sardonic laugh rustled in his throat. For the span of three heartbeats he could do nothing but stare at her in muted astonishment.

The woman wanted to discuss his search for a bride? Here? Now? When his mind was back at Charity House, focused on two small children who were...

Far better off than they'd been three weeks ago. Given their new, happier circumstances, he supposed there wasn't much more to say on the matter.

That didn't mean he wanted to talk about his *bride hunt,* as Callie called it. The term didn't sit well with him, made his search seem calculating, perhaps even callous. His brows pulled together in a frown.

Was his approach cold and self-serving? Or was his approach part of a wise, forward-thinking plan?

He shook his head to clear his thoughts, but found he couldn't focus. Not with Callie's pretty green eyes sweeping over his face. "Now is not a good time for this particular conversation."

"I daresay there's no good time for this particular conversation."

She couldn't know how much he agreed with her on this. "No. I suppose not."

Thunder rumbled overhead, a dismal warning that the storm wasn't over. The wind kicked up again, matching his dark mood and bringing an unseasonable chill to the air.

Callie clutched her arms around her, and attempted to hide a slight shiver behind a roll of her shoulders. Reese caught the movement. "Are you cold?"

"A little."

Honesty, even in the small, seemingly unimportant matters, it was one of the things he liked most about this woman. He wasn't supposed to like her. She was only a friend.

You are allowed to like your friends, he reminded himself.

Not this much.

When she shivered again, he realized he'd been staring. He quickly shrugged out of his coat and settled it around her shoulders. "Better?"

She nodded. "Yes, thank you."

"Let's get you home."

She opened her mouth, probably to say something along the lines of, *but we aren't finished with our conversation yet.* He raised a hand to forestall her. "We will continue our discussion in one of Mrs. Singletary's parlor rooms, where we'll be considerably more comfortable than out here in the elements."

Callie's lips twitched, as if she had something more to say. Another protest, no doubt. Again, he gave her no chance to voice her thoughts aloud. "I have found," he said, "that I think far more clearly when I am warm and dry."

A heavy sigh escaped her. "I do, as well."

"Then, we're in agreement. Off to Mrs. Singletary's we shall go." He tucked Callie's gloved hand in the bend at his elbow and guided her in the proper direction.

Her long-legged strides easily kept pace with his. Though he knew many men preferred small petite women, Reese rather liked a woman with some height and substance to her.

He'd have to remember to let Callie know of his preference.

For now, he concentrated on getting her home before the rain let loose.

Upon entering the widow's house, Winston materialized on the threshold. Reese and Callie had barely entered the foyer when the fastidious butler clucked his tongue in disapproval at the mud they'd tracked in on their shoes.

After a brief smile at Callie—which she returned with a wide one of her own—the man turned his full attention onto Reese. "Mr. Bennett." Displeasure sounded in his voice. "Mrs. Singletary is not at home. Nor was she expecting you today."

"I'm not here to see the widow." He removed his coat from Callie's shoulders and handed it to the other man. "My business is with Miss Mitchell."

"Ah." A disapproving sniff. "I see."

Reese suspected the man did, indeed, see the situation clearly. Perhaps even clearer than he himself did.

"We'll be in the blue parlor," he announced.

Another sniff. "Very good, sir."

Before the butler could say more, Reese took Callie's arm and escorted her up the winding staircase, down the twisting corridors and into the blue parlor. With each step, he shored up his fortitude, knowing the next half hour would require patience.

Extreme patience.

The only saving grace to this highly awkward situation was the realization that Reese could better control his bride search with Callie in charge. Unlike Mrs. Singletary, the younger woman would listen to him, respect his wishes and, thereby, address his needs above her own agenda.

He refused to entertain thoughts to the contrary.

Lips pressed into a flat line, he steered her toward a chair angled in such a way as to catch the heat wafting from the fireplace.

"I see someone anticipated us." He nodded to the crackling fire.

"This is one of Mrs. Singletary's favorite rooms." Callie smoothed out her skirt and then glanced up at him. "She insists a fire be prepared in the hearth, regardless of the time of year or the weather."

Caught in that beautiful sea-green gaze, Reese found no ready response, other than to say, "Ah."

He folded his large frame in the chair situated next to hers. "I believe you wanted to discuss my search for a bride."

"Indeed, yes." She released a slight smile that highlighted a glint in her eyes, a glint that hinted at an impish, playful spirit beneath the carefully bland exterior.

Reese couldn't think of a worse thing to notice. Why did this woman call to a part of him he'd thought long buried?

Why her? Why now?

He cleared his throat. "Where would you like to begin?"

Face scrunched in a delicate frown, she tapped her chin with a fingertip. "I suppose we should start by reviewing your list of requirements for your future bride."

The censure in her voice was unmistakable. It was the same tone she'd used the previous evening when she'd read his list aloud. "We have already done that, just last night."

"Yes, but as I mentioned then, I believe your qualifications are too vague and unclear, it's as if you threw them together in a matter of minutes."

He steeled his jaw. "I assure you, I spent considerable time drawing up my list."

"Oh, really?" She gave him a look that reminded him of an unbending, ruthless schoolmarm. "Just how much effort did you put into the task?"

"I don't see how that signifies in our discussion."

"Then you won't mind telling me." There was that schoolmarm look again, matched with a tone that would make any young boy cringe.

Fortunately for Reese he was no longer a young boy. "I took a full thirty minutes. However—"

"Thirty minutes? On each item?"

"No." Absurd. "I spent thirty minutes drawing up the entire list."

She gaped at him. "That is all the thought you put into something as important as your future bride?"

"Yes, that is all. *However,*" he repeated, determined to state his case before she interrupted him again, "I have thought on the matter for years."

She went back to tapping her chin, seemingly lost in thought. "Can I assume, then, that you are able to recite all seven items on the list?"

"Of course."

"Excellent." Now the schoolmarm showed up in her posture, rigid and unyielding. "Proceed."

"You are *quizzing* me?"

Her response was a lift of a single eyebrow. "You said you wanted my help. I cannot help you if you refuse to cooperate with the process."

A surprised laugh escaped him. The woman was relentless. A formidable adversary as any he'd encountered in the courtroom.

Did she know he liked nothing better than matching his wits with a worthy opponent?

"Very well." He shut his eyes a moment, controlled a familiar wave of anticipation. "She must be well-educated and articulate, which will also make her an excellent hostess. She should love children as much as I do, and want several of her own, at least five."

Her eyes full of appreciation, Callie nodded. The first sign of approval since they'd sat down.

Reese found himself emboldened by her silent endorsement and continued with more fervor. "She must come from a good family and value strong family ties. As you know, my father is very important to me. She must get along with him, and he with her."

Once again, Callie blessed him with a nod of approval.

His pulse roared in his veins. In his heart, Reese knew he was on the verge of something real, something emotional and exciting.

There was no reason he couldn't enjoy the process

of finding himself a wife. With Callie at the helm, he might even have moments of great fun.

As soon as the thought materialized, Reese instantly changed his mind. He did not want to incite questions from Callie, or go into detail as to his reasoning behind the remaining items on his list. Or rather, *one* of the remaining items on his list. The most important one. The one that was not up for discussion or would ever be subject to compromise.

But if he wanted to find a suitable woman to marry, he must press on. He drew in a tight breath. *Press on, Reese. Press on.* "She must be conventional, steady and predictable. I will not, under any circumstances, consider a known risk taker or—"

"Wait. Just wait a minute." Callie stopped him with a hand in the air. "Why are you dead set against a risk taker?"

"That is my business." He turned his head away, shut his eyes a moment, and fought for control. "Accept my wishes on this, or we're done."

Callie didn't know what she heard in Reese's voice. Not anger, precisely, but a hint of underlying pain.

She wanted to reach to him, to offer him comfort and soothe away that haunted look in his eyes. It was the same sensation she'd experienced when he'd arrived at Charity House today.

She still didn't have the right to push past his guard.

Oh, but the urge to go to him persisted. Warning bells were going off in her head by the dozen, even as she reached her hand out and closed it over his.

"Reese, I'm not asking you to explain." She spoke in her softest voice, the timbre barely above a whisper.

"I'm sure most men, given a choice, would wish for their wives to act in a manner that would keep them out of harm's way."

"Then you understand."

Far better than she cared to admit. Oh, how she knew what came from taking risks.

"I do," she said, quickly amending her response and adding, "I suppose so."

Although she knew the dangers of taking risks in her own life, she didn't understand why Reese wanted a steady, predictable woman in his.

What terrible tragedy had he endured? Had he watched his mother die in an accident? Someone else?

As the questions rattled around in her brain, Callie realized how little she knew about this man, nearly nothing about his past. Why was that? Why did she know so little about him when he'd once been betrothed to her own sister?

Perhaps Fanny hadn't been the only one who'd kept herself hidden from her intended. Perhaps Reese had done so, as well.

Something to think about. "You haven't mentioned two items from your list. Do you remember what they are?"

She didn't need him to voice them again. Except, she did. She had a point to make.

A very large point.

Leaning back in his chair, Reese stretched out his legs and turned his head back to hers. His gaze had gone completely blank, free of all emotion. "She must have a good moral compass."

That one still perplexed Callie. "Do you mean to

say, she should be a godly, Christian woman with an unshakable faith?"

He didn't answer her question, but instead said, "And finally, she should be a witty conversationalist."

"Because…?"

"I should think it obvious." He crossed one ankle over the other, rested his elbows on the arms of the chair and began tapping out a rhythmic staccato with his fingertips. "If I am to spend the rest of my life with a woman, I must be able to tolerate her company."

Callie blinked at him in astonishment. "Let me get this straight. You believe that if a woman is a good conversationalist, then her company will be pleasing, as well?"

He inclined his head. "Stands to reason."

Could the man truly be that obtuse? Didn't he know there was more to a happy marriage than witty banter?

Apparently not.

Perhaps she should attack the subject from a different angle. "I noticed you left out love as a requirement, both last night and again today."

"Love is not a necessary component to a successful union."

"You would be happy trapped in a loveless marriage?"

"I didn't say I wanted a loveless marriage."

Confounding, baffling man. "But, Reese, you just said—"

He cut her off midsentence. "I expect to like and admire the woman I marry."

Oh, really. "You did not put that on the list."

He waved his hand in dismissal. "It's understood."

Oh, really.

Callie remembered Mrs. Singletary's initial response when she'd read through Reese's list. She'd muttered something about him being her toughest case to date. Ah, but he wasn't the widow's problem anymore.

He was Callie's.

She studied his handsome face. Dear, misguided, stubborn, *stubborn* man.

He shifted in his seat, scowled. "Callie, why are you looking at me like that?"

"How am I looking at you?"

"As if you fancied the notion of tossing me over a cliff."

She bit back a laugh. "You do realize that would be physically impossible."

His scowled deepened. "I meant it as a metaphor."

She hummed her response from deep in her throat. "Uh-huh."

"Callie, I mean it. I don't like that look in your eyes. It's disconcerting and bodes of—"

"Shh." She held up a finger. "I am trying to think."

His response was a hum so similar to hers she nearly laughed. Wagging her finger at him, she mentally shuffled through the names of various women she knew in town, women who met every one of his requirements, uninspired as they were.

She came up with four names with very little effort. Lovely girls, all of them, at least on the surface, until one spent more than a few moments in their company. Another point of contention Callie had with his list. Reese had failed to include a single personality trait for the woman with whom he planned to spend the rest of his life.

So be it. She would present her initial batch of women.

It was nothing less than he deserved.

Feeling a bit remorseful—but only a very little bit—she leaned forward and captured his gaze. "For your prospective bride, what say you to Miss Catherine Jameson?"

"Catherine Jameson? You cannot be serious."

Not in the least, but she persisted, anyway. "She meets every requirement on your list."

"She also laughs like a hyena."

True. But Callie couldn't resist this chance to drive home her point. "I assume you have heard a hyena laugh?"

He shot her a warning glare. "At least once a year, whenever I visit the zoo."

"How wonderful that you have cause to visit the zoo that often."

He did not respond to this, but instead shot her another warning glare.

Callie simply smiled. "What about Grace Mallory? She's very pretty."

Beautiful, actually. And again, fit every one of his requirements.

"No," he said through tight lips.

"No?"

"Her mother is trying."

"You won't be marrying her mother," Callie pointed out oh-so-helpfully, which earned her a third warning glare, this one especially fierce.

She presented her next option. "That brings us to Penelope Ferguson."

"No."

"What's wrong with Penelope?" As if Callie didn't know. The girl had been beyond intrusive at Mrs. Singletary's dinner party last night.

She expected Reese to remind her of this important little detail, but he went with a vastly different argument. "Her name begins with *P*."

Callie bit back a laugh. "You would reject the girl merely because you don't like the first letter of her name?"

"It's unimaginative on her parents' part, giving each of their daughters a name that starts with the same letter as the mother. It's impossible to keep any of them straight."

"Oh, honestly, Reese." Callie pursed her lips. "You must realize that once you are married to Penelope you would at least be able to tell her apart from the others."

"No Ferguson girl. I am firm on this." He wound his hand in the air. "Who else did you have in mind?"

She thought for a moment. "Natalie Blankenship."

Reese held silent a full five seconds. Callie could see his mind working up a reason to reject Natalie along with the others.

"Natalie is charming," Callie added, a little miserably, because the girl was actually suitable. "She's lighthearted and smart and comes up with insights into human nature that are almost always correct."

More silence.

"She's pretty, too." Callie sighed. "Raven hair, blue eyes, exquisite skin."

Reese dragged a hand over his face. "Natalie is too…" His gaze filled with a triumphant gleam. "Short. My neck would not be able to withstand a lifetime of looking so far down just to meet her eyes."

"Now you're just being difficult. She's exactly the same height as Fanny."

"And we both know how that turned out."

Callie gaped at the man.

He held her stare, unflinching, then drew his feet back under him and leaned toward her. "Any other prospects you wish to run by me? Perhaps—" he leaned in closer still "—a woman I will actually consider?"

Well, well. Wasn't he clever? He'd been on to her game all along. She made a face at him. "I was merely trying to clarify my argument about your list of requirements, which as you must realize by now are too vague."

He sat back. "You have made your point."

Nevertheless, she wasn't through. "You must be more specific, Reese, or we will be at this for ages."

"Understood."

"Then you will revise your list at once?"

"I will."

Her pulse quickened at his ready agreement. She'd just bought herself some time. But how much? Enough to contact Fanny and convince her to return home? "And you won't rush the process," she ventured. "But you will truly think through each of your requirements?"

"Yes."

It was her turn to lean into his space. "When can I expect your changes?"

"Soon."

"Could you be more specific?" She must know exactly how much time she had to lure Fanny home.

"Monday," he said through a tight jaw. "I will deliver my revised list to you on Monday."

"Too soon," she muttered, threads of panic weaving through her control. "You must treat this process seriously."

"I *am* treating it seriously."

"Of course you are." She gave him a pitying look. "If you're hoping to end up with a bride whose name begins with the letter *P*."

A reluctant laugh escaped him. "You, Callie Mitchell—" he pointed his finger at her "—are a ruthless opponent."

"Thank you."

"I did not mean that as a compliment."

She sighed. "I know."

His well-cut lips curved. "I will present my new list to you only after a full week of consideration."

Better. So much better. "Deal."

He held out a hand. "Shall we shake on it?"

Why not? She pressed her palm to his and her heart took an extra hard thump. Her mind reeled.

From this moment on, Callie knew her life would never be the same. She'd won today's battle against Reese, but feared she'd already lost the war...for her heart.

Chapter Twelve

Reese kept busy the following week. He had a calendar full of appointments and court dates. Each client meeting required complete focus, the court appearances extensive preparation. In addition, there were contracts to review and business transactions to negotiate.

Even with the vast amount of work demanding his attention, Reese's mind kept returning to the other, more personal task before him, a task he'd put off all week, though he couldn't fathom why. Eight days after his conversation with Callie and the dreaded bride list—as he was coming to think of it—*still* needed rewriting.

Shoving away from the desk in his private study, he swiveled around and gazed out over the back lawn. The early morning sunlight glistened off the dew-covered grass. With the snowcapped mountains in the distance, the manicured lawn was picture perfect, as if painted by a master artist.

Reese rolled his shoulders. The idyllic scene was

too perfect, too untouched. Where were the signs of everyday activity? Of life itself?

If he squinted, he could almost see his future children racing across the lawn, their rousing game of tag turning up the grass and leaving divots. Two of the girls would be taking turns on the swing he would one day hang from a high tree branch. Meanwhile, Reese would be tossing a ball around with one of his older sons, his wife looking on, smiling and laughing, their youngest perched on her hip.

He rubbed a hand over his face, blew out a hiss and rolled his shoulders again. Had he waited too long to make such a dream come true? Had time run out?

No children would fill this rambling old house with laughter if he didn't find a woman to marry soon, which would never happen if he didn't get on with the business of drawing up his new list of requirements.

In her cheeky, impertinent way, Callie had pointed out the flaws in his original approach. He had, indeed, been too vague.

She'd won that battle fairly, extracting his promise to dedicate a full week to his new list. A week that had come to an end yesterday afternoon.

He'd delayed long enough.

Lips pressed in a grim line, he swiveled back around and pulled out a blank sheet of paper. He would approach the new list as he would any other assignment, with ruthless efficiency and rigid attention to detail.

He stared at the blank page a full five minutes.

What did he want in a wife?

He thought he knew. Now…he wondered. Perhaps he should start with personality. She should be kind and fiercely loyal. Excellent. He wrote those down.

What else?

He shut his eyes, sorting through possibilities. She should have a soft, feminine manner and know how to talk to frightened children, using the same amount of gentleness as Callie had with Gabriella Velasquez.

Reese opened his eyes and wrote down *soft, feminine manner* then added *patient, gentle and nurturing*.

She should smile often. Yet another image of Callie materialized. Reese liked all her smiles, the sweet ones, the teasing ones, but he especially liked the one she'd given him on the back porch of Charity House. His future wife should also know how to build him up, rather than tear him down. When Callie had praised him for his efforts on Daniel's behalf, Reese had been ready to conquer the world.

He wrote down *pretty smile* and *full of encouraging words*.

A familiar knock on the doorjamb had him turning the paper over, facedown.

His father stepped into the room. "You're up and at it early this morning."

Rising to his feet, Reese glanced at the clock on the mantelpiece, noted the time. Half past eight. "No earlier than usual."

"It's Sunday, son."

Because he wanted to avoid a lengthy dissertation on the importance of honoring the Sabbath—the same argument his father presented every Sunday morning—Reese kept his face blank. "I know what day it is."

"Then why are you already hard at it?" His father's gaze flicked across Reese's desk, narrowed over the stack of contracts he'd brought home with him Friday evening. "The Lord set aside this day for rest."

"I took most of yesterday off. I am sufficiently refreshed."

"You know that's not what I meant."

Reese opened his mouth to speak, then stopped. His father was a brilliant attorney, best known for his litigation skills. Further discussion on the matter would only turn into an argument, which would eventually end in a stalemate.

"You work too hard, son."

Feigning boredom, Reese leaned back against his desk, folded his arms across his chest. "No harder than you did at my age, or the subsequent twenty-five years following."

"My point, precisely." Remorse shifted in the other man's eyes. "I don't want you ending up like me."

"It would be an honor to follow in your footsteps." Reese uncrossed his arms. "You took what grandfather started and built Bennett, Bennett and Brand into a prestigious law firm with a reputation for honesty and integrity."

"That may be true." Eyes full of unspoken regrets slid past Reese, brushed over the stacks of papers on his desk, then shot back. "But there's no pleasure in a lifetime of hard work if all you have to show for your efforts are a large sum of money in the bank and a stellar reputation."

Hearing the underlying message beneath the words, Reese realized his father was lonely. Why had he not noticed that before?

Would he welcome grandchildren in this house? Would that be enough to fill the void in his life? Surely, it couldn't hurt. "You will be happy to know I plan to marry by the end of the year."

His father stilled. "You are courting a woman, someone in particular?"

"Not yet, but I will be in the foreseeable future."

"Do I know her?"

Reese wasn't sure how to answer that question. Both he and his father could very well already know the woman Reese would eventually marry. Or they may not. Best to skirt the question altogether.

He could, however, offer a bit more information to assuage the older man's curiosity. "I have enlisted Mrs. Singletary's assistance in my search for a suitable bride, at least originally, however—"

"You what?" His father stared at him, mouth gaping open. "Have you gone mad, allowing Beatrix Singletary that much control over your life?"

"She isn't in control of anything." Reese clenched his jaw so tight he felt a muscle jerk. "In fact, she has handed over the task to her companion."

His father looked at him for a long moment, his face perfectly stunned. "Callie Mitchell is helping you find a bride?"

Reese bristled at the shock in his father's voice, ready to defend himself—and Callie—until he noted the hint of delight in his father's gaze and the twinge of some other emotion that bordered on...satisfaction?

"Why Callie is, she's—" his father gave a small, amused laugh "—the perfect choice."

Perfect? Reese begged to differ. Bossy, pushy, entirely too feisty? Absolutely. "I trust she'll steer me in the proper direction."

"No doubt, no doubt." The echo of a smile filled

his father's voice and, for once, he let the matter drop without giving his opinion in agonizing detail.

"I had better be going, or risk arriving late to church." He pulled out his pocket watch, made a grand show of checking the time, then glanced back at Reese. "Will you come with me?"

"Can't." Reese pulled a stack of papers forward, feigning a need to get back to work. "I have several contracts to review before tomorrow morning."

"Attending church is expected of a man in your position."

Reese set down the paper, very slowly, very deliberately.

Getting married was expected. Attending church was expected. He was sorely tempted to behave in a manner that was decidedly unexpected.

He stifled the urge, as he always did. "You know why I don't attend church anymore."

"I do. And I understand your reticence." He gave Reese's shoulder a sympathetic squeeze. "What Reverend Walton said to you at Miranda's funeral was unforgivable."

Reese held silent, irritation burning hot. He shrugged out from under his father's grip and prowled the length of the room with clipped, angry strides.

Reverend Jeremiah Walton had started out as expected, giving Reese familiar platitudes and pat words of condolence. Miranda was with the Lord, safe in Jesus's arms, living in a better place where there was no more pain or sorrow.

Reese had heard it all before, had even prayed there was truth in the rhetoric. But when the man pulled Reese aside at Miranda's funeral and suggested she'd brought on her own death with her reckless behavior, Reese had walked out of the church. Either that, or punch the pompous, self-righteous man in the mouth.

Though he knew Jeremiah Walton was only one preacher, and had left town years ago, Reese had avoided church ever since.

"You'd like Beauregard O'Toole's sermons. They're inspiring without being overly preachy."

Perhaps he *would* get something out of returning to church, especially if he attended Beau's church. He liked the man, respected him, enjoyed debating complicated theological matters with him. In truth, Reese had been feeling empty lately. Perhaps he could use some Godly inspiration and sound, Biblical direction.

Was today the day?

Needing a moment to think, Reese stalked over to his desk and put his hand on the closest stack of papers. On top was the agreement between Mrs. Singletary and Jonathon Hawkins. His associate Garrett Mitchell had drawn up the initial contract and had done a stellar job. The verbiage put the widow and young entrepreneur in a legally binding partnership that benefited both equally.

With Mrs. Singletary's financial backing, Hawkins would soon expand his hotel empire into major cities beyond Denver, Chicago and St. Louis.

"Son? Did you hear what I said?"

Reese had nearly forgotten his father was in the room. "I'll attend church with you soon."

"You say that every Sunday."

He dismissed the perfectly compelling argument with a flick of his wrist. "Perhaps I mean it this time."

His father persisted. "Mrs. Singletary and her pretty companion will be there."

Reese didn't want to see Callie this morning. She would no doubt ask him about the dreaded bride list.

"I'll attend Beau's church with you in the next few weeks," he said again, more firmly. "It is a promise."

His father went to the door and spoke without looking back. "I'm going to hold you to that."

"I'd be disappointed if you didn't."

Chuckling, his father left the room. Reese moved around his desk and turned over the new list he'd begun for Callie.

He'd made a good start, but was it still too vague? Perhaps.

Rationally, he knew finding a woman to marry wasn't going to be as simple as creating a string of qualifications and then plugging in the most suitable candidate. But he had to start somewhere.

He fished out his original list from a drawer, read through it, his gaze returning several times to the line about children.

He wrote his desire for children on his new list. No use pretending he didn't crave a large brood of happy, healthy offspring. His children would never have to wonder whether their father loved them or not, something Gabriella and Daniel Velasquez had never experienced.

The twins touched Reese in ways he couldn't explain, urging him to do something about their situation, even knowing there was little he could do. They were in good hands.

Callie understood his sense of helplessness. He'd seen it in her eyes, those bright, deep green catlike eyes. There were times when she seemed open and available, transparently vulnerable yet full of inner strength and grit.

She was also full of mischief, as evidenced by her sassy opinions over his bride list. Opinions that rang a bit too true. He couldn't afford another mistake. One failed engagement was bad enough.

Two, unacceptable.

Callie claimed she needed specifics? Well, Reese would give her specifics.

He picked up a fresh sheet of paper and went to work.

Bright and early Monday morning, Callie stared in disbelief at her closet, her incredibly *bare* closet. No more oversized, ill-fitting dresses, no more ugly frocks or aprons or bonnets or coats or wraps, nothing but the two gowns Mrs. Singletary had loaned her.

The widow had followed through with her threat. She'd gathered up all of Callie's dresses and taken them away, presumably to donate to charity.

Callie felt violated.

Why, *why* must Mrs. Singletary insist on making her into a new creation? Why was it so important that Callie stand out from the crowd?

There was no reason for people to notice her, no need to garner unnecessary attention.

Her past mistake with Simon had taught her a hard lesson. It was best to remain quiet and small, easily ignored. The Bible supported her position on this in several places. *Clothe yourselves in righteousness.* As well as the command from the Apostle Peter, *Do not let your adornment be merely outward, rather let it be the hidden person of the heart.*

Sage words to live by.

She blinked at her closet, reached out, let her hand drop. This was terrible, another blow, as shocking as the one Fanny had dealt Callie by not responding to her most recent letter requesting she return home at once.

How long was Callie going to be able to stall Reese's bride search? More to the point, what was she supposed to wear today?

Had she not stayed up so late compiling her list of suitably unsuitable women for Reese, she would have taken the time to lay out her clothes before she'd gone to bed. Had she been her usual, efficient self she would have made this shocking discovery the previous evening.

She moved aside the borrowed dresses—they were not hers, regardless of what Mrs. Singletary said—thinking perhaps the widow had missed one of Callie's more suitable gowns.

She came away empty.

With profound reluctance, she stepped back and shut the closet door.

Resentment filled her. She was the widow's companion, not her current *project*. Not some doll to be dressed up and paraded out into the world.

"Meddlesome, interfering, intrusive woman."

"Who would that be, dear?"

Callie whirled around. Mrs. Singletary stood in the doorway, brows lifted, eyes twinkling with good humor.

More than a little miffed at her employer, Callie couldn't find it in her to feel embarrassed over her softly muttered words, words meant for her ears only.

As her own mother always said, eavesdroppers never heard anything good about themselves.

Still…

Callie shouldn't have spoken so plainly. The widow meant no harm, even if her tactics were a bit heavy-handed. "What have you done with my clothes?" she asked, proud that her voice came out calm and mildly curious.

"We discussed this, Callie." The widow moved deeper into the room. "I have sent the bulk of your wardrobe to the Home for Destitute Widows and Orphans. Though, I must say, I felt a little guilty doing so."

"As well you should," Callie muttered.

The widow lifted a delicate shoulder. "Your clothing was beyond ugly, ghastly really. Those poor women deserve better."

Outrage had Callie sputtering. "That, why that is just—"

"True?"

"Mean."

"And yet, also true."

With no ready comeback, Callie paced through her room. Back and forth, back and forth. She ended up at her closet again, threw open the door and scowled at the two gowns hanging there. "What am I supposed to wear today?" She touched the crimson grown. "This one is too fancy and the blue is too…"

Fetching, she nearly said. Thankfully, she refrained. Too telling and, depending on her tone, could be misconstrued as ungrateful.

Though she didn't appreciate the widow's tactics,

she knew Mrs. Singletary had acted out of kindness rather than ill will.

Nevertheless, Callie would have to visit a local dress shop as soon as possible, or perhaps Neusteters department store. She could not do so in her night-gown. She would have to wear the blue dress, after all.

"Not to worry, Callie." Mrs. Singletary drew alongside her and linked arms. "I have made an appointment with my personal seamstress. She will be here tomorrow morning at nine o'clock sharp."

"I am quite capable of shopping on my own."

Mrs. Singletary laughed in delight. "We both know my fashion judgment is far superior to yours."

At the widow's teasing tone, Callie felt her own laugh work up through the layers of frustration and anxiety. She pressed her lips tightly together.

"In the meantime, I have found several other dresses in my wardrobe that will suit you."

"But of course."

"What did you say, dear?" The widow asked the question while motioning someone into the room from the hallway.

"It was not important, Mrs. Singletary."

The widow hummed in response, even as she guided one of her maids into the room.

Callie didn't recognize the petite black-haired girl. No more than seventeen, maybe eighteen, she held two dresses draped over her arms, one in a rich emerald-green and another made in the most beautiful shade of lavender Callie had ever seen.

She eyed both creations, her gaze hovering over the lighter of the two. "I thought you said no pale colors."

"Lavender is the exception." The widow led Callie

to her dressing table, pressed her gently into the chair. "Julia, could you please come here."

The maid carefully set the two dresses on the bed and did as Mrs. Singletary requested.

"Callie, this is my newest maid, Julia."

The two women greeted one another with a smile.

"Julia comes highly recommended by Polly Ferguson and is considered a wonder with hair."

Knowing where this was headed, dreading it all the same, Callie held silent. What could she say, anyway? *My hairstyle is perfectly acceptable, Mrs. Singletary.*

The widow was a force to be reckoned with in this mood. Runaway freight trains could learn a thing or two from her.

"I trust my friend's opinion, of course," Mrs. Singletary said to Julia. "But, alas, before I allow you to work your talents on my hair, I wish to test your skills on my companion."

"Yes, ma'am, perfectly understandable." Julia turned her attention to Callie. Picking up a small clump of hair, she studied the curling blond locks with squinted eyes. "You have beautiful hair, miss, the color is extraordinary."

"Thank you."

"You are in good hands, Callie dear. I shall be off." The widow beamed at her before heading to the doorway. "I have much to do before my attorney arrives."

Callie didn't bother sighing at the way her heart lifted at this pronouncement. She was actually growing used to the sensation.

Mrs. Singletary paused at the doorway then turned back around and moved toward the bed.

In silence, she considered the newest two dresses,

bouncing her gaze between Callie and the bed. At last, she picked up the lavender dress. "You will wear this one today. And this one—" she fingered the green gown "—when we attend the theater this evening."

"Yes, Mrs. Singletary."

"One last request." The widow captured Callie's gaze in the mirror. "I would find it most helpful if you would sit in on my meeting with Mr. Bennett today. I will expect you in one hour and twenty minutes."

A week ago, Callie would have thought Mrs. Singletary's request strange and disconcerting. Not today.

A week ago, Callie would have worried that Mrs. Singletary had an agenda in asking her to join her business meeting with Reese.

Not. Today.

Because, today, Callie accepted the truth about her employer. Beatrix Singletary was shrewd and cunning.

And she always, *always* got her way.

Chapter Thirteen

Whenever Reese met with Mrs. Singletary at her home, he kept the conversation brief and to the point. Today was no exception. With a complete lack of fanfare, he laid out the particulars of Jonathon Hawkins's requests. "The hotelier wants three changes to the initial contract Garrett Mitchell designed."

Concern shifted in the widow's gaze. "Do not tell me Mr. Hawkins is having second thoughts."

"Not in the least. I don't believe you will find the stipulations troublesome."

This seemed to satisfy the widow's misgiving. "Carry on."

"The first is minor, a simple case of rewording." He pointed out the newly worded passage with his index finger. "The second is a bit more complicated. It states if either of you decides to sell your share of the properties, you will give the other first rights to the purchase."

The widow considered the changes in silence, her eyes tracking over the page.

At last, she nodded her head. "I see no problem with either provision."

"Agreed." He flipped to the next page. "The third change is no more complicated than the other two, but could prove a problem if you aren't in agreement with Mr. Hawkins on the matter. He wants—"

The widow held up a finger as if she had something to say, then brought it back down. "Go on."

"Mr. Hawkins is insisting the hotels retain the Dupree name and asserts this point is nonnegotiable." Since Beatrix Singletary did not take ultimatums well, Reese continued before she could speak. "As you already know, the original Hotel Dupree was owned by Marc Dupree before he married Laney and joined forces with her at Charity House."

"Ah, yes, hence the hotel's name." The widow's brow furrowed. "That still doesn't explain why Mr. Hawkins insists on keeping the name."

"He was one of the first residents of Charity House."

The widow blinked at him in surprise. "I knew he had a personal connection with the Duprees, but…" Mrs. Singletary stopped to draw a breath. "I had not realized it was so direct."

"He believes his success in business is in large part due to Marc and Laney's influence in his life, especially Marc's. Maintaining the Dupree name on all current and future properties is his way of honoring their legacy."

The widow turned her head to the side, giving Reese her profile as she mulled over this last piece of information. "And if I refuse to maintain the Dupree name?"

Reese inhaled slowly. "The deal will fall apart and Mr. Hawkins will withdraw from further discussions."

She turned back to face him. "Maintaining the Dupree name is that important for him?"

"Yes."

"Very well." She picked up the quill beside her hand, dipped it into the ink pot and then flipped to the last page of the contract.

Reese couldn't refrain from asking, "You are not put off by Mr. Hawkins's refusal to negotiate on this point?"

"Indeed not—I admire the man's sense of loyalty." With a flourish, she signed her name on all three copies, set down the pen and then leaned back in her chair. "I believe I will very much enjoy working with him on this project."

"I will deliver the signed contracts to him this afternoon."

At the same moment he reached for the pages, a knock came from the other side of the door.

Mrs. Singletary flashed him one of her cagey grins. "The young woman has exquisite timing."

Reese's stomach lurched. He wasn't sure what the widow meant by the comment, but he had no doubt who the young woman was with exquisite timing.

In anticipation of Callie's entrance, Reese rose to his feet. He straightened the contracts into one neat pile then flipped open the lid of his briefcase.

Feeling a strange tightness in his chest, he shoved the contracts beneath the revised bride list.

Soft footsteps stopped a few feet behind him. "Hello, Reese."

He looked over his shoulder. Felt his gut roll again

as he turned around fully. The sight of Callie in a perfectly cut, fashionable, light purple dress ratcheted his heartbeat to an alarming pace. She'd done something different to her hair again. This newest style highlighted her long neck and arresting features.

The impact was like a punch to his heart. "Good afternoon, Callie." He wasn't surprised by the rustiness of his own voice. The woman made him uneasy, now more than ever. "You look quite lovely today."

"Thank you." She produced a slightly nervous smile.

Reese swallowed, hard.

He shouldn't be this attuned to the woman. She was Mrs. Singletary's companion, tasked with the duty of finding him a bride. She was only in his life to assist him in sorting through potential candidates. She would eventually fade into the background while Reese wooed another woman.

The thought didn't sit well.

Callie was not a porcelain doll on some shelf, to be dragged out when needed, then flung aside when she'd done her duty.

She deserved better.

As though reading his mind, she stared at him intently, almost defiantly, her green, green eyes running across his face, as if her entire focus was on him. No one but him.

He felt a spark of something long hidden away, a desire to toss away lists and ledgers, to once again discover the joy of a spontaneous act.

Dangerous, dangerous thinking. Riddled with disaster.

Reese was no longer a boy of eighteen. He and Callie had only just become friends. He must ignore this surge of affection and focus on his goal. To find a wife who would make him a decent companion and a proper hostess, a woman who would help him fill his nursery.

Mrs. Singletary shoved her way between them.

Reese balked at the intrusion. In a show of silent solidarity, he moved to stand beside Callie.

The widow smiled fondly at them both. "How is the bride hunt coming along?"

Oh, she was a sly one, broaching the subject with the calmness of one announcing it looked like rain coming on the horizon. One day, Reese would like to see Beatrix Singletary on the wrong end of a match-making plot.

Callie stepped forward. "We have hit a slight snag in Reese's bride search, but not an insurmountable one." She smiled over at him. "I have charged Reese with the task of revising his original list of requirements. We will proceed once he's finished."

"Which, you will be pleased to discover, I am." He dug inside his briefcase, pulled out the slip of paper on top. "I present to you—" he thrust out his hand "—my new list."

Callie's mouth formed a perfect O, but no words came forth. Nor did she reach for the paper.

Why not? She'd told him to draw up a new list and take his time doing so. He'd followed her directive, coming up with the most exacting specifics with the most precise language possible.

He pressed the paper into her palm.

She lowered her gaze. Almost instantly, her head shot back up. For a moment her mask of exquisite, maddening control fell away and emotion shone through.

There. There in her eyes, he saw astonishment and alarm and, most baffling of all, hurt.

Somehow Reese had managed to hurt her. That hadn't been his intent. He might have been a bit too precise with a few of the items, for levity's sake only. He'd thought Callie would see the intended humor.

He touched her arm, wanting her to understand.

She shifted out of his reach. His hand dropped away.

Uncomfortable silence hung between them.

"I see you two have much to discuss." Mrs. Singletary inserted herself into the conversational void, her voice a mix of flatness and droll irony. "I'll leave you to it."

Reese held himself motionless as the widow exited the room. Only after she shut the door did he shift his stance. He'd never been restless or edgy. Until Callie.

She turned to him, her gaze unreadable.

It was then that he realized she wasn't telling him he'd been too vague this time around. Nor was she pointing her finger at him in outrage, or scowling at him like a schoolmarm—pity, that—or telling him he'd still gotten it all wrong.

Reese had a brief insight that if he would only let down his guard, and open his heart, even a little, this woman would light up his world as no one ever had before.

He cleared his throat, as he seemed to do far too often when he was alone in Callie's company. "Is there something wrong with my list?"

"No." She shook her head. "Or rather, yes. I mean, no."

"Which is it? Yes or no?"

"Oh, Reese, your new list. It's so very…specific."

Annoyance burst into life. "Which is what you said you wanted. You told me my requirements were too vague. You insisted I should be more specific."

A sigh leaked past her lips. "I see you took my words to heart."

"Of course I did. You were right, Callie, I hadn't spent the proper amount of time or thought on the first go-round. Any number of women could have fit my original requirements, including highly unsuitable women. So I—"

"Reese." She held up her hand to stop him from continuing. "I'm afraid you might have been a bit too specific this time around."

He scowled. "Which item are you referencing?"

Lowering her head, she studied the page. "You have listed you desire a woman with brown hair."

"What's wrong with brown hair?" Miranda's had been a wild flaming red. Fanny's, pale blond. It made sense for him to avoid both colors.

"Do you realize how many shades of brown hair there are?"

He eyed her warily. "Is that a trick question?"

"There are scores. Golden brown. Reddish brown. Dark brown. Black brown."

Why was she harping on hair color? "Any shade of brown will do."

Something flashed in her eyes, something that looked like hurt. A protective instinct took hold of him, followed by a desire to make her smile. Before he could stop himself, he took her hand, brought it to his lips. "Attend the theater with me tonight."

"I…" She cocked her head *"What?"*

"Callie Mitchell." He pulled her closer, pressed her palm to his heart. "Would you do me the honor of being my guest?"

She drew her hand free, tucked it against her waist. "I am already attending the theater with Mrs. Singletary."

"Then you two must sit with me and my father in our box. I insist," he added when it looked as though she might protest. "If the play is boring, we will discuss my bride list further."

It was the last thing he wanted to do but, at the moment, seemed the absolute right thing to say.

"I'll let Mrs. Singletary know of your invitation." She lifted her chin. "The final decision will be up to her."

"Fair enough." He would make sure the widow accepted. Callie *must* sit beside him tonight.

The desire to have her close, sitting in the seat next to him, shouldn't fill him with such anticipation. But it did.

Reese refused to analyze his motivation.

So he wanted to provide Callie with an evening that brought her joy and happiness? They were friends, after all. It made sense that he would want to please her. To restore her pretty smile. A night at the theater seemed the perfect place to start.

What could possibly go wrong?

All this talk of marriage was beginning to depress Callie. She needed a distraction, if only for an afternoon. With Mrs. Singletary taking tea with a friend, that left her several hours to fill before she had to dress for the theater.

Any activity would do, as long as it took her mind off of Reese's latest list of requirements. Brown hair, indeed, what was the man thinking?

Twirling a lock of her pale blond hair, Callie tried not to think about his other requirements. Most of which she would never hope to meet. She could not speak at least two other languages besides English, only Spanish, and not very well. She could not play a musical instrument.

She could not sing in tune.

Really, Reese had been alarmingly specific this time around.

Telling herself she was merely curious, Callie picked up his list and read it again, from top to bottom, more slowly this time. Other than wanting children, there was only one other requirement she met. Her name did not begin with the letter *P*.

She rolled her eyes to the ceiling, a bubble of laughter escaping through her pursed lips. The man was impossible. Really quite funny. And oh-so-endearing.

She looked back at the list, sighed miserably.

No scandal in her past.

The fatal blow. A gut punch, as her brothers would say.

Technically, Callie hadn't actually ignited a scandal when she'd run off with Simon. But her behavior had been shameful. At the very least, her judgment would forever be suspect. *Bad company corrupts good character.*

What would Reese think if he found out what she'd done?

Tears pricked at the back of her eyes. She wrapped her arms around her middle and tried not to cry.

Shoring up her emotions, she retrieved her Bible from the nightstand. She searched around in the Psalms for some verse, any verse, to make her feel less dismal. Nothing. She landed on *1 Peter*. She read for a while, mostly skimming the passages until she was in the fourth chapter. Everyone had a talent, so the Apostle claimed, gifted to them by God.

Perhaps tapping into her talent might help with her sour mood.

Lowering to her hands and knees, she fumbled around beneath her bed, found the box of paints, brushes and round canvases she'd tucked away. She sat back on her heels and ran her palms over the rectangular wooden box.

Back at school, Callie had loved art classes. It wasn't until she'd taken a course in miniature portraiture that she'd discovered her true talent. One she pursued for her own enjoyment.

She took out a blank, three-inch oval canvas and positioned it on the small writing desk near the window. Natural light was always best for the intricate detail work required for small portraits.

Once her paints were mixed and sitting in colorful piles on the palate, she began.

Time evaporated.

Confusion and hurt disappeared, leaving only the creative process. She'd nearly forgotten the joy of putting an image on canvas, of making a picture out of nothing but an idea, the closest she would ever come to understanding the beauty and order of the world God had created with His hands.

Hours later, when the sky had faded to a dull purple

and the light in her room took on a gray cast, Callie sat back and studied her handiwork.

A bride and groom stared back at her. The bride wore white, in the same style as the crimson gown Mrs. Singletary had loaned her. Callie looked closer at the image. Without realizing it, she'd painted her own face on the bride.

The groom wore a black formal suit with tails, a crisp white shirt and bow tie beneath. His hair was nearly as black as the suit, his eyes one shade lighter and his face...

She leaned in closer still, gasped.

The groom's face belonged to Reese.

Callie had painted a wedding portrait of them together.

A sound of dismay whistled in her throat. To dream of more than friendship with him was one thing, but to put that secret hope on canvas? Insufferable.

As she cupped the tiny canvas in her palm, she admitted the truth at last. Her heart yearned for Reese.

Which meant her heart was headed for disappointment.

Even if, by some strange twist of events, he turned his attention onto her, Callie could never win him for herself. He belonged to Fanny. And even if he didn't, her past mistake would always be with her, looming as a dark reminder of her true nature.

"Miss?" Julia popped into the room, holding several magazines against her. "Where are you?"

"Over here," she called out.

"Why are you sitting in the dark?"

"Time got away from me." She swiped at her eyes. "I hadn't realized dusk was upon us."

Julia walked through the room, turning on lamps and wall sconces as she progressed. "Mrs. Singletary sent me to style your hair for this evening's event."

As if waiting for her cue, the widow herself sauntered into the room. "Let's try something more festive for our evening at the theater." She took one of the magazines from the maid. "Something like, say—" she flipped through the pages "—this one here."

Julia leaned over the magazine. "That would look rather nice on your companion, but what about this one instead?" She flipped the page and placed her finger on another image.

While the two consulted over Callie's hairstyle, ignoring her completely, she took the opportunity to slip the portrait she'd painted in the back of a drawer of her writing desk. She then stored her paints under her chair as stealthily as possible.

Thankfully, neither woman paid her any attention.

"I hear the Gibson Girl is all the rage out East," Julia remarked, turning the page once more. "It looks like this."

"Oh, my, yes. That would suit Callie quite well, quite well indeed." Mrs. Singletary's voice filled with satisfaction. "It is decided. Carry on, Julia. You have one hour to transform my companion into a Gibson Girl."

Having issued her command, the widow swept out of the room.

Much to Callie's relief, Julia performed her duties in silence. She wasn't in the mood for conversation.

When she was fully dressed, Callie turned in a tight circle and faced the mirror. She hardly recognized herself. Sighing in pleasure, she stroked her hand down the silk damask in a stunning emerald green. The color was exquisite and added a golden tone to her skin.

The dress itself had a rounded neckline bordered by a thin row of lace and pale green flowers. She'd never worn anything so lovely, had never seen her hair look both disheveled and elegant at the same time.

The maid looked at her expectantly. "What do you think?"

"You are very talented, Julia."

The girl grinned. "It's as if the hairstyle were created just for you."

Callie touched her hair, most of which was piled high on her head in a loose topknot with a waterfall of curls caressing her cheeks. *Soft* and *romantic* were the words that came to mind.

A wave of pure happiness crashed over her. Why not embrace her transformation, if only for tonight? Why not revel in being an attractive woman?

She studied her image in the mirror a moment longer. She looked young, beautiful and innocent. For that one instant, she felt as if she was all three.

Chapter Fourteen

Reese thought he'd conquered the dangerous leanings of his youth. For fourteen years, he'd consciously avoided situations that might lead to messy, emotional entanglements.

Yet here he stood, raging inside, battling against his very self, merely because Callie Mitchell had entered the theater's atrium. Every effort to hold off the rush of feeling sweeping through him proved useless.

He hardly recognized himself.

The way his heart dipped in his chest did not belong to the man he'd become, a man renowned for his restraint, who adhered to a rigid set of rules and personal standards.

Dressed in a deep green dress that highlighted her blond hair and trim figure, Callie called to the part of Reese he'd locked tightly away. She sparkled like a precious jewel, her entire being lit from the inside out.

He was not the only man who noticed.

A jolt of possessiveness shuddered through him, making him uncomfortably aware that he loathed the idea of sharing Callie with anyone tonight.

When their eyes met over the crowd, Reese felt another catch in his throat. He took the moment in, like a dream, then shook himself free.

"Ah, Mr. Bennett, there you are." Mrs. Singletary shouldered through the crush of theater patrons, Callie following beside her. "Please tell me you have not been awaiting our arrival down here in the crowded atrium."

"I have, indeed." His voice was that of a man doomed to a fate he could no longer prevent. "I wanted to make certain you found your way to my box without incident."

"How very gentlemanly of you."

He inclined his head.

Callie shifted closer to him, presumably to be heard over the din. Whatever reason, Reese's collar felt too tight.

"Has your father joined you this evening?"

Reese enjoyed the way her winged brows knit delicately together as she asked the question, the way she looked him straight in the eye.

"He is already upstairs. Come. Allow me to escort you the rest of the way." He offered his arm to Callie, waited until she threaded her gloved hand through the crook of his elbow before turning to Mrs. Singletary and going through the process a second time.

Keeping both women near, he focused on conquering the stairs at a sedate but steady pace. By the time they reached the final landing the crowd had thinned to a mere smattering of theatergoers seeking out their reserved seating.

Reese released the women. "Ladies." He moved the curtain aside. "After you."

Inside their box, his father immediately took over the pleasantries. Reese hung back.

Propping a shoulder against the wall, he watched Callie laugh at something his father said. She looked comfortable. Relaxed and happy.

Reese was no longer a fanciful man, yet the sight of her unfettered joy gave him immense pleasure.

The more time he spent in Callie's company the more he grew to appreciate her understated beauty and unique personality. Beneath the starch was a kind, pure heart and an intelligent mind.

She took his breath away.

The sensation had little to do with the change in her outer appearance. Something profound was happening to the woman, an overcoming of her innate shyness that brought her inner beauty to the surface.

What must it have been like, he wondered, to live in the shadow of a sister like Fanny?

Reese studied Callie's lovely face. She looked a lot like Fanny. And yet, not at all.

Callie was far more beautiful.

Reese couldn't believe it had taken him this long to notice.

Smiling, she turned her head toward him. Their gazes merged and Reese was caught once again inside a pair of beautiful sea-green eyes.

His pulse thundered in his ears.

Still smiling, Callie broke away from his father and Mrs. Singletary.

The thunder turned into a roar.

Out of the corner of his eye, Reese saw his father take Mrs. Singletary's arm and guide her to the seats in front of the railing in their box. Their bent heads and hushed voices indicated they were in a deep conversation.

Neither looked back at Reese and Callie. They might as well be alone.

He fought back a bout of uncharacteristic nerves.

"Reese?" Callie's hand came to rest on his forearm. "Are you unwell?"

How like her, he thought, to react with genuine concern.

"I am perfectly well." How like him, to immediately deny anything less than faultless control.

"You are sure?" Callie persisted. "You seem different tonight, not quite yourself."

How right she was.

"Busy day at work. My head is full of—" *you,* he nearly blurted out, catching himself just in time "—complicated legal matters."

She squeezed his arm, the small gesture one of quiet understanding and affection. "You work too hard."

"I suppose, sometimes I do." The admission did not come easily, but even in this small matter Reese didn't want to mislead this woman.

Her mouth gentled and her eyes warmed and he thought his head might explode from the wonder of her.

"Are you a fan of comedies?" he blurted out.

Two perfectly winged eyebrows arched upward. "Changing the subject?"

Absolutely.

Reaching to one of the plush velvet chairs behind his father and Mrs. Singletary, Reese picked up a playbill. "I was referring to tonight's performance. Shakespeare's *As You Like It.*" He read the title aloud, then slid his gaze across the lead actor's photograph. "A Simon Westgrove is playing the role of Orlando."

"What?" Callie yanked the two-page brochure away from Reese, ran her gaze wildly over the cover. "It can't be. It's just not possible."

Her stunned reaction was completely unexpected, as was the way her face had paled to a dingy gray.

"Callie." He took her arm and steered her to the back of the box, away from his father and Mrs. Singletary to afford a degree of privacy. "What is it? What's wrong?"

"It's. Oh, Reese, I…" She glanced up at him, her eyes glassy and unseeing, as if she was lost in another time, another life. "I do not like this play. Or—" she choked out a bitter laugh "—this particular actor."

Although the play wasn't especially a favorite of Reese's, either—the plot relied too heavily on deception—he sensed the lead actor was the real cause of Callie's sudden anguish.

"You have seen Simon Westgrove perform this play before?"

She nodded, her eyes miserable.

"When I was attending school in Boston I frequented the theater often. I…" She broke off, blinked several times, took a slow, deep breath and then squared her shoulders.

Another slow breath, a jerk of her chin, and then the rigid, controlled Callie Mitchell slid into place.

Gone were the soft eyes and warm smile, replaced with a cold, rigidly blank stare.

Reese suspected he knew why. "Do you know Simon Westgrove, personally?"

"Yes." She didn't expand, but the shadows lurking

in her eyes spoke volumes. The famous actor had done something to hurt Callie.

Reese wanted to whisk her out of the theater, to someplace safe, somewhere that would restore her sweet smile and the kind, approachable woman who hugged frightened children.

"Do you want me to tell Mrs. Singletary you are ill?"

Her spine stiffened. "Don't be absurd."

The lights flickered, indicating the start of the play. They silently took their seats in the chairs directly behind Mrs. Singletary and Reese's father. He leaned close to Callie. "I will escort you home and—"

"That won't be necessary." She spoke without looking at him. "I am perfectly happy to remain in my seat for the entire performance."

Happy? No, she wasn't.

Wishing to soothe away her pain, he reached for her hand. He acted on impulse and entirely without an agenda other than to offer Callie his silent support.

She barely acknowledged him, except to close her fingers tightly around his.

Musical notes filled the theater. A hush came over the audience.

The curtain began its ascent.

Callie shut her eyes briefly, drew in several deep breaths, and then several more. Reese knew the technique well, employed it often himself. She was gathering her composure, and having phenomenal success.

She barely flinched when Simon Westgrove entered the stage and recited his opening line.

She was so in control, so brave, Reese wanted to

pull her close. He leaned over her instead and said, "You are safe with me."

He wasn't sure where those words came from, but he sensed they were the ones she most needed to hear right now.

She held perfectly still for one beat, two. Then, slowly, very, very slowly, she turned her gaze to meet his.

The impact of her misery was like a punch to his gut. "Callie—"

"Thank you, Reese." She pressed a fingertip to his lips. "You cannot know how much your presence means to me."

Tears pooled in her eyes. Blinking rapidly, she ruthlessly held them in check.

Compelled, he lowered his head, brought her hand to his lips then straightened. Though he didn't look at her again, he kept their fingers entwined.

She did not attempt to pull away.

Only when the curtain descended over the stage for intermission did she unclench her fingers from around his.

Staring straight ahead, she did not applaud the performance. She did not move a muscle.

Reese ached for her.

"Well, I say." Mrs. Singletary stood and turned to smile at them. "That Simon Westgrove is everything the rumors contend. Marvelously talented, indeed."

Though her reaction was nearly impossible to detect, Reese felt Callie stiffen beside him.

The widow's eyes narrowed. "Are you not enjoying yourself, Callie?"

She produced a broad smile. "I am having a grand time."

Her voice sounded brittle.

The widow's eyes narrowed even more, but she must have caught Reese's imperceptible shake of his head because she merely patted Callie on the shoulder and said, "I am glad to hear it, dear."

She turned to Reese's father. "Come, my friend, I have a mind to see who else is in attendance tonight."

The older man's lips curved. "The usual suspects, I presume."

"You jaded old man." She slapped playfully at his arm.

"You think me wrong?"

"I dare say, no." She linked her arm through his. "But I refuse to admit defeat until I have checked for myself, which I do not wish to do alone."

Reese's father chuckled. "And so you won't."

They left with no further fuss.

Reese waited an additional three minutes before breaking the heavy silence in the box.

He could go for the direct approach, or attempt to interject some levity into the situation.

"The play was wretched. The worst I've suffered through in years." He waved a hand in dismissal. "Predictable storyline and dreadful acting, especially from the untalented male lead."

His tactic worked. Callie laughed. It was a strained, paltry sound, and lacked all signs of joy, but Reese claimed it a victory.

"Thank you, Reese." Callie swiped at her cheeks. "That was exactly what I needed to hear."

"Want to talk about it?"

She shook her head.

"I'm a good listener."

She craned her neck forward, glanced at the box on their left, then over to the one on their right. "So, I would humbly suggest, are many others here tonight."

Message received. Reese began a lengthy exposition on his reasons for disliking the play.

Simon. Of all the actors, in all the acting companies traveling across America, Simon Westgrove was in Denver, performing the role of Orlando. The same character he'd played the night Callie had first met him.

Her breath snagged on a skittering heartbeat, even as the memory of her folly took hold.

Her inability to see beyond Simon's slick surface, to the man beneath the handsome face, had nearly led her into ruin. She'd fallen for his considerable charm, his charisma, his skill in donning a role and making it his own. There was no denying he was a brilliant actor. On and off the stage.

She'd believed him when he'd said she was beautiful, when he'd called her the most extraordinary woman of his acquaintance. She'd thought him in love with her, had never once questioned his devotion, until she'd run away with him and he'd made it shockingly clear he had no intention of marrying her.

The moment she'd discovered his duplicity she'd immediately left him. She'd returned to her dormitory before dawn, thereby avoiding others finding out about her foolishness. Not even Fanny had been aware of her absence.

Callie had been so naive, so gullible.

She wanted to cry.

And there sat Reese, a man worth a hundred Simons, offering his silent support, not even knowing why she needed it.

If he knew the cause of her despair, would he remain by her side, offering his allegiance?

She didn't dare test him.

Reese drew her to her feet. "You look like you could use a change of scenery."

She didn't argue as he led her to the back of the box. However, when she realized he was directing her out onto the landing and possibly beyond, she pulled him to a stop. "I'm sorry, Reese. I don't think I can bear facing other people right now."

She could hardly bear her own company.

Nodding, he let go of her hand. "Will you tell me what's wrong?"

"I want to." She really, truly did. "But you will think differently of me if I do."

Not that, Lord. Anything but that.

She couldn't stand knowing he might think less of her after she told him what she'd done. Her life had been far easier when Reese hadn't thought of her at all.

"I'd rather discuss anything but me." She took the cowardly approach and deflected the conversation back onto him. "For instance, your most recent bride list."

Something flickered in his eyes, something that looked like annoyance. He shook his head, even as he reached out and drew her against him with heartbreaking tenderness.

As they stood hidden from view, one of his hands cupped the back of her head and urged her to rest it against his shoulder. He said nothing, simply held her in silence. The moment couldn't have been more profound or poignant had he kissed her.

Encircled in Reese's arms like this left her dizzy with emotion. Nothing had ever felt more right, or so wonderful.

"I think you should strike hair color off your list." She whispered the words into the lapels of his suit, trying desperately not to cling to him.

"Any particular reason why I should?"

Because I don't have brown hair.

Tears burned behind her eyes, but she held them back. "You must remain open-minded to all possibilities, or risk missing out on the perfect woman to marry."

"Are you suggesting I consider even women with streaks of gray in their hair?"

He was trying to make her laugh. The dear, dear man. She swallowed back a sob. "Especially them."

A sound of amusement rustled in his chest. "I'll take that under advisement."

"Reese?"

"Hmm?"

She pulled back to look into his eyes. "I heard from Fanny last week."

Why had she inserted her sister into this tender moment? Callie knew the answer, of course. Because she couldn't allow herself—or Reese—to forget who stood between them.

Surely he would set her away from him now.

He did not.

He did, however, loosen his hold. "I'm glad, Callie." He swept his gaze over her face. "I know how important your relationship with your sister is to you."

But just how important was *his* relationship with Fanny?

"Jonathon Hawkins personally delivered her letter to me the other night at Mrs. Singletary's dinner party."

Reese's eyes never left her face. "Did she write something that upset you?"

Her answer came immediately. "Yes." She shook her head. "I mean, no. Not really."

Clasping his hands behind his back, he took a step away from her. The distance between them was no more than a few feet. It felt like a gaping, impossibly large chasm that could never be breached.

Callie sighed. How appropriate they were having this conversation at the theater. "Fanny claims she broke your engagement because she was merely playing a role with you and couldn't be sure who she really was beneath the facade."

"That's what she told me, as well, when we spoke last."

Why didn't he appear more upset? Why did he seem detached, indifferent even?

"Don't you want to know what she else said?"

"No, Callie, I'm not curious in the least." He held her gaze with unwavering resolve. "I'm quite comfortable with the way Fanny and I left things between us."

"You seem sincere."

He held her gaze for several more heartbeats, some silent message in his eyes. "I am, very."

Okay. "About your bride hunt…"

He took a deep breath. "What about it?"

She looked over her shoulder, assured herself the adjoining theater boxes were completely empty before continuing. "I have come up with several names I wish to run by you."

His expression cooled. "Perhaps we should sit down for this."

"If you wish."

They returned to the plush velvet seats they'd left only moments before. As Callie settled into her own chair and waited for Reese to follow suit, she looked out across the auditorium to the box she'd occupied with Mrs. Singletary a few weeks ago.

So much had changed since then.

What had started out as infatuation for a man she only knew as her sister's ex-fiancé was building into something more, something stronger and lasting. Callie was beginning to understand Reese on a whole new level.

He was more than a brilliant attorney, more than a man of unquestionable integrity. He was kind and loyal, a man who worked too hard but found time to play baseball with orphans.

He deserved happiness. If not with Fanny, then with the woman of his own choosing.

Callie would no longer hinder the process. She would find him the perfect bride. Fanny had made her decision. She'd had her chance and had thrown it away. Callie was through protecting her interests where Reese was concerned.

"I think you should consider Violet Danbury." The twenty-year-old met all of his requirements, on *both* his lists.

"No."

"She is perfectly suitable," Callie argued.

"She is named after a flower." He spoke as though that was reason enough to cross her off his list.

Callie blinked at him, confused. "Does that mean you won't consider Lily Manchester, either?"

"No flower names. They're ridiculous."

He was actually rejecting two perfectly suitably women because they were named after flowers? After also refusing to consider women who names began with *P*?

Why was he being so difficult?

Callie's breath backed up in her throat.

Was it possible that Reese was intentionally sabotaging the process? He winked at her. *Oh, my.*

She stared into those smiling eyes, eyes full of silent affection directed at her. Hope spread to the darkest corners of her soul. Would he, possibly, maybe, consider Callie a suitable candidate?

Oh, please, Lord. Please.

As soon as she lifted up the silent prayer she caught sight of Simon's photograph on the playbill. Reality slammed into her. Callie was many things. Suitable she was not.

Chapter Fifteen

Callie endured the following morning of dress fittings with a philosophical mind-set. Four times, she stretched out her arms and held perfectly still while Mrs. Singletary's personal seamstress draped and pinned fabric over her.

But, really, what did it matter if Callie wore fashionable gowns or tattered rags? Who would ever care if her hairstyle was copied out of current magazines or pulled tightly against her head in a severe bun?

Her future was set. Her foolish mistake with Simon would forever cast a shadow over the rest of her life. She slumped forward.

"Stand up straight, miss." The dressmaker, a small woman with a beak nose and rust-colored hair, scolded her in a thick Irish brogue. "Or we will be at this all day."

It was a sufficiently terrifying threat. They'd been *at this* for what felt like hours already.

Callie dutifully stiffened her spine and stared straight ahead, feeling more like a doll than ever before. Dressed up, paraded out at parties, manipulated in every direction, then randomly discarded.

Mutiny swelled at the apropos metaphor for her life. She was worthy of more, so much more. She'd made a mistake. One. Mistake. She wasn't alone in that, the Bible even taught that *all fall short of the glory of God.*

Her past did not have to define her future. She was a child of God, forgiven and loved.

She'd been betrayed by a fast-talking, charming actor trained in playing a role and deceiving others. She could either spend the rest of her life feeling shame over her lapse in good judgment, or accept the Lord's mercy.

The past was the past. The future, hers for the taking.

Why couldn't she reach for what she wanted? For *whom* she wanted?

An image of chocolate-brown eyes, broad shoulders and attractive, sculpted features came to mind. Her heart gave several hard, thick beats. Reese. *Oh, Reese.*

A wistful sigh escaped her lips.

"Did you say something, dear?"

"No, ma'am." Callie caught Mrs. Singletary's gaze in the mirror. "Just deep in thought."

"Ah. I completely understand." The widow picked up her cat and cuddled the animal close. "More times than not, I have found an evening at the theater often calls for reflection the following morning."

Refusing to give anything away, Callie schooled her features into a bland expression. "Very insightful."

"Yes, yes. Now, let me see where we are." Stroking Lady Macbeth's head, the widow circled around Callie.

"Excellent work, Mrs. O'Leary. That particular shade of blue suits my companion quite well."

"I thought it might." The dressmaker tucked a piece of fabric at Callie's waist, pinned it into place and then stepped back to study her handiwork. "Perfect."

The widow agreed. "When can we expect the finished garments?"

"This one will be ready by the end of the week, the others within two more."

Nodding in satisfaction, the widow captured Callie's gaze in the mirror once again. "You have been very patient today. When we are through here, I will treat you to lunch at the Hotel Dupree."

Callie would rather stay at home and rest. Her muscles ached from holding them in stiff, awkward poses. But she'd never been a patron at the restaurant where she'd once worked. It would be nice to see the other side. "I'd very much enjoy accompanying you, Mrs. Singletary."

"Excellent."

An hour later, dressed in another of Mrs. Singletary's castoffs, this one a gold sateen with blue-and-green trim, Callie followed her employer to a table in the Hotel Dupree dining room. Settling in her seat, she took in the elegant decor, ran her fingers over the fine china and silver place settings.

She'd barely set her napkin in her lap when Jonathon Hawkins joined them at the table. He greeted Mrs. Singletary first, then turned his smile onto Callie. "Miss Mitchell, it's a pleasure to see you again."

"And you, as well." To her surprise, Callie meant every word. She'd half expected to feel animosity toward the man. But the anger simply wasn't there anymore. Mr. Hawkins had merely offered Fanny a job in another city, and only *after* she'd broken off her engagement.

"I have taken it upon myself to order for the three of us," he said, dividing his attention between Callie and Mrs. Singletary. "My chef makes a memorable sea bass, as I'm sure Miss Mitchell can attest."

"Indeed, he does."

"Well, then, I bow to your expert opinions," Mrs. Singletary said. "We shall indulge in the sea bass today."

After a few more pleasantries, the widow and Mr. Hawkins proceeded to discuss the new decor of the restaurant, which segued into other changes he had in mind for the hotel.

Apparently, Callie had been invited to a business luncheon, where she understood only a third of the terms. When the conversation turned to types of lumber best suited for crown molding, she decided to take a short break.

"If you will both excuse me." She set her napkin on the table. "I'd like to freshen up before our meal is served."

"That'll be fine, dear." Mrs. Singletary waved her off with a distracted sweep of her hand.

In no particular hurry, Callie made her way through the restaurant and into the lobby. The hotel was teeming with activity. Groups of people lounged on the luxurious leather furniture. Some of the guests were reading books, others newspapers, while still others partook in animated conversations.

Everyone looked happy, satisfied and completely at their leisure. The Hotel Dupree had become a destination in and of itself. She was proud to have once played a small part in its success.

Recognizing the employee behind the registration desk, Callie decided to say a quick hello. She hadn't seen Rose since taking the position as Mrs. Singletary's companion. It would be lovely to catch up with the other woman.

Callie's steps faltered when she realized she wasn't the only person heading in the same direction. A few steps ahead of her was someone else, a man. Her throat turned dry as dust. She recognized that bold swagger, that arrogant tilt of the head.

The sight of *him,* the dark figure from her past, sent her into an air-gasping fluster. She swallowed hard against the biting pressure rising in her stomach, cinching around her heart.

Simon was here.

In the Hotel Dupree.

What were the odds? *What were the odds?*

Callie swayed, her balance momentarily thrown off. She stumbled backward, then quickly righted herself. She had to get away before he noticed her, before he could hurt her again.

The force of her panic frightened her.

Spinning on her heel, she retraced her steps. Shame and fear made her movements clumsy, awkward. *I have to get away.*

"Callie? Callie! Come back."

She ignored the call, keeping her head down as she hurried back the way she came, praying no one noticed the urgency in her steps.

"Callie." A hand clasped her arm and whirled her around.

Infuriated, she yanked free of the offensive grip. Her stomach roiled. Her eyes stung. She tried to move, but she was hit with a spasm of immobility, her feet frozen in place. All she could do was stare at the man who'd once been the sole player in her dreams, now the lead actor in her nightmares.

His face was more handsome than she remembered, his demeanor more polished and slick. Oh, but his eyes were the same steel-blue. How had she not seen how cold and detached they were?

How had she missed the depravity in his gaze?

"We meet again, my beautiful, beautiful girl. Or as I like to think of you—" his lips curved into a sly, knowing grin "—the one who got away."

The intimacy of his words made her feel tainted. Was it any wonder she'd spent the past four years avoiding masculine attention? Her eyes stung with the threat of tears. She swallowed them back. "Excuse me, Simon. My employer will be wondering where I am."

"Wait." His hand returned to her arm.

She shrugged away from him.

He tucked his hands into his pockets. For a moment, the brilliant actor slipped away and all that remained was a spoiled man who always got his way, by any means possible.

"I have never forgotten you, Callie." He said her name in a low voice as he moved in close, far too close. "I have always regretted losing you."

She couldn't fathom why he would say such a thing. What could he possibly hope to gain? Surely he couldn't think she would fall for his lies a second time? "I don't believe you, Simon, not after the way you callously deceived me."

His shoulder lifted in a leisurely shrug. "We had a misunderstanding."

"A misunderstanding?" She nearly spat the word. "Is that how you remember it?"

Another lift of his shoulder. "Had you not bolted out of the hotel so quickly I would have explained my position in greater detail."

"You explained yourself quite well." To her utter humiliation, a tear leaked out of the corner of her eye.

His hand came to her face, wiped at her cheek.

She slapped him away.

He gave a dramatic sigh, but didn't reach for her again.

"You have become even more beautiful in the years since we last met." Like a hungry cat seeking easy prey, his eyes roamed over her face. "I made a grave mistake letting you go."

"I left *you,* the very moment I discovered your wicked agenda."

And that, Callie realized, was what she'd nearly forgotten through the years since leaving school.

She hadn't given in to Simon that night. She hadn't fallen completely for his lies. She'd walked away on her own steam, with her virtue still intact.

"My sweet, sweet Callie." Simon's smile didn't quite meet his eyes this time. "Still so pure, so untouched, so wholly innocent. Other than your beautiful, exquisite face, those were the traits that most intrigued me about you."

He moved in closer, reached for her.

She took a large step back.

Undeterred, Simon closed the distance between them once more. *Again,* Callie stepped back.

So involved in their conflict, she didn't notice that a third party had joined their scuffle until an angry masculine voice dropped into the fray.

"Touch her again, Westgrove, and I'll make sure it's the last thing you ever do."

Callie jerked around so hastily she lost her footing. Reese caught her, steadying her at the waist. Once her balance was restored, he let her go, though it took Herculean control not to whisk her up in his arms and carry her out of the hotel lobby.

"Reese." Her thunderstruck gaze met his. "What… what are you doing here?"

"I have a meeting with Jonathon Hawkins."

"Oh." She looked away, but not before he saw the humiliation in her eyes.

He'd never seen Callie wear such an expression before, a combination of shame, regret and fury. Emotions he knew were directed at the man standing behind her.

Reese's gaze focused and hardened on Simon Westgrove.

Had he any doubts as to whether Callie knew the famous actor personally, they'd been dispelled the moment he'd walked into the Hotel Dupree. Even from across the lobby, Callie's obvious panic told its own story, a story Reese knew he wasn't going to like.

Now was not the time for questions, save one. "Are you all right?"

She nodded miserably.

His chest filled with a need to protect, to wipe away that look of anguish on her face. He drew her close, securing her beside him. Trembling, she leaned into him.

Westgrove arched a brow. "It appears I have been replaced in your affections, Callie, my love."

She stiffened, either at the words or the endearment, Reese couldn't be sure. One thing he did know, Callie wanted nothing to do with the actor, who was grinning with far too much intimacy in his gaze.

"It's time you left, Westgrove. Callie doesn't want you here."

"I say we let the lady speak for herself."

The silence that met those words seemed to last a lifetime.

Then, Callie snapped her shoulders back and straightened her spin. "Mr. Bennett is correct. I don't want you here, Simon. I never want to see you again."

"You heard the lady." Reese took a hard breath. "Off you go."

"How sublime." Westgrove barked out a laugh. "I've landed in a badly scripted play with a couple of two-bit actors on stage with me."

The other man could malign him all he wanted, but Reese wouldn't stand for him disrespecting Callie. He started forward.

"No, Reese." Callie rested her hand on his arm to stop his pursuit. "He's not worth it." Before he could respond she turned her head and glared at the other man. "Go away, Simon."

"Is that your final word on the matter?" His gaze shifted from her to Reese then back to Callie. "I cannot persuade you to run aw—"

"*Go.*"

The man paused. A shadow flickered in his eyes, then was gone. "Right. Your loss, sweeting."

After throwing an audacious leer in Callie's direction, Westgrove sauntered away. He moved through the lobby with a casual, relaxed stride as if he hadn't a care in life.

Reese drew in several steadying breaths, debating whether to stay with Callie or follow after the actor and have a private...*word* with the man.

Callie's struggle to catch her breath made the decision for him. Reese gently lifted her chin until she looked him directly in the eyes. As she blinked up in silence, he ran his gaze over her face, taking careful inventory.

"What did Westgrove do to you?" Reese was surprised by the rage in his voice.

Callie lowered her head. "I don't think I can tell you."

He could see she would rather keep her secret safely hidden. How well he knew the need to conceal parts of the past, to suffer through the tormenting pain alone.

If he didn't encourage Callie to unburden herself with him, would she turn to someone else? With whom could she confide? None of her brothers were in town. Fanny was gone. The only support in Callie's life was Mrs. Singletary. Her employer.

A frown tugged at Reese's brow as he pondered how alone Callie was in the world right now, with only the widow to champion her.

And him. Callie had him, too. He badly wanted to give her his unwavering support, his unconditional acceptance. The trick would be convincing her to let him.

"Let's sit down, over there." With a jerk of his head, he indicated the far right corner, where two wing-back chairs were surrounded by large potted plants. The makeshift alcove was private, but not indecently so.

When Callie nodded her agreement, Reese took her arm and guided her across the marble floor, their footsteps striking in a shared rhythm like hammers to nails.

She sat primly, her spine perfectly erect. Regardless of her stiff posture, Reese was struck by the graceful way she entwined her fingers together in her lap. There was nothing hard about this woman, nothing coarse or brazen. She personified gentleness and goodness.

He placed his hand over hers. "Tell me what happened with Westgrove."

Lowering her head, she held silent a moment. Then, slowly, she looked back up. Her gaze was full of unspeakable pain. "You'll think differently of me once I do."

She'd said much the same thing once before.

What had Westgrove done to her? "I meant what I said at the theater last evening. You'll get no judgment from me, no condemnation."

"I don't know quite where to start." Her voice was very low, very quiet. The sound called to mind broken trust and betrayed innocence.

Emotion wrapped around him, a bone-deep urgency to protect Callie—always. If Westgrove appeared again, Reese would likely beat the man to a pulp.

For now, he focused on earning Callie's trust. One step at a time. "How did you meet him?"

"I met him in Boston. Fanny and I were in our final year at Miss Lindsey's Select School for Women. I was mad for the theater back then, and went as often as I could." She smiled ruefully, and a little sadly. "A friend of a friend worked at the theater and introduced me to Simon. I was instantly dazzled by his charm and wit. He seemed equally enamored and said all the right things to turn my head. I believed I was special in his eyes."

With slow, deliberate movements Reese sat back in his chair. "You let him court you?"

"I suppose that's what you could call it. He was very persistent, very convincing with his attentions, he…" She broke off, darted her gaze around the lobby.

"Go on," he urged.

There was another moment of hesitation before she continued. Reese didn't interrupt her again, but let her tell the tale of Westgrove's treachery.

With each new piece of evidence pointing to the man's despicable nature, anger stormed inside Reese. He tried not to show it, but the discovery that Callie had been lied to so completely—*used* so dishonestly—filled him with a protective fury unlike he'd ever experienced before.

Over the next part of the story Callie's voice hitched. "When Simon asked me to run away with him, I thought he meant to marry me."

She continued on, explaining in a halting tone all the events of that evening.

Reese's hands balled into fists. "Westgrove should answer for his behavior."

"Oh, Reese, I carry my own share of the blame." She choked on a sob. "The part of me raised by Godly, Christian parents should have known not to agree to run away with him. I should have *known* not to meet him in a hotel."

"You were young, Callie. He preyed on your innocence."

"And I let him." She dropped her gaze and then, as

if determined to fight off her embarrassment, boldly lifted her chin. "Once I realized he had no plans to marry me, I immediately left the hotel lobby and returned to my dormitory."

"He didn't follow you?"

"No, and he never tried to contact me again. Ironic, isn't it?" Her glassy-eyed gaze shifted around, landing in no particular spot. "After all these years, I cross paths with him in another hotel lobby?"

"I'm sorry, Callie." It angered him that a woman who deserved only affection and tenderness had been treated with disrespect, with such ugly intent.

Reese had never been prone to violence, but he felt his temper rising with vicious force, urging him to crush the man who'd hurt this beautiful, special woman.

"Now you know my secret." She met his gaze. "And the full extent of my shame."

"You have no reason to be ashamed." Reese carefully took her hands in his. "You were lied to and betrayed. But when the real test came, you resisted temptation. That doesn't make you dishonorable, it makes you incredibly brave."

"You…you think me brave?"

"Callie Mitchell." He brought her hands to his lips, kissed both sets of knuckles. "You are the bravest person I know."

Chapter Sixteen

Several days after her altercation with Simon, Callie's emotions were still in turmoil. In truth, she didn't know quite what she felt about the encounter. Relief, to be sure. She'd faced her past. Though she could have handled Simon on her own, Reese's timely appearance had been a blessing. His kindness afterward had given Callie the confidence to set aside her shame and freely accept God's grace.

Where did that leave her now?

She'd spent so much time looking back, allowing her past to define her present, that she didn't know how to move forward.

Live your life. One day at a time.

Yes. Yes!

Drawing in a long breath, she looked around the overly decorated parlor in Polly Ferguson's home. As usual, Callie had accompanied Mrs. Singletary to her weekly meeting of the Ladies League for Destitute Widows and Orphans. She attempted to focus on the earnest discussion about poverty among single, unattached women in Denver, but she'd lost the gist of the debate.

Though she had her own opinions on the subject, and cared a great deal about the plight of the poor, her efforts to sort through the various positions proved unsuccessful.

Her mind kept wandering back to the Hotel Dupree, to the makeshift alcove out of the main traffic area. Reese had been incredibly gentle with her and so sweetly outraged on her behalf. His defense of her had meant more than he could know.

He'd even called her brave.

Reese really was a wonderful man.

Now, she could not stop dreaming of him, of hoping one day he would see her as more than a friend, perhaps even consider her for his bride. Problem was, if he did propose to her, Callie couldn't accept. Not as long as he insisted on avoiding a love match. She would accept nothing less.

They were at cross purposes, she and Reese, facing an obstacle perhaps even greater than his previous relationship with Fanny.

"Pass the scones, Miss Mitchell."

"Oh." She jerked at the command. "Yes. Of course, Mrs. Ferguson."

After placing one of the buttery pastries on her own plate, she handed the serving tray to the woman sitting on her left.

In her role as hostess, Polly Ferguson presided over today's meeting from a brocade settee on the opposite side of the room. The matriarch was bracketed by two younger copies of herself. Phoebe and Penelope even wore gowns in the same shade of pale pink as their mother.

Philomena Ferguson, the third oldest daughter, was also in attendance. She sat on Callie's right. Barely twenty years old, Philomena was well-spoken, well-educated and, in Callie's estimation, the most likeable of the Ferguson sisters. With her unusual hazel eyes and flawless complexion, she favored her brother Marshall in both looks and temperament.

Callie believed she and Philomena could forge a friendship, given time. If pressed, she would also admit the girl suited most of Reese's requirements for a wife. Her hair was a beautiful golden *brown,* with natural caramel streaks that complemented her pretty eyes. Or course, her name did start with the letter *P.*

"Is the rumor true, Beatrix?" Polly Ferguson eyed Mrs. Singletary with a stare that had a bit of cunning wrapped around the edges. "Is Reese Bennett Junior actively seeking a wife?"

Callie winced. While she'd been lost in thought the conversation had turned in a more gossipy direction.

Had someone overheard her conversation with Reese at the theater last week? No other explanation made sense. She groaned inwardly. She'd been careful to keep her voice low, barely above a whisper. Not careful enough.

Mrs. Singletary—*bless her*—deflected her friend's question with ease. "Now, Polly, wherever did you hear such a tale?"

"It makes sense, doesn't it?" Mrs. Ferguson leaned forward, her narrowed gaze giving her a hawklike appearance. "Mr. Bennett is the most eligible bachelor in town. And now that he's in sole charge of his family's law firm, he must be in search of a wife."

"I have no doubt my attorney will make some young woman a wonderful husband." Mrs. Singletary cast her gaze to the ceiling. "It's certainly something to ponder, at any rate."

Oh, Mrs. Singletary was good. She actually sounded as though this was the first time she'd considered Reese for one of her matchmaking schemes.

Clever ploy.

But her friend wasn't fooled. "Now, Beatrix, I find it hard to believe you aren't personally involved in Mr. Bennett's search. Everyone knows you enjoy making a good match."

The widow chuckled. "Everyone would be right. But, regrettably, I am not in league with Mr. Bennett."

"Is that so? Well, according to my source, he was overheard discussing a list of qualifications he wishes in a bride. If he wasn't speaking with you, Beatrix—" Mrs. Ferguson's gaze turned shrewd "—then who?"

Mrs. Singletary cocked an eyebrow. "It's quite the mystery, isn't it?"

Pretending grave interest in her plate, Callie pinched off a small bite of scone. Oh, but her insides turned over, making knot upon knot upon knot. She'd inadvertently put Reese at the center of Denver's gossip mill.

She must warn him.

"It would be a great coup—a feather in your matchmaking cap, if you will—to make a match for Mr. Bennett, especially if the bride was one of my lovely daughters."

Phoebe and Penelope twittered among themselves,

openly plotting how best to gain Reese's attention. But as it so happened, their names started with *P*.

Now that the subject had been broached, a barrage of questions began. Callie almost felt sorry for her employer. Except Mrs. Singletary didn't appear the least bit troubled by the verbal attack. In fact, she looked secretively amused as she fielded the onslaught of questions with her usual aplomb.

At one point, her delighted gaze caught Callie's.

Callie frowned in return. She found none of this amusing. Every woman in the room was now speculating as to which young lady in town Reese would ultimately choose to marry.

He must be informed of this horrible turn of events, before the competition to win his heart began in earnest.

As Callie decided how best to approach the subject with him, Mrs. Singletary skillfully turned the conversation to her annual charity ball next month.

It was a smooth transition, aided by Philomena, who suggested a portion of the funds raised be used to buy winter coats for the destitute widows and orphans in town.

The group was debating which one of their members should head up the decoration committee when Laney Dupree entered the parlor. "Sorry we're late." She shoved her hair off her face. "A busy morning at the orphanage."

"Well, you are here now." Mrs. Singletary patted the empty seat beside her. "Come, sit by me."

Laney hesitated, perhaps because she wasn't alone. A young woman about Callie's age accompanied her. The newcomer was quite beautiful. Her black hair offset her pale white skin and heart-shaped face, while her eyes were an unusual shade of blue, nearly lavender. Callie had only read about such a color in books.

Laney made the introductions. "This is Miss Temperance Evans, our newly appointed headmistress for the Charity House School."

Miss Evans's responding smile was dazzling. "Thank you for including me in your meeting. I look forward to helping your cause however possible."

The cultured British accent fit the beautiful face to perfection, as did the yellow silk organza gown.

"We were just discussing my annual charity ball before you arrived." Mrs. Singletary directed her words at Laney. "You have such an eye for detail, I wonder if we can lure you into heading up the decorations this year."

"I'd love to take on the duty." Laney claimed the seat next to the widow. "I already have several ideas."

"As do I," one of the older women declared.

A shuffling of seats followed.

While the older women deliberated over the benefits of roses versus lilies, and gold accent over silver, Penelope and Phoebe eyed Temperance Evans with suspicion.

Proving herself the more gracious of the Ferguson daughters, Philomena scooted over to make room for Temperance next to her.

Once she took her seat, Callie offered the woman a scone.

"Thank you."

Callie smiled. "Tell me, Miss Evans, what made you decide to settle in Denver?"

"My parents brought me here as a child so I could

experience the great American West. I fell in love with the area, especially the mountains. When I learned about the headmistress position at Charity House, I decided to leave London—" she lifted her hands in a show of surrender "—and here I am."

There was more to Temperance's story. Callie heard it in her overformal tone.

So, apparently, did Phoebe Ferguson. "You traveled halfway across the world to run a school for prostitutes' children?"

"I did."

"Why?"

"I have a fondness for children." Miss Evans did not explain herself further.

Penelope took over the interrogation, screwing up her face into a disbelieving scowl. *Not* a becoming expression on the girl. "You seem awfully young to run a school."

"I am twenty-three."

"I would have guessed eighteen."

"That's quite enough." Philomena didn't actually snort, but she came perilously close. "Leave the poor woman alone."

An argument immediately broke out among the three sisters, the two oldest joining forces against the younger. Philomena held her ground throughout the fray. Clearly, she harbored a quiet strength and a spine of steel beneath the serene expression she usually wore.

When Phoebe stomped out of the room, and Penelope followed her in a near identical display, Callie gave in to a sigh.

"Good riddance," Philomena mumbled.

With Miss Evans leading the way, conversation turned to the rigors of sea travel during the rainy season. Philomena warmed to the subject.

Callie listened in silence. Both women made excellent observations and seemed perfectly levelheaded. If she presented their names to Reese as potential candidates in his bride search, would he seriously consider them?

Or would he find a reason to reject them as he had all the others? A prayer flashed through her mind, coming straight from her heart. *Oh, please, Lord, let him find fault with every woman I present.*

Unable to focus on the contract beneath his hand, Reese swiveled in his chair and looked out his office window. People of every shape and size hurried along the sidewalks en route to their respective destinations.

There was a rhythm to their steps. Not so, inside his head. Thoughts buzzed around chaotically, with no apparent destination to drive them in a satisfying direction.

Shutting his eyes, he attempted to clear his mind. But his thoughts kept circling back to Callie. And the trauma Simon Westgrove had put her through.

After discovering the full extent of the actor's treachery, Reese had been tempted to hunt down the man and make him pay for what he'd done to her. Fortunately for Westgrove, the acting troupe had left Denver that very afternoon. Reese had missed the train's departure by a full hour.

At least the man couldn't hurt Callie anymore. Reese hoped she would forever let go of the shame she'd been carrying through the years. Her only mistake had been to fall in love with the wrong man.

Callie's situation was additional proof that love was a dangerous prospect, especially when deeply felt. For Reese, the emotion had been so strong he'd nearly gone mad when he lost Miranda.

Loving like that couldn't be good. Of course, love came in many forms. It didn't have to hurt, or end in tragedy, or bring about pain.

Perhaps he could even love his wife, as long as he kept the emotion from growing too deep, or becoming too fervent.

If his head ruled his heart, he would find a suitable woman to marry—a woman who would make a good wife, a proper partner in life and a devoted mother to their children.

Was he being overly optimistic?

Ever since holding Callie in his arms, he'd felt something shift inside him, urging him to expect more from his wife than companionship.

Looking back, Reese could admit his feelings for Miranda had been entirely too strong, while his feelings for Fanny had not been enough.

He needed to find a balance.

In that regard, the bride list made practical sense.

Then why did the thought of checking off qualifications until he found the most suitable candidate not seem as wise as it had before?

Blowing out a hiss of frustration, he stood and moved closer to the window. Leaning an arm on the frame, he looked out unseeingly over the city then focused on the mountains beyond.

"I've come to warn you."

By now, he should be used to the way his gut rolled at the sound of Callie's voice. He swallowed once, twice, three times.

Once he had his reaction under control, he glanced over his shoulder.

Callie stood in the doorway of his office, her hands twisting together at her waist, her brows scrunched into a frown.

Something was wrong.

Had Westgrove returned?

Reese hastened toward her. Whatever had happened, he would stand by her. The intense urge to alleviate her worries nearly flattened him.

He'd once thought this woman hid a world of feeling behind her cool facade, but Reese now knew the truth. The world of feeling was inside him, bubbling to the surface whenever he was in the same room with her.

This was not the way things were supposed to be. He wasn't supposed to want to champion this woman, to protect her from all harm, to make her happy above all other pursuits.

Yet he couldn't bear any other man having that honor.

Reaching out, Reese took her hands, lowered his gaze over her. She was wearing the blue dress she'd worn weeks ago. The beginning of her transformation. He noted again how the color highlighted the green in her eyes and made her skin glow.

Everything in him pinpointed to one specific goal. Erase her misery. "Callie, what's upset you?"

"I… I don't know where to start."

"Has Westgrove—"

"No." She shook her head. "It's not Simon. He is good and truly gone from my life."

The relief quickening through Reese's blood nearly brought him to his knees.

"Oh, Reese, I'm afraid something terrible has happened and it's my fault."

Her unease cut him to the core. Still focused on his goal, he pulled her into his office and, despite knowing it was a bad idea, shut the door behind her. They were alone.

Completely.

Alone.

And yet, all he could think was how to soothe away that look of worry in Callie's eyes. He resisted placing a hand on her face, though he desperately wanted to cup her cheek and tell her everything was going to be all right.

He couldn't know that for certain. Not until she told him why she'd come to him. "Tell me what has happened."

"We were overheard."

Someone had been listening to them at the Hotel Dupree? The monumental consequences immediately struck him. Although Callie hadn't actually done anything wrong with Westgrove, she'd agreed to run away with the man, had gone so far as to meet him at his hotel. Her actions, if taken out of context, could prove her ruination. "Who heard us?"

Perhaps it wasn't too late to stop the gossip. If he could address the person directly, explain the situation, perhaps he could prevent the worst of the talk from spreading.

Callie sighed. "I don't know for certain. But Mrs.

Ferguson brought up your bride search this morning at the Ladies League for Destitute Widows and Orphans tea." She sighed again. "Penelope and Phoebe are already plotting how best to win your heart."

His bride search? That's what they'd been overheard discussing? So relieved to find *he* was the center of gossip, and not Callie, Reese threw back his head and laughed.

Callie's mouth dropped open. "How can you find this amusing? Women all over town will be throwing themselves at you now."

"I can assure you, I don't find any of this amusing. But the idea of any woman plotting ways to win my heart? It's absurd."

"Love is not absurd."

"No," he agreed, sufficiently sobered. "It's very serious business. But I meant what I said, Callie, I am not seeking a love match."

Pressing her lips tightly together, she eyed him for a long silent moment. Something flickered in her eyes. Hurt, perhaps? Disappointment? A combination of the two?

"Why are you so resistant to falling in love?" she asked.

"I've already explained my position."

"You are being incredibly single-minded." She punctuated the accusation with a scowl.

He suspected she was attempting to appear fierce. The expression only managed to make her look wholly adorable. Unable to resist, he reached out and placed a hand on her shoulder.

She stared up at him, her gaze searching his. "I told

you about Simon. I shared my past with you. Won't you trust me with yours?"

Perhaps it made him a hypocrite but he couldn't, he wouldn't, talk about Miranda with Callie. "No."

"Whatever happened, I'll not pass judgment."

He believed her. Sorely tempted to unburden himself, he opened his mouth but couldn't get the words to form together logically in his mind. "I appreciate your offer, Callie, but still, no."

"Will you at least discuss your bride search with me?"

He gave her a wry smile. "Isn't that what brought on this latest snag we find ourselves in now?"

She sighed. "The floodgates are open, Reese. Every woman in town will soon be vying for your attention."

He chuckled at the dismay in her voice, placed his other hand on your shoulder. "Surely not *every* woman. Let's not forget, I can often be stern and overly rigid."

"Untrue. You are handsome, kind, gentle, especially with children, not to mention upright and full of integrity. Any woman in her right mind would consider herself fortunate to receive a marriage proposal from you."

Her defense of him was charming. "Some would say I dislike chaos."

"You simply appreciate lists."

He chuckled again, the sound rumbling from the depth of his soul. This beautiful, sweet, fiercely loyal woman understood him. "You do know me well."

Compelled, he drew her into his arms.

"Reese." She spoke his name on a whisper. "I don't think this is a good idea."

"No, it's not."

"Nor do I think—"

"Now, see, that's the problem. You think too much.

We both do." Maybe, just this once, they needed to stop thinking and indulge in a bad idea…together.

Course set, he pressed his mouth to hers.

Callie stiffened in his arms. Less than a heartbeat later, she leaned into him.

All thought disappeared.

For a second, Reese allowed himself to indulge in the sensation of holding a woman he cared about, whose company he thoroughly enjoyed.

After a moment, he lifted his head and stared into Callie's wide green eyes. Caught inside her beautiful gaze, a condition he was growing to appreciate, he forgot all about lists and timetables and adhering to tight schedules.

He jerked back.

Callie Mitchell was a dangerous woman.

As if coming out of a trance, she drew in a slow, careful breath of air. "I better go, before Mrs. Singletary worries."

She turned.

"Callie, wait. We have to talk about what just hap—"

"Please, Reese. Please don't say another word." She wrenched open the door and all but ran out of his office.

Watching her scurry down the hall, she looked as though she couldn't get away from him fast enough. The realization brought a moment of searing pain. A pain so similar to grief Reese had to reach for the doorjamb to steady himself.

One lone, coherent thought emerged, bringing with it a bright spurt of hope. He'd been searching for a wife in the wrong place and in the wrong way.

Time to start a new list.

Chapter Seventeen

Throughout the next week, whenever Callie found herself alone—a state that occurred far too often for her peace of mind—her thoughts returned to Reese.

Sitting in the hard, straight-back chair facing her writing desk, she pulled out the miniature portrait she'd painted, cupped it in her hands and studied the image in the bright morning light.

She'd painted Reese smiling.

The expression reminded her of the way he'd looked when she'd informed him that word had gotten out about his bride search.

His reaction to the news still mystified Callie. He'd seemed completely unconcerned that women all over town would soon be throwing themselves at him.

Was he that immune to falling in love? That resistant? Did he actually believe his life would be happy without it?

God's second greatest commandment called His children to love one another. Love was important, necessary, a prerequisite for a good, healthy life.

Callie knew Reese had the capacity for deep emotion. She'd seen him with the orphans at Charity House. No man had that much patience without love in his heart.

A terrible thought occurred to her. Had someone broken his heart?

Was Fanny the culprit? He claimed not. But what if Reese was still pining for his former fiancée?

Callie wasn't sure she had the courage to push them together, not anymore, not after all she and Reese had shared in the past month. Besides, her sister refused to come home and make things right with him. Fanny had thrown away her chance with Reese.

But…if he truly loved her sister, how could Callie stand in their way? How could she not do everything in her power to bring them back together? Reese deserved happiness. As did her sister.

Lowering her head, Callie studied the miniature portrait in her hand, ran her fingertip over his face. She paused over his mouth, remembering how in the midst of their talk about love he'd kissed her.

Her finger shook as the memory refused to fade.

He'd been so gentle with her, both at the theater and at the Hotel Dupree. And again when he'd held her in his arms and pressed his lips to hers. He must care for her.

Of course he cares. We are friends.

Friends don't kiss friends, not the way Reese had kissed Callie. His behavior baffled her. He seemed almost calculating in his pursuit of a bride, but Callie knew he wasn't that heartless. He was wonderful, extraordinary.

She thought she might cry.

Why had he pursued Fanny first? Why, all those

months ago, hadn't he looked at Callie the way he had in his office the other day?

Would she have accepted his suit at the time?

She didn't know. She truly didn't know. Ever since returning home to Colorado she'd allowed her mistake with Simon to define her.

Had she spurned Reese without even knowing it?

"Callie, are you ready to go?"

Jumping at the question, she quickly tucked the miniature away in her desk and looked up at her employer. "Nearly there. I just have to finish pinning my hat in place."

"Hurry, hurry, dear, we don't want to be late for church."

"I'm coming." Callie secured the final three pins and checked her reflection in the mirror. She was growing used to her transformation, even appreciating the changes Mrs. Singletary had insisted upon. But it was more than just the outer wrappings.

The new Callie no longer hovered around the edges of life. She no longer melted into the shadows. She held her head high, wore dresses tailored specifically for her and styled her hair in the latest fashions of the day.

Smiling at her reflection, she picked up her reticule and turned. "All set, Mrs. Singletary."

She was talking to the widow's back.

Callie scurried after her employer, eventually catching up with her outside the mansion. Since they were only a few blocks away from the church building, and the day was already warm, Mrs. Singletary suggested they walk. Callie agreed. They took the most direct route and thus managed to arrive a full ten minutes before service started.

Now they were no longer walking, Callie looked up at the sky. The sun shone bright, hugging the church building in its golden arms. The pretty steeple pointed straight toward the pristine blue heavens. The mountains in the distance marched in a craggy row, looking like sentinels on duty, safeguarding all who moved in their shadows.

"Lovely," she whispered to no one in particular.

Mrs. Singletary hummed her agreement as she waved at someone she knew.

Callie started up the steps. She conquered only two when she realized her employer hadn't joined her. "Aren't you coming, Mrs. Singletary?"

"Go on ahead, dear. Sit wherever you like. I wish to speak with Laney Dupree before I head inside." She took off toward her quarry.

Callie smiled after her employer.

When she'd first taken the position as the widow's companion, she hadn't expected to attend church with her. She'd assumed her employer would wish for a more formal service than the one they enjoyed at Denver Community Bible Church.

Mrs. Singletary had surprised Callie, stating she'd supported the church loosely connected with Charity House and always would as long as she had breath in her lungs.

Denver Community was led by Reverend Beauregard O'Toole, a member of a famous acting family who'd chosen ministry over the stage. All were welcome in Pastor Beau's church, no matter their current situation or what they'd done in the past.

It was a sentiment Callie had agreed with in theory, but she was only just now coming to understand what it meant to accept God's grace fully. Or, as the good reverend often said, "Who better to appreciate God's unlimited mercy than the lost, misguided and hurting?"

A movement caught Callie's eye. She turned, felt her smile widen. Reese had come to church with his father today. The elder Mr. Bennett was already engaged in an animated conversation with Mrs. Singletary and her friends. Reese stood off to one side.

He did not look happy. Actually, his eyes had taken on a hunted look. Perhaps that was due to the fact that he was being quickly surrounded by a swarm of women, all of whom were openly competing for his attention. They'd sufficiently corralled him.

Other than plow someone over, he was good and truly stuck. A captured audience.

Easy prey.

As a friend, Callie should hurry over and rescue him. She decided to let him suffer a few moments longer. It served him right for laughing at her, when she'd only sought to warn him of this very thing. Now that word was out he was actively seeking a bride, he might as well get used to the female interest.

With slow, even steps, she approached the perimeter of the crowd surrounding him and lifted up on her toes.

"Mr. Bennett," she called over the uproar. "Mrs. Singletary has insisted you and your father sit with her this morning. Stop dawdling, please, and do come along."

Thoroughly trapped, he spread out his hands in a helpless gesture. A silent plea filled his anxious gaze.

"Oh, honestly. Step aside, ladies." Callie shouldered her way through the bulk of the crowd. Angry female objections arose.

Callie ignored them.

Taking hold of Reese's sleeve, she tugged. Hard.

A little stumble on both their parts, more objections, then—finally—she managed to pull him free.

For a moment, his gaze turned inward, as if to contemplate how he'd ended up on the wrong end of his bride search.

Callie resisted the urge to remind him she'd warned him this would happen. Instead, she silently looped her arm through his and attempted to guide him toward the church entrance. He refused to move. For a moment, there was an alarming intensity to the man, his features severe with concentration as he stared into her face.

"I believe I owe you an apology." His voice held a sheepish tone. "You were right."

"Though I never get tired of hearing those three little words, I'm afraid you've lost me." She sent him a smiling glance. "What was I right about?"

"I have become the center of unwanted female attention." He sounded so perplexed and baffled she didn't know whether to laugh or quiet his concerns.

She chose something in between.

"You'll be fine," she said in her most soothing tone, patting his arm with her free hand. "That is, as long as you never leave your house again."

His lips dropped into a frown. "Not funny."

"I thought so."

They entered the church before either could say more. All heads turned in their direction. Or rather, all *female* heads turned in their direction. Although the attention was unnerving, Callie knew most were looking at Reese. Speculating as to why he was with her.

Refusing to be intimidated, she lifted her chin and moved deeper into the building. The pew she usually shared with Mrs. Singletary and Reese's father was still empty. They were probably still chatting outside.

A loud squeal of delight rent the air. "Miss Callie. Mr. Reese. Over here. Hey, we're over here."

Seated in the back row with several of the other Charity House children, Daniel Velasquez bounced up and down while waving his hands frantically in the air. His sister copied his every move.

Dressed in their Sunday best, their hair combed and eyes shining, the twins looked adorable. They also looked set apart, with a large empty space between them and the other children in the pew.

Daniel shouted their names again, this time adding, "Won't you come sit with us?"

Callie would like nothing better, but it wasn't her decision alone. She turned to discuss the matter with Reese, but he was already pulling her toward the children.

There was a moment of jostling and organizing and arguing over who would sit where. In the end, Callie and Reese ended up in the middle of the pew with Gabriella on Callie's lap and Daniel on the other side of Reese.

As if on cue, the first strains of organ music wafted through the air. Everyone stood. Callie attempted to set Gabriella on her feet, but the girl clung to her, wrapping her arms around her neck in a death grip. Shifting her hold, she settled the child on the church pew.

With her arm around the little girl, Callie had to sing the hymn from memory. Obviously sensing her predicament, Reese held out his hymnal so Callie could see it, too.

She breathed in slowly, restraining a sigh. He smelled so good, clean and fresh, soap mixed with pine. She took another short breath, leaned in closer and began singing the selected hymn in earnest. Her voice melded with Reese's. They sounded good, as if they'd been singing together all their lives.

Despite her efforts to stay focused on the song, her thoughts turned fanciful. She imagined her and Reese together like this every Sunday, with their many children beside them, taking up an entire church pew.

Shocked at the direction of her thoughts, Callie shook away the image.

Out of the corner of her eye, she glanced at Reese, only to discover he was watching her. Something quite nice passed between them, a feeling that instilled utter contentment.

The singing came to an end. There was another round of jostling for position, whereby the children ended up in the same places they'd started.

Reese shared a smile with Callie over their heads. He then nodded to his father and Mrs. Singletary as they passed them on their way to a pew closer to the front of the church.

Pastor Beau took his place behind the pulpit amid more than a few female sighs. It was the same reaction he received every Sunday. Not only was the preacher on fire for the Lord, but he also had the trademark O'Toole tawny hair, classically handsome features and mesmerizing eyes.

As was his custom, he began with a bang. "The scandals of our lives can become the story of God's redemption. But only if we allow Him full access to our pasts."

Callie nearly gasped. It was as if Pastor Beau was speaking directly to her, giving her permission to release the shame of her past once and for all.

"Today is a new day, meant to be lived under grace."

Heads bobbed in agreement, Callie's among them.

"Ah, but living under grace is not as easy as it sounds." He lowered his voice and nearly everyone in the congregation leaned forward. "We often let our pasts hold us back from living a victorious life. We cling to the memory of our mistakes and wallow in the pain of our broken dreams."

Reese stiffened. Callie slipped a glance in his direction, surprised to find he looked as though he'd been punched in the face.

She reached out and covered his hand. He remained rigid under her touch.

"God is the God of our todays and tomorrows," the preacher continued. "But He's also the God of our yesterdays. He reaches into our pasts, forgives our offenses and settles all claims against our conscience."

Reese shifted in his seat. Cleared his throat. Mumbled something under his breath.

"The Lord's goal is not to condemn us, but to heal us. But God doesn't do any of this without our permission. We must be willing participants in our own redemption. I ask you this…" A pause. "Do you have the courage to put the pain of your past into His hands?"

Reese leaned over and said something in Daniel's ear. The boy nodded, then moved in beside Callie as Reese slipped out of the pew.

The sermon continued, but Callie couldn't concentrate on the rest of the message.

She desperately wanted to go after Reese, but she couldn't up and abandon the children.

What seemed an endless amount of time later, the sermon came to a close. "Let us pray."

Callie bowed her head, lifted up her own silent prayer for Reese, for whatever trouble haunted him enough to exit the church in the middle of the message.

"Lord," Pastor Beau began, "help us forget those things which are behind us, and reach forth unto those things which are before us. Teach us to forgive ourselves as You have already forgiven us. We ask this in our Savior's name, Amen."

After the closing hymn, people began shuffling out of the church. Though Callie wanted to run out of the building and seek out Reese, she stayed with Gabriella and Daniel until one of the older children promised to see the two back to Charity House.

"But we want to stay with you, Miss Callie."

Smiling down at Gabriella, she smoothed a hand over the glossy dark head. "I'll stop by the orphanage later this afternoon. We'll bake cookies."

"Will Mr. Reese be with you?" Daniel asked.

Since she didn't know where he'd gone, Callie hedged. "I'll see what I can do, but no guarantees."

When she was outside and once again alone on the steps, Callie's gaze roamed the immediate area. People lingered, clumped in groups, but she saw no sign of Reese. Driven by a strange urgency, she walked around the side of the building, where the cemetery was located.

Her gaze landed on a tall figure nearly hidden in the

shadow of a large ponderosa pine tree. Reese. Head bent, he was staring down at a grave. A second later, he sat on the ground beside the weathered headstone.

The pang in her heart was fueled by sorrow. Sorrow for Reese, for the evident loss he suffered of a loved one.

Callie watched him several minutes longer before setting out in his direction.

Reese had no idea how long he sat beside Miranda's grave. He figured not long, maybe only ten minutes. The final strains of the closing hymn still quivered on the air. People were only just spilling out onto the church steps. He didn't want anyone seeing him here in the cemetery. No one would, unless they came looking for him.

Callie would come. He'd seen the worry in her eyes as he'd shifted around her in the pew. A part of him wanted her to find him so he could share his burden with her.

Another part wanted her to stay far away.

Of all the days he'd chosen to return to church, he had to come when Beau gave a sermon about forgiveness and letting go of the past. One line had hit Reese especially hard. *God reaches back into our pasts, forgives our offenses and settles all claims against our conscience.*

Could it be that simple? Could it be a matter of releasing the pain of his past to the Lord, asking for healing and then…what? What came next?

Did he boldly reach for a different kind of future than the one he'd been pursuing for fourteen years?

Reese lifted his gaze to heaven, a wordless prayer

forming in his mind. He was tired of remembering Miranda's death, instead of celebrating her life. Tired of the lingering grief that hit him when he least expected it. He wanted…

He wanted…

Freedom.

He wanted to set the past firmly behind him. That, he realized, was why he now sat at Miranda's grave. He needed to settle the past, to finally let his wife rest in peace. Not because he wanted to be free of his memories of her, but because he wanted to be free of the broken dreams that kept him from living fully in the present.

Where did he start? What words did he use? His heart felt numb in his chest.

He and Miranda had been so young when they'd married. Her recklessness had fueled his impulsiveness. Fire to fire, flame to flame, they'd burned bright, too bright.

Frowning over the memory of their shared impetuousness, their foolish thoughts that they were immune to misfortunes, he picked up a stone and rolled it around in his fingers. The dirt covering the rock felt hot and dry against his skin, much like his long ago dreams of a happy marriage with the beautiful Miranda Remington.

A shadow blackened the sun overhead. "Reese?"

At the sweet familiar voice, the riot of emotions swirling inside him calmed. Callie had found him, perhaps thinking she'd come to his rescue. And maybe she had.

In that moment, Reese knew he would tell her about Miranda, and he would do so today. But at what cost?

Callie would want to know the truth, all of it, and that would require giving her a piece of his soul.

She lowered to a small wrought-iron bench situated between him and the tree, but said nothing.

From his position on the ground, he looked up at her. Her gaze was fastened on Miranda's headstone, sweeping quickly over the etchings. Reese didn't have to follow the direction of her gaze. He knew every word, every line by heart, including the final three. *R.I.P. Miranda Remington Bennett. 1863 to 1881.*

Callie's brows pulled together, as if calculating the dates in her mind. Reese saw the exact moment she made the connection.

Her eyes filled with a hundred unspoken questions. She spoke but one of them aloud. "Miranda was your—" her gaze returned to the headstone "—sister?"

"My wife."

Chapter Eighteen

Despite her shock over Reese's astonishing revelation, Callie did not push him to explain himself further. Not yet. He needed time to gather the words that would best tell his story—a story she doubted few people had heard. Perhaps only his father knew the full tale. And maybe not even him. Maybe Reese carried his terrible loss deep within him, where no one could know the magnitude of his pain.

Oh, Reese.

Wanting to ease his suffering, but not sure if he'd welcome her interference, Callie patted the empty space on the bench beside her. He gave one firm shake of his head, clearly preferring to sit on the ground beside his wife's grave.

Callie's heart took a tumble at the obvious implications. She did not try to coax him away again. However, a few moments later, he joined her on the bench, after all.

Holding silent, he stretched out his long legs and rolled his shoulders, but he didn't look in her direction.

She studied his profile. Enveloped in shadows cast by the tree overhead, his face appeared pale and gray.

Callie's heart took another tumble.

Whatever had happened to Reese's wife was clearly a tragic tale. When he continued staring straight ahead, she could stand his silence no longer. "Your wife died, back in—" she cut a glance at the headstone "—1881?"

"That's right." At last, his eyes met hers. "Miranda and I were married September of that same year."

Fourteen years had come and gone since his wedding, more than half of Callie's life. Reese's wife had died the same year they'd married, when Reese had been no more than—Callie calculated the years in her head—eighteen years old. *So young.* It explained much about his current approach to finding a bride.

"I'm sorry, Reese." She reached out and covered his hand with hers. "I'm truly sorry for your loss. There aren't words for what you've suffered."

"None that have been invented, at any rate." His stilted tone hinted at a storm of pent-up emotion held firmly in check.

"Will you tell me about your wife?" As soon as she asked the question, Callie realized she was quite possibly asking him to bare his soul. "Unless, of course, you'd rather not."

"I want to, Callie. I really want to tell you about Miranda." He clutched tightly at her hand. "But I don't think I can do it without your help. Ask me whatever you wish and I'll try to answer honestly."

"All right." The muscles in her stomach quivered as she cast about for her first question. "How…how did you meet?"

His brows pulled together in concentration, as if

he was following the memories back through time, all the way to the beginning. "I met her at a party at the Carlisles'. What prompted the occasion doesn't matter. I remember being furious at my father for insisting I attend. Because I had other plans that evening."

He went quiet as he drew his hand free of hers and set it on the arm of the bench. "Plans, I have no doubt, that would have landed me a night or two in jail." He let out a wry chuckle. "It wouldn't have been the first time."

"I shudder to ask."

"Probably for the best." He shifted a bit, released another laugh, this one self-deprecating. "I was an outrageous rebel in my youth. Impulsive, bone-stubborn and determined to find trouble wherever I could."

Callie could hardly imagine the person Reese described. He was such a deliberate man now, upright and straight, full of staggering patience. She couldn't imagine him behaving in a manner that would *land him a night or two in jail.*

"Go on," she said softly when she realized he'd fallen silent again.

His gaze lost somewhere in the past, he blinked at her in confusion.

"You were telling me about the party where you met your wife," she prompted. "Your father insisted you attend, and…"

"Right." He nodded. "The party. The moment I saw Miranda from across the room I fell completely, hopelessly in love. I know that sounds clichéd, but it's the truth. I was smitten from the moment I laid eyes on her."

His own eyes shuttered to slits, his gaze once again somewhere faraway.

After a moment, still glassy-eyed, he continued. "She was laughing when I walked up to her. I was captivated by her beauty." He smiled softly. "She had unruly red hair and startling, pale blue eyes. I asked her to marry me that very night. She said yes. We were wed a week later."

A flood of surprise washed over Callie. "So quickly?"

He smiled again, and Callie felt it deep within her soul, the pull of attraction she felt for him. Pray he didn't see her feelings written on her face.

"I was young, Callie. Impetuous. Miranda was equally spontaneous and untamed. We had one glorious, wild, uninhibited month together." He bent his head. "Then she was gone."

One month? He'd only been married one short month? So little time for happiness, Callie thought, so few days to be with the one he loved. "How did she die?"

He wiped a hand across his mouth. "Miranda loved horses. They were her greatest passion. She insisted we ride every day, sometimes twice a day, sometimes even more. I happily obliged her. It never occurred to me do anything else."

"Of course not. You loved her and wanted to make her happy."

"I did." He ran his hand over his mouth a second time. "She found great pleasure in challenging me to race at the most unexpected moments. It didn't matter where we were, in the heart of town, near an open field, in the midst of a crowded neighborhood. She died on one of our races."

There was sorrow in his eyes, unmistakable guilt in his voice. "Reese." Callie turned slightly to face him.

"I was raised on one of the largest ranches in Colorado. I know horses better than most. Accidents happen, no matter how careful the rider is or how skilled."

"Nevertheless," he continued as if he hadn't really heard what she said, "Miranda's death could have been prevented."

"You don't know that for sure."

"We were racing in a field we'd never ridden across before. Neither of us cared. We never cared. We were both that reckless."

You were both that young, she thought, remembering her own penchant for wild, spontaneous acts.

"Miranda was winning, as usual, laughing at me over her shoulder. But then her horse stumbled and went down hard." He tilted his head to the sky, released a slow breath of air. "After a series of rolls, Miranda ended up under the animal. It happened so fast. By the time I caught up to them, the horse was back on his feet. Miranda lay still on the ground."

"She... You..." Callie's voice broke over the words. "When you found her, was she dead?"

He shook his head. "Not dead, but nearly. She hung on for three days. Three endless days that crawled along at a slow, wretched pace. Yet when I think back to that time, those collective moments seemed to have passed in a single heartbeat."

"Oh, Reese."

"I willed her to live. I prayed unceasingly. I begged God to take me instead of her. To no avail. She breathed her final breath in my arms."

"I'm sorry." The words felt so inadequate.

"For months afterward, I wanted to die, too." He turned his haunted gaze onto Callie. "Maybe a part of me did die. The impulsive boy of my youth was gone for good, replaced by the man you see before you now."

A man who valued lists and structure above spontaneity and recklessness. So telling, Callie thought, so incredibly heartbreaking. Because after fourteen years, Reese still blamed himself for his wife's death.

In that, at least, Callie could ease his mind. "Reese," she began, thinking the best route just might be to lead him to the truth, instead of simply telling him. "Whose idea was it to race across that field?"

"I… I don't remember."

"I think you do," she said softly.

Angry shock leaped into his eyes. "You know nothing about what happened that day. You weren't there."

Knowing how badly he was hurting, Callie was tempted to back down. But no. This was too important. *Lord, give me the courage to continue.*

She took a deep breath and repeated the question. "Reese, whose idea was it?"

"Hers," he hissed. "It was Miranda's idea to race across that empty field."

"And yet—" Callie gentled her voice to a whisper "—you're still blaming yourself for her death."

"Of course I blame myself. I didn't have to agree to her challenge that day." His chest heaved with the vehemence of his response. "I could have discouraged her. I *should* have insisted we turn around."

"Would it have mattered?"

"I—" He broke off, lowered his head. "No."

Callie brought one of his hands to her face, pressed her lips to his open palm. "Maybe it's time you forgave yourself for your wife's death."

He continued staring at her, pressing his lips into

a grim line. He looked down at his hand, at the spot she'd kissed, then folded his fingers into a fist.

"Are you still in love with her?" Callie asked.

"A part of me will always love Miranda. I'm who I am because of her." He unclenched his fist, spread his fingers out wide. "But Beau's sermon released something inside me, something that's been coming on for some time, a need to put the past behind me, once and for all."

Callie knew just how easy it would be for Reese to continue holding on to the blame for his wife's death, instead of allowing God to heal his pain. Hadn't she done much the same thing with Simon?

"I left the church and came here to Miranda's grave with the idea of letting her go." He flexed his hand. "It's time I forgave her for dying on me."

"And time," Callie ventured, knowing she was risking his ire, "you stopped blaming yourself for not preventing the accident that took her life."

He nodded. "Yes. It's time I forgave myself, as well."

Did he know what a huge step he'd just taken? Did he realize the ramifications? "You recently called me brave. But you're the one who's brave, Reese. So very, very brave."

He didn't respond.

Cupping his face between her palms, she kissed him firmly on the lips. "Thank you for telling me about Miranda."

She dropped her hands, blinked away the sting of tears and attempted to stand.

"Don't go." He pulled her back down beside him. "I still have something to say, something important."

Callie waited, holding her breath, fearing what was

about to come out of his mouth yet knowing he needed to have his say.

"On several occasions you've asked me why I don't want a love match. Now you know the answer."

She did. But she didn't like it.

"I've already loved once in my life. Once was enough. I know how much it costs to give someone my heart, and the terrible price that must be paid when love is lost. I'll not willingly go through that pain again."

Callie lowered her head a moment, her heart beating wildly against her ribs. "I understand." She pushed the words past the lump in the throat. "I'll continue helping you find a suitable bride, but I won't expect you to fall in love with her."

He eyed her for a long, tense moment. "Thank you."

She nodded, feeling helpless and sad and more than a little defeated.

"Come on." Rising, he reached out and pulled her to her feet. "We had better return before my father and Mrs. Singletary get it into their heads to send out a search party for us."

Callie tried to laugh, but the sound came out scratchy and rough. A perfect match to her mood.

Tucking her hand in the crook of his arm, Reese led her out of the cemetery and around the building to the front of the church.

His father and Mrs. Singletary were waiting for them on the front steps.

"Ah, there you two are." Mrs. Singletary dropped a large, satisfied smile over them. "Mr. Bennett and I were discussing where we should partake in our noonday meal. We have decided upon the Hotel Dupree because, as Callie can attest, the chef makes a memorable sea bass."

The elder Mr. Bennett smiled. "I enjoy a good sea bass."

The idea of food made Callie's stomach churn, as did the prospect of sitting through a meal making small talk. She opened her mouth to refuse, thinking she would claim a headache, when she remembered her conversation with the Velasquez children. "That sounds lovely, but I'm afraid I won't be able to join you."

Mrs. Singletary, being Mrs. Singletary, insisted on an explanation. "Why ever not, dear?"

"I promised a couple of the Charity House children I'd bake cookies with them this afternoon."

The widow continued holding Callie's gaze.

The penetrating look caused her to add, "I mustn't disappoint the children."

"No," the widow said in an ironic tone. "We wouldn't want that."

Callie extricated her arm from Reese's only to have him reach out and take her hand. "I believe I'll join Callie at the orphanage."

"You will?" she asked, shooting him a surprised look. "Why?"

"I have a fondness for fresh baked cookies. And—" he divided a long, steady stare between his father and Mrs. Singletary "—a massive dislike of sea bass."

Beatrix watched two of her favorite young people depart on their walk to Charity House. A short walk, indeed, seeing as the orphanage's backyard spilled onto church property.

Oh, but it did her soul good to witness the changes in their relationship. Not long ago they were quite awkward in one another's company. Now they fell into perfect step, matching each other's stride, as if they'd been strolling together like that all their lives.

She smiled fondly after their retreating backs. At last they were comfortable together. Indeed, they made a far cozier picture than when she'd insisted Callie walk Mr. Bennett to the door after her dinner party. They'd barely looked at one another that night. Now, their heads were tilted close in hushed conversation.

Only after they turned the final corner did she allow her smile to turn smug. "They are falling in love."

She predicted an autumn wedding, the plans already materializing in her mind.

If his masculine snort was anything to go by, apparently the man standing beside her had a differing opinion. "You think you're so clever, Beatrix."

Not prone to feigning false humility, she answered the odious question without hesitation. "I am clever, Reese, dear, as evidenced by my vast and ever-increasing fortune, which, as you may recall—" she lifted her nose in the air "—has greatly benefited your own overflowing coffers."

He started to say something, probably, *I earned most of the money without your help,* but she cut him off.

"Do you object to your son marrying my companion?"

"I think they make a lovely couple. I am quite fond of Miss Mitchell. I hope something comes of it." The corner of his mouth turned down. "That's not the point."

Her brows rose. "But of course that's the point."

He jabbed a finger in the air between them. "You shouldn't meddle in other people's lives."

"Don't be ridiculous. If not me, then who do you suggest should guide otherwise stubborn individuals to their happily-ever-after?"

His lips tightened. "You should leave the future up to the Lord. Stop playing God."

The very idea. It was insulting. "I am but a humble servant of our Lord, directing misguided men and women in the proper direction. I never force a match."

"No?"

"I nudge."

"Beatrix, you cannot continue interfering in other people's lives. One day you will make a false step."

She waved this off with a flick of her wrist. "Don't be silly. I know exactly what I'm doing."

For the barest second he looked appalled that she would dare claim such a thing, then, in a stern tone, he said, "No one is infallible. You will make a mistake. It's only a matter of time. I urge you to cease and desist—"

"Reese Bennett, you may be smart. You may be highly successful in your given field." *You may be entirely too handsome for your own good.* "But you will not tell me what to do."

He stared at her.

"I mean it."

To her great surprise, he laughed.

Finished with their conversation—with the man himself—she turned on her heel and headed down the pathway to her home. Walking, or rather marching, with her head held high, served the very necessary purpose of cooling off her temper.

"Beatrix, darling," the odious man called after her. "Haven't you forgotten something?"

Her feet ground to a halt. Instead of turning around completely, the man didn't deserve that much courtesy, she shot a haughty look over her shoulder. "What would that be, Reese, *darling?*"

"You promised to introduce me to the Hotel Dupree's famous sea bass."

"You still wish to dine with me this afternoon?"

"I would like nothing better." The smile he gave her was quite devastating.

She pressed her lips tightly together in what turned out to be a failed attempt at returning that handsome smile.

"Come, Beatrix." He reached out his hand. "My carriage is ready and waiting to take us across town."

Well, why not? She spun back around and, in silence, head still lifted, took his outstretched hand.

When their fingers connected, then entwined, the smirk he shot her was full of masculine arrogance.

"You should know I am only accompanying you because, once given, I never break a promise." She looked at him with narrowed eyes, daring him to comment.

With nary a word, he helped her into the carriage and settled on the opposite seat. His gaze warmed. "I apologize for upsetting you, Beatrix. It was unconsciously done."

She noted he didn't actually ask for forgiveness for what he said, merely for upsetting her. As apologies went, she supposed it wasn't the worst she'd ever heard. Not the best, but certainly not the worst.

She could continue making him suffer, but no one would ever accuse Beatrix Singletary of carrying a grudge. "Apology accepted."

"So quickly?" He leaned back in his seat and chuckled softly. "You do realize I was prepared to grovel."

Ha, she knew better than that.

"Nevertheless," she began, feeling far more generous than he deserved, "at times such as these, it helps to have a short memory."

He inclined his head. "You are graciousness itself."

"Of course I am."

Having seized the last word, she leaned back in her seat and set out to enjoy a fine meal with equally fine company at a very fine hotel.

Chapter Nineteen

With each step she and Reese took toward Charity House, Callie felt the tension seep out of him. He seemed more relaxed, as if a dark shadow had been lifted from his heart.

How well she knew the feeling, and how happy she was to see the light restored in his eyes. Ignoring the little flutter in her heart, she smiled up into his face.

He smiled back.

They were a single unit in that moment, united by the revelation of their individual secrets to one another. If only Reese wasn't resolved to lead with his head, Callie thought.

If only she could settle for less than love in her own life. Perhaps then they could forge something lasting, something that would keep them together forever.

When they turned the final corner to the orphanage, she pulled him to a stop. "Tell me the real reason you chose to come with me to Charity House instead of dining with your father and Mrs. Singletary."

"I *really* dislike sea bass."

She laughed. "Very funny. But, seriously, Reese, why?"

He shot a glance over her shoulder, smiled secretively. "I've been thinking it's time Beatrix Singletary found herself on the other end of a little matchmaking."

"You're joking."

"Not even a little." Returning his gaze to hers, he lifted an elegant shoulder. "My father seems the perfect choice."

She couldn't think why. "But they disagree on most topics."

"Precisely." He leaned forward, lowered his voice. "Take a moment and think about it, Callie."

Contemplating the notion, she tapped her chin with her fingertip.

"Mrs. Singletary and your father, as a couple? Why that's brilliant." Half appalled, half amused, another bubble of laughter slipped past her lips. "A bit startling, but brilliant."

"I've been known to think fast on my feet." He leaned over and gave her a boyish grin. "A talent that can be quite handy in the most startling, brilliant ways imaginable."

Laughing in perfect harmony, they entered Charity House side by side. But then Reese pulled away, mentioning something about needing to find Marc.

Callie reluctantly let him go.

Feeling slightly abandoned—all right, a lot abandoned—she adopted a more leisurely pace than the long, clipped strides that had taken Reese so quickly away from her.

She'd barely moved into the main parlor when a

small hand tugged on her skirt. A surge of affection seized her heart.

"Hello, Gabriella." Callie crouched down to eye level, studied the pretty little girl. "I forgot to tell you this morning, but you look quite lovely in that dress. I particularly love the pink bow tied at your waist."

"Look what I can do." The child executed a perfect twirl.

"Very impressive." Callie hugged the girl's thin shoulders.

Gabriella clung for several seconds, then squirmed free.

"Where's your brother?" she asked, mildly concerned. It wasn't typical to find one Velasquez child without the other nearby.

"He's in the tiger room. He and the other boys are playing with toy soldiers."

"Sounds like…fun?"

"Uh-uh." The little girl scowled adorably. "I'd rather bake cookies with you."

"Already halfway done," said a familiar voice from the doorway.

Smiling, Callie straightened to her full height. Temperance Evans stood silhouetted in a ray of sunlight, looking really quite beautiful as she returned the gesture.

"Don't tell me you cook, too?" Callie asked.

"No, no, no." The headmistress gave a brief shudder. "My mother always used to say that if you can make sense of a recipe, you can make any dish. But I've discovered it's a bit more complicated."

Callie didn't disagree. Even something as basic as deciphering simple measurements could present a challenge to someone unschooled in the various abbreviations.

Miss Evans frowned down at the child holding onto Callie's hand. "You are not to be in the main parlor, Gabriella. It's against house rules."

Though her words were somewhat stern, Miss Evans ran a gentle hand over the child's hair as she added, "You must rejoin the other little girls playing jacks on the back porch."

Gabriella buried her face in Callie's skirt. "I want to stay with you."

Frustration flashed in the headmistress's gaze, followed by a genuine note of sympathy.

Before Miss Evans could decide which emotion to give in to, Callie spoke first. "What do you say, Gabriella?" She pried the little girl away from her skirt. "Want to come with me and see what's happening on the back porch?"

"No." The child stared at the floor. "I want to go find my brother."

Miss Evans sighed.

Callie leaned down and captured the child's gaze with her own. "You don't want to play jacks?"

The child's eyes welled with tears. "I want Daniel."

"Go on, Miss Mitchell. Take the child to her brother."

Less than five minutes later, Callie stood on the edge of the tiger room, named after the massive mural painted on the far wall. The scene depicted a large jungle cat prowling through a detailed world of vines, trees, beautiful waterfalls and all sorts of colorful, exotic animals.

The boys, grouped into two separate teams, were

facing off in what looked like a ferocious battle of some sort. They weren't alone, either. Reese and Marc Dupree were on the floor with them, squaring off with one another from opposing sides.

They were so involved in their game, nobody noticed Callie and Gabriella. Callie took the opportunity to watch the skirmish in silence. Or rather, she watched Reese.

Her heart dipped to her toes. Reese. Oh, Reese. This was what he would be like as a father. Sprawled out on the floor, tin soldier in hand, playing as if he were another one of the children, caring little for the dirt and smudges on his clothes.

Daniel, sitting on Reese's left, caught sight of his sister. "Gabriella, come be on my team. We're playing marshals and outlaws."

The little girl rushed over to her brother and plopped down beside him.

After patting her on the head, Reese handed Gabriella a tin soldier. "We're the good guys, *Marshal* Velasquez."

The little girl beamed up at him.

"You have too many people on your side," the boy sitting beside Marc whined.

"Yeah," another one added. "That's not fair to us."

"Callie, come quick." Marc motioned her to take the empty spot next to him. "It's up to you to even out the numbers."

Even out the numbers. That had been nearly the exact same argument Mrs. Singletary had used when she'd insisted Callie attend her dinner party all those weeks ago.

Much had changed in her life since that night. She

was no longer a piteous wallflower content to hide in the shadows. Nor was she satisfied with camouflaging her light behind ugly clothing.

The woman she was today fully embraced the transformation her employer had originally hoisted upon her. Happily willing to accept she was a child of God, worthy of love.

Reese had been instrumental in the change. Was it any wonder she loved him?

She loved him? Why, yes. She did. Callie loved Reese. The realization should have come as a shock, but instead it spread through her like warm honey, sweet and appealing yet also a little sticky.

Callie knew while she might never win Reese's heart, she had to try.

"Move aside, boys." She settled in beside Marc, and then locked her gaze on Reese. "Let the battle begin."

This was the woman Reese had always suspected lurked inside Callie. Beneath the ugly clothing and off-putting facade was a beautiful, fierce warrior princess. A woman who bravely stepped out of the shadows and tackled life head-on.

Mesmerized, Reese watched her take up her position as one of the *outlaws*. Appropriate, given that this woman could easily steal his heart if he didn't take care.

There were far worse fates a man could suffer.

Why, Reese wondered, had he avoided her all these years? Why had he kept his distance for so long?

He knew, of course.

Deep down, he'd sensed her fighting spirit, her passionate loyalty for the people she loved. That hidden ferocity had alarmed him. He'd been too hobbled by guilt over Miranda's death to recognize the beauty of Callie Mitchell. By thinking he needed to maintain control at every turn, he'd steered clear of this charming, daring, magnificent woman.

In an ironic twist, it was Callie who'd helped him let go of Miranda and allow his wife to finally rest in peace.

Toy soldier in hand, a husky growl came out of her throat, followed by a delighted giggle. Reese couldn't take his eyes off her.

He made a mental note to add *not afraid to get dirty* and *willing to play with toy soldiers* to his latest bride list.

Even dressed in her Sunday best, Callie battled as valiantly as any of the boys in the room. But, alas, her efforts—and those of her team—weren't enough. The good guys won.

Daniel and Gabriella jumped up and down, cheering with the rest of their teammates.

As Reese watched the siblings' uninhibited celebration, joy and relief filled him. He couldn't be more pleased by their transformation.

Wondering if she'd noticed the change in the children, as well, he glanced over at Callie. A mistake. He'd let his guard drop a second too long. In the next instant, he was tackled playfully by his teammates. Fingers and elbows jabbed at him. He took a foot in the gut, one in his chest, and all he could think to do was…

Laugh.

It felt good to laugh. Freeing.

Not only was Miranda finally at peace but so, too, was he.

Hovering from a spot overhead, Callie peered down at him with one of her prettiest smiles. "Want help up?"

He rolled out from under the tangle of arms and legs, then stretched out his hand. "Please."

The moment their palms pressed together he felt it, the sensation of coming home, of finding his place in the world, of letting go the fight.

Strangely lightheaded, he let Callie pull him to his feet. Staring into her eyes, his throat began to burn with unexpected emotion. He swallowed. "You are a fierce opponent, Miss Mitchell."

"Something you should keep in mind, Mr. Bennett."

"I like a good challenge."

"Then considered yourself warned. One day, victory will be mine."

"Watch yourself, Reese." Smiling, Marc clasped him on the shoulder. "The Mitchells give no ground. They take no prisoners. It's a marvel we lost the game."

Eyes narrowed, Callie pointed a finger at Reese. "We'll get you next time."

He started to say something along the lines of *you're welcome to try,* when he caught a movement in the doorway. The new schoolmistress stood beside Laney Dupree, watching the shenanigans from a safe distance.

Both women were smiling, but only Laney carried the smile into her eyes.

In fact, Temperance Evans looked excessively stiff. Her gaze was distant, as well. Standing intentionally apart from the action, she reminded Reese of Callie.

Or rather, the old Callie. The new Callie was the most approachable woman he knew. He was growing quite fond of the changes in her.

"I see we missed out on all the fun," Laney said with a hint of remorse in her tone.

Miss Evans looked more than a little relieved.

Carrying two of the younger boys upside down in either hand, Marc sauntered over to his wife and kissed her square on the mouth with a loud smacking sound.

"Oh, stop." She playfully pushed at his chest. "You're embarrassing yourself."

That earned her a dry chuckle from her husband.

Grinning, Marc set the boys on their feet. At the same moment, Laney announced, "Milk and cookies are waiting in the kitchen."

Cheers erupted, followed by a mass exodus toward the door.

Marc halted the stampede with a piercing whistle. "Everyone, freeze."

Silence dropped over the room like a cannonball falling from the sky.

"You know the rules."

"No running inside the house," half the children said, while the other half grumbled under their breath.

Shoving away from her spot at the door, Miss Evans took charge.

"Follow me, children." She turned on her heel, then glanced back over her shoulder. "Remember, we walk in an orderly fashion, single file, no pushing or shoving."

She didn't raise her voice, or speak overly harsh, yet every child obeyed her directives, lining up one by one, single file, tallest to shortest, Gabriella near the rear behind her brother.

Marveling, Reese stepped aside to let the children pass.

Once the last little boy trooped into the hallway, Marc let out another, softer whistle. "I bow to your expertise," he said to his wife. "Miss Evans was a perfect hire."

"I do so love being right."

He gave her another loud peck on the cheek. "I know that, my love."

Everyone laughed.

"You know, Laney—" Marc wiggled his eyebrows "—playing Marshals and Outlaws is hard work. I could use a cookie myself. What about you, Reese?"

Reese adopted the same hopeful tone as the other man. "I wouldn't say no."

Marc leaned around him. "Callie? What about you?"

"I also enjoy cookies."

"Then follow me." Laney motioned them into the hallway. "Quickly, now, before they're all gone."

As if in silent agreement, Reese and Callie took up a position side by side and fell in step behind the Duprees. Only as they wound their way to the stairwell did Reese realize Callie had grown unnaturally quiet. The fight hadn't exactly left her, but she seemed less... bold. Not quite as feisty.

He glanced over at her, noticed her face held a thoughtful expression. A lot was going on in that complicated mind.

Wondering if he was the cause of this alteration in her mood, he waited until they hit the first-floor landing then tugged her off to one side.

Marc halted, as well, a question in his eyes.

"I need to speak with Callie before we join you in the kitchen."

Brows traveling toward his hairline, Marc's gaze turned suspicious.

Reese rolled his shoulders in annoyance. "We'll stay out in the open. Where you can see us."

This time, Marc looked to Callie for confirmation.

"I have no objection," she said.

"Out in the open." Marc pointed at Reese. "Move too far away from my line of vision, and I'll come looking for you."

"Understood." As soon as Marc rounded the corner, Reese took Callie's shoulders and turned her to face him. "All right, out with it."

Her eyes widened. "Out with what?"

"What's on your mind? And don't say 'nothing,' I see the inner wheels spinning."

She pressed her lips tightly together and said nothing.

"Come on, Callie. You're thinking so loud my ears hurt."

Sighing, she lifted a delicate shoulder. "I'd rather not speak of it here."

He touched her arm. "You can tell me anything."

She drew her bottom lip between the teeth, glanced at a spot behind him. Shaking her head, she pulled him into the shadows and lowered her voice to a mere whisper. "It's Miss Evans."

"The schoolmistress?" He jerked in surprise. "What about her?

Callie went silent on him again, but her eyes held a troubled light. That couldn't be good.

"What's wrong with Miss Evans?"

"Nothing. Not a single thing. If you must know." Callie looked left, then right, then left again. "I like her."

So she'd found a new friend. That was nice. But why was she telling him? Why the stealth and whispered conversation?

As if reading his mind, Callie gave him a meaningful stare. "She's perfect."

"Please." He made a sound deep in his throat. "No one is perfect."

Another sigh, this one full of female frustration. "She's perfectly suitable. For you. You must realize she fits all your requirements for a..." She mouthed the word *bride*.

For several heartbeats, Reese stood in stunned silence. She was foisting Miss Evans on him? *Now?* After all that had happened between them? When his head was so full of Callie he couldn't think straight?

"Say something," she whispered.

He couldn't think what to say, so he went for levity. "Uh...*something?*"

Lips pursed, she shook her head at him. "She fits every one of your requirements and a few you haven't listed."

Did this woman not realize how miserable she sounded? Did she not realize how heartening it was for him to discover Callie didn't want him pursuing Miss Evans? "I don't like her."

"What's wrong with her?"

She's not you.

He nearly blurted out the truth in his heart, but decided now wasn't the time. Not with them skulking in shadows as if they had something to hide.

"Her smile rarely meets her eyes," he said. "Doesn't bode well for easy, lighthearted conversations."

"Oh, honestly." Callie threw her hands in the air. "Are you trying to be difficult?"

Actually, he was. But, again, now wasn't the time for that particular conversation. He had a new bride list to finalize, with an entirely different set of requirements, ones Callie would surely approve of this time around. Seeing as she was his inspiration.

He looked over his shoulder again, back into the kitchen. Miss Evans was handing a cookie to one of the smaller children. The smile she gave the little girl was warm and friendly and completely rendered his earlier argument moot.

Callie followed the direction of his gaze and sighed heavily. "She's very beautiful and appears to have a great affinity for children."

She was so adorably upset by this admission he couldn't help but tease her a little. "I may have responded in haste. Perhaps I'll allow her further consideration, after all."

"Did you know she can't cook?"

Amused at Callie's sudden switch in position, Reese pretended to consider this new piece of information. "Not at all?"

"She can't even follow a simple recipe."

Reese stifled a laugh. "She's a smart woman. I'm confident she can learn."

Lowering her head, Callie sighed a third time. Or was it the fourth? He'd lost count. "If you really like her," she began, "I suppose I could teach her the basics."

"You'd do that for me?"

She nodded, looking profoundly unhappy. He didn't think he could adore this woman any more than he did right now.

"That's very generous of you, Callie." And very, very educational.

She was jealous of Miss Evans. Simply because she thought the woman would make him a suitable bride.

A plan began formulating in his mind. It would take time to implement and would require much preparation on his end.

Reese was a patient man, highly skilled at carrying out a properly prepared plan.

Beginning tomorrow, he would start over with his bride hunt. He would pursue just one woman from this point forward. The *only* woman he wanted, the most suitable woman for him.

The trick would be to convince Callie that *he* was equally suitable for *her.*

Chapter Twenty

Over the following weeks, Callie noticed a discernible change in Reese. He seemed more attentive, making a point to seek her out at parties or the theater or whenever their paths crossed. If he had a meeting with Mrs. Singletary, he lingered over mindless discussions with Callie about the weather, both before and after his appointment.

At Charity House he found ways to include her in whatever game he'd chosen to play with the children.

He always behaved above reproach, treating her as though she was a woman worthy of his respect. Other than that one time in his office, he didn't attempt to kiss her again. No, he treated her with generosity and tenderness, as if she was precious in his sight. As a result, Callie was getting to know Reese on a whole new, deeper level.

She was also falling more in love with him by the day. Not the man she'd wistfully watched from afar, but the man she knew him to be now. A man who worked hard, cared deeply for his family and friends, and who adored all children.

What he didn't do was discuss his bride hunt with Callie. No matter how many times she broached the subject, no matter what tactic she employed to get him talking, he managed to dodge the conversation altogether.

Only two causes made sense. Either he'd turned to Mrs. Singletary for help once again. Or he'd made up his mind and had chosen a woman to become his bride. The latter seemed unlikely. With all the attention he'd been paying Callie, how would he have time to pursue any woman? How could he—

A gasp flew past her lips. She quickly pressed a hand to her mouth. But... Oh. Oh. Reese was pursing...*her*?

"Oh, my!"

Situated behind the desk in her private study, Mrs. Singletary looked up from the guest list she held in her hand. "Did you say something, Callie?"

"No, I... I just..." She couldn't form thoughts in her mind. Her heart beat wildly in her ears, stealing what little concentration she had left. "I...thought of something I forgot to do for tonight's ball."

The widow placed the list on the desk in front of her. "What is that, dear?"

Think, Callie. Think. "I...haven't picked out my hairstyle yet."

"That's leaving it a bit late. The ball will be starting in a few hours."

Callie stood, looked frantically around, pivoted toward the exit. "I need to consult the magazines Julia left in my room."

Without waiting for the widow's response, she hurried out of the office and strode quickly through the winding corridors. She desperately needed the sanctuary of her own room, where she could sort through the chaotic thoughts running around in her head. Reese had chosen her.

He'd chosen *her* for his bride.

But…why hadn't he made his decision known to her? *He's had weeks.*

What could he hope to gain by not informing her of his intentions?

So focused on puzzling out his strange behavior, she nearly tripped over the cat trotting beside her. Fluffy tail pointed straight up in the air, Lady Macbeth barely swerved out of the way.

Callie smiled down at the skittering cat. "Seeking escape, are you?"

The spooked animal darted in front of her feet once again. Prepared for the move, she redirected her steps, skirting disaster by less than a foot.

Lady Macbeth rushed ahead of her, pausing at her bedroom door. The moment she twisted the doorknob, the cat shoved inside and dashed under the bed.

Callie didn't blame her for wanting to get away from the household commotion. For three days straight, Mrs. Singletary's home had turned into a hive of activity in preparation for her annual charity ball.

Vast quantities of people came and went throughout the day, bringing with them large amounts of food, an assortment of desserts, flower arrangements and who knew what else.

Rugs had been rolled up and tucked away in the attic. The floor in the main ballroom had been waxed and polished, twice. Buffet tables had been set up in several rooms on both the main and second levels of the house.

Aside from the outside help, Laney Dupree had also put Mrs. Singletary's staff to work on the decorations, including Callie. Her fingers were numb from polishing scores of silver candlesticks, dishes and serving trays.

As the widow's companion, Callie would be expected to act as one of the hostesses this evening. Until then, she would enjoy a bit of solitude. She quickly shut her bedroom door and clicked the lock in place.

"It's safe to come out now."

Lady Macbeth peered out from under the bed, gave Callie a narrow-eyed glare then dashed back into her hiding place.

"Can't say I blame you, you're out of harm's way under there, might as well stay put."

That way Callie wouldn't have to worry about tripping over the skittish animal as she took to pacing. Her heart overflowing with emotion, she tracked around the perimeter of the room.

Reese was actually courting her. How had she not made the connection? The gentleness, the sweet, affectionate attentiveness, all spoke of a man wooing the woman he preferred above all others.

She wanted to be his bride, so very much, but only if he loved her. She didn't want him to propose because he deemed her suitable according to some list he'd drawn up as he would a legal brief.

She wanted his heart, all of it, and would settle for nothing less. Unfortunately, he'd given the bulk of it away already, when he was more boy than man. *I've already loved once in my life. Once was enough.*

Oh, Reese.

Callie spun in a tight circle, retraced her steps, maneuvering around the furniture when necessary. She knew Reese cared for her, but that wasn't the same as love.

The fact that Callie refused to settle for second best in his heart was really his own fault. He'd taught her to accept her worth as a cherished child of God.

"Typical man. He's ruined everything. *Everything.*"

Marching over to her writing table, she yanked open the drawer and pulled out the portrait she'd painted of her and Reese. She'd titled the picture Bride and Groom.

Wishful thinking. If Reese proposed and she refused him, would he marry someone else? The thought was a black stain upon her heart.

"Callie? Are you in there?" A rapid knocking sounded at the door. "Do let me in, dear. I'm worried about you."

Sighing, she carefully set the painting on her desk. She should have known Mrs. Singletary would follow her after that hasty departure. The widow was nothing if not perceptive.

"Coming," she called.

The moment she opened the door, Mrs. Singletary grabbed her by the shoulders and stared into her face. After several seconds of intense scrutiny, she released a slow exhale. "You're all right."

"Of course I'm all right."

"You left so abruptly I wasn't entirely sure." She looked over Callie's shoulder. "May I come in?"

"Yes." Callie stepped back and let her pass.

After a brief glance around the room, Mrs. Singletary chose to perch herself on the edge of Callie's bed. "Won't you tell me what's upset you?"

Surprisingly close to tears, she sank down beside her employer and drew in a steadying breath. "It's hopeless."

"Nothing is ever hopeless." The widow draped her arm around her shoulders. "With God all things are possible."

Then why did her situation feel so completely *impossible?*

"I'm in love with Reese." She was astonished at how easy the admission came.

"I know." Mrs. Singletary removed her arm from around Callie's shoulders and took her hands. "Love is a marvelous thing. A treasured gift from God. Something to be celebrated."

Not when it was one-sided. Giving in to her sorrow, she buried her face in her hands and let the tears come at last.

"Oh, dear. Those aren't tears of joy."

Callie had never cried in front of her employer, but now that she'd begun she couldn't seem to stop the flow. "I'm in love with Reese, but he's not in love with me."

"Well, that's just silly. Of course he loves you. I dare say he's besotted."

The woman sounded so confident that Callie experienced a small flutter of hope. "Why… How…?" She dropped her hands and gaped at her employer. "How do you know?"

"It's quite simple, dear. I've watched him watching you. He does it all the time, especially when he thinks no one is paying attention." The widow leaned in close. "I *always* pay attention."

Something tugged at Callie's heart, something new and wonderful. Something that felt like anticipation. "He—" she swiped at her cheeks "—watches me?"

"Indeed, yes. He can't keep his eyes off you. At the theater he watches you instead of the play. Moreover, you're the first person he seeks out at any gathering and the last he speaks to before he departs."

If half of what the widow claimed was true, Reese could very well ask her to marry him soon. It was a gloriously wonderful thought and so horribly terrible.

She knew he cared for her, perhaps even deeply. But that wasn't the same as loving her. "He was married once before. Did you know that, Mrs. Singletary?"

Her words were met with several beats of silence. "You jest."

"Fourteen years ago."

"How did I not know about this?"

"The marriage lasted only a month before his wife died in a riding accident. He was only eighteen at the time, and…" Callie blinked rapidly to stave off another onslaught of tears. She'd cried enough. "His wife was the love of his life."

They both fell silent, staring at one another. Callie saw the widow processing this new piece of information, saw that keen mind of hers evaluating what it all meant. "You are sure about this?"

"He told me himself." *I've already loved once in my lifetime. Once was enough.*

"Well, hmm. That certainly explains a lot." The widow rose, then began to pace through the room, following nearly the same route Callie had taken.

Eyes burning with unshed tears, she tracked the woman's progress until she could stand the suspense no longer. "Do you now understand why the situation is hopeless?"

Mrs. Singletary held up a hand. "Hush, dear. I need a moment."

Callie gave her two. Then said, "But, Mrs. Singletary, you have always claimed that we each have only one true soul mate."

"I know what I said. But perhaps it's time I reevaluated my opinion on the matter." She halted at the writing desk, picked up the miniature portrait Callie had made of her and Reese. "Did you paint this, dear?"

"Yes."

"It's quite lovely." She set the portrait back on the desk and returned to sit beside Callie. "Despite his previous marriage, I still believe Mr. Bennett is in love with you."

Callie squeeze her eyes tightly shut, trying desperately to hold back the burst of hope spreading through her. "I want to believe you."

"It seems you have an important decision ahead of you."

Callie opened her eyes. "I…do?"

The widow rose, peered out into the hallway, then came back to stand over her. "You can either let your fears determine your future and thus live the rest of your life alone. Or you can take a leap of faith and seize a lifetime of happiness with the man you love. The choice is yours."

"But even if Reese does love me—"

"Oh, he does."

"How can I trust it's enough? How will I know if

I'm enough? What if Reese…" She broke off, unable to finish the rest her thought.

No, she must continue. She must speak aloud her greatest fear. "Mrs. Singletary, what if Reese grows to resent me?"

"For what, dear?"

"For being alive?" She swallowed. "For not being Miranda."

"There are no guarantees in life, or in love. That's where faith comes in. You must allow the Lord to direct your path. In the meantime, let's get you dressed." Mrs. Singletary stuck her head back in the hallway. "Julia. Hurry, hurry, our time is running short."

The maid popped into the room, breathing harder than usual, as though she'd run the entire length of the long corridor.

"My companion must look her very best this evening." Mrs. Singletary took the maid's hand and dragged her toward Callie. "She should wear her hair up, I think, with perhaps a few tendrils hanging loose around her face."

"Whatever you think best, Mrs. Singletary."

"Then up it shall be." She headed toward the door, paused. "Think about what I said, Callie. The only way you will lose this battle is if you refuse to fight."

With those sage words, the widow swept out of the room.

Reese entered Mrs. Singletary's home behind an unfamiliar couple. It seemed all of Denver had been invited to the widow's annual charity ball.

Handing his hat and gloves to one of the hired butlers, he entered the crowded foyer and looked around.

Women were dressed in formal gowns made of colorful silks or satins. They wore elbow-length white gloves and fancy adornments in their hair. Jewels glittered around their necks.

In contrast, the gentlemen wore formal black tailcoats and trousers with white vests and matching white bow ties.

Looking for one woman in particular, Reese scanned all the female faces but didn't find the one he wanted most to see.

Shouldering his way through the bulk of humanity lingering in the open foyer, he continued searching for the only woman he wanted to see tonight. The crowded drawing room on his right was filled to capacity with clusters of people chatting among themselves.

No Callie.

Although, he had to admit, there were an uncommon number of attractive young women in attendance tonight. He felt the bulk of their gazes following him as he moved on to the next room. The overabundance of female interest in him had failed to die down in the weeks since news had gotten out of his bride search.

It seemed everyone wanted to know who he would marry.

He planned to end the speculation tonight.

He had his final list tucked inside an interior pocket of his jacket. After weeks of writing and rewriting, agonizing over what to put in and what to take out, he was ready to present his requirements to Callie.

He needed to find her first.

Music floated through the house. Tables draped in gold-and-silver satin lined nearly every room. Trays of fruit and cheeses were surrounded by piles of smoked fish, roasted fowl and thinly sliced cuts of beef. Several tables were dedicated to desserts.

At last, he caught sight of Callie in the grand ballroom. She was dressed in a gossamer gown that was neither blue nor green but a mesmerizing combination of the two. The bodice was form-fitting, trimmed with lace, while the skirt draped in flowing waves of fabric past her slippered feet. Her hair was piled on top of her head with a loose waterfall of curls hanging around her face.

As he'd seen her do countless times in the past, she watched the dance floor from a discreet distance. The sight made his gut twist. She should be taking a turn around the ballroom with the other couples, with him as her partner.

Easy enough to rectify.

She must have sensed his gaze on her because she turned her head and smiled at him. She was different tonight, bolder, more sure of herself. As inevitable as the day giving way to night, his heart picked up speed. His blood raced through his veins.

His throat seized over an unsteady breath.

He set out in her direction.

She set out in his.

They met halfway and he took her hand. "You are a vision tonight."

Though she boldly held his stare, the slight tremble in her fingers spoke of her nervousness. "Thank you, Reese. You're looking quite handsome yourself."

"I look like every other man in the room."

She smiled again, an expression of infinite caring and affection. "Perhaps in what you are wearing, that is true. But you stand out above all others, in looks and character."

He'd asked himself many times over the past few weeks, why this woman was the one he wanted to marry. *Why her?*

Now, as he stood entrapped in her gaze, he wondered why he'd ever doubted his decision to pursue her.

"Shall we dance?"

She bit her lip. Even without that telltale sign, he could sense her hesitation. He silently willed her to say yes.

Her answer came in a brief nod. He drew her into his arms and spun her out onto the dance floor.

Gazes locked, they danced in silence for most of the song. It came to an end all too soon and they stepped apart.

Reese wasn't through holding her. "Dance one more with me."

"I have been tasked with refilling the dessert tables whenever they fall low. I cannot neglect my duties." She sighed. "Nor can I monopolize you all evening."

The strains of the next waltz filled the air. "Once more," he insisted.

"People may misunderstand your intentions."

"My intentions are wholly honorable." Sweeping her into his arms, he gave her no more chance to argue. "Besides, you owe me a respite."

Her eyebrows arched at haughty angle. Ah, there she was. *His* Callie.

"Countless women have been showing up at my law firm all week with the sole purpose of insisting I dance with them at the ball this evening."

Letting out a delighted laugh, she shook her head.

Then, as if concerned he might actually be telling the truth, her eyes rounded. "Surely not."

"I might have exaggerated the number." His tone came out more amused than he'd felt at the time. "It wasn't *countless* women, just two."

Eyes narrowed, head titled, she considered this a moment. "Let me guess, their names begin with the letter *P*."

"Right on the first try." He spun her in a circle.

She matched him step for step. "I forbid you to dance with either Phoebe or Penelope Ferguson tonight."

He drew back in laughing surprise. "You forbid me?"

"Don't think you can defy me on this, either." The mock scowl she gave him was as endearing as the rest of her. "I will make a scene if you do."

"I wouldn't dare risk a scene."

They danced the next twelve notes in companionable silence.

"I've made up a new bride list," he said.

Her feet stumbled to a halt and she blinked up at him in horrified silence.

It was hardly the response he'd expected.

At last, she found her voice. "You did what?"

"I have designed a new list. I brought it with me." He took her arm and guided her off the dance floor. "I thought we might review it together later, perhaps when the ball is winding down."

"You have revised your list," she repeated.

"You'll be pleased to discover that I put much thought into this last and final one. It's very detailed. I'm hoping you'll approve of the changes."

She glanced at him without smiling. "So you are still seeking a bride?"

"Not precisely." He was attempting to tell her he'd picked out his bride—*her*—but he was making a hash of it. "I've already made my decision. You see, Callie, I—"

A small commotion at the front of the ballroom cut off the rest of his words. Reese swiveled his head and, for a perilous moment, his mind went blank.

He'd expected this evening to be memorable. Had hoped and planned for it to be so.

But he hadn't foreseen this shocking twist.

After months of being gone, after innumerable unanswered letters from her sister, Fanny Mitchell had chosen tonight to make her return to Denver.

As she took the dance floor with her partner, Reese clasped Callie's hand and watched his ex-fiancée waltz back into their lives.

Chapter Twenty-One

Fanny looked spectacular, Callie thought glumly. She was poised and sophisticated beyond her twenty-two years, and even more beautiful than when she'd left town. The blue silk gown she wore complemented her delicate beauty, while the artfully arranged mass of blond curls set off her exquisite face and startling amber eyes.

As if she didn't know—or perhaps didn't care—that she was the center of attention, she twirled around the dance floor in Jonathon Hawkins's arms. A triumphant return, timed for utmost effect.

But to what end?

If Fanny had come to the ball in an effort to halt any remaining gossip over her broken engagement, she'd failed. The ballroom buzzed with whispers and speculation. Gazes swung between Fanny and Reese.

Callie thought she might be sick.

Not wishing to add substance to the rumors already circulating through the ballroom, she discreetly tugged her hand free of Reese's.

He continued staring straight ahead. "Did you know she was coming tonight?"

"No. Did you?"

Reese shook his head.

They fell silent again, both of them watching Fanny, as were most of the other party guests.

Callie stared blankly at the spinning couple, her thoughts in turmoil. Why had her sister chosen tonight to make her long-awaited return? Why had she not let Callie know she was coming home?

Was Reese happy to see Fanny? His stiff posture hinted that he was more taken aback than pleased. Callie couldn't drum up the courage to look at him to find out one way or the other.

The whispering intensified around them, turning into open speculation. She thought she heard her name linked with Reese's, followed by an unfounded conjecture that she'd played a role in her sister's broken engagement.

Now gazes were turning to study her and Reese, making a connection that wasn't there. Or hadn't been there until recently.

The music played on and Fanny continued whirling around the dance floor with Mr. Hawkins.

Callie's stomach churned in perfect rhythm with their steps. She wanted to be glad her sister was home, truly she did, but did Fanny not realize that her sudden appearance would generate talk, much of it ugly? Did she not hear the whispers following her across the dance floor?

"Why did she have to come back tonight?"

Reese shook his head, obviously as baffled by Fanny's behavior as Callie. "Your sister has interesting timing."

Indeed.

If Fanny had arrived even hours before the ball had begun, Callie would have been better prepared for the whispers. She would have found a way to temper the gossip...somehow. She loved her sister—she did. Hadn't she sent innumerable letters begging Fanny to come home?

Now that her sister was here, Callie wished she would have stayed away.

Guilt washed through her at the thought, turning her heart bleak. Where was the joy over seeing Fanny again?

Her sister was her best friend, the woman who knew her better than any other. Yet, Callie still wanted her gone.

This time, a spark of resentment followed the thought, leaving an unattractive blight on her soul. This insight into her character was not a pretty one.

"I must greet her properly," she said, mostly to herself, but Reese responded, anyway.

"As should I." He shook his head in resignation. "She's given us little choice."

They shared a bleak smile.

"Come." He took her hand and set it on his arm. "The waltz is drawing to a close. We'll catch up with her as soon as she steps off the dance floor."

More than a few curious glances followed their progress across the room.

They approached Fanny and Mr. Hawkins on the very edge of the parquet floor. Neither seemed to notice their arrival. They were each looking steadily into one another's eyes, a silent message flowing between them. With a shaky smile, Fanny lowered her head.

Mr. Hawkins cleared his throat. "Thank you for the dance, Miss Mitchell."

Fanny continued staring at her toes. "It is I who should thank you, Mr. Hawkins. I'm afraid I didn't sufficiently think through my actions. Had you not asked me to dance I don't know what I would have done. You saved me from certain humiliation."

"I'm glad I could help." He started to say more, but caught sight of Callie and Reese. "Ah, Miss Mitchell. Mr. Bennett." He divided a look between them. "Always a pleasure to see you both."

Callie greeted him with her a short nod and then turned her attention to her sister. "Welcome home, Fanny."

"Callie." Fanny's head lifted and a look of unfiltered relief filled her gaze. "I'd hoped you would be here this evening."

As she stared into her sister's eyes, Callie recognized the discomfiture there, the worry that her return would not be received well. Whatever lingering anger she'd been holding toward Fanny suddenly disappeared. All that was left was love. Love for her sister. Love for her best friend. Fanny had made her share of mistakes recently. Then again, so had Callie.

Judge not, lest you be judged.

"Oh, Fanny." Callie pulled her younger sister into a warm, tight embrace. "I've missed you so."

"I've missed you, too, Cal. So very much."

They clung to one another for several seconds, neither caring that they were making a spectacle of themselves with their joyful reunion. Or that the whispers and chatter had increased.

Fanny stepped back first.

Her gaze dropped over Callie, traveling from head to toe. "Why, Callie, you're beautiful. And your dress..." A smile curved her lips. "It's absolutely stunning and so perfect for your coloring."

A few months ago, the compliment would have alarmed Callie. She would have retreated behind her cool mask, concerned she'd attracted unnecessary attention. Now, she accepted her sister's admiration with a gracious smile and a genuine thank-you.

"My, how you've changed, Cal." Fanny clasped her hands delightedly. "Is this newfound confidence due to Mrs. Singletary's influence?"

"And Reese's." Callie answered without hesitation, not quite realizing what she'd revealed until the words had passed her lips.

Reese. He stood silently beside her, his shoulders not quite touching hers. Tall, strong and vigilant, ever watchful, she found strength in his presence.

She dared a glance in his direction, but he wasn't looking at her. He was looking at Fanny, his expression unreadable.

Fanny turned to face him directly.

A hush fell over the surrounding crowd, spreading through the ballroom like yeast through leavened bread. It was as if the entire room was poised in anticipation, eager to witness firsthand this unexpected reunion between the estranged couple.

"Hello, Fanny." Reese gave her a brief nod, his smile slipping only a fraction. Callie doubted anyone noticed but her. "Welcome home."

"Thank you, Reese." Fanny looked momentarily disconcerted, then returned his smile with a bright one of her own. "It's wonderful to be back in Denver."

"Is your return permanent?" Callie asked, hoping to alleviate the tension falling over their awkward little group.

"I haven't yet decided." Something flickered in Fanny's gaze as she glanced at Mr. Hawkins. "The terms of my employment aren't quite settled."

Mr. Hawkins frowned, the gesture one of genuine masculine puzzlement. "Miss Mitchell, I am more than willing to meet your requests."

Fanny lifted her eyebrows. "*All* of them?"

After a slight pause, he nodded.

"Wonderful." Her eyes lit with triumph. "Nevertheless, I wish to think it over before I give you my answer."

Her response earned her a frown. "I understand. However, you should know…" His face took on an unbending expression. "I will not wait indefinitely for your answer. You have a week to make your decision."

Fanny gasped. "But, Mr. Hawkins, I—"

"One week. Not a day more."

After a quick word of farewell to Reese and Callie and a brief nod in Fanny's direction, he was gone.

Additional tension descended in his wake. Expectant silence hung heavy on the air. Not quite understanding what she'd just witnessed, Callie shared a confused glance with Reese.

He lifted a shoulder, then, ever the gentleman, stepped into the void. "Fanny, would you care to dance?"

Eyes still on Mr. Hawkins, hands clenched at her

sides, Fanny drew in a sharp breath. "Thank you, Reese, I believe I would. Very much."

As he guided her sister onto the dance floor, Callie was filled with admiration for Reese. The sensation was followed immediately by gloom. Though Reese had merely been smoothing over an awkward moment, Fanny was once again in his arms.

Callie's worst nightmare realized.

Melting to the edge of the dance floor, then farther back into the shadow cast by an oversize flower arrangement, she watched her sister and the man she loved waltz together.

They made a striking pair.

Reese's masculine build stood in stark contrast to Fanny's slight frame, his dark to her light, their steps flawlessly in sync with the music. The romantic waltz seemed to have been composed for this moment.

Callie sighed unhappily. Mrs. Singletary had commissioned entirely too many waltzes for this evening's ball. Why couldn't she have insisted upon quadrilles, where couples spent more time apart than together? Or, better yet, a scotch reel, where they didn't touch at all.

Reese and Fanny executed a well-timed series of turns. The action sent a fold in Fanny's skirt wrapping around his legs. He said something to her that made her laugh.

Callie had a peculiar feeling in her stomach, one of dread, as if her world was about to cave in around her.

A faint sigh slipped past her lips.

"You're frowning, Miss Mitchell. Please tell me I'm not the cause."

"Indeed not." She swung her gaze to meet Marshall Ferguson's. "I was merely caught up in the music."

"By the expression on your face I take it you don't like this particular arrangement."

She considered how best to answer the question. "If you must know, I find it a bit melancholy for my liking."

He shut his eyes a moment, as if attempting to listen to the music without any distraction. "The composer has relied too heavily on the minor chords," he said, opening his eyes. "That, I believe, is why the piece has a sad tone."

"You know your music, Mr. Ferguson."

"A bit." He gave her a sheepish grin. "Don't tell my mother, but I have been known to tap out a ditty now and then on the fiddle."

Picturing him with a fiddle beneath his chin, plucking out a jaunty tune, she laughed softly. "I should very much like to see that."

"One day, perhaps I shall satisfy your curiosity." Smiling, he gestured to the flurry of dancers. "Would you do me the honor?"

Her first impulse was to refuse, to lean back against the wall and retreat into the shadows she'd once worn as a protection from future heartache. She'd hidden from life itself, cloaking her true self behind ugly clothes and severe hairstyles. She'd allowed a false sense of shame to keep her trapped in the mistake of her past.

She was not that woman anymore.

"Why, thank you, Mr. Ferguson, I would love to take a turn around the floor with you."

Reese knew the exact moment Callie and Marshall Ferguson joined the whirl of dancers. He felt it in his gut, in the kick of possessiveness that hit him square in the heart. *Mine. She is mine.*

He had half a mind to cut in, to stake his claim in front of everyone assembled, as beastly as that sounded even in his own head.

Alas, he must finish this dance with Fanny first. A multitude of gazes were on them. Tongues wagged. Speculation abounded.

"Why did you come home, Fanny?"

He didn't ask the question for himself. They'd said everything that needed saying months ago. There was no point in rehashing the past, especially since matters were settled between them. But Fanny's ill-timed arrival had brought unkind speculation onto Callie.

That, he would not tolerate.

Her gaze not quite meeting his, Fanny lifted her chin and said, "I came home because I missed my family."

He believed that was partially true. The Mitchell brood was a tight-knit group. Fanny had always been close with her siblings. But her explanation brought up another, more significant question. "Why did you choose tonight, and this ball in particular, to make your return?"

"I…" She sighed delicately. "It's hard to explain."

"Try."

She fell silent.

Reese took the opportunity to eye her more closely. He dropped his gaze over her face, searching for the woman he'd thought he knew. The one with manners and grace, who would never think to cause a public spectacle as she'd done tonight.

"You must have known your entrance would create a resurgence of the gossip."

She remained silent.

"That isn't like you, Fanny." He spoke her name softly, hoping to instill her trust, at least enough to get the truth out of her. "You've never been one to draw unnecessary attention to yourself. Again, I have to ask why you chose to do so tonight?"

"Oh, Reese." She lowered her gaze to a spot near his left shoulder. "I guess I thought if I faced the gossip head-on, in a public setting, with half of Denver in attendance, my return would go...easier."

"Easier?" The muscles in his shoulders tensed. "You mean easier for you."

"Yes."

"It was selfish of you not to warn anyone of your arrival, especially your sister."

"I'm sorry, truly I am. I didn't mean to throw speculation in her direction. And I definitely didn't mean to hurt Callie."

Again, he believed her. Fanny was not inherently selfish. She would never do anything malicious. Nevertheless, her actions had hurt her sister. Not just tonight, but for months.

"Your absence has been hard on her." He steered around a slow-moving couple gawking at them. He chose to ignore their interest. "Despite how things were left between you and Callie, she's missed you."

"I've missed her, too. I hadn't realized how much until I saw her again tonight." Sighing, Fanny leaned her head to one side and scanned the dance floor. "She's changed since I left, for the better."

"She's come into her own." He caught Callie's eye

across the dance floor. She smiled at him over Ferguson's shoulder.

The tautness in his chest lightened as he returned the gesture.

Fanny followed the direction of his gaze. "I hadn't realized you and my sister..." She broke off. "That is, I hadn't considered that you two would form an...an affection in my absence."

He rolled his gaze back to her. "We don't need your permission."

"No, you don't. I meant what I said the last time we spoke, Reese. I wish you nothing but the greatest happiness in life. If my sister makes you smile like that, more the better."

His feet paused, the barest of seconds, before sweeping them into a series of fast turns that left no opportunity for further conversation.

Fanny broke the silence between them as the music hit the final chords. "Reese?"

He guided her through a simple, three-step turn. "Yes?"

"I'm glad we never married." She angled her head and studied his face. "I believe you are equally relieved."

He nodded. "We would have had a comfortable life together. But I have recently discovered I want more out of marriage."

He glanced over at Callie and saw his future unfold, a future full of laughter and happiness, children and family, freshly baked cookies and battles with toy soldiers.

He turned his gaze back to his dance partner. "I should have never proposed to you, Fanny."

"I should have never said yes."

The waltz came to an end, as did the remaining threads of uneasiness between them. They'd needed this final confrontation. Had needed to meet again and say their proverbial farewells.

Reese could go forth into the future confident his relationship with Fanny was firmly in the past. He offered his ex-fiancée his arm.

She took it without hesitation. "Thank you for the dance."

"The pleasure was all mine."

Chapter Twenty-Two

"The evening is an unqualified success." Mrs. Singletary made this pronouncement from the edge of the dance floor.

Callie stood restlessly by her side, wondering when the ball would come to an end. Not for several hours at least. The clock had just struck midnight and the crowd showed no signs of thinning. In fact, the heavily populated dance floor seemed to have grown denser in the past half hour.

She stifled a sigh and struggled to arrange a pleasant look on her face. "Everyone seems to be having a marvelous time."

"Of course they are, dear, we left nothing to chance. The decorations are lovely, the food superb, the music divine." As if she were a queen and the party guests were her beloved subjects, the widow cast a fond smile over the room. "I am quite pleased with the turnout. I predict the new hospital wing will be fully funded by the end of the night."

A blessing, to be sure. Yet Callie couldn't shake the terrible sense of foreboding that tugged at her.

She hadn't spoken with Reese since he'd danced with her sister. There'd been no real opportunity. Fanny's sudden arrival seemed to have sparked even more female interest in Reese. He was the most desired dance partner at the ball.

For the past hour he'd wound his way through hordes of smiling admirers. He barely took a step away from one woman when another appeared by his side. They each received a word or two, some a request to dance. He was so gallant, so handsome, so *sought after.*

"...and despite the brief scene your sister's arrival created." Mrs. Singletary continued the conversation, ignoring Callie's lack of response. "Or perhaps because of her ill-timed appearance, tonight's ball will be talked about for months to come."

Though Callie had missed most of the widow's words, she couldn't argue that last point. Fanny had made quite the memorable entrance. Hours later, people were still whispering about her return. Many openly wondered what the estranged couple had said to one another during their sole dance together.

Callie would like to know the answer to that question herself.

The widow clasped her hands together in glee. "I believe this year's ball has proven even more eventful than last year's, when your brother accomplished quite the coup d'état."

Callie's smile came easily as she remembered how Garrett had dropped to one knee right in the middle of the dance floor. A hush had fallen over the crowd as he'd taken his childhood sweetheart's hand and uttered seven simple heartfelt words. *Molly Taylor Scott, will you marry me?*

Of course, Molly's answer had been yes.

Wistfully, Callie wondered if Reese would utter similar words to her. *Callie Anne Mitchell, will you marry me?*

Perhaps he wouldn't propose at all now that Fanny had returned. There'd been no chance to discover how he really felt about her sister's appearance.

For the past hour, Callie had been relegated to watching him take a turn across the floor with seven different partners. She'd counted every one of them. Now he was dancing with Temperance Evans.

"Speaking of your family…" Mrs. Singletary turned her head to Callie, a question in her gaze. "Where is Fanny?"

Though her sister had danced nearly as many dances as Reese, with as many different partners, she'd gone missing in the past ten minutes.

"I'm not sure," Callie admitted. "Perhaps she's at one of the buffet tables."

"Perhaps." Something came and went in the widow's eye, something a little sneaky. "It would seem Mr. Hawkins has gone missing, as well."

Before Callie could respond, Reese's father appeared.

He greeted the widow first. Then turned and bent over Callie's hand next, giving her curled fingers a polite kiss. The gesture was very smooth and perfectly executed.

"Miss Mitchell." He straightened. "May I have the honor of this dance?"

"Oh, I… You wish to dance with me?" She'd assumed he'd come over to ask the widow.

"Other than your exquisite employer—" he winked at Mrs. Singletary "—you are the most beautiful woman in the room."

The compliment warmed her bruised heart. Until he'd uttered those kind words Callie hadn't known how much she needed to hear them.

Shielding her gratitude behind lowered lashes, she took his offered hand. As they pirouetted across the floor, Callie allowed herself to enjoy the dance, *another* waltz, with a partner she liked and admired a great deal. If Reese did ask her to marry him, if he truly loved her as Mrs. Singletary claimed, Callie would take great pleasure in having this man as her father-in-law.

He effortlessly took her through a series of turns then smiled into her eyes. "I trust you are enjoying yourself this evening?"

Her gaze caught hold of Reese and Miss Evans twirling together just off to their left. Why did he have to look so…pleased with his dance partner?

Callie forced a tremulous smile on her lips and focused her full attention on her own partner. "While tonight has had its special moments—" the loveliest when she'd danced with Reese "—to say I'm enjoying myself might be a bit of an overstatement."

"Ah." His eyes took on a sympathetic light. "Your sister certainly caused a stir with her arrival."

"I believe that was her aim." Now that she'd had time to consider Fanny's behavior, Callie thought she understood her motives. "She probably assumed it would be best to face the bulk of the gossip all at once."

Even as a child, Fanny had tackled the worst of any situation first, saving the less challenging tasks for last. Her favorite saying had always been *Let's get this over with, shall we?* The more Callie chewed on the notion, the more she thought she understood why Fanny had arrived at the ball unannounced.

Had her sister explained her actions to Reese? Callie's gaze sought his. He wasn't looking at her. He was too busy smiling at something Miss Evans said.

Sniffing in irritation, she swung her gaze back to her partner.

Another gleam of sympathy sparked in Mr. Bennett's eyes. "Do not despair, my dear. My son can be slow on the uptake, but he's a very smart man. He will come around, given time."

Did she want Reese to *come around?*

No, she wanted him to love her without reservation. She wanted him to give her his heart freely. She wanted him to ask her to marry him without having to "come around" to the idea after the elimination of other potential brides.

If Reese continued to hold on to his determination not to love again, they could never be happy together. One, or both of them, would grow to resent the other.

Hopelessness filled her very bones, but Callie refused to allow her misery to show on her face.

"Have faith, Miss Mitchell." Mr. Bennett gave her another kind smile. "The Lord has the particulars of your future already worked out. When the time is right, you and Reese will find your way to happiness."

"How can you be so certain?"

"I have prayed on the matter."

"You…have prayed for Reese and me?"

"I have, and I'm fully confident all will turn out well." The waltz ended. Mr. Bennett stepped back and dropped his hands to his sides. "Smile, Miss Mitchell. Here comes my son to claim the next dance."

The moment after she thanked him for his kindness, she was swept into strong arms and spun in time to the strains of yet another waltz. It was a glorious moment, one she never wanted to end.

Callie let the music pour over her as Reese skillfully guided her across the floor. Clutching breathlessly at his broad shoulders, she gazed into his eyes and simply allowed herself to enjoy this time with him.

He smiled down at her with a look of admiration, affection and something else. Something she didn't dare name.

Dimly, she heard someone mention how wonderful *they* looked together. Was the comment directed at her and Reese?

"You look happy." His deep voice was like a soft, warm caress across her cheek.

"I am. Oh, Reese." She opened her eyes and smiled up at him. "At this moment, here in your arms, I am very, very happy."

"You're beautiful, Callie. You take my breath away." He spoke the words reverently, with a look in his eyes that denoted deep emotion, the kind that would endure a lifetime. But was it love he felt for her? Or something closer to affection?

He pulled her close. "Before the night is over," he said near her ear, "I wish to speak with you alone."

Oh, my. She experienced a small flutter of anticipation. "What's stopping us from finding a private spot now?"

"What, indeed?" He spun her to the edge of the dance floor and released his hold. His eyes were filled with a question, and just the barest hint of nerves.

He'd never been more attractive to her than in that moment.

He took her hand.

She let him lead her out of the ballroom, through the attached drawing room and, eventually, into the main corridor. "Where are you taking me?"

"To the place where my bride search officially began and where I hope—" he smiled over at her "— it shall end."

The sweet pain of hope filled her heart. And she knew in that moment that not only did she adore this man, but she would also love him with all her heart for the rest of her life.

He stopped outside the blue parlor and peered inside. "Excellent. No one here but us." He pulled her into the room with him and shut the door behind them. "At last, I have you all to myself."

This was it, Callie realized. He was going to propose.

But would she say yes?

Now that he had Callie alone, Reese felt a roll of apprehension slide along the base of his spine. He'd planned for this moment. Had carefully considered the exact words he would use.

He wanted Callie for his wife—no one else would do—but he was no longer sure how to introduce the subject of marriage. His proposal would be something he and Callie would retell over and over again, sharing the particulars with their family and friends, their children and grandchildren.

The list.

He should start with the bride list he'd tucked in his jacket before leaving his house earlier this evening.

He reached his hand inside the pocket. At the same moment, Callie turned to face him fully, and he balked at the look of vulnerability he saw in her gaze. "Will you tell me what you and Fanny discussed during your dance?"

Of course she would want to know. Moreover, she *deserved* to know.

He thought back over his conversation with her sister—it seemed a lifetime ago—and chose to give Callie a brief summary rather than a word-for-word retelling. "She explained why she showed up here tonight without warning."

"I think I can hazard a guess."

He lifted a brow.

"She decided it would be best to confront as many people as possible rather than suffer endless individual meetings over the coming weeks."

"You know your sister well."

She continued staring up at him. "Was that all you discussed?"

"Mostly that. We also both agreed we should have never become engaged."

"But, Reese, you were engaged." She sat on a nearby settee, her posture still and erect. "We both know you would have married Fanny had she not begged off."

Refusing to begin their life together with a lie, he made no attempt to disagree. "I won't deny that I once thought your sister and I would suit. We were well-matched in many ways."

Callie lowered her head. "Yes, you were."

He came to stand next to her. She didn't look at him, but kept gazing down at her slippered toes. "That's not to say I would have been happily married to her."

"You once told me companionship in marriage was more important than happiness."

"I was wrong. Callie, because of you, because of our time together, I can no longer settle for a comfortable marriage with a suitable bride."

She lifted her head, hope shining in her gaze. "Truly?"

"I want more."

He wanted the dream he'd only glimpsed in his youth. A dream lost to him in a split-second riding accident.

Now that he'd put the past behind him, and the grief, Reese wanted something different for his future, something new and real and lasting. A deep, abiding relationship. With Callie, only her, no one else would do.

"The woman who meets these requirements is the one I hope to marry."

He retrieved his most recent bride list and thrust it toward her with a surprisingly shaky hand.

She drew back from the paper as if it was a poisonous viper.

"Go on, take it." When she continued to recoil, he placed the list gently in her hand. "Once you read what I've written, I believe you'll understand everything."

He hoped.

For the first time in years, he lifted up a prayer to

the Lord. *Please, Lord, let her see the contents of my heart in the list I've created.*

"Oh, Reese, I can't go through this with you anymore." She spoke in a quiet, even voice that sent a chill up his spine. "I just can't."

She attempted to return the paper to him, unread. He clasped his hands behind his back. "Read the list, Callie."

She blew out a breath.

"Please."

Some of his desperation must have sounded in his voice, because she lowered her head and began to scan the paper in silence.

He waited as she perused the front of the page. Over half of the thirty-seven items were written there. The rest were on the back.

Some of his requirements were intentionally vague. *She should sing hymns in church with a clear, bold voice.* Others were incredibly specific. *She must have blond hair, green eyes and have worked as Beatrix Singletary's companion for at least two months.*

For levity, he'd even included a few items that bordered on the silly, yet would hopefully mean something to Callie. Items such as *her name must begin with the letter C.* And...*she must be prepared to battle with toy soldiers on a weekly basis.*

Eyebrows scrunched in concentration, she flipped over the page.

When her lips pressed into a grim line, Reese felt the first stirrings of concern. Callie should be smiling by now. Surely, she recognized that he'd made the list with her in mind.

He held his breath, fighting an urge to rush her.

Finally, she set the paper on her lap and lifted her head.

What he saw in her eyes made his throat burn. Her gaze was completely closed off. She looked numb, hurt.

Somehow he'd injured her.

"Did you read item number thirty-seven?" That had been the most specific of the bunch. *She must be Callie Anne Mitchell, no other woman will do for me.*

"I did." Her voice was hollow and distant and so full of pain he felt a similar sensation strike at his own heart.

Panic tightened in his chest. "Have you nothing else to say?"

She looked down again, read the last line aloud in a flat, pained tone that spoke of heartbreak. He felt something rip inside him.

Sighing, she lifted her head. "Tell me why you want to marry me, Reese."

Her question confused him. "It's right there, on the paper, all thirty-seven reasons. What more do you want me to say?"

She flinched as if he'd slapped her. "I need you to tell me why I should marry you, in your own words."

"Those *are* my own words."

When she didn't respond, he realized he'd made a mistake. Somehow he'd botched this and yet he couldn't pinpoint exactly how.

The silence between them grew. His heart lurched as he watched her eyes fill with tears.

He dropped in front of her and placed his palms flat on her knees.

"Don't cry, Callie." He took her hands and drew them to his lips. "Please, don't cry. I want you for my bride. Only you. There is no other woman for me. I will never want anyone but you."

Her wet, spiky lashes blinked at him. The sadness was still there in her gaze. *Why* was she still sad?

He rose, dragged her into his arms and kissed her on the mouth. After a moment, he pulled slightly away, looked her straight in the eyes and said, "Callie Anne Mitchell, will you marry me?"

"Oh, Reese. I've been waiting to hear those words for a very long time." She laid her head on his shoulder and whispered into his coat, "I love you."

His heart soared.

Then dipped. Something was wrong. Callie wasn't saying yes to his proposal. She was crying again. He could feel the tension thrumming through her.

She stepped out of his arms, lifted her chin and, after snuffling a little, placed steel in her spine. "Do you love me, too, Reese?"

For a moment he stood staring at her, speechless. Most of him wanted to answer yes. *Of course I love you,* his heart whispered.

He loved her more than he thought himself capable. But one small, stubborn part of him couldn't push out the words.

For an alarming moment, he was frozen between past and present, his very future at stake. And still, he couldn't seem to make his mouth work properly.

Callie's lower lip trembled. "Your hesitation is answer enough."

He reached for her, but she spun away from him and hurried out of the room.

Following hard on her heels, he called after her. "Callie, don't go. I love you. I—"

She couldn't hear him. She was already halfway down the corridor, slipping around the corner. He followed after her, but he was too far behind. She'd disappeared into the crowd before he could call to her again.

His heart turned to ice. His mind reeled. He knew this feeling. *This is what grief feels like. This is the agony that comes with loss.*

No different than a death.

He'd vowed never to experience this type of pain a second time in his life, only to have it become his reality once again.

Throat thick, Reese stared at the sea of bobbing heads, wondering how he would convince Callie he loved her with all his soul.

It wasn't going to be easy, but convince her he would. He couldn't lose Callie. He'd do whatever it took to keep her in his life forever. But he would not give her another list. No. More. Lists. He would win her over with words spoken from the deepest depths of his heart.

He prayed it would be enough. It *had* to be enough.

Chapter Twenty-Three

Still dressed in her ball gown, Callie lay on her bed, blinking up at the ornate, perfectly square ceiling tiles overhead. Tears leaked out of the corner of her eyes. She let them come, let them spill freely.

Let them blur her vision.

She was so tired. So scared and confused. Reese loved her. He *had* to love her. All the signs were in the list she held clutched against her heart. She had no doubt he'd put considerable thought into each and every item. She even understood what he'd been trying to tell her. The dear, sweet, wonderful man.

His marriage proposal had been simple, the exact words she'd dreamed of hearing from him. But there was still no guarantee he would give her his heart completely.

Without his full commitment to her, their life together would be nothing more than an empty shell of unrealized possibilities.

Why couldn't Reese embrace the gift they'd been given, a deep, abiding love that was meant to last forever?

Rolling onto her side, Callie crumpled the list

tightly in her hand and continued to cry. Dawn's gray light cast its gloomy hue over the room. The quiet was unearthly, especially after the crushing din of the party that had only just concluded an hour ago.

Callie was going to lose Reese. The prospect was so awful that she squeezed her eyes tightly shut and begged the Lord for relief from the pain in her heart. All she wanted was for Reese to admit he loved her. Why couldn't he say three simple words? *I love you.*

Perhaps she was asking too much of him. Perhaps he'd expressed his feelings in the only way he knew how, in a list of thirty-seven requirements that only she could meet.

"Callie?" A light scratching came from the other side of her door. "Are you in there?"

She pressed her face into her pillow.

The knocking increased, growing louder with each blow of fist to wood.

"Go away, Fanny."

"I'm afraid I can't do that." The door creaked on its hinges. Light footsteps sounded on the wood floor. And then, her sister stood next to the bed.

Callie rolled to her other side. "I don't wish to speak with you right now."

"But you're crying."

"I'm fine."

"You've never lied to me before, Cal, don't start now."

At the disapproval she heard in her sister's voice, something inside Callie snapped. "Go. Away. Fanny." She swiped at her eyes. "It's an easy enough request for you to follow. You're good at leaving."

As soon as she said the words, she regretted them. But before she could offer an apology, Fanny laughed softly. "A valiant effort, but you won't run me off that easily."

Callie swiveled her head to meet her sister's gaze. "I didn't mean to criticize you for leaving town."

"Yes, you did." Fanny smiled affectionately down at her. "I can't say I blame you."

"You did what you thought was best at the time."

"Very true." Fanny came around to the other side of the bed and sat down beside Callie. "But that doesn't take away the fact that I was impossible to live with during those initial days following my broken engagement."

"You weren't *that* bad."

"Oh, I was. I was surly, short-tempered, about as inflexible as a wood plank. I only thought of myself. When I made my plans to leave Denver, escape was all I cared about. I know that's no excuse for my behavior, but I couldn't stand the gossip another day, or—" she gave Callie a meaningful gaze "—the censure."

"You mean the censure from me."

"I mean from everyone. You. Garrett. Even our parents." Fanny twisted around and stretched out on the bed beside her. "I knew I was letting everyone down, but there was nothing I could say, no explanation I could express that seemed to satisfy any of you."

Callie squeezed her sister's hand. "I'm sorry I was so hard on you."

"I understand why you were." Fanny turned her head. "You thought I was making a mistake, the biggest of my life."

Callie frowned at the memory of that difficult time. She'd said a lot of things to her sister, all of them true, none of them tactful. Looking back, she wished she would have spoken with more grace, less disapproval.

"I'm sorry," she said again. "I could have chosen my words better."

"Apology accepted."

They fell silent, each staring up at the ceiling.

"Callie, do you still believe all the things you said about Reese?"

"I—" She cut off the rest of her words and considered the question seriously, trying to remember exactly what she'd said about Reese back then. The same she would say about him now. "Yes, I believe he's a good man, decent and loyal, the best I've ever known."

"You're in love with him."

She kept her gaze focused on the ceiling. "I am."

Fanny laughed delightedly. "That's terrific, Callie."

"It doesn't bother you that I'm in love with the man you once planned to marry?"

"Not in the least. What Reese and I shared would not have sustained a marriage in the long run. You two are far better suited. I wish you nothing but happiness together."

Callie had needed to hear those words from her sister, she realized. Yet her heart remained locked in despair. "Reese and I will never be truly happy if he continues to hold a portion of himself back from me. It's not that I want him to forget his first wife. I just want him to—"

"His first wife?" Fanny hopped off the bed and spun around to gape at her in open-mouthed shock. "What are you talking about? Reese has never been married."

Mind reeling, Callie sat up and swung her feet to the ground. "You don't know about Miranda?"

"Who's Miranda?"

"The woman Reese married when he was eighteen.

She died a month later in a tragic riding accident. He never told you about her?"

Fanny's eyebrows drew together. "In the entire time we were engaged, not once did he mention that he'd been married before."

"And yet he told me the whole story." Callie processed this new twist in her relationship with Reese, felt a spark of hope ignite.

"You do realize what this means?" Fanny sat down on the bed beside her. "Reese loves you, Callie. Why else would he trust you with the secret of his past?"

The secret of his past. Yes, Reese had shared much with Callie, including the pain and grief he'd experienced after Miranda's death.

He claimed he'd loved once and once was enough. Yet, he continued to love deeply. He loved his father. He loved the children at Charity House.

He loved Callie.

He'd tried to tell her as much with his bride list. His feelings for her were written in that bold, looping script of his, the truth all but glaring at her from every item. He'd done so much more than speak three simple words. He'd spelled out his love thirty-seven unique, individual times.

She must find him and tell him she understood. She would tell him she loved him and convince him that she didn't need him to say the words back. She would—

"What's that you're twisting around in your fingers?" Not waiting for an answer, Fanny took Reese's list and began reading it aloud. "'My bride must meet the following requirements. Number one, she must—'"

"Give me that back." Callie snatched the paper out of her sister's hands. "It's for my eyes only."

"What is it? Something Reese gave you, I can tell. I recognize his handwriting."

Callie's heart slammed hard against her ribs. Of course Fanny would recognize Reese's handwriting. There were a lot of things her sister knew about Reese. It would take Callie a while to get used to Fanny knowing him so well.

Not as well as you. He never shared himself with her as he has with you.

The peace that flowed through her brought another wave of tears.

"Thank you, Fanny." Callie pulled her sister into her arms and gave her a tight, heartfelt hug. "Thank you so very much."

"You're so very welcome. But, Callie, what are you thanking me for?"

"For breaking your engagement with Reese."

"Ah, that." Fanny stepped back and grinned. "You're most welcome, dear sister, most welcome indeed."

They shared a laugh.

"Oh, Fanny." Callie's heart swelled with sisterly love. "I pray you find happiness one day with the man of your dreams."

"I pray that, as well. I even think I know the man already." A turbulent expression fell over her face. "But I may have already ruined my chances with him."

For the first time since her sister's return, Callie realized Fanny had changed. Not outwardly. She was still as beautiful as ever, perhaps even more so. But there was a sadness in eyes, one that denoted heartache. Callie recognized the look. She'd worn it herself for years. "Has someone hurt you, Fanny? A man, perhaps?"

"Yes and no."

"That's an interesting answer that tells me absolutely nothing."

"It's complicated, Callie. Suffice it to say I misunderstood someone's intentions and now I must either move on with my life or wallow in self-pity."

Callie gripped her hands. "If you need to talk…"

"I know I can come to you." She firmed her chin. "Yes, yes, but enough about me. What about you. What are *you* going to do about Reese?"

"I'm going to take the biggest leap of faith in my life. And leave the rest up to the Lord."

"Now that's the fighting Mitchell spirit. But before you approach Reese, I highly recommend you consider changing that dress." Fanny's gaze narrowed over her. "You may also wish to splash cool water on your face."

"Is that your tactful way of telling me my gown is wrinkled and my eyes are puffy?"

Fanny pursed her lips. "You'll also want to rethink your hair."

The first thing Reese did the next morning was return to Mrs. Singletary's, back to the place where he began his search for a suitable bride.

Callie had been with him every step of the way. It seemed fitting she was where his journey ended. He would not leave the widow's mansion until he secured Callie's hand in marriage.

A bleary-eyed Winston let him in. "Good morning, Mr. Bennett."

"A fine good morning to you, Winston."

The butler blinked, his brows pulling together in obvious confusion. "I wasn't aware you had an appointment with Mrs. Singletary this morning."

"I've come for Miss Mitchell."

The confusion dug deeper across the man's forehead. "That presents a problem, sir. Miss Mitchell left the house nearly thirty minutes ago."

Reese's heart took a plunge. Of all the scenarios he'd taken into account, he hadn't expected Callie to be out when he returned this morning.

He forced down the thread of panic weaving through him and made himself speak slowly. "Do you know where she went?"

The butler's gaze shifted around the entryway, then fell back on Reese. "I believe Miss Mitchell mentioned she was heading to your house, sir."

Callie had gone in search of him? Joy wound through his apprehension, the sensation so profound Reese nearly lost his footing. "Thank you, Winston."

A renewed urgency in his steps, he exited the house, his sole intent to find Callie as quickly as possible.

Halfway home, he caught sight of her across the street. His heart slammed against his chest, as it always did whenever she was near.

She hadn't seen him yet. That didn't stop Reese from cataloguing her every feature. The tall, lithe frame. The exquisite face and sea-green eyes. The pale blond hair pinned beneath a jaunty, feathered hat, her loose curls hanging down her back in pretty waves.

Callie. His Callie.

For too many years, she'd stood on the edges of life, content to observe rather than participate. She'd hid her true self behind drab clothes and severe hair.

Never again. He would make sure she had no reason to camouflage her true nature. She was a beautiful, kind-hearted woman meant to live each moment to the fullest. With him by her side.

Pulse roaring in his ears, he crossed the street. "Callie."

Her gaze connected with his and her feet ground to a stop. For a moment, neither of them spoke. Neither of them moved.

Reese swallowed.

The pretty speech he had planned vanished from him mind. Everything he'd been, everything he was, everything he desperately wanted to become, pinpointed to this one moment. To this declaration of his heart. "I love you."

"Oh, Reese." She leaped into his arms. It was more a collision than an embrace and defined their relationship perfectly. No half measures for them.

He held her tightly to him and simply breathed her in for several long moments.

"I love you, too," she whispered in his ear. "So very much."

They kissed, right there, in the middle of the neighborhood, for entirely too long to be considered proper.

Reese loved every scandalous, reckless second.

When he pulled back and looked into her eyes, he saw his whole future staring back at him. With their combined love and commitment to one another, they would raise their children in a happy, somewhat messy, boisterous home.

He had much to say to her, but first…

He pulled her close again and whispered the contents of his heart another time. "I love you."

"I don't think I'll ever get tired of hearing that." She sighed into his neck. "I came looking for you this morning, but you weren't home. I was on my way to your office."

He set her at arm's length. "Winston kindly told me where to find you."

"You went to Mrs. Singletary's in search of me?"

"I came to give you the words you deserve to hear." He took her hands, placed them next to his heart. "I love you, Callie Mitchell."

"That's the third time you've said that."

"I plan to tell you every day for the rest of my life, three, four, five times a day, even more on special occasions."

She laughed. "What a pair we make. I went to your house to tell you I already know how you feel about me. You don't have to say the words, Reese."

"Callie, my love, I want to say them. I *need* to say them." He drew her hands away from his heart and kissed each set of knuckles. "After Miranda died I foolishly vowed never to love again, at least not with the careless abandon that had led to my unspeakable grief. I was wrong to close myself off from the possibility of loving again."

"It was an understandable response to your loss. I don't want to replace Miranda in your heart." She smoothed her fingertips over his face, flattened her palm against his chest. "I believe there's room in there for both of us."

This woman understood him in a way no one ever had before. "Miranda was the love of my youth, but you, Callie." He dropped his head and placed a kiss on her palm. "*You* are the love of my life."

"Oh, Reese."

"Callie Anne Mitchell." He bent to one knee. "Will you marry me?"

"Yes. Oh, yes, Reese." Tears filled her eyes, spilled down her cheeks. "Of course I'll marry you."

"Don't cry, Callie." He rose, wiped at her tears with the pad of his thumb. "You're supposed to be happy."

"I am. I'm ecstatic." She turned her head slightly away. "But I've never been a pretty crier. I must look a mess."

He cupped her face in his hands. "You've never looked more beautiful in my eyes."

"Oh, Reese, stop. Stop being so wonderful. You're going to make me cry harder."

"I love you, Callie." He pulled her into his arms, rested his chin on her head. "I'll love you until the day I die."

This time, she pulled back. "I'll love you just as long, Reese, until there's no more breath in my lungs."

His heart stilled, and his mind clouded over with abject terror. No. He would not allow fear to prevent him from reaching for a lifetime of happiness with this woman.

"Whether you live one day, fifty years, or a hundred and fifty, my life will be richer for having you in it."

She lifted on her toes and kissed him on the mouth. "I'll do my very best not to die on you anytime soon."

He knew it was a promise that came straight from her heart, but there were no guarantees in life. "We'll live each day to the fullest and face every moment, whether good or bad, together."

"That sounds like a wedding vow."

"All that's left is the ceremony." He kissed her forehead. "How do you feel about short engagements?"

"I think they're the very best possible kind."

He kissed her temple. "We're in agreement."

She laughed.

He kissed her nose. "One month from today you will become Mrs. Reese Bennett, Jr. and I'll become the happiest man on earth."

"I love you, Reese."

He kissed her mouth. "I love you, too, Callie. I will love you for the rest of my life, with all my heart."

It was a pledge he would never grow tired of giving.

Epilogue

Exactly one month after the day he'd proposed, Reese stood at the front of the church. His father was on his left, Pastor Beau on his right. All three men were really very handsome, but the most attractive in Callie's eyes was Reese.

He looked magnificent in his gray morning suit.

In a matter of minutes he would become her husband.

Fanny gripped both her shoulders and kissed her on the cheek. "Ready to get married?"

If asked, Callie would say a month engagement was twenty-nine and a half days too long. "I'm more than ready."

"Then you better follow me." Fanny spun around, winked at Callie over her shoulder then waltzed down the aisle.

Not a single whisper rose up in her wake, not one comment about the maid of honor having once been engaged to the groom. Reese and Callie had invited only family and close friends to their wedding, as much for Fanny's sake as theirs.

The dress Callie wore had been a gift from Mrs. Singletary. The widow had spared no expense on the gown. The yards of cream-colored satin overlaid with imported lace was the finest Callie had ever owned.

Mrs. Singletary had been with her at every fitting, and had helped her plan every detail in the short time between Reese's proposal and today's ceremony. Through it all, she'd gloated over her role in making what she called "the match of the season."

Callie would miss the woman dearly. She took great comfort in knowing that Reese was still Mrs. Singletary's personal attorney and Callie was still a member of the Ladies League for Destitute Widows and Orphans. She would have chance upon chance to socialize with the widow, especially if Reese's father would take the hint and start pursing her with more enthusiasm.

Once Fanny took her place at the front of the church, the organist switched her sheet music and began playing the wedding march.

The guests rose to their feet and swung their gazes in Callie's direction.

"That's our cue." Her father kissed her on the forehead. "This is where I would normally give you one final chance to change your mind. But there's no need for such silliness here."

Callie laughed softly. "No, sir. No need at all."

He offered her his arm. "Shall we?"

"We shall."

Head high, shoulders square, Callie began her march down the aisle on her father's arm.

Gabriella and Daniel waved from the pew they shared with the other Charity House children. Of course, she waved back. Their big, happy smiles were proof the children were finally settling into life at the orphanage.

At the end of the aisle, Callie caught sight of her mother's eyes filling with tears of joy. She had to look away or risk crying herself.

Her father kissed her one last time, and then passed her off to her groom.

Smiling broadly, Reese leaned over and whispered her three favorite words in her ear, low enough that only she could hear.

Her heart lifted, sighed.

Pastor Beau cleared his throat. "Shall we begin?"

As one, they turned to face the altar.

After they recited the traditional vows, and the rings were exchanged, Reese took Callie's hand in his.

"I love you," he said simply.

She made the same pledge from the depths of her soul. "I love you."

"With the Lord as my guide," he continued in a gruff voice, "I'll stand by your side, Callie. I'll stick with you through the joys and sorrows of life, through every first and every last, through births and deaths and everything in between."

"And I'll stand by your side, Reese, I'll never waver, never question your devotion. I will be your helpmate and honor you always."

Pastor Beau concluded the ceremony with a few words. "Reese and Callie, may your love always be sincere, full of kindness, grace and mercy. Make it your mission to esteem one another above yourselves. Be joyful in hope, patient in affliction and faithful in prayer. Live in harmony with one another and your neighbors." He paused, smiled, then finished with, "I now pronounce you man and wife."

A loud cheer rose up from the Charity House pew. Not to be outdone, Callie's brothers added their own hoots and hollers of approval.

"On that joyful sound." The preacher gave a hearty laugh. "You may kiss your bride."

"Gladly." Reese pulled her into his arms and gave her a long, drawn-out, soul-searing kiss.

When he eventually stepped back, Callie smiled up at her husband. "We're going to have a lovely life together."

"While we're at it—" he pulled her back into his arms "—let's have a little fun, too."

She eagerly agreed. "That's a splendid idea."

With their family and friends shouting to *kiss her again,* Reese touched his mouth to hers.

It was a perfect start to their marriage. A moment Callie would cherish all the rest of her days.

* * * * *

An avid reader by age seven, **Clari Dees** loved to hang out at the public library, and the local bookstore staff knew her by name. Her fascination with books and libraries continues, and Clari now works as a public librarian by day and a writer by night. When she's not locating books for an overdue term paper or tracing down a missing genealogy link for patrons at the library, she can be found at her computer plotting the lives and fortunes of hapless fictional characters.

THE MARSHAL
MEETS HIS MATCH

Clari Dees

He healeth the broken in heart,
and bindeth up their wounds.
—*Psalms* 147:3

Weeping may endure for a night,
but joy cometh in the morning.
—*Psalms* 30:5

To my Lord and Savior, Jesus Christ,
who gave me the desire of my heart.

To my mother, who taught me to read.

To my father, who taught me to love God's Word.

To my brothers and sisters, who believed
I could write and encouraged me along the way.

I Love You So Much!

Chapter One

Little Creek, Colorado
Spring 1883

Meri McIsaac stepped through the doors of Van Deusen's Dry Goods and Mercantile into the enveloping aromas of dried spices, leather goods and pickle barrels and straight into the even more enveloping arms of Mrs. Van Dteusen.

"Oh, it's so good to see you. It's been an age since you've been in town." The diminutive, white-haired proprietress ambushed Meri with an exuberant hug. "Are you going to be at the church picnic a week from Saturday?"

Meri shrugged. She'd forgotten about the annual church picnic that heralded the end of a long winter and the welcome arrival of spring. "I don't know, yet. The weather's been so wild lately…"

"Oh, the roads are drying up nicely now, and you just have to be there. The new marshal has arrived, and you *have* to meet him. I've told him all about you. And if you don't like him, there are a several other new single men who'll be at the picnic, as well. You can look them all over and see which one strikes your fancy. You're not getting any younger, my dear, and it is high time you found someone to marry. Your dear mother wouldn't want you grieving for her any longer. She'd say it's time you got on with your life. You don't want to spend your entire life as an old maid, so be sure to come to the picnic where you can meet all the new bachelors at once." The woman's head nodded sharply to emphasize her point as she finally took a breath.

Meri struggled to hide her annoyance at the well-meaning assault, but the old maid comment flicked a raw spot, sparking her temper. Ducking her head and taking a deep breath, she pretended to study the list of needed ranch supplies and hastily changed the subject before losing control of her tongue. She was already feeling guilty for snapping at her father on the ride into town. He'd innocently mentioned a lighthearted memory of her mother, but it had stung the still fresh wound of her loss, and she'd saddened him with a harsh reply. She didn't need another biting retort on her conscience.

"I have a list of things we need at the ranch. Faither asked me to leave it with you. He'll stop by after he finishes at the bank to load the order into the buggy. I've got another errand I need to run, so if I can leave it with you, I'll be on my way." Meri thrust the list into Mrs. Van Deusen's outstretched hand.

"Of course, dear. Are there any special instructions?" The woman was already perusing the list.

"No. I think the list is pretty self-explanatory." She hid a relieved sigh. As pushy and nosy as Mrs. Van Deusen could be, she was also easily distracted by a long list. She prided herself on filling orders to the exact detail and fretted if something was not in stock. If Meri could get away before the proprietress finished reading the paper, she would escape another round of unwanted advice about her unattached status.

Mr. Van Deusen walked out of the supply room and around the end of the long counter. "We'll see to the order, Miss McIsaac. You feel free to go about your other errands. Naoma can catch up with you when you return." His wink went unseen by his wife.

Meri managed a weak smile and a thank-you and escaped out the door. This was supposed to be a fun trip to town to get away from the ranch for a little while after a long, hard winter, but she was out of sorts and already regretting the trip. She'd forgotten Mrs. Van Deusen's escalating matchmaking efforts and the terms *old maid* and *spinster* beginning to be linked to her name. Being twenty-nine years old and unmarried— by choice, mind you—did not make one an old maid!

Feeling her temperature rise as she dwelt on the subject, Meri ducked down the alleyway between the mercantile and the clock maker, taking the back way to the livery stables. She wasn't in the mood to deal with any more nosy, opinionated females at the moment, or she'd have a new title to add to the irksome ones of old maid and spinster. Something along the lines of the *cranky* and *snippy* old maid.

Meri walked past the line of businesses and out-buildings that made up the north side of First Street and reached the pastures belonging to Franks's Livery Stable and Smithy.

Franks, a former slave freed during the War Between the States, had worked his way west during the turbu-lent years following the war, eventually settling in Little

Creek. No one knew for sure how old he was, but he seemed ageless to Meri with his unlined chocolate skin, sharp black eyes, closely cropped black hair with a few touches of gray and an upright frame rendered massive by years of working with horses and blacksmith's tools. He could be intimidating to those who didn't know him, but a gentler, kinder man didn't exist outside of Meri's father, in her opinion, and Franks had become a close friend. He never failed to calm her down when she was riled, cheer her up when she was sad or just be available with a listening ear, a shoulder to cry on and words of wisdom when she was ready to listen.

It had been weeks since she'd had an opportunity to chat with him due to the stormy weather of late winter. Her father had remarked that any other female would want to visit their "women friends" after being cooped up at the ranch for weeks, but Meri preferred Franks's company to anyone else in town.

Franks ran the livery stable and had also acquired enough land to allow him to breed horses on a small scale. No one knew horses like Franks, and Meri loved to discuss every aspect of them and their breeding with him, which would have scandalized the finer sensibilities of the prim-and-proper matrons of town if they could overhear.

She reached the corner of the closest pasture and slipped through the fence boards. Franks's pastures ran almost the entire length of the town, with the livery located at the northeast end. A walk through the pasture to the livery would be just the thing to soothe her irritation.

She hadn't covered much ground before she attracted the attention of Franks's horses. They trotted over, curious about the newcomer to their pasture. "Hello, fellas. I don't have any treats, but how 'bout some scratches?" Warm, eager bodies surrounded her, and she was kept busy for several minutes giving hearty scratches behind ears and across shoulders, backs and bellies. As the horses shifted and stretched to allow access to itchy places, Meri felt the tension begin to drain from her own body.

"Hey, Abe." She scratched a tall, rawboned black gelding. "Who's the new guy?"

A large muscular bay with a white star peeking through a long black forelock was eyeing her coolly from the edge of the herd.

"Aren't you a handsome fella?" she cooed, slowly advancing toward him. The tall horse, probably over sixteen hands high, snorted and stepped cautiously away from her. Meri mirrored his actions and backed off to take away the pressure she'd inadvertently put on him. "A little shy, are you? Okay, I'll leave you alone, but we'll be friends soon just like these other fellas. Come here, Abe. Why don't we take a ride to the barn?"

Abe, hovering just behind her shoulder in hopes of another scratch, stepped in front of Meri and dropped his nose to the ground in silent invitation. With a little jump, she landed on her stomach across his lowered neck. Raising his head calmly, he lifted Meri off her feet. Using Abe's movement, she slid down his neck toward his withers, twisting her body and swinging one riding-skirt-clad leg up and over his back to slide into riding position.

Meri rubbed his neck. "You're such a smart boy."

Settling herself and flipping her black, flat-brimmed hat off her head to hang down her back by its rawhide strap, she grabbed a hunk of mane and turned the sensitive horse in the direction of the barn using the lightest pressure from one calf muscle. "Let's go find a treat."

Abe sprang into a smooth lope that defied his rather gangly appearance, and Meri relished the feel of his muscles rippling under her and the wind across her face. This was much better than the rough buckboard ride into town and more soothing to her frayed emotions than visiting with "women friends."

Franks's land was divided into multiple pastures, and a fence was quickly coming closer. A gate provided access to the next pasture, but instead of slowing and heading toward it, Meri leaned over Abe's neck urging him into a gallop. Nearing the fence, the horse bunched his muscles and jumped, leaping up and over as if on wings, clearing the obstacle with plenty of room to spare and eliciting a delighted whoop from Meri.

Smoothly landing on the other side, she allowed Abe to gallop several more strides before sitting back and tugging on his mane to slow him to the smooth, rocking lope for the remainder of the ride. All too soon they reached the barn gate, and Abe halted, turning sideways to allow Meri to reach the latch. Meri patted Abe on the neck and leaned down to unfasten the gate.

"Hold it right there!"

Meri flinched hard at the unexpected voice, startling Abe and sending him sidestepping away from the gate. Her hand had tightened around the latch in surprise, and she was unceremoniously dumped on the ground when Abe moved, smacking her head against the gate as she fell. Shocked by the unfamiliar occurrence of falling—she hadn't come off a horse in years—Meri struggled to get her bearings and sit up, massaging the ache in her scalp. Pushing loosened strands of hair away from her face, she snapped, "What is your problem, scaring us like that?"

"I make it a point to scare rustlers."

"Rustlers? Where?" Meri scrambled to her feet, and the world spun wildly. Grabbing for the gatepost to steady herself, she closed her eyes against the dizziness blurring her vision and pulsing in her ears.

"I'm lookin' at her," replied the now-muffled voice.

"You're not making a lick of sense." Meri tried to shake off the vertigo. Moments before, she'd been flying across the pasture on Abe's back, and now she was crawling off the ground, attempting to make sense of a confusing, disembodied voice.

"I mean—" the voice slowed as if addressing a simpleton "—when you steal a horse, you deserve to be scared off of that horse."

Her whirling vision finally began to clear. Meri looked up and up again before she located the source of the voice. A tall man, boot propped on the bottom rail of the gate and arms folded along the top, stood looking down at her. He wore a tan cowboy hat that cast a deep shadow over the upper half of his face, but the lightly tanned skin around his mouth was creased in a small smirk.

"I am not stealing a horse." Meri blinked away the last vestiges of dizziness.

"That's not how it looked from here," he replied. "I watched you sneak through a fence, snatch a horse and try to ride it out of the pasture without renting it at the livery first."

"I was riding it *toward* the barn. If I were stealing

it, why didn't I just jump the far fence and ride away from town?" Meri flung her hand to gesture toward the bottom end of the pasture.

"I can't begin to try to explain the workings of the criminal mind, ma'am," he said politely.

"C-criminal mind?" she sputtered. "I'm not a criminal, and I wasn't stealing that horse!" She reached for the latch and pushed on the gate. Neither it nor the man budged.

"Let me out!" Meri gritted, shoving against the gate once more. She'd controlled her tongue with Mrs. Van Deusen, but she was quickly losing any desire to do so with this infuriating stranger.

"Sorry. I'm not in the habit of releasing horse thieves, especially ones who don't have any manners." A tinge of laughter denied the validity of the apology, and a dimple winked in his left cheek.

Meri had had enough of this ridiculous conversation and turned. Abe stood behind her, head cocked, looking a little perplexed at all the commotion, but awaiting further directions. She placed her hand under his chin, gently urging him forward until he stepped up to the gate.

"Abe, open the gate." She held the latch open and pointedly ignored the stranger as she added sweetly, "Please."

The horse pushed his chest into the gate, forcing the tall man to hurriedly step out of its arching path. As the gate swung wide, Abe calmly stepped through and to one side to allow Meri to close and latch the gate behind him. Remounting in the same manner as before, she looked down at the shadowed, grinning face watching her. With tart civility she uttered two words. "Good day!"

At the touch of her legs Abe loped toward the barn and his stall. Meri ignored the chuckles coming from behind them and welcomed the protective shelter of the barn.

Wyatt Cameron watched the fiery female disappear into the shadows of the barn. She had caught his attention when she'd crawled through the fence, and as Franks had been helping another customer at the time, Wyatt had stepped outside for a closer look. The horses had blocked his view of her, however, until she'd appeared as if by magic atop the black gelding and come flying toward him.

Where had she learned to ride like that? She rode with all the skill and effortlessness of an Apache warrior. He'd commanded cavalry soldiers who hadn't ridden half so well. Wyatt leaned against the fence replaying her jump. She was clearly a capable rider, but that jump had been foolhardy. The ground in the pasture was still muddy enough that the horse could have slipped and fallen on either the takeoff or landing. At least the soft ground would have cushioned her fall. He grinned as he remembered her rubbing her head. Or maybe not.

He hadn't intended to frighten her off the horse, he'd only aimed to tease her a bit, but she'd come up fighting, again like an Apache. Reminded him a bit of his sister when he'd pushed her too far as a kid. Either that or a wet cat. Not that she resembled anything close to an Apache warrior or a wet cat. She was attractive, though not in the same overdressed style as the women he'd met around town so far. There was a fresh, carefree prettiness about her with her honey-brown hair twisted back in a windblown braid and her cheeks flushed with exercise.

Who was she? He'd not seen her before. And he'd seen every female in Little Creek. Or maybe it only felt that way because he was the newest single man in town. He certainly hadn't lacked for dinner invitations since arriving.

He was at the barn door before he realized his feet had followed her. He paused as Franks's voice rumbled in response to something the woman had said. His job as Little Creek's new marshal did not include following the first attractive woman that caught his attention. His feet stepped closer to the door. As marshal, however, it *was* his job to follow up on suspicious activity. He would just verify that Franks knew who she was before he left. *If the horses knew who she was, then surely Franks knows her.*

He ignored the logical thought, as the voices inside the barn grew more distinct.

"You is gonna spoil that hoss, missy!"

"Don't try to fool me, Franks. I know Abe is your favorite. I can't spoil him any more than you've already done."

The woman was gently running a brush over the black horse as Wyatt slid into the shadows inside the barn door. Was this the same woman who'd tried to snap his head off outside? Her prickles had disappeared, and there was a smile in her voice.

Franks chuckled. "Abe don' agree with you none. He dun say he is de mos' abused hoss on de place."

Their banter sounded like an oft-repeated ritual. Now that he knew she had told the truth, he could leave. But his feet continued to have a mind of their own and stayed put.

"You're both telling tall tales. Speaking of tall tales, some saddle tramp just made Abe dump me at the gate and accused me of being a horse thief. Have you seen any drifters hanging around? I don't think I've ever seen him before, but the way my head was spinning from bumping that gate, I could be wrong."

Franks sounded choked when he spoke. "Real tall fella?"

Wyatt had to swallow a chuckle of his own.

"Yes…" She straightened slowly, watching Franks as she exited the stall. "Do you know who he is?"

"He's helpin' out 'roun' here for a while," Franks hedged, avoiding her eyes and looking straight into Wyatt's.

Wyatt laid a warning finger over his lips and moved on cat's feet to stand behind her. He'd learned a thing or two about dealing with Apaches in his years as a cavalry soldier.

"Franks, do you know anything about this man? What if he's an outlaw on the run or something?"

Franks's dark eyes snapped. "Now, missy, I'se seen a lot of things in my time, and I knows how to read a man. I likes what I sees in this un. Just cuz you is upset over comin' off old Abe don' mean you can go accusin' people a bein' outlaws. Yo mama dun raise you better'n that!"

Wyatt decided it was time to announce his presence before she accused him of any more crimes. "Hear, hear." The violence of her startled jump almost made up for her attack on his character.

She spun around, grabbing her head as she blinked

rapidly. When she looked up at him, surprise widened her brown eyes, and she backed away. "Sneaking around, scaring a person out of their wits, doesn't speak too highly of your character, Mr...."

The prickles were back in full force. But he hadn't become a captain in the U.S. Army Cavalry because it was easy. He could handle prickles. "Wyatt Cameron, Marshal of Little Creek, at your service." He doffed his hat and dipped his head in a small nod.

She stared then blinked like a sleepy owl. "The marshal?" Her eyes narrowed. "Where's your badge?"

He pointed to the vest he'd discarded earlier when he'd gotten warm in the barn. It lay over the edge of a stall, a five-pointed star glinting dully in the shadowy structure. "And might I add, you don't seem *too* witless to me, ma'am." He had a few prickles of his own. He also had years of military strategy and Apache fighting up his sleeve. Keeping the enemy on the run prevented them from launching a successful attack, even if the enemy was only a single diminutive female. Because a female on the run couldn't chase him.

"*Witless?* What...? What *are* you talking about?"

"You said I scared you out of your wits, but I think you're just *manner*less not witless."

"Mannerless...?"

If the confusion on her face was any indication, his military strategy was working. But never before had he had the desire to laugh when trading fire with hostile natives. "When a gentleman introduces himself, a lady is expected to reciprocate the gesture."

There it was again! The tone that made it sound as if he was talking to a simpleton!

Meri straightened to her full height, glaring at the man towering over her. She wasn't short at five foot seven, but this man, his shoulders nearly as broad as Franks's and standing several inches taller, made her feel unusually small. Now that he'd removed his hat, she could finally see his features.

She sized up the irritating stranger. Thick wavy brown hair glinted with cinnamon highlights and framed a nicely put together face. Smiling hazel eyes were set under arched brows of the same brown hue as his hair. Sun-bronzed skin stretched over high, sculptured cheekbones and directed her eyes to a nose that looked to have been broken once. Firm lips tucked up at one corner in a lopsided grin set off a very determined chin.

Glancing down, she noted a red neckerchief, faded blue shirt belted into dusty brown canvas duck-cloth trousers and well-broken-in boots. All of which clothed a broad shouldered, lean muscled form. Hearing a chuckle, her eyes snapped upward to find a full-blown smile showcasing pearly white teeth. Feeling a blush burning its way up her cheeks, she frantically tried to recall what had been said. Now was not the time to be distracted by a handsome face.

"I said, when a gentleman introduces himself, a lady is supposed to reciprocate." The dimple winked at her again, highlighting his smirk.

Meri was growing tired of that smirk. "Well, there's your problem—you're not a gentleman!" Spinning around, she faced Franks who hastily straightened grinning features. "I thought you said he was 'helpin' out' around here?"

Franks hearty laugh boomed out. "He's helpin' out cuz his horse is here, but he is de new marshal shore 'nuff."

The marshal stepped into her field of vision. "And don't let me catch you trying out that stunt you pulled with Abe on my horse, or I really will run you in for horse theft. That is, after I get done pickin' you up off the ground when he tosses you on your head."

Her back stiffened at the insult. "I've never met a horse that could toss me on my head!"

He cocked his head, frowning slightly as if searching his memory. "I seem to recall you being tossed not more than a few minutes ago and by a horse, too, if my memory serves me correctly." A twinkle lit the hazel eyes, and Franks chuckled.

"Abe didn't toss me! You startled us!" Meri fought the urge to stamp her foot. She had no idea why they thought this was so funny. Gritting her teeth, she looked at Franks and scraped together the ragged remnants of her dignity. "Thank you for the use of Abe. I can see you're busy, so I'll run along."

"No need to go runnin' off in such a all-fired hurry. I was hopin' to sit an' chat a spell." Franks's eyes glinted with suppressed laughter as he glanced between Meri and the new marshal.

"I'm supposed to meet Faither at the mercantile. He's probably waiting on me." Meri planted a quick kiss on Franks's cheek and beat a hasty retreat down the aisle to the livery entrance.

"Bye, Miss Meri," said Franks.

"Good day, Miss Meri," echoed the marshal.

Meri froze momentarily before turning slowly. "A *gentleman* does not call a lady by her first name unless given express permission. The name is *Miss McIsaac* to you!"

Wyatt grinned. "See, that wasn't so hard was it?"

Meri huffed disgustedly and dropped the haughty tone. "What wasn't so hard?"

"Acting like a lady and introducing yourself."

The man was as annoying as a splinter in a wool sock. "Don't you have work to do, Marshal? Or is harassing people your only job?"

Hooking his thumbs behind his belt, he rocked back on his heels. "I've already apprehended a dangerous horse thief this mornin'. All in all I'd say not a bad day's work, *Miss McIsaac.*"

Meri shot a quick glance at Franks. "I said you didn't know enough about him. When the town council learns how delusional he is, they'll fire him on the spot. He'll have so much time on his hands you can put him to work mucking out all the stalls. He should be good at it, judging by what he's shoveled out since I arrived!"

Taking advantage of the instantaneous silence, she spun on her heel and marched out of the barn, biting back a victorious smirk of her own. Finally! The last word!

But as she cleared the doorway, she heard Franks speak. "Hoo whee, Marshal, you dun riled her up sumpin' fierce! Her mamma would'a warshed her mouth out with soap for dat!"

Color flew high in her cheeks as she continued her march away from the livery stable, followed by the irritating sound of the marshal's laugh. Franks was right. Her mother wouldn't have been happy about the last comment she'd let fly. Catriona McIsaac had always admonished that just because ranch life could be crude and dirty, one's speech didn't have to be crude and dirty. Meri let out a deep breath as her shoulders slumped. She should not have lost her temper, but—

honestly! The man had called her a horse thief! Between that, her lately volatile emotions and…and those unnerving eyes, it had been like waving a red flag at a bull, and she'd attacked.

Something Mrs. Van Deusen had said earlier flitted across her memory, stopping Meri in her tracks.

"…the new marshal has arrived, and you *have* to meet him. I've told him all about you."

No! Oh, no, no, no!

Mortified consternation swamped the last dregs of temper. She should have never left the ranch this morning. Faither had better be done with his business, because she wanted to slink out of this town as fast as possible. Mrs. Van Deusen could find some other unsuspecting female to throw at the new marshal. Meri wanted absolutely no part of him! Not that he'd want anything to do with her after this morning. It was going to be hard enough to come back in for church services, to say nothing of the picnic.

Dread slithered down her spine, and she groaned. Just the thought of sitting in the same church building with that man made her feel queasy enough maybe she'd just stay home from church for a while. She definitely wouldn't have to feign not feeling well! And who needed a picnic, anyway? Staying away from town was sounding better all the time.

Crack!

The sound of a gunshot slammed into her ears. Meri's heart stopped as the direction of the gunfire dawned on her.

She broke into a dead run.

Chapter Two

Wyatt examined the repaired holster before strapping it around his waist and holstering his pistol. "Looks good, Franks. I figured I'd have to replace the whole thing, but I can hardly see where you fixed it. Thanks."

Crack! The gunshot interrupted Franks's reply.

Wyatt pivoted toward the barn door, wishing for his rifle from his office.

"Wait! You might need dis." Franks tossed a rifle to Wyatt, a second rifle in his other hand.

"Thanks." Wyatt snatched the rifle out of the air and sprinted out of the barn, hearing Franks pound the ground behind him.

As they turned the corner onto the main street, Wyatt dodged the running figure of Miss McIsaac. Where did she think she was going?

"Stay back!" He barked as he passed her. He spared a split-second glance over his shoulder, pleased to see her slow down. Good. He didn't know what was going on, but the fewer spectators he had to deal with the better.

A man jumped astride a horse to ride away from the bank, throwing hot lead around and forcing curious onlookers to scurry for cover. Wyatt threw up his rifle, slamming the butt of the gun into his shoulder. As he laid his finger against the trigger, someone ran between him and the mounted gunman. He jerked the barrel of the rifle up and held his fire. He had no clear shot, but the shooting horseman needed to be stopped before someone was killed.

Wyatt pulled his pistol and fired twice in the air, aiming far above innocent heads. The bullets came nowhere near the gunman, but he sank his spurs into the horse's sides as he yanked violently on the reins and plunged down an alleyway.

The shooting stopped, and heads poked out of doorways like so many prairie dogs. "Anyone hurt?" Wyatt shouted as he ran toward the bank.

"No. But I think the bank's been robbed." An unidentified voice yelled back.

Wyatt slammed the bank doors open, Franks and several other men hot on his heels. No one was in the front room, but the door to the office stood open, and the banker was slumped on the floor just inside it. He moaned and tried to sit up as Wyatt entered. He gave the banker a quick glance then looked around the office.

"Franks, help him." He pointed to the banker and moved to a second man lying motionless and bleeding on the floor beside the massive desk.

There was blood on the floor around the white-haired man's head and more blood staining his side, but he was breathing. The wound on his side was bleeding freely, and Wyatt pulled off the red neckerchief he wore, wadding it up and pressing it against the wound to staunch the blood. "Somebody fetch the doctor!"

A commotion sounded at the office door. "Faither! No!"

The piercing cry pulled Wyatt's eyes up. Miss McIsaac sank to her knees on the other side of the bleeding man, her face a mask of disbelieving horror.

"Is this your father?"

A silent nod was his only answer as her eyes frantically ran over her father's form. Her hand gripped a tiny hideout pistol. Where had that come from? More important, what had she planned to do with it? Take on the bank robber herself? *Probably.* "If you'll put that gun away, I need you to hold this while I check on the banker."

Miss McIsaac looked at the pistol as if seeing it for the first time, blinked, then tucked it away in a pocket. She looked back at him, shock darkening her eyes.

Wyatt grabbed her unresisting hand and placed it over the bloody neckerchief. "Hold this down as tight as you can. It'll slow the bleeding. The wound doesn't look too bad, but he's got a gash on the back of his head, as well. Looks like he hit it on the desk when he fell."

Her face drained of color, and he heard her breath hitch in her throat. "You're not going to faint on me, are you?" He deliberately forced a hint of scorn into the question.

It worked. The muscles along her jaw clenched as she took a deep breath, and when she spared a glance at him, some of the spark was back in her eyes if not in her voice. "I don't faint."

She might be foolhardy, but she was tough, too. He disliked leaving her with her wounded father, but he had a gunman to follow before he got any farther away. He pushed to his feet and took a last look at her lowered face as she focused determinedly on her hands.

Her lips were moving soundlessly, but she was keeping steady pressure on the makeshift bandage.

"Doc's comin'," someone cried from the back of the crowd.

Relieved, Wyatt went to try to glean information from the banker.

Wyatt wondered if he smelled as rank as the men wearily riding alongside him. Then again maybe the odor came from himself alone and not his companions. Three days chasing an elusive quarry wasn't conducive to rest, much less keeping clean, and he would dearly love a bath, food and sleep; not necessarily in that order. Unfortunately it might be a while before he was able to acquire any of them. The townsfolk were going to want to know the results of the three-day chase. Returning to town with nothing to show for the posse's efforts but weary horses, weary bodies covered in trail dust and a glaring lack of a culprit and loot was not an auspicious beginning to his career as Little Creek's marshal.

In the minutes following Mr. McIsaac's removal to the doctor's office while men had scrambled for horses, Wyatt had fired questions at the assembled crowd. The banker had been too shaken up to give any helpful information, and none of the onlookers could add anything to what Wyatt had seen himself as he was running toward the bank. Armed with this pitiful lack of information, but a veritable arsenal of assorted firearms, Wyatt and the hastily assembled posse rode out of town, hot on the trail of the bank bandit.

Following the tracks of the fleeing horse and rider until night had forced a halt, they'd made a cold, dark camp lest the bandit had circled around to take a few shots at them in the glow of a campfire. Canteens of water and strips of jerky had provided their meal before they'd taken turns standing guard or grabbing a few hours of sleep. As soon as the sky had begun to lighten, they'd continued their pursuit, but had lost the trail when it had merged with a sea of tracks left by a passing cattle herd being pushed toward the Denver stockyards.

Splitting up the posse, they'd spent the rest of the day cutting for sign on both sides of the cattle trail. They'd even caught up with the herd, but the drovers had denied seeing either hide or hair of anyone but themselves and the posse.

Another day of tedious searching for sign had ended in failure when a heavy rainstorm had rolled through leaving them wet, cold, tired and discouraged. Wyatt had hated to head back empty-handed and without any idea of the whereabouts of the bandit, but washed-out sign, dwindling supplies and a dispirited posse had left no other option.

Twilight descended as they rode into town, and Wyatt thanked the men for their participation before the posse broke apart, each man heading for his own home while Wyatt continued toward the livery. His horse deserved a good feed and some rest. It had been a hard ride for them both.

Franks met him at the front doors of the livery. "From de looks ob things, I specs you dun lost dat fella."

"That about sums it up." Wyatt wearily scrubbed a hand over his face, feeling the rasp of three days' growth of beard. "How's everything here in town?"

Franks unsaddled, rubbed down and fed the weary horse as he talked. "Well, Mr. McIsaac's still out cold, and Doc is shore 'nuff worried. Miss Meri ain't left his side de whole time. De banker is okay, but he's sayin' he cain't do nuttin' 'bout the loss ob de money, and we'd better hope you foun' it. Everythin' else has been quiet like."

Wyatt gave Franks a quick rundown of the fruitless search before adding, "I think I'll check in at Doc's office then try to find a meal and my bed, if no one needs me. Thanks for the use of that horse. He was a good fella. I appreciate you keepin' one handy for me until Charger recovers from our trip up here." Wyatt shook Franks's hand, bid the man good-night and made his way to the doctor's house.

A light was burning in the front window, and he tapped softly on the door. Dr. Kilburn opened it and, upon seeing who it was, quietly invited him in. "Did you catch him?"

"No. We lost his tracks," Wyatt ruefully admitted. He had a feeling he was just beginning to hear this question. He changed the subject. "How's McIsaac?"

Doc shook his head. "I wish I knew. I removed the bullet from his side, and it isn't such a bad wound, barring infection. It's the blow to his head that has me concerned. He hasn't shown any sign of consciousness, and I'm worried there might be swelling inside his skull due to the severity of the blow he took when he fell. It's become a waiting game, unfortunately."

"May I see him?"

"You can peek in the door, but be quiet about it. Miss Meri had just dozed off when I checked on them a few minutes ago. She hasn't slept much since it happened, and I'd like her to get some rest."

Wyatt nodded, and Dr. Kilburn led him down a short hall and quietly opened a door. A lamp glowed softly, throwing its feeble beam on the two figures occupying the room.

Mr. McIsaac, his head swathed in white bandages, was lying motionless and silent on the small bed. His face looked unnaturally pale even in the dim light of the lamp's lowered flame. Wyatt threw up a quick prayer for God's healing and turned his gaze toward the room's other occupant.

Miss McIsaac—he liked Franks's "Miss Mary" better—the woman who'd hopped on a bareback, bridleless horse to go flying across the field, snagging his attention like no gussied up, eyelash-batting, flirting female had ever done. He'd found himself distracted and thinking about her at the oddest times while tracking with the posse, remembering her reaction when she'd fallen off the horse at his feet. He'd expected tears and pouting but she'd come up fighting, and he'd kept at it just to watch her spine stiffen, her chin come up and her brown eyes spark and sizzle.

Tonight, though, the fiery spirit and ramrod-straight spine were missing. The slender young woman drooped sideways in the large rocking chair, weary distress creasing her sleeping features. Her head leaned awkwardly against her shoulder and the back of the rocker in a way that was sure to leave a crick in her neck by morning. Someone had draped a blanket over her, but her slender hands gripped the arms of the rocker. Even in sleep there was a tension about the fragile-looking figure and an obvious lack of peace that made his heart ache.

Wyatt forced his gaze back to Mr. McIsaac. He was not in Little Creek to be distracted by a female. He was here to do a job and continue to squirrel money away toward his goal. He'd seen the stress the families of army soldiers and lawmen had undergone. Long ago he'd decided not to put someone he loved through that and to avoid female entanglements until he was no longer in a dangerous profession. When he found a place to settle down and pursue his dream of raising prime horseflesh, then he would think about a family. Until that happened, however, he was riding alone. And enjoying it.

A hand on Wyatt's shoulder reminded him Doc was waiting. Stepping back, he allowed the man to softly pull the door closed and followed him to the front room.

"Now, young man, you go find yourself a meal and a bed. There's nothing you can do here tonight, and I'd like to catch some sleep myself before anyone else decides they need me."

Taking his advice, Wyatt bid the doctor good-night and left the house, praying as he walked through the dark, quiet town for God to heal Mr. McIsaac, to give Miss McIsaac strength and to help him bring the thief to justice. He reached his office and decided a meal and a bath could wait; sleep was more important. Retreating to the small rear room that held his few belongings, Wyatt wearily shed hat, boots and pistol holster. Placing his pistol and rifle within easy reach, he flopped across his bed and let out a gusty sigh. Like the doctor, he wanted rest before anyone else needed him. Dumping the questions and worry swirling through his mind at the feet of his Heavenly Father, he was sound asleep within minutes.

Please, God, don't take him, too! Please don't take him, too!

Time slowed, and the ticktock of the bank clock grew louder and slower until it was all Meri could hear as she desperately pressed the blood-soaked cloth against the bleeding wound and struggled to pray. She jerked when a second pair of hands covered hers, and she glanced up wildly.

"You can let go now." Dr. Kilburn's kind, bearded face peered into hers as he lifted her hands away. "I need to take a look."

Meri sank onto her heels, clenching bloody hands together while he examined her father. After a cursory look at the wounds, he pulled a thick cloth from his bag, folded it into a square pad and pressed it over the gunshot wound. Looking up, he motioned to two men who hurried over with a litter, and Meri scrambled to get out of their way.

"Take him to my office. Tell my wife to prepare for surgery. I'll be right behind you as soon as I examine the banker." Turning to Meri he added, "You walk alongside and keep pressure on that pad to slow the bleeding."

Unseen hands lifted Meri to her feet as she struggled to make her limbs obey her brain. Moving to her father's side, she frantically tried to keep up with the litter bearers as blood spurted over her hands. The harder she pressed, the faster the blood poured.

"Stop. Please stop!" But there was no one around to

hear. She was kneeling over her father in the middle of a deserted street.

"Please, God, don't take him, too. I can't lose him. Don't take him, too!"

A rooster crowed as Meri searched for something else to staunch the bleeding. The rooster crowed again, and Meri jerked awake, a cold sweat covering her skin from the vivid dream. Aching from the rocking chair and the unaccustomed inactivity of the past few days, she slowly pushed herself to her feet and gingerly stretched protesting muscles and joints before straightening the nightgown and wrapper Mrs. Kilburn had loaned her. A tap on the door warned her, and she turned as Dr. Kilburn and his wife entered.

"Good morning, dear. I have breakfast almost ready. You have a few minutes to wash and freshen up if you like. I also washed and pressed your clothes for you. They're hanging in the spare room." Mrs. Kilburn smiled softly at Meri as she issued the invitation before hurrying back to her kitchen.

Meri delayed leaving the room, hovering over the doctor as he examined her father. "Still no change," he muttered.

"Is there *anything* we can do?" Meri asked in frustration as she looked at the pale, quiet figure of her father.

"Yes. We can pray for God's healing and wait for it to occur. Your father had a pretty big shock to his system, but so far he's holding his own." The doctor moved away from the bed and patted Meri's shoulder reassuringly. "Go freshen up and get some food in you. I'll leave the door open. We'll be close enough to hear if he stirs."

Meri allowed herself to be ushered from the room

to the spare room across the hall. By the time she'd finished her morning ablutions, dressed in the neatly pressed skirt and blouse and headed for the kitchen, another voice had joined those of Dr. Kilburn and his wife.

Pastor James Willis was sitting at the table drinking coffee but stood when she entered the room. "I'm sorry for disturbing you so early, I wanted to check on Ian and see if there's any way I can be of assistance."

"Doc says all we can do now is pray and wait." The words felt like shards of glass in her throat.

"They've been keeping me apprised of Ian's condition—" he waved his hand toward Dr. and Mrs. Kilburn "—and the church family has been lifting him up in daily prayer, but what can we do to help *you?*" Pastor Willis gently asked.

"I don't know…" Meri choked as the pressure of the past three days suddenly clawed its way up her throat and overwhelmed her. The need to get away before she screamed and made a complete fool of herself robbed her of any semblance of social skills.

"I'm sorry, I… Excuse me!" Meri rushed out the door of the kitchen into the backyard.

"What about your breakfast, dear?" Meri heard Mrs. Kilburn ask as she cleared the door.

"Let her go. Food's the last thing on her mind right now."

Dr. Kilburn's voice faded as Meri left the yard, running blindly. She didn't know where she was going; she just followed her feet as they carried her away from the place where her father lay unconscious.

Adrenaline had carried her through the past couple of days, but the uncertainty of her father's health could not be ignored any longer. The doctor said wait and pray.

She'd *been* waiting.

She'd *been* praying.

Why wasn't God listening? She'd prayed and waited and waited and prayed through her mother's illness but lost her anyway. Now here she was again, in the same position with her father. She couldn't go through this again. She *couldn't!*

Fear and grief met with the fury of a mountain thunderstorm and raged in Meri's chest. Her breath came in ragged gasps, and her eyes and throat burned. She needed to get away from curious eyes. She needed to be on the range where she could run and scream. Where no one could hear and accuse the "old maid" of finally snapping.

Where could she go? For that matter, where was she?

Disoriented, Meri glanced around and realized she'd run from Pastor Willis, straight to the church building. Well, maybe praying at an altar would be more effective than the silent, incoherent pleas ricocheting around her brain the past three days.

Trying the handle of the spick-and-span little white building, she walked inside, pausing to let her eyes adjust to the dimmer light. The room that rang with preaching and singing on Sundays, and the schoolchildren's recitations the rest of the week, was unnaturally quiet and dim. The sun had just started peeking over the horizon, not yet bright enough to illumine the interior.

Collapsing onto the nearest bench, her eyes fastened on the flag at the front of the room as her mind tried to find the words to pray. Gradually her ragged breathing began to quiet.

"Heavenly Faither…" The words echoed hollowly in the empty room. "I don't know what to say that I haven't already prayed. I don't want to lose Faither. I've already lost Mither. Isn't that enough for a while?" The anger in the question surprised Meri. She was scared and sad, not angry. Meri's voice rose though she tried to temper her tone. "Please! You *have* to heal Faither!"

Unable to sit any longer with the emotions tumbling around inside her, Meri got up and paced the aisle of the little building. An open Bible lying on the edge of the desk at the corner of the platform caught her attention. It was a school day, and the teacher would soon be here to prepare for the children who would fill the benches when the bell rang. She needed to leave before she was caught yelling at God, but maybe she could find quick comfort in His word.

Grabbing the book, her eyes roamed the open pages for several seconds…

…searching… There.

Romans 8:25–28.

But if we hope for that we see not, then do we with patience wait for it.

Wait. There was that word again. She was tired of waiting. She wanted her father healed now.

Likewise the Spirit also helpeth our infirmities: for we know not what we should pray for as we ought: but the Spirit itself maketh intercession for us with groanings which cannot be uttered. And he that searcheth the hearts knoweth what is *the mind of the Spirit, because he maketh intercession for the saints according to* the will *of the God.*

Pastor Willis had preached one Sunday how Jesus Christ prayed to the Father on behalf of believers. He didn't forget to pray like a person might, He always knew what and how to pray, and the Holy Spirit interpreted the muddled, incoherent prayers, which might be all a believer was capable of in times of trouble.

A hint of peace tiptoed through her heart. Someone was praying over her, and that thought brought the first comfort she'd felt in days. Her eyes continued down the page.

And we know that all things work together for good to them that love God...

She didn't know how any of the awful recent events could be good, but maybe she'd make it through them without running screaming down the main street of town.

Rereading the verses slowly, she hugged the reassurance of them to her heart before placing the Bible back on the desk. The weight on her shoulders wasn't gone, but it was more bearable, and Meri felt she could face the day and the people in it.

Hunger pangs reminded Meri of missed breakfast, so she left the little church—her return to the doctor's house much slower than her departure. Fear and worry still nibbled around the edges of her heart, but the verses she'd read seemed to be keeping the worst of it at bay.

A burst of embarrassment over her abrupt exit hit her as she slipped through the kitchen door.

"There you are. I've got your breakfast keeping warm on the back of the stove if you feel like eating." Mrs. Kilburn looked up from the bread dough she was kneading.

"I am hungry, but I need to apologize for the way I ran out so rudely," Meri said softly.

Wiping her hands off on a towel, Mrs. Kilburn walked over to where Meri was standing and wrapped her in a hug. "Oh, honey. You don't owe me an apology. I'm not upset. You've been cooped up in this house for days and have a ton of worry pressing on you. Frankly, my husband and I were beginning to worry that you hadn't let any of it out. I think that maybe you have this morning. You look like you feel better." She pulled back and peered into Meri's face.

"A little. Thank you for saving breakfast for me, and for taking the time to clean my clothes." Meri swallowed past the lump in her throat as the warmth of Mrs. Kilburn's hug sank into her heart.

"Enough of that. We keep this up, and we'll both be crying while your food spoils." Mrs. Kilburn dabbed her eyes with her apron and tugged Meri to a seat at the table before placing the plate of breakfast in front of her. "You eat while I tend to this bread, and then you can help me do the dishes. Busy hands help keep the mind off heartaches."

Meri's mouth watered as the aromas drifted up from the plate in front of her, and she bowed her head briefly. Digging into her meal, she listened to Mrs. Kilburn quietly hum the new tune "Blessed Assurance."

Mrs. Kilburn was in her late forties with curly blond hair arranged in a thick bun, and soft eyes that seemed to look at the world with a calm assurance and acceptance Meri wished she could emulate. Meri had not spent much time around the woman outside of church gatherings, but she knew Mrs. Kilburn was familiar with heartache. She'd miscarried several times and knew the grief of loss and childlessness, so her words of compassion rang with authentic empathy.

Mrs. Kilburn assisted her husband with his patients, and Doc frequently said he wouldn't be able to practice medicine without her. He bragged she was his right hand and the best nurse he'd ever worked with. Watching her over the past few days, Meri couldn't help but agree.

Finished with her meal, Meri washed and dried the dishes while Mrs. Kilburn kneaded and shaped the dough into loaves and slid them into the oven. Meri could hear Dr. Kilburn's office door open and the sound of boots getting closer.

"Come into the kitchen," Dr. Kilburn was saying to someone. "We can grab a cup of coffee while you wait for Meri to return."

Meri finished drying the dish in her hands as she glanced toward the door. Dr. Kilburn entered followed by the tall figure of Marshal Cameron. Meri stiffened her knees and spine, fighting an abnormal thudding in her heart that destroyed the measure of peace she'd found earlier.

"Ah, she's back already. Meri, the marshal stopped by to speak with you. Both of you have a seat, and I'll get us some coffee." He stepped to the stove where the coffeepot simmered.

Meri set the dish down and wiped her perspiring hands on the towel, the marshal's cool, searching eyes making her uncomfortable.

"If she can be spared for a few minutes, I need to speak to her in private." He addressed Dr. Kilburn, but his hard gaze remained on Meri, watching, waiting. He motioned toward the back door. "If you'll step outside into the garden, I have a few questions to ask you about the bank robbery."

Chapter Three

Wyatt studied Miss McIsaac, and replayed the morning's events in his mind. Questions concerning the holdup had driven him from his bed before dawn. After time spent praying and searching the Scriptures for wisdom, he set his Bible aside and pored over the wanted posters and notices filed in his desk. He had glanced through them as time permitted over the first days on the job, but early this morning, he'd studied each one carefully, looking for any descriptions that matched what he knew of the bank robber.

Sounds of an awakening town had finally caused him to push back from the desk, stretching as he stood. He needed more information about the holdup and the culprit; rushing to follow the trail of the thief hadn't left time for a comprehensive investigation. Talking with witnesses again might provide additional information to tie to the wanted posters. Buckling his holster around his waist and settling his prized Stetson on his head, Wyatt blew out the lamp on his desk and walked out the door. He'd learned the café was a favorite morning spot for many of the single tradesmen in town, and Wyatt decided to combine two chores at once: breakfast and information gathering.

The food was tasty and plentiful, but Wyatt didn't learn anything particularly useful, and he answered as many questions as he asked. Finishing his breakfast, he left the gathered diners speculating among themselves about the how and who of the robbery, and more importantly, when the marshal was going to find their missing savings.

His next stop was the bank, and though the doors were closed and locked with a sign that read Closed Until Further Notice, his knock brought Mr. Phineas Samuels to the door.

"I'd need to discuss the bank robbery if you have some time this morning."

Mr. Samuels motioned him inside and closed the door before speaking. "I see you failed to catch the scoundrel who robbed my bank, Marshal."

He ignored the accusation in the banker's voice and followed the man across the front room holding the cashier's desk to Mr. Samuels's office. As they entered, Mr. Samuels waved Wyatt toward a chair before circling his desk and taking his own seat.

"I'm sorry, Mr. Samuels, but we lost the tracks in a passing cattle drive. That's why I'd like to go over the events of that day again. I need all the information I can find. Maybe I can match him to accounts of other holdups and alert surrounding marshals to keep an eye out for anyone matching his description. Would you start at the beginning and tell me everything you can remember, please?" Wyatt perched his hat on his knee and pulled a small notebook and pencil from his shirt pocket.

"I don't see how that's going to help you now. Seems to me you're shutting the barn door *after* the cow has escaped." Mr. Samuels rocked back in his chair, folding his soft pudgy hands over his brocaded paisley vest.

"Humor me, if you would."

The man's tone was irksome, but Wyatt kept his demeanor passive. The balding, wire-rimmed-spectacle-wearing banker perched behind his massive desk like a king on his throne, and Wyatt felt sympathy for anyone who'd ever had to ask this banker for a loan.

Mr. Samuels grudgingly began to recite the events of the day of the bank robbery. "Mr. McIsaac and I were finishing up our business here in my office when a man walked in, pulled a gun and demanded that I open the safe. I argued, but he threatened to shoot me, so I opened the safe. When he turned his back and started grabbing money and throwing it into a bag, Mr. McIsaac pulled his own gun from beneath his jacket to stop him. Unfortunately the thief turned in time to see it and shot him. I thought he was going to shoot me next, but instead, he hit me on the head. Next thing I remember was you and Franks coming in."

"How did he get into your office without the teller seeing him?" Wyatt questioned.

"My bank teller quit a couple weeks ago to move closer to his widowed mother. I hadn't replaced him yet, so it was just Mr. McIsaac and me in the bank that morning."

"What did he look like?"

"He had a black hat pulled low over his head, a blue bandanna covered the rest of his face and he was wearing a dirty leather jacket over brown shirt and pants."

Wyatt looked up from his notes when Mr. Samuels stopped speaking. "Did you notice anything else?"

"Yes, I did. I saw the horse he rode away before I blacked out. It was wearing the McIsaac ranch brand." Mr. Samuels rocked his chair back. "If it wasn't for the fact that McIsaac was shot, I'd wonder if he had anything to do with it. Or maybe one of those derelicts he's hired as ranch hands decided the pickings were better here!"

Wyatt hid his surprise at this bit of news. "Let's not jump to conclusions just yet. If you'd been hit on the head, how did you see the horse he rode?"

"I managed to get to my feet to call for help as he left, and I saw him through the window but then I must have blacked out." The man puffed up like a little banty rooster. "I am the victim here, Marshal! Are you questioning my word?"

Wyatt hastened to smooth his feathers. "No. I'm simply trying to get the events straight in my mind. How much did he get away with?"

"Everything in the safe! You saw it that day. He cleaned me out! I've had to close the doors because I have nothing to do business with. And then you couldn't manage to catch him or get the money back! I'm beginning to have serious doubts about the town council's choice for marshal!" Mr. Samuels slammed his palms down on the desktop as he stood.

"Everything?" Wyatt let his surprise show this time. "How could one man carry everything from the safe? How much was everything?"

Mr. Samuels instantly went on the defensive. "This is a small Western bank, not a big Eastern city bank. We don't have the same amount of capital as bigger cities, and until I've contacted my investors, I'm not at liberty to divulge the dollar amount of what was stolen. Now if you'll excuse me, I need to get back to my papers. I'm explaining to my backers what's happened to their money!"

"If I'm to recover the stolen money, I need to know how much was taken, Mr. Samuels."

"*When* you have a suspect in custody, Marshal Cameron, I will divulge that information to you. Until then, I've told you everything I know. Good day, Marshal!"

"I need to know the amount that was taken, Mr. Samuels," Wyatt said implacably.

"I said good day, Marshal!" The man was sulled up tighter than a mad, wet hen.

Wyatt eyed him for a moment before reluctantly deciding to retreat from this particular battle until the man had calmed down. "Thank you for your time, Mr. Samuels. If you think of anything else that might be helpful, let me know." He picked his hat off his knee, stood, nodded to the disagreeable man and walked out the bank door.

Outside he returned his hat to his head and tucked the notebook back into his pocket.

Whew!

If other townsfolk felt the same way, it was going to be rough around here until the culprit was apprehended and the money returned. He already knew one person in particular who was definitely not going to be happy to see him when she found out the reason for his visit.

Miss McIsaac's father was still unconscious as far as he knew, but their ranch had been implicated in the bank job, and he needed answers. He really needed to talk to Mr. McIsaac, but only God knew when—

or if—that would happen. Looked like Miss McIsaac would have to do.

Sending up a quick plea for help, he'd headed toward the Kilburns'.

Now Wyatt watched Miss McIsaac's reaction carefully as he motioned toward the back door. "If you'll step outside into the garden, I have a few questions I need to ask you about the bank robbery."

Her face showed the fatigue of the past several days' vigil, and there was a hint of redness around her eyes as if she'd been crying. But aside from the wariness that had appeared when he'd come in, Wyatt saw no other emotions at his words. If her ranch was somehow involved in the robbery, no hint of it showed on her face.

"Oh, goodness, there's no need for that. Sit down and enjoy your coffee." Mrs. Kilburn placed her hand on her husband's arm. "Come, dear, I'll help you straighten that mess you call a desk."

Miss McIsaac's voice halted their departure. "I'd rather you both stayed. Whatever the marshal has to say, he can say it in front of all of us. If he has a problem with that, he can leave." She enforced the last remark with a defiant look in his direction.

There was that feisty spirit he'd seen at the livery. "If having the Kilburns here makes you more comfortable, that's fine with me. I would ask, however, that you keep this conversation confidential."

Dr. Kilburn pulled out a chair for his wife. "I always protect the privacy of my patients, and as Ian and his daughter are under my care, my wife and I consider it our responsibility to protect their privacy." Mrs. Kilburn nodded her agreement.

"Very well. Miss McIsaac, would you care to have a seat, and I'll get straight to the point?" The woman still stood in the same spot, gripping the towel.

Slowly and deliberately, she turned and hung up the damp dishrag, smoothing it unnecessarily before turning back around, running her palms down her skirt and walking to the work-worn table. He saw her stiffen as he reached to hold a chair for her, sliding it in smoothly when she sat opposite of Mrs. Kilburn. Seating himself at the end, to the right of Miss McIsaac, he reached for the coffee the doctor placed in front of him. Taking a quick sip, he fired up another quick prayer that God would give him the right words. Swallowing the hot, bitter brew, he began.

"I just spoke with Mr. Samuels concerning the bank robbery, and another detail came to light that I really need to discuss with your father, Miss McIsaac. Since that's not possible at the moment, I need you to tell me everything you know." Pausing, he watched Miss McIsaac dart a look at him from the corner of her eyes before returning her gaze to the cup wrapped in her slender hands. Was she avoiding his gaze because she knew something, or because she found his presence as unsettling as he found hers?

Her long honey-colored hair was smoothed back into a braid that fell halfway down the back of the high-necked, wheat-colored blouse and dark green riding skirt she'd worn the day of the holdup. Distractedly he wondered how she managed to look so neat and fresh after several days in the same outfit. Forcing his thoughts back to the task at hand, he pulled the notebook out of his pocket and flipped it open. "Tell me what you saw after you left the livery stable that day."

A hint of pink warmed her cheeks, and he felt a glimmer of satisfaction. So, he wasn't the only one who hadn't forgotten their first encounter.

She raised her cup slowly, took a sip and lowered it, gazing into its contents. "I heard a shot fired before I reached the street. When I rounded the corner, I saw something happening at the bank. I had just headed toward it when you and Franks passed me."

"That reminds me. I told you to stay back, yet you still showed up at the bank. You don't follow orders very well, do you?"

Miss McIsaac set her cup down into the saucer with a little more force than necessary, but still didn't look directly at him. "My…" Her voice caught, and Wyatt saw her swallow hard. "My father was in that bank. *Nothing* would have stopped me from getting to him…" The words *even you* hung in the air unspoken.

"How did you know your father would be there?"

"I didn't know for sure he was still there, but he'd told me he had business at the bank, and when he was through he'd meet me at the mercantile. When I heard the shots and saw the commotion at the bank, I was afraid he was involved."

"What do you mean, 'involved'?"

Miss McIsaac went very still then turned her head slowly and finally looked him full in the face. Wyatt felt the heat immediately.

"What exactly are you trying to imply?" Fire may have been in her eyes, but her words were encased in ice.

Wyatt softened his tone and replied calmly, "I'm

not implying anything. I'm simply asking what you meant by 'involved.'"

Miss McIsaac searched his face for several moments before looking down and releasing a heavy sigh. "I mean, I was afraid he was still there when the holdup occurred. Unfortunately I was right." Her voice caught again, and he saw the muscles along her jaw clench.

"Did you see or notice anything as you ran to the bank?"

"I saw a man riding away from the bank, firing his gun." She painstakingly aligned the bottom of the cup with the ring of flowers on the saucer.

"Did you notice anything familiar about him?"

"No. Why should I?" Miss McIsaac glanced back up at him, her forehead creased in a frown.

"Did your father ride his horse to the bank?"

"No. We drove the buckboard in, parked it at the mercantile. Faither walked to the bank."

"Did any of your ranch hands ride in with you?"

"No. Are you trying to get at something, Marshal? Why don't you just ask what you want to know? Quit beating around the bush?"

Wyatt searched her eyes for a long second, ignoring the confused glare in them, and continued to watch her when he finally spoke. "When I questioned Mr. Samuels, he said the thief rode off on a horse that wore the McIsaac brand." He heard the soft exclamations of surprise from the Kilburns' lips as Miss McIsaac shoved her chair back and lunged to her feet.

"That's a lie!" She gasped, shaking her head.

Dr. Kilburn stood and placed a gentle hand on her shoulder. "Calm down, child. The marshal is just doing his job. He has to investigate what he's been told. Let's sit back down and hear the man out."

She sat with a thud. "There is no way it was one of our ranch hands. I'd trust every one of them with my life."

"The banker didn't seem to recognize the man who robbed him, but he did say the horse was a McIsaac ranch horse. Did the horse look familiar to you at all?'

She shook her head.

Wyatt wondered if she truly hadn't recognized the horse or if she merely refused to tell. He'd known this wasn't going to go well. He'd been correct. He was beginning to feel like ducking when those eyes turned toward him firing sparks. Wyatt ran a hand through his hair. It wasn't singed, yet. But the day was still young.

"I'm sorry to have to question you when your father is unconscious, but I need to gather as much information as I can to bring you father's shooter to justice."

"It's not your questions that bother me. It's the implication that our ranch was involved in the holdup. It's not true!"

"Again, I'm not implying anything. I have to follow any and all leads I have and, unfortunately, that means asking you these questions. It also means I'm going to need directions to your ranch."

"You are not going to harass our hands with baseless accusations."

"I'm not going to accuse anyone, but you haven't been home in three days, and if it *was* one of your ranch horses, your hands might know something about it. If you won't give me directions to your place, I'll get them from someone else because I *will* follow up on this."

"Then I'm going with you. You are not questioning our hands without me there." Miss McIsaac got to her feet again, and Wyatt could feel anger radiating from her.

He could sympathize; he was beginning to feel the emotion himself. He pushed back his own chair and stood. "This is my job. I can handle it without your interference. Besides, you can't leave your father, can you?" Wyatt saw a retort die on Miss McIsaac's lips, and her shoulders slumped. His shot had found its mark.

Dr. Kilburn interrupted then. "Actually it might be a good idea for Miss McIsaac to go with you. She needs to get away for a little while. This would give her a chance to check on the ranch." Turning to Miss McIsaac, he continued, "Your father is stable, and it could be a while before he wakes up. Even when he does, it will be some time before he's ready to travel. This will give you a chance pick up anything you'll need for an extended stay."

She looked indecisive. "What if something happens while I'm gone?"

"You can make it to the ranch and back in just a few hours. I don't expect any changes with your father, good or bad, in that amount of time, and a change of scenery will do you good. If anything does happen, I'll send someone to bring you back."

Miss McIsaac looked at Wyatt. The glare was gone, replaced by a steely determination to accompany him. He doubted he'd seen the last of her temper, but the change of scene was already doing *him* some good.

His irritation cooled. "All right, you can ride along.

I'll go get a buggy from Franks and be back to pick you up in about half an hour."

Grabbing his hat from the back of the chair where he'd hung it when he'd entered, he thanked Mrs. Kilburn for the coffee and headed to the front door.

Meri leaned against the edge of the livery stable doorway and worked to control her rapid breathing. She'd overheard the marshal tell Dr. Kilburn that he would ask the gunsmith to keep an eye on the town before getting a buggy from Franks. After a quick check on her father and a hurried explanation to the Kilburns, Meri had taken advantage of the marshal's plan and slipped out the back door.

Cutting through alleys at a run and keeping an eye out for a certain lawman, she'd made it to the livery unseen where Franks had helped her saddle two horses. She had no intention of riding with the man in a buggy all the way to the ranch. Horseback would be quicker, and it would allow her to keep her distance.

The intense fear and uncertainty of the past few days lifted enough to allow her to feel a tiny amount of smug satisfaction. She'd managed to regain some control of her life. Even if that control were only that she'd ride to the ranch *on* a horse instead of *behind* a horse.

The thought of sitting shoulder to shoulder with the marshal sent a funny shiver along her spine. That would be too much like courting, not that she knew anything about it. She wasn't girly enough to attract that kind of attention. When you could outride, outshoot and out rope the boys, they tended to treat you like one of the boys. And when it came time to go courtin', they went after the sweet-smelling, dainty town ladies.

Movement caught her eye, and she stepped back into the shadows of the barn as the long-legged figure of the marshal strode into view. "He's here, Franks." Meri gathered the reins of the two horses and mounted Abe in one fluid motion. "Thanks for the use of Abe. I'll have him back this afternoon. I'll also bring Sandy in with me if you can spare the room."

"I always got room for that puppy you call a hoss, honey. You be careful now, and I'll be a prayin' for yo daddy." Franks patted her knee and turned back to his forge as she rode out to meet the marshal, leading a second horse.

His eyes narrowed as Meri rode up to him and handed him a set of reins. He ignored them and shoved his hat back as he looked up at her. "Aren't you supposed to be at the Kilburns' waiting for me to return with a buggy?"

Chapter Four

"We can get to the ranch quicker this way. That is, if you'll quit standing there asking pointless questions and get on the horse." Meri tossed the ignored reins at him.

He snatched them neatly out of the air, his hazel eyes never wavering from her face. "How did you get here so fast?"

"I know a shortcut. Can we go now? Daylight's wasting." She was growing a little nervous under his scrutiny.

"Is it that you naturally don't like to follow orders…"

"You didn't issue an order. You only said you'd be back with the buggy. I decided this would be quicker." Meri's lips twitched in a nervous half grin.

"…or that you didn't want to ride in the buggy with me?" He continued as if the interruption hadn't happened.

Meri felt heat stain her cheeks at the accuracy of his guess, and a crooked grin began to spread across his face. "Standing around talking won't get us to the ranch," she blurted, and touched Abe. The horse jumped away from the grinning man into a ground-eating trot.

Glancing back, she saw him leap into his saddle without benefit of the stirrup and spring after her. Controlling the urge to race home, Meri kept the big black gelding at a respectful trot as she rode along the pasture fence to the outskirts of town and Little Creek Bridge. Maybe she *should* have stayed put and waited on the marshal and the buggy. It would have spared her the embarrassment of his accurate guess. Then again, this way she could get away from him for a minute, even if it didn't last long. She peered over her shoulder again. He was staying back, though he'd probably catch up to her once they were on the trail out of town, but it would be enough time for her cheeks to cool.

Abe's hooves thudded across the planks of the bridge spanning Little Creek, the clear-running stream that lent the town its name and marked its western boundary. Meri drew a deep breath. Dr. Kilburn was right. She *had* needed to get away and clear her head, and a horseback ride to her beloved home was the perfect way to do that even if she did have to put up with the meddlesome marshal.

"I thought I had a squirrel in that hole." Apparently he wasn't going to let her ignore the fact he'd guessed her real reason for riding horseback.

She felt her cheeks heat again at his satisfied tone. So much for having time for her blush to fade. If this kept up, she'd just have to get used to the sensation of her face being on fire.

Or…she could…

Meri flexed her heels against Abe's ribs, and the gelding switched to the rocking-chair lope that temporarily carried her away from her tormentor. The escape didn't last long. Franks had provided the marshal with a horse every bit Abe's equal, and in minutes the horses were side by side. The road wasn't in good enough shape from the recent deep mud to indulge in a full-out gallop, so Meri contented herself with the current pace and the wind in her face, thankful when the marshal remained silent.

The fresh pine-and-cedar-scented breeze began to weave calming fingers through Meri's hair as the beautiful scenery slipped past. Some of the tension melted from her shoulders, and the silence grew less uncomfortable in spite of feeling his eyes on her from time to time.

When he spoke, his comment caught her off guard. "I was sorry to hear about your mother."

Meri looked at him, but for a change, he wasn't looking at her. Somehow that made it easier to answer him. "How did you know?"

"Some of the men on the posse mentioned it—said it hadn't quite been a year since her death?"

Meri felt the weight of guilt and grief crash back down as she nodded. Her father had teased her on the way to Little Creek that her mother would have scolded her for wearing riding attire instead of a dress since she was going into town in a buggy. The words had reminded Meri of their loss, and she'd snapped that her mother wasn't around anymore.

She'd immediately regretted it. Instead of apologizing, however, she'd sulked, not understanding how less than a year after her mother's death, her father could tease about her mother's memory and seem to be handling her death so much better than Meri was. How she wished she'd guarded her tongue that day. She'd not apologized, and now it might be too late.

"What was her name?"

Meri welcomed his interruption of her depressing thoughts. "Catriona."

"So, both of your parents were from Scotland?" He was watching the passing landscape as if memorizing every detail.

"Why did you say Scotland? Most people guess Ireland."

He looked at her then. "My name *is* Cameron. My grandparents came from Scotland. I recognize the brogue."

"I don't have a brogue."

"You do when you say *faither,* and I'd be willing to guess you used the Gaelic *mither* instead of *mother.*"

Meri nodded. "They came to America before I was born so their accent had softened, but when I was little they used a lot of Gaelic." A memory surfaced. "I did have a brogue by the time there was an actual school to attend. I remember the kids teasing me because they thought I was hard to understand. I worked hard to sound more like them, but I never quit using *mither* and *faither* to address my parents." She cocked her head. "I had forgotten about that."

Their horses topped a rise, and below them lay the McIsaac ranch nestled among the foothills of the Rockies. Marshal Cameron pulled his mount up, and Meri followed suit as they gave their horses a breather from the hour-long, gradually climbing ride and surveyed the property below them.

A large log ranch house was surrounded by orderly, well-kept outbuildings that included a couple of barns, a bunkhouse, a summer kitchen, a smokehouse and sundry smaller buildings. White fencing encircled a pretty garden already showing the effects of early springtime planting, and corrals housed horses and a few cattle. Empty pastures and hay fields radiated out from the ranch buildings and disappeared into trees and over foothills.

"So, this is home."

Meri nodded. "Beautiful, isn't it?"

"Absolutely." Silence reigned a few moments as both riders drank in the scene below them. "I do have a question, though." A puzzled look sat on his face.

Meri was becoming wary of his questions but was curious about the cause of the expression. "What?"

Marshal Cameron pointed toward the barn corrals. "What in the world is that…critter?"

A spontaneous laugh burst from Meri's lips when she looked in the direction he indicated. "Those are Highland cattle from Scotland. Faither imported them several years ago. They come from the mountainous region, and their thick wooly coats make them quite hardy in our cold snowy winters. Several ranches around Colorado raise them. There's even talk about starting a breed association. They're very self-sufficient cattle and thrive on the grazing that we have here. They're also easy to work with because they're so friendly."

"Well, it certainly is the hairiest beast I've ever seen, outside of a buffalo." He was watching Meri closely, a peculiar, distracted look on his face.

"And what have you ever seen *inside* a buffalo?" Meri kept a straight face but couldn't resist the question.

"What?"

A chuckle escaped her. "Never mind."

The dreaded smirk reappeared, and his searching gaze never left her face. "Oh, I got it. You…just surprised me. I didn't realize you were—"

He broke off abruptly. Meri wondered what he'd intended to say, but a distant shout prevented her from asking. Meri waved at a figure standing in front of the biggest barn.

"Come on. I'll introduce you to our foreman. He can answer any questions you have about the men and our horses."

Wyatt followed Miss McIsaac the rest of the way down to the ranch yard, enjoying his view of the spunky lady. So, this was the woman Mrs. Van Deusen wanted to introduce him to at the church picnic. Her full rich laugh and the way her face had lit up as she'd explained the cattle had nearly made him blurt the realization aloud. He had managed to catch himself, thankful for the distraction of the ranch hand's shout that had prevented Miss McIsaac from asking the question he'd seen on her face.

When he'd arrived in town, his bachelor status instantly made him the most popular person for invitations to a meal to meet someone's daughter, or niece, or sister or granddaughter. He'd quickly started turning a politely deaf ear when the conversation changed to, "Oh, I have someone you just have to meet…"

Mrs. Van Deusen had been somewhat more subtle but just as persistent. She never mentioned names or invited him to a meal to meet some female, but she'd mentioned her dear departed friend's lovely daughter every time Wyatt happened to cross her path. He'd let the hints go in one ear and out the other, but as he'd looked down at the ranch a moment ago, Mrs. Van Deusen's voice had echoed through his memory.

"If they can get in from their ranch," Mrs. Van Deusen had said, "they raise those strange cattle from Ireland or Scotland or someplace foreign like that, you know—I'll finally be able to introduce you to her at the church picnic."

That tidbit had snagged his attention since his own family tree originated in Scotland, but that was the extent of the notice he'd taken of it at the time. With the disturbance of the holdup, he'd not had time to realize Mrs. Van Deusen's hints added up to the spirited, rides-like-the-wind Meri McIsaac. After the onslaught of gushing, flirting females breathing down his neck the past few weeks, Miss McIsaac's prickly reaction had been a fresh change and had actually snagged his attention. Not that he planned to do anything about it; he still had a dangerous job and no home to offer a woman.

Wyatt mentally scoffed at himself. Even if *he* were willing to think about going along with Mrs. Van Deusen's schemes, he was quite sure her quarry had no intention of being caught. Besides, he had enough trouble on his hands trying to catch a bank robber and find the missing money.

"Howdy, miss, how's the Boss man?" A familiar voice cut through Wyatt's musings.

"Still unconscious. I came to pick up a few things and get an update on the ranch. Faither will want to know when he wakes up. Where's Barnaby?" Miss McIsaac kept her voice brisk and businesslike, but Wyatt heard the underlying fear.

"He's riding range with a couple of the boys, said he might be back for lunch."

"This is the new marshal. He needs to ask Barnaby some questions. He seems to think the horse the bank robber rode was one of ours." Miss McIsaac and Wyatt dismounted simultaneously. "Marshal Cameron, our top hand, Jonah Chacksfield."

"There's no need to introduce us, miss. I've known Captain Cameron since he was a lowly shavetail lieutenant fresh from the East." Jonah snapped a sharp salute.

"At ease, Sergeant." Wyatt put out his hand and grabbed the man's burly paw in a hearty handshake. "It's good to see you. What are you doing out of the army? You were one of the best sergeants I ever served with, figured you'd be in uniform until you got too old to climb into a saddle."

The stocky barrel-chested ranch hand looked away momentarily. When he looked back, Wyatt thought he saw a sheen of wetness in the man's eyes. "I just didn't have the heart to reenlist after my Sally passed."

Wyatt gripped the sergeant's shoulder and cleared his throat against a sudden hoarseness. "I wondered why I quit getting letters from her. I assumed you'd been transferred, and they were getting lost." He stopped and swallowed hard. "She was a quite a lady. I'll miss her."

Jonah was the first to break the silence that shrouded the little group, saying gruffly, "Now, sir, what's this about one of our horses being used in the bank job?"

"Drop that 'sir' stuff, and call me Wyatt. When I questioned the banker this morning, he said the horse the thief used wore the McIsaac brand. None of the other witnesses I talked to mentioned that. Maybe they assumed Mr. McIsaac had ridden in on that horse and the thief stole it. However, since that wasn't the case,

I need to know if you've noticed any horses missing and where all the ranch hands were that day."

"I told you before, none of our hands would be involved in anything criminal." Miss McIsaac flared up again.

Jonah wrapped a beefy arm around Miss McIsaac's shoulders and gently squeezed. "He's just doing his job, Miss Meri. No need to get upset about it. You've got enough on your plate. Let me and Barnaby handle the captain and his questions. You go in and chat with Ms. Maggie. That housekeeper's been frettin' around here for days like a hen that's lost her chicks."

Wyatt waited for the inevitable argument, but her shoulders drooped as she exhaled noisily. "You'll let me know if anything's wrong, and send Barnaby to see me when he comes in." It wasn't a question.

"I will. Now go let Ms. Maggie fuss over you for a bit." Jonah gently turned Miss McIsaac toward the house and gave her a gentle push. "Scat."

Wyatt watched in amazement as Miss McIsaac meekly walked to the house and disappeared inside. "I've seen you wrangle raw, rowdy recruits and turn them into well-disciplined troops, but until today I never fully appreciated the extent of your skill." Wyatt looked at Jonah with newfound respect. "How exactly did you manage that?"

Jonah's hearty laugh thundered out. "She's a handful, but I'll take a strong, opinionated female over a silly, pampered flibbertigibbet any day of the week."

"As will I, but that doesn't explain how you managed to get her to go so quietly."

"A good sergeant never reveals his secrets, Captain. Besides, I have a hunch you'll figure out how to handle her. Half the fun of courting my Sally was figuring out how to deal with her strong temperament."

"Sorry to disappoint you, but a lawman's life doesn't leave room for courtin'."

"Are you still stuck on the notion you have to have a 'safe' job before you can have a wife?"

"It's not a notion. I saw more than one bride-to-be hightail it back East when she saw her future living quarters. I saw wives leave their husbands because they couldn't handle the long absences, and I saw women devastated when their husband rode in draped over the back of a horse. I won't do that to a woman."

"You saw a couple of bad examples and focused on them instead of the good ones. What about my Sally?" Jonah sounded a bit offended.

Wyatt hurried to soften his remarks. "You were the exemption to the rule. Sally was special."

Memories glistened in the tough old sergeant's eyes. "That she was, that she was."

Wyatt changed the subject. "Back to the reason I rode out here—what do you have to tell me that you didn't want Miss McIsaac to hear?"

"You always were one of the sharper knives among that lot of army brass. We *did* have a horse go missing for several days before showing up among some of our cattle all covered in dried sweat. I don't want Miss Meri to be worryin' about it just now since there's nothing she can do. I've questioned all our hands, but no one noticed anything unusual, and I trust our men. We've got a few who can be a little wild occasionally, but they're all honest fellows. Mr. McIsaac has given all of us a hand up when we were down on our luck, and not a one of us would do anything to hurt him or Miss Meri."

"Are any of the men available that I can talk with them?"

"Barnaby, our foreman, and most of the hands are out doing various chores. If you're hungry, we can grab a sandwich from our cook, and I'll introduce you to the ones in for lunch. Barnaby should be back in as well, and you can ask 'em any questions you have. Afterward, I'll take you out and show you where we found that horse."

"I'd appreciate that."

Over lunch Wyatt met the handful of cowboys that assembled for food. None of them knew anything more than what Jonah had already told him, and to a man, they had nothing but concern and well wishes for their wounded "Boss man."

When everyone drifted back to their various tasks, Jonah brought up a couple of fresh, saddled horses. "Ready to ride, Captain? Barnaby hasn't made it back, but I'll wager we'll run across him before we return to the ranch."

Wyatt mounted the horse. "You've probably told me as much as he can, but I'd appreciate getting a chance to meet him. And I thought I told you to call me Wyatt?"

"Too many years in the army. Captain comes easier to the tongue."

Jonah led the way across the ranch yard, and as they passed the main house Miss McIsaac stepped out on the porch. "Hold up! I'm going with you," she called out.

"No. Stay put. Jonah's going to show me around, let me get a feel for the land out this way and maybe catch up with your foreman. I'll be back to escort you to town before it gets dark." Wyatt lifted his hat and loped his horse away, ignoring the protests from the woman on the porch and Jonah's sardonic snort.

Chapter Five

Jonah waved a hand toward the land in front of them. "This is where we found that horse day before yesterday. He'd been ridden hard and still had the dried sweat, saddle and spur marks to show for it. Made the boys livid. Not only had someone stolen one of our remuda from under our noses, they also used it badly in the process. Our hands pride themselves that when they *do* use their spurs they do it with such gentle finesse they never leave a mark or a sore spot on the horse.

"I backtracked the rider and found where he'd had a fresh mount waiting. After he'd swapped, he set ours loose. Both sets of tracks led into and out of that churned-up ground where the trail herd circled town a few days ago."

Wyatt nodded. "That's where we lost him when we were tracking him. We caught up with the drovers, but they said they hadn't seen anybody, and we couldn't find where he'd turned off before it started raining."

"He was pretty slick about it. I might not have found it if he hadn't used the same route coming and going from the cattle trail. He used an offshoot of Little Creek to hide his tracks, but he was a little less careful after he swapped horses. I was able spot the signs of his previous trip when I trailed the new horse back. I didn't follow him any farther after he hit that trail— figured we had our horse back and that was the end of it. We let the surrounding ranchers know to keep an eye on their own remudas and left it at that. Never thought about it being connected with what had happened in town."

"The tracks'll be washed out, but show me where you trailed him so I can get an idea of where he was and where we lost him."

"Sure 'nuff. We'll go right through the area Barnaby was plannin' on workin' when he left this morning. If he's still there, we'll stop and chat."

They did meet up with Barnaby and several other hands moving cattle to another area for fresh grazing. Wyatt was impressed with the graying, quiet-spoken man, but again didn't learn anything new. Barnaby promised to keep his men alert to anything that might be of interest to the marshal. He also told Jonah to ride in with Wyatt and stay in town where he could keep an eye on the Boss man and Miss Meri.

The rest of the afternoon passed quickly, and Wyatt got a feel for the land. It was beautiful mountain-valley country, and he was impressed with the way the land was being utilized to its fullest potential. Every time he saw the strange-looking woolly red cattle, the memory of a laugh rang through his thoughts.

The McIsaac ranch lay west and slightly north of Little Creek and the bandit had ridden out of town heading east. The trail herd had bypassed the town on the west before veering northeast toward Denver.

"Do the trail herds always go this direction?" Wyatt asked. "Seems like it'd be shorter to go around the east side of town."

"We don't have as many now that the railroads are getting more accessible, but a few still come around the west side and across a portion of our range because McIsaac allows them access. There are more farmers on the east side now, and they don't appreciate their crops getting torn up. Most of the trail bosses do their best to ensure they do the least amount of damage possible," Jonah replied.

Wyatt studied the land. "When we first lost the tracks, we continued east in the direction he'd been traveling. We followed the trail herd until we caught up to the drovers, then we backtracked and had almost made it to where you're showing me he cut out before it began to rain. If we'd come this direction first, we might have found his trail before it rained and been closer to catching him." Wyatt was frustrated. "Why did he circle back around the town and stay in the area when he knew a posse was after him? Why didn't he get as far away as he could, as fast as he could?"

"Maybe he did. By coming this way, he did the unexpected and bought himself more time," Jonah mused.

"This is *definitely* not an auspicious beginning to my job as Little Creek's marshal, and if I don't catch him and get the bank's money back, it'll be a very short-lived job. The good citizens are understandably nervous about that money," Wyatt groaned.

"Well, there is someone we can talk to who'll be

able to point us in the direction we need to go for you to catch him," Jonah said, turning his horse to face Wyatt.

"Who?" Curiosity filled Wyatt's voice.

"Him." Jonah glanced up briefly before bowing his head, and Wyatt felt peace descend and frustration melt away as he listened to the former master sergeant bend his knee before the Master of Heaven, asking for God's wisdom and guidance in the task before the marshal.

He echoed the prayer in his heart and uttered a hearty Amen when Jonah finished. "Thank you for realigning my perspective, Sergeant. You were always good at that, if I recall."

"I did straighten out a few smart-mouthed lieutenants in my time. Although I must say, I had less polishing to do on you then some I ran across. Your mother'd done a pretty good job already." Both men chuckled as they headed back.

Riding into the ranch yard, Wyatt cast a glance at the lowering sun. "Miss McIsaac is going to be champing at the bit to get back into town."

"If she hasn't already left." Jonah grinned.

"I told her to wait—that I'd ride back with her. I don't want her, any woman, out on these roads alone, at least until we catch this fella."

Jonah snorted. "I'll be much surprised if she waited around more than a few minutes after you threw that order at her."

"Why didn't you say something earlier? Stop her from going in alone?"

"Figured it was about time you learned you can't bark orders at a woman as if she's a soldier. It just don't work. Besides, Boss man has a standing order. When someone sees her ride out, which is frequently, they are to let the bunkhouse cook or Ms. Maggie know and then follow Meri to make sure no one bothers her. Boss man couldn't cure her of riding alone, something he loves to do himself, so he makes sure someone is always keeping an eye on her. I think she figured out his little scheme a long time ago, but as long as they stay out of her way, she tolerates it."

The men stopped their horses in front of the main house and a sturdy, dusky-skinned woman, black braids wound in bands around her head, stepped onto the porch carrying a tray with a pitcher and several glasses. "Thirsty? I have fresh lemonade here," she said in a lightly accented voice.

"Yes'm, Ms. Maggie! Sounds great! Captain Cameron, meet the real ramrod of the McIsaac ranch, Maggie Running Deer, the McIsaac's housekeeper." Jonah took the tray and set it on a table between several comfortable-looking rocking chairs. "Ms. Maggie, the new marshal of Little Creek."

Wyatt doffed his hat and bowed slightly to the woman. "Nice to meet you, ma'am. Is Miss McIsaac ready to head back to town?" He took the glass of lemonade Jonah handed him and swallowed half of it in a single swallow, choking when he heard the woman's answer.

"She left a couple of hours after you rode out. Barnaby rode in, and after talking with him, she tossed a bag on Abe and took him and Sandy back to town."

A sly grin appeared on Jonah's face, but he refrained from saying *I told you so.*

Wyatt hastily swallowed the last of the tangy drink

before setting the glass down. "Thank you, Ms. Maggie. That hit the spot."

"Sit down, Captain, and take a load off." Jonah disposed of his own glass. "I've got to put a few things in my saddlebags before we head to town." Thanking Ms. Maggie, he headed for the barn leading the two horses.

Wyatt quelled the urge to rush back to town and slowly sat down. Miss McIsaac had, by now, probably already arrived back in town, but his hands itched to give her a good shaking—the little scamp. Instead he controlled his impatience and accepted the refilled glass Ms. Maggie handed him before heading back to her baking.

One of the cowhands he had met earlier ambled up leading the horse he'd ridden from town, along with another saddled horse, and tied them to the rail in front of the house. "Jonah'll be 'long direc'ly." The man sauntered away.

The minutes dragged by as he gazed unseeingly at the tidy ranch yard, fingers drumming on the arm of the rocker. Flower beds sported a few early delicate blooms, a kitchen garden boasted rows of emerging greenery, and neat fences spread out and away, delineating pasturage. All lent a well-cared-for air to the place, yet they failed to register beyond a vague awareness as Wyatt turned the day over in his mind. He needed to separate the few pieces he'd found and examine them thoroughly; see if, and where, each piece fit into the puzzle of the bank robbery.

"You gonna sit staring into space all day, or do you want to ride in with me?" Jonah laughed at his blink of surprise when he looked up to see the sergeant already mounted.

Wyatt hurried off the porch and swung into the saddle. "Don't get uppity, Sergeant, or I'll put you on report!"

Jonah's laugh rang as they turned their horses toward town.

Meri imagined the look on the marshal's face when he realized she was gone, and grinned. She'd eaten lunch while Ms. Maggie fussed about the holdup and Boss man's injury and had just finished packing a bag when she'd seen the marshal and Jonah riding out. Planning to ride with them and speak to Barnaby herself, she'd instead been ordered to stay put. She'd tried to argue they could get back to town quicker if they combined their tasks but had been completely ignored as the overbearing man had ridden away at a lope. She'd nearly gone back to town then and there but had curtailed the impulse. The job she'd left her wounded father's side to do wouldn't be completed to her satisfaction until she'd spoken with Barnaby.

Time had crawled as she'd prowled the barns and grounds, repeatedly answering the question, "How's Boss man?" from worried ranch hands who wanted the information straight from her. Impatience had finally gotten the best of her, and she'd been saddling Sandy to go find the foreman herself when he'd ridden in. Having already heard the latest update on McIsaac from Jonah and the marshal, Barnaby had quickly filled her in on ranch happenings. He had things well in hand and had promised to send a rider in frequently with news of the ranch and to check on Boss man. Faither would be pleased, but not surprised, at Barnaby's capable management in their absence.

Thanking him for his diligent care of the ranch, she'd tied her bag to Abe's saddle, shoved her .44-40 Winchester carbine into the rifle boot, mounted Sandy and left the annoying marshal to fend for himself. The nerve-rattling tension was absent on this leg of the journey, and Meri smugly congratulated herself on getting back to town on her own terms. She shoved away the ridiculous notion that the trip seemed rather dull in comparison to the ride to the ranch.

Heavenly Father, please heal Faither so we can return home and life can get back to normal...without that bossy marshal.

The silent prayer evaporated before she finished, and the peace she'd tasted earlier was nowhere to be found. All the joy she normally experienced when riding her lovely palomino failed to materialize, and even the satisfaction at having outsmarted a certain lawman tasted stale.

The unexpectedly disappointing ride finally neared the end, and Meri breathed a sigh of relief as she approached the edge of town. Pausing, she heard echoing hoofbeats behind her. Spying a suitable hiding place in the brush alongside the road, she situated herself and Sandy, tied Abe's lead rope around his neck and tapped his hip to send him on down the road. She was rewarded shortly when the cowboy who'd been surreptitiously following her rode into view. He pulled his horse up short when he saw Abe grazing along the roadside alone. He glanced around suspiciously.

"You can head home now, Shorty. Tell Barnaby and Ms. Maggie I made it to town in one piece," she said dryly, nudging Sandy out of hiding.

Shorty touched the brim of his hat and turned his horse, a sheepish smile at being caught on his face.

Meri grinned at him. It had become a game to see if she could spot the rider tailing her. Some were better at staying hidden then others, but she knew someone was always within earshot on her "solitary" rides.

There had been Indian trouble in several areas of the newly formed state, but they hadn't had a problem in this area for many years. She felt so safe on the ranch, she often forgot she lived in what Easterners called the "Wild" West and took off alone on Sandy. Her father allowed this, as she was always armed, but quietly arranged for additional protection. Meri suspected her father, himself, followed her from time to time and was one of the riders she felt but never saw or caught.

Faither.

Her throat ached with a sudden tightness as she remembered him lying so still, blood pooling on the bank floor. She couldn't handle losing him, too.

Meri turned her head in the direction of the cemetery where her mother's body lay. The burial ground sprawled along a high slope a little over a half a mile from the western edge of town, out of danger of any floodwaters from Little Creek.

Retrieving the happily grazing Abe, Meri detoured and headed that direction. She'd not been back to her mother's grave since the funeral. She knew only the shell of the loving wife and mother was there, but the loss seemed so bitterly final there that Meri only wanted to avoid it. The cemetery represented nothing but death and heartache to her.

She missed her mother so much she physically

ached sometimes. She missed her hugs, her laugh. She missed the way her mother would lovingly call her by her full name—America Catriona. She didn't need a cold gray headstone to reinforce her loss.

Today, however, she forced herself to keep riding toward it. She should at least check on her mother's plot. Then when Faither awoke, she'd be able to tell him she'd checked on the ranch *and* Mother.

Nearing the graveyard, she noticed movement between the tree line bordering the top edge of the cemetery and a ridiculously ornate crypt. Meri halted Sandy. The crypt was the local oddity, having been built by an eccentric miner who'd struck it rich. He'd resided around Little Creek long enough to see it completed before moving on to follow rumors of another gold strike and leaving the empty, imported-marble monstrosity looking disdainfully down upon meager creek-stone or wooden markers. Two marble lions guarded the door of the vault, but they proved inadequate protection against curiosity seekers and mischievous boys.

Meri fully expected to see a couple of those boys now, but instead, Mr. Samuels appeared around the side of it, head down, walking slowly. She felt her eyes widen in surprise. He hadn't been out and about much since the theft at the bank, owing to his own head injury, and he must have walked because she didn't see his buggy anywhere. Why was he wandering around up there anyway? His wife's grave plot was down near the front of the cemetery not far from her mother's plot. Had the blow to his head left him a little confused?

He glanced up, saw her and flinched as if startled.

Meri lifted her hand to wave, but he ducked his head and scurried down the slope of the graveyard. Reaching his wife's grave, he knelt, turning his back to her.

Meri felt for him. She understood how it was when someone intruded on your private grief and quietly turned the horses away from the cemetery with a sense of relief for the reprieve. She could always come back later when she wouldn't be interrupting anyone, and she really needed to get the horses tended to and return to Faither. She'd been gone far too long already.

Several minutes later Meri dismounted in front of Dr. Kilburn's and looped the reins around the hitching post. Taking her satchel off Abe, she saw a tall boy walking toward her. "Billy?"

"Yes, ma'am?"

"Are you available to run an errand for me?"

"Yup, I was keepin' a lookout for ya. I'm to let Mrs. Van Deusen know when you get back here 'cause she's gonna bring you a plate of supper, and she'll give me my choice of candy next time I'm in the store." Billy nodded, grinning. "I reckon I kin do that when I run your errand."

Meri grinned in response to Billy's freckled, friendly one. "Yes, I reckon you can. I'll give you a nickel if you'll walk Sandy and Abe over to Franks's, and tell him I'll come see him as soon as I can."

"Yes, ma'am! I'll take real good care of 'em! And Mrs. Van Deusen'll bring you a real nice supper when I tell 'er you're back." Billy's grin stretched even wider as Meri placed the promised nickel in the grimy outstretched hand.

"By the way, why is Mrs. Van Deusen bringing me supper?" Meri asked.

"On account a Mrs. Kilburn havin' to sit with some-body who's sick, I guess. Mrs. Van Deusen said she'd take care of you and Doc this evenin'." Billy carefully untied Abe and Sandy.

Meri took her bag and slid her carbine out of the saddle scabbard, stepped back and watched as the lanky adolescent proudly led the two steeds down the middle of the road, whistling and calculating whether to spend or save the precious nickel.

"I'm glad you're back so soon, Meri," Dr. Kilburn said gravely as he opened the front door and waved Meri inside.

Meri's heart lurched in fear. "Faither?"

"He's taken a turn for the worse." His tone was sober and regretful.

If Dr. Kilburn was worried, it must be bad. Fear swallowed Meri. This couldn't be happening. Not again!

She ran for the room where her father lay. Reaching for the door handle, she stared at her full hands. She'd forgotten she was still carrying her bag and carbine. Her frantic brain wasn't able to coordinate the task of setting down the items to turn the knob.

Doc reached around her and opened the door before gently relieving her of the items. Meri hastened over and collapsed to her knees at the edge of the bed. Her father looked so much worse since just this morning. His breathing was labored, his skin flushed and damp with perspiration and creases slashed across his drawn face in cruel lines.

It was only a bump on the head and a slight wound! People recovered from worse. Why wasn't her father recovering? Looking up at Doc, she croaked, "Why…?"

Doc seemed to understand what she couldn't voice. "He's fighting infection in that bullet wound, and his fever is rising. He's not responding to anything I've given him."

A soft tap sounded on the door frame, and Pastor Willis stepped into the room. "I stopped to check on Ian."

Doc repeated what he'd told Meri. As he finished speaking, Pastor Willis dropped to his knees alongside Meri and placed his hand on McIsaac's shoulder. Speaking quietly, he prayed aloud for healing and restoration, wisdom for Doc and peace for Meri. When he finished, he turned to her. "Is there anything I or the church members can do for you besides keeping people informed and praying?"

Meri shook her head then stopped as an idea pierced through the fog in her brain. "Uh, maybe. Do you remember the sermon you preached once about calling for the elders of the church?"

"Yes, I do—James 5:14 and 15. 'Is any sick among you? let him call for the elders of the church; and let them pray over him, anointing him with oil in the name of the Lord: And the prayer of faith shall save the sick, and the Lord shall raise him up…'"

"That's the one. Would you do that for Faither?"

"Of course, dear. All you had to do was ask. I'll go notify the men of the church and bring them back here as quickly as possible." Pastor Willis patted Meri on the hand, pushed himself to his feet and left the room.

"Is there anything I can do to help Faither while we wait?"

"I'll get some fresh water, and you can sponge his face and neck to give him some relief from the fever.

That's what I was doing when I heard you arrive." Picking up a basin and wet cloth from the bedside stand, he left the room.

Meri dropped her face into her hands. Fear sat so heavy on her chest it was difficult to draw a breath, and she trembled all over. Her heart labored with hard, painful thuds. She couldn't have stood to her feet if she were forced at the point of a gun.

A gun.

The nasty urge to find the man who'd injured her father swept over Meri in a black rage. Oh, how she wanted to hurt the man who'd done this! Do to him what he'd done to her father! Anger surged through her temporarily replacing fear, and Meri shot to her feet as Dr. Kilburn reentered the room carrying a fresh cloth and basin of water.

"Here, keep your hands busy and your father a little cooler."

Meri moved to do his bidding, tenderly wiping her father's face repeatedly with the cool wet cloth while chewing on the anger raging through her and envisioning what she would do when she got her hands on the person who had caused her father's injury.

It was some time before she paid any attention to the quiet nudging in her spirit to pray, to forgive, and when she did, she couldn't push any words past her clenched teeth or her even tighter heart. The man who did this didn't deserve to be forgiven, her emotions argued.

Giving up the halfhearted struggle, anger and fear once again vied for dominance, and the bitter ache that had resided in her heart since her mother's death shaped itself into a hard, defiant, angry knot.

Meri lost track of time and jumped when she heard

subdued voices and multiple feet entering the house. Laying aside the wet cloth and grabbing a nearby towel, she hastily dried her hands, smoothed back her hair and straightened her clothes. She wished she'd taken a moment to change into fresh attire, but she was out of time. A knock sounded, and she stiffened her spine and took a deep breath before stepping to the door to open it.

Pastor Willis entered the room followed by six more men, all showing signs of having recently and hastily washed up from their day's labors. The men included Mr. Benhard, the Western Union agent; Mr. Allen, the surveyor; Mr. Gumperston, owner of the café; Mr. Hubert, the barber; Mr. Van Deusen and Franks. All were members and elders of Little Creek Baptist Church, and hearing the clock chime from the parlor, Meri realized that these men, in all probability, had delayed their supper by coming to pray for her father. The knot in her chest softened just a bit at this display of concern and care for him, and she struggled to swallow past the lump that blocked her throat.

Dr. Kilburn was last through the door, behind the solemn little troop, and ushered Meri through the now-crowded room to seat her in the rocker. Pastor Willis stood at the end of the bed and pulled a small Bible out of the pocket of his black frock coat. After flipping through the pages, he stopped and read aloud the passage from James 5 before asking the assembled men to take turns praying.

Closing her eyes, Meri listened to the humble prayers. Men she had been acquainted with only in a cursory way through church and town activities now knelt at the Throne of Grace asking for healing for their Brother in Christ. Men like Mr. Van Deusen who never spoke more than a few words at a time poured out their hearts to God as they prayed for her father. Their fervent requests made the small room ring, and the simple eloquence of their prayers further loosened the knot that had formed in her chest.

When Franks stepped up to pray, Meri's eyes startled open, and her gaze flew to his face when he mentioned her. "Father God, I ask in faith, dat you heal Brother Ian, dat you raise 'im up from dis bed a sickness. And Father, I ask dat you heal Miss Meri from de hurt a losin' her Mama, and dat you give her de abil'ty to forgive de man dat did dis crime. I ask dis in de precious, holy name ob Jesus!"

How had Franks known she was struggling with forgiveness? She hadn't realized it herself until moments before the men had arrived. Meri forced her eyes shut as Pastor Willis began to pray and wrap up the solemn little service. He reiterated the requests for the full recovery of Mr. McIsaac and for peace, grace and the ability to forgive for Meri, and finished by thanking God for his promise of healing and for the willingness of the gathered men to humble themselves in prayer for Ian McIsaac.

Meri stood and moved around the end of the bed at the gruffly chorused Amen and watched as the men surreptitiously wiped at their eyes. Her own eyes were dry, but her throat was painfully tight as she tried to express her thanks to men who, one by one, came up to her, shook her hand and thanked *her* for the opportunity to help, to pray.

Pastor Willis urged Meri to let him know when there was any change or any further way he could be of service, and then he exited the room behind the men, leaving Doc and Franks with Meri. Doc leaned over and checked on Ian, and Franks reached down to draw Meri into a gentle hug. How she wished she could give in to the desperate urge to cry. Her eyes and throat burned but no relief of tears came. She heaved a dry, sobbing sigh.

"Hush now, chil'. I know you is hurtin', maybe wurse den yo' pa, but our God'll heal you, if you let 'im. Jis as surely as de sun rise in de mornin'. You jis place yo' faith in His promise!"

Chapter Six

Meri forced her aching eyes open. It had been a long night of no rest as she'd kept vigil, bathing her father's feverish face repeatedly. Mrs. Van Deusen had delivered supper and given Meri a chance to wash up, change clothes and eat, and then had insisted on staying the rest of the night. Meri had tried to dissuade her, dreading the woman's chatter, but Mrs. Van Deusen had refused to leave. To Meri's grateful surprise, however, the shopkeeper had seemed to realize Meri was near the end of her rope and had merely added her quiet prayer to those still echoing in the room before pulling out her knitting.

In the early-morning hours her father's fever had broken, his breathing had grown easier and Dr. Kilburn had declared the immediate crisis over. Mrs. Van Deusen had dozed off and on during the long night and had ordered Meri and Doc to their rooms for some rest, promising to wake them if there were any changes. Stumbling to a spare room, Meri had collapsed on the bed fully clothed, asleep as soon as her head hit the pillow.

Now, trying to focus her weary eyes on the small clock on the bedside table, she was surprised to see it was after nine o'clock. She'd slept the morning away. Sitting up, she tossed aside the blanket someone had laid over her and moved to the dressing table. Fresh water was in the pitcher, and she gratefully splashed the cool liquid on her face before brushing her hair and pulling it off her face in a hasty braid. Changing into a fresh skirt and blouse, she hurried to her father's room.

Dr. Kilburn looked up from his examination of her father as she came in.

"Has his fever come back?" she asked fearfully.

"No." Doc's voice was hushed and held a strange note. "In fact, if I hadn't seen it yesterday, I wouldn't believe he ever had a crisis."

"What do you mean?" Meri asked in confusion.

"I mean there is absolutely no sign of infection, the wound is clear and healing well, there's no hint of fever, his color has improved and his breathing and pulse are all normal for someone who's just asleep." Doc moved to the nearby basin and washed his hands, muttering under his breath. "We asked God to intervene yesterday, but I guess I didn't expect it to happen so fast. I claim to have faith, but..." Doc shook his head, a rueful expression on his face.

"I don't understand. If he's better, why is he still unconscious?"

"Your father was in a coma from the head injury and then had complications from the infection. Today the infection is gone, the lump from the blow to the head is nearly gone, the symptoms that indicate a coma are gone, and he's responding to stimuli. Your father exhibits all the signs of a man who is simply sleeping."

"Then why don't you wake him up?" Meri whispered in frustration.

"He stirred some during my examination but didn't wake completely. Sleep is healing to the body, and I'd like him to wake on his own."

Taking her by the arm, he ushered her out of the room, gently closing the door. In the kitchen he poured two cups of coffee. Handing one to Meri, he sat down, took a sip of the steaming brew and heaved a huge sigh of satisfaction. "My wife should be home shortly since the patient she was watching last night is on the mend, and with your father looking so much better, I'm feeling quite the successful practitioner this morning." He chuckled. "I don't think I had all that much to do with any of it, though. A greater Physician than I has been at work this morning."

Meri tentatively sipped the bitter drink and hid a grimace. She really didn't like the stuff, but maybe it would wake her up since she seemed to be walking through a dream. As the liquid hit her empty stomach, it growled loudly in protest. "Excuse me!"

"No. Excuse me. I forgot to tell you breakfast is waiting for you at Naoma's. She left early this morning after I returned from checking on my other patients. We let you sleep as long as you wanted. You are under doctor's orders to get some fresh air, stretch your legs and have a hearty breakfast."

"What about your breakfast, and Faither—I need to be here when he wakes up."

"I had a lovely breakfast with my wife when I checked on her and her patient, and you sitting around waiting for your father to wake up won't change things or hurry them along. I don't want you as a patient, too, so follow my prescription and go get some hot breakfast."

"But what if he wakes up while I'm gone?"

"I'll be right here, and he'll still be here when you return. You're only going to Naoma's, not around the world. You'll be back before you know it. But don't run there and back. Walk."

Feeling her stomach rumble again, Meri took his advice, and after checking to see that her father was still asleep, she walked toward Thomas and Naoma Van Deusen's home.

"Well, good morning. I wondered where you were hiding." The marshal's voice rang out, startling her and causing a couple of passersby to turn and look at the man walking toward her.

"I wasn't hiding, but maybe I should have." A grin lit the marshal's face at her feisty reply, and she fought the unexpected urge to grin right back. *No,* she warned herself. *Don't encourage him.*

"I saw Doc when he did his rounds earlier. He said your father was doing better. Is he awake yet?" He fell into step alongside her.

She shook her head. "Doc *says* Faither is better, but he hasn't woken up." She winced at the childish whine in her voice, but the fear that Dr. Kilburn might be shielding her… Meri turned to head back. She should not have left her father.

Fingers touched her arm, halting her steps. Almost as soon as she registered the contact, his hand withdrew, and he shoved it into his pocket. "Is Dr. Kilburn a liar?"

"What? No! Of course not." The worry whirling inside her dissipated at the unexpected question.

He parked his free hand on the butt of his pistol. "Because I'm the man to see if you want to file a complaint against him."

The absolute ridiculousness of filing a complaint against Dr. Kilburn caused a rueful grin to tug at her mouth. "And who do I see if I want to file a complaint against you?"

He rubbed at his chin thoughtfully. "Now, I don't rightly know. I've never had anyone complain about me before."

The grin tugged harder, turning up the corners of her mouth as she forced her feet to continue to Mrs. Van Deusen's house. "You are incorrigible."

"Well, thank you, but that's not exactly what I'd call a complaint." His long, easy stride brought him alongside her again as she neared the little cottage tucked behind the mercantile.

Mrs. Van Deusen stepped onto the porch and waved. "Good morning, Marshal. Come in and have some breakfast with Meri."

"No, thank you. I ate at the café this morning."

Meri hid a relieved sigh. The thought of sharing breakfast with him did funny things to her insides.

"That was hours ago. I know because I saw you leaving when I headed home. I have plenty of hot biscuits, sausage and gravy, and I won't take no for an answer."

He shrugged. "Who can refuse an offer like that?" He stepped onto the porch and held the door open for her. "After you."

"Thank you," she said to the marshal. As they entered the kitchen, she turned to Mrs. Van Deusen. "I'm sorry you had to go to all this trouble after being up all night."

"Fiddle-faddle. I left early enough this morning that I had a chance to take a nap after Thomas opened the store. I had just gotten up when I looked out and saw you coming. Now quit apologizing and dig in." She set two steaming plates of food in front of them. "You two keep yourselves company. I, ah, I need to take something to Thomas. He's so absentminded you know."

Meri knew nothing of the kind. Thomas might be quiet and reserved, compared to his voluble wife, but absent-minded he was not. Naoma scurried out the door leaving a painful silence behind her.

"Shall I ask the blessing?" At her nod Wyatt bowed his head and prayed a quick prayer before picking up his fork and digging into the fragrant food on his plate. He ignored the bowed head and pink cheeks on the woman across the table.

She took a halfhearted bite of food, keeping her head down. The food must have sparked her appetite, because after the second bite, she dug in eagerly. When her plate was almost empty, she laid her fork down and leaned back, still avoiding his gaze.

Wyatt stood and gathered his dishes. Since she didn't seem inclined to break the silence, military strategy called for a diversion to end the standoff. "Why did your parents leave Scotland?"

Miss McIsaac dabbed her mouth with her napkin, a feminine move that might have distracted a less disciplined soldier. "They were evicted off the land and put on a boat to Canada during the potato famine."

"How'd they wind up in Colorado?" He placed his

dishes in the tub of soapy water and began to wash them. He didn't want Miss McIsaac to think he was going along with Mrs. Van Deusen's matchmaking scheme, but it was only polite to do the dishes in return for such a fine meal.

"They worked their way down to the States, where I was born, and saved every penny they could. Faither worked as a hired hand, and Mither took in laundry. When they heard about the gold rush, they followed it out here."

"Did they strike it rich?"

"Not in gold. Faither tried panning for gold, but he found he could make more money driving freight wagons of supplies to the miners." She grinned slightly, remembering. "Mither panned more gold dust than Faither ever did."

She should smile more often. Then again, it might be safer for him if she didn't. "What do you mean?"

"Mither took in washing and mending from miners who couldn't or wouldn't do their own. She said she would pan her wash water before dumping it out to collect the gold dust she'd washed from their pockets."

Wyatt chuckled. "Smart woman."

Her smile disappeared. "She was." Her eyes took on a distant look. "I was little, but I remember how tough those years were. They scrimped and saved, and when the Homestead Act was passed, Faither staked his claim on a piece of land he'd seen while hauling freight. For the first time in his life, Faither owned his own piece of ground. He kept driving freight wagons for a while to bring in money, buying a couple head of cattle at a time to stock his ranch. It was slow, but he built a home and solid herd without going into debt.

Later when they modified the Homestead Act, Faither was able to acquire more land. The ranch is nearly a thousand acres now—bigger than the estate their landlord owned in Scotland."

"And stocked with the furriest cows I've ever seen."

Mrs. Van Deusen's return interrupted whatever reply Miss McIsaac might have made. "Aren't you the sweetest man? A marshal who does dishes. I knew I liked you. Our town is so blessed to have been able to get you to fill the position of our marshal."

She picked the remaining dishes off the table and handed them to him to wash, never taking a breath as she turned toward Miss McIsaac. "He resigned his commission in the army and moved back to Virginia when his father died and his mother grew ill. When she died, he came back West and was working down in Texas as a deputy. The first Sunday he was here after arriving to meet with the town council about the position, he came to church services. He has such a lovely voice and sings right out on the hymns. We had him over for lunch that very day. Thomas is on the town council you know. Marshal Cameron won my husband over right away! Now Thomas isn't easily impressed. He reserves judgment on people 'til he's known them awhile. Why, he still hasn't warmed up to Banker Samuels, and we've known him for nearly ten years!"

If he hadn't been so anxious to get out of the kitchen, Wyatt might have been impressed at how long the woman could talk without stopping for air.

"Thank you for the wonderful breakfast, but I really should get back to Faither." Without waiting for an answer, Miss McIsaac hurried to the kitchen door and through the house to the front door. Mrs. Van Deusen followed hot on her heels.

Wyatt took a deep breath and exhaled noisily. Much more of that and he would have been the one blushing.

Mrs. Van Deusen's voice carried through the house. "He's thirty-three, you know."

"Mr. Samuels?" Miss McIsaac sounded as confused as Wyatt felt. He swiped his rag over the last dish. He had better make good his own escape before the woman returned.

"No, dear. Marshal Cameron. He's never been married, and you two are so close in age."

"I'm not thirty yet, Mrs. Van Deusen!" Miss McIsaac's voice was growing fainter.

"You're not? Hmm… I thought you were. Oh, well, you're not very far from it. Goodbye, dear."

Wyatt dried his hands on a towel. Dishes or no dishes, it was time to retreat before the matchmaker returned and trained her guns on him. He strode to the open front door. Miss McIsaac was nearly running in her attempt to put distance between her and Mrs. Van Deusen. He would have laughed if he hadn't been so impatient to escape himself.

"Marshal?" Mrs. Van Deusen turned to reenter the house and nearly ran him over. "Oh, there you are. You aren't going to let her traipse all the way back to Doc's by herself, are you?"

"No, ma'am. Thanks for the meal." He sidestepped her and hurried down the steps to follow the other fleeing victim of the matchmaker's ambush.

He tried to keep his retreat dignified but quickly realized he would have to hustle to catch Miss McIsaac. She might be shorter by almost half a foot, but she could sure cover some distance when she wanted. She had passed the mercantile, the newspaper office and the hotel, and was nearing the barbershop when Jonah exited it and called out to her.

She stopped, giving Jonah and Wyatt a chance to catch her. "What are you doing in town?" Wyatt noticed she wasn't even breathing hard.

"I rode in yesterday evening with the captain. Barnaby sent me in to check on you and Boss man and be available when you needed me. I caught Doc this morning as he headed out to check on patients. He said Boss man was doing better, and you were finally getting some sleep. I was just headin' back there to check on you both."

Several townsfolk had wandered over while Jonah was speaking and now voiced their desire to hear how Mr. McIsaac was faring. When Miss McIsaac repeated Doc's assessment from this morning, there were replies of surprise and amazement peppered with an occasional Praise the Lord here and there. The gathering crowd then turned its focus on Wyatt.

He willingly answered the pointed, sometimes accusing questions concerning the still-at-large thief and their missing savings. However, after a few minutes he subtly turned the inquisition into an opportunity to interrogate the crowd about what they had seen that day or whether they had noticed anyone matching the description of the holdup man since. The crowd began volunteering to contact friends or family in neighboring towns as to whether or not they knew anything that might lead to the discovery of the bank robber's identity.

As the impromptu meeting began to discuss the

ramifications of the theft, Wyatt noticed Miss McIsaac surreptitiously edging to the side of the crowd and slipping down a side street. Catching Jonah's attention, he motioned with his head to indicate he was following her and made his own way through the dispersing crowd.

She had her head down when his longer strides overtook her and didn't notice him at first. Remembering the spark that had shocked his hand when he'd touched her arm earlier, Wyatt kept his hands firmly at his sides, denying the itch to find out whether it had just been a chance occurrence. He cleared his throat to get her attention.

She visibly flinched as her head flew up and swiveled toward him. "I do wish you'd quit sneaking up on me, Marshal!"

"I wouldn't have to sneak up on you if you stayed still once in a while." He lengthened his stride to keep up with her quickening pace. "Speaking of which, I seem to recall telling a certain young lady to stay put yesterday, but she flagrantly disobeyed that order. You wouldn't know anything about that, would you?"

She avoided his eyes. "I seem to recall a slightly out-of-his-jurisdiction marshal hollering something over his shoulder as he rode away from the ranch yesterday, but as he couldn't be bothered to wait for me, I came back."

"I can see how a would-be horse thief might have trouble following orders from a marshal and worrying about where his 'jurisdiction' is or isn't."

They reached the doctor's house, and she paused, turning to face him. She tilted her head slightly. "Now that's just a bit of the pot calling the kettle black, don't you think, Marshal?"

The innocent confusion on her face tempted Wyatt like a mouse to cheese, but her sugary-sweet tone warned him of the trap. "How so?"

Opening the front door, she stepped across the threshold and turned to face him, saying quietly, "I seem to recall you riding out of my ranch yard yesterday…on a horse that did not belong to you!" She firmly shut the door in his face.

Wyatt grinned in spite of himself at Miss McIsaac's verbal riposte.

"I'm beginning to think you provoke that woman on purpose just to watch her reaction." Jonah had caught up with them and now made his presence known.

Wyatt shot a grin at him, but didn't reply as he reached for the door that had so recently been shut in his face. He did enjoy getting a reaction out of her and liked the fact she didn't back down from him even when rattled or frustrated. If he were in a safer occupation, had a place of his own… Wyatt broke off the thought. But he wasn't, and he didn't. He might enjoy sparring with the pretty female, but that's all there was to it.

He ignored the little voice that whispered, *for now.*

There was no one in the front office when they walked in, but the far door stood ajar, and Wyatt heard Miss McIsaac speaking. She sounded pleased, but he couldn't make out what she said before a second unknown voice responded.

"That's Boss man. He's awake!" Jonah exclaimed.

Chapter Seven

They hurried to Mr. McIsaac's room, and coming to a standstill in the doorway, watched as Miss McIsaac gingerly hugged the man sitting propped up in the bed. Dr. Kilburn leaned against the opposite wall, hands tucked into his vest pockets, a beaming smile lighting his usually earnest expression.

The little tableau brought a sting of moisture to Wyatt's eyes, and he quietly thanked God for sparing this woman more grief by restoring her father to her. Only the soft crooning of Mr. McIsaac broke the silence, and Wyatt recognized the quiet words as Gaelic. As a child he'd heard his grandfather use the language of the Old Country when his emotions got the better of him. Jonah's noisy sniff brought Mr. McIsaac's attention to them, and Meri quickly pulled away, busily straightening the coverlet.

Mr. McIsaac batted away her hands. "Quit fussin', darlin' girl. Ye'll make these gentlemen think yer faither's a feeble auld man."

Miss McIsaac gave a very unladylike snort. "You are feeble, and while you may not be old, you've definitely aged me the past several days, so I can fuss if I feel like it."

Mr. McIsaac gave her a glare that Wyatt recognized. He'd earned that same look from the man's daughter. He grinned. It was rather fun to see her on the receiving end of it for a change.

"Watch your sass, lassie! Ye're not too big to turn over me knee." Laugh lines radiated away from dark eyes twinkling in response to Miss McIsaac's growl.

"Faither…"

"Excuse me, darlin'," he interrupted her, "Jonah, don't just stand there. Come in and introduce the fellow with ye."

As the two men moved farther into the room, Dr. Kilburn left with the admonishment that he'd let them talk for a few minutes, but when he returned, they'd need to leave and allow Mr. McIsaac to rest.

Jonah introduced Wyatt and was summarily ordered by Mr. McIsaac to bring a couple more chairs so he wouldn't have to break his neck looking up at them.

"It's nice to finally talk with you, Mr. McIsaac. It's a privilege to meet the answer to so many prayers." Wyatt shook hands with the man as Jonah left the room in search of chairs.

"I'm pleased to meet ye, Marshal Cameron, but call me Ian. Now, I want to know what happened after I was shot. Did ye get the man?"

"No, sir, and call me Wyatt. We were unable to catch him that day, and I haven't tracked him down yet. I've got a few questions I'd like to ask you if you feel up to it."

"I think you should wait, Marshal, 'til Faither's a

little stronger before you bother him with your questions," Miss McIsaac interjected.

"America Catriona McIsaac! A measly scratch does not make me senile. I can certainly handle a few questions. Now stop interrupting, and let's hear what the man has to ask."

Mr. McIsaac gave a stern glance at his daughter, and Wyatt cleared his throat to hide his chuckle at her look of chagrin. He'd certainly learned the source of her fiery spirit. From his vantage point it looked like she'd inherited her mother's features and her father's temperament.

Ian McIsaac had an unruly thatch of white hair above snapping dark eyes and thick, white brows. Meri's eyes held the same snap but were a light brown with delicately arched brows, and her head was crowned with thick wavy light brown hair that reminded Wyatt of honey when it was held up to the sun. McIsaac had broad, weathered features that were in contrast to Meri's refined features of high cheekbones and straight delicate nose, full, rosy lips and a neatly rounded, but decidedly determined chin.

The pale yellow shirtwaist she was wearing made her lightly bronzed skin glow, and the way it skimmed her figure down to the waist of her full blue skirt highlighted the curves of her slender frame. She was beautiful. And her name was America, Meri for short. The two words sounded alike, but he'd assumed Franks was saying "Miss Mary" when he addressed her.

"Marshal?"

His thoughts snapped back to attention. "Yes?"

"Ye had some questions for me?" Mr. McIsaac's

eyes bounced between his daughter and Wyatt with a speculating gleam that disappeared so quickly Wyatt almost missed it.

Wyatt sat in the chair Jonah shoved toward him and cleared his throat. Pulling the little notebook from his pocket, he prepared to take notes and asked Mr. McIsaac to recount the events on the day of the robbery.

"I left Meri at the mercantile and stopped in to the bank to discuss some business with Mr. Samuels. I was just finishing up with him when someone entered the bank. Mr. Samuels left me in the office to see who it was. After a minute or two he walked back in at the point of a gun."

"Do you remember what the man was wearing?" Wyatt asked.

"I do. He'd changed clothes since he'd drifted through the ranch a week or so before, but I remember what he was wearing both times."

"What?" Wyatt voiced the startled question in chorus with Miss McIsaac.

"He came through our ranch?" she asked incredulously.

"Yes. Ye were out riding at the time. He drifted in about lunchtime. I didn't like his looks or his attitude. He seemed to be up to no good. I caught him prowling about the barn. When I confronted him, he gave me a hard-up story. Our policy is to feed strangers, so I had Cookie, our bunkhouse cook, fix him a plate, but the man kept trying to get information about the ranch, the surrounding neighbors and the town. Most drifters are more interested in who might be hiring, not how many head I run, how big the spread is or how big me neighbors' spreads are. When he'd finished his meal, I suggested he keep riding."

"How long ago was this?" Wyatt questioned.

"What day is it?"

"It's Saturday. The holdup happened on Tuesday, and you've been unconscious ever since." Miss McIsaac reached to touch her father's hand from her place on the other side of his bed as if to reassure herself he was truly awake.

"Then it was two weeks last Wednesday that he rode through the ranch," McIsaac said after a quick calculation.

Wyatt made a note of that. "You said he was wearing something different at the bank. Are you sure it was the same man?"

"Aye. He was wearing a black hat, a blue shirt, brown pants and a yellow bandanna when I first met him. He was still wearing the black hat when he robbed the bank, but this time he had a leather coat covering a brown shirt and pants and had a blue bandanna pulled up over his face. Most of his face was covered by the hat and cloth, but I recognized his voice and the way he carried himself."

"Did you learn his name when he was at your ranch?"

"No. That was another thing that made me suspicious of him at the time. Every time I asked his name, he'd pretend not to hear me and ask another question or change the subject."

"What happened after he came into the office with Mr. Samuels?"

"He waved the gun at Mr. Samuels and ordered him to open the safe there. Mr. Samuels refused, but the man grabbed him and shoved him toward it, put the gun to Mr. Samuels head and again ordered him to open it or he'd shoot him. Mr. Samuels obeyed him, and then the scoundrel shoved him out of the way, pulled a cloth bag out of his pocket and started filling it. I had been sitting by the desk, but when they came in, I stood up. He ordered me not to move, but didn't search me and didn't realize I was carrying a gun under me coat. I was slipping it out when Mr. Samuels looked me way and shouted…something. I can't remember exactly what. At his shout the man turned and fired. I remember falling, and I think I heard both men yell something again before I passed out."

Wyatt finished writing and flipped back a couple of pages to read some earlier notes. "Samuels said you tried to stop it by pulling your gun, but he didn't mention shouting. He said the man turned, saw you pulling your gun and fired."

McIsaac thought for a moment. "No. I definitely remember he didn't turn until Samuels shouted."

Wyatt scratched a few more words in his notebook.

"What did Samuels say happened after I was shot?" Ian McIsaac leaned forward intently, winced a little and sank back against his pillows.

"Mr. Samuels said the bandit hit him over the head after shooting you and left after grabbing the rest of the money out of the safe. He doesn't remember much after that because of the blow to his head."

"I definitely remember voices right after I fell." McIsaac muttered. He was quiet for a moment, thinking. "By the way, what happened to me gun?"

"I didn't see it when we got there. Do you have it, Miss McIsaac?"

"No. I didn't even think to look for it although I know he usually carries one. I haven't even thought about it since."

"That was me favorite pistol," McIsaac grumbled. "I sure would like it back."

"I'll ask around," Wyatt said. "Maybe someone else picked it up that day and forgot to mention it."

"You said the thief cleaned out the safe?" McIsaac asked.

"Yes. Mr. Samuels said he got everything."

"That must have been a lot of money to carry if he took everything."

"How much do you think he got away with?" Wyatt looked from his notes.

"I have no idea, but Samuels had just been bragging how well the bank was doing. I assumed there was quite a bit of money in that safe."

Dr. Kilburn walked in and cleared his throat. "It's time to let Mr. McIsaac get some rest. I don't want him to overdo things on his first day awake, even if he has made a remarkable recovery from yesterday."

"Now, Doc, I haven't had a chance to speak to Jonah about the ranch," McIsaac protested.

"Jonah can drop back by after you've had some rest. Your ranch will still be there." Doc's stern tone brooked no argument.

Getting up from his chair where he'd been quietly listening, Jonah hastily assured McIsaac that the ranch was fine and not to worry his head about it as Barnaby had things well in hand.

Wyatt asked Mr. McIsaac to describe the physical characteristics of the man who'd visited his ranch, and after writing down the information, he closed his little book and slipped it and the pencil back into his pocket. "If you think of anything else, let me know. Until then you have my word that I'll do whatever it takes to track down the culprit."

Doc shooed them out, ordering Miss McIsaac along with them. "I want to examine your father, and then he needs to rest. You go get some fresh air or take a nap, but run along."

Wyatt was mulling over what he'd learned from Meri's father as he and Jonah walked to the front door, aware that Miss McIsaac had followed them. Stepping aside to allow her to precede him, he watched her blindly walk through the door Jonah held open. She looked a little lost and unsure what to do with herself. He followed her into the brightly lit outdoors, admiring the glints of gold that danced to life in the honey-colored thick braid as sunlight touched her uncovered head.

"What are you going to do, Miss Meri?" Jonah asked.

Meri glanced around, seeming to search for an answer before replying with forced cheerfulness, "I think I'll enjoy Mrs. Kilburn's garden for a bit, and then I might take that nap Doc suggested."

Jonah patted her on the shoulder. "You do that, miss. I'll come back by later this afternoon, and if your pa's feeling up to it, I'll give him the details he wants about the ranch." Turning, he walked down the street.

Her gaze followed him for a moment before she looked at Wyatt. "Good day, Marshal." She walked toward the corner of the house where Mrs. Kilburn's well-nurtured flower garden began.

"My name is Wyatt. Do you think you could use it instead of Marshal?"

As soon as he uttered the words, he wondered why it even mattered and half wished he'd left well enough alone. When she continued to walk away without responding, though, the silent challenge was too strong to ignore. "I could order you to use my name."

She paused and glanced over her shoulder at him. Was she trying not to smile?

"You could try—" she started walking away again "—but it wouldn't work."

"Hmm… Then I'll have to come up with something else. But… Miss McIsaac?"

This time when she stopped, she turned to face him squarely. "Yes, *Marshal?*" She threw the gauntlet with a bland inquisitiveness that failed to mask completely the glint in her darkened eyes.

Wyatt accepted the challenge, throwing down his own gauntlet. "I won't *order* you to use my name, but make no doubt about it…you *will* use my name!"

Meri never made it back to her room for a nap after Jonah and the marshal departed. All vestiges of weariness had vanished as swiftly as the lawman after his self-confident pronouncement. She prowled the garden oblivious to the beauty of new green leaves and tender buds, arguing with the man in her thoughts.

Of all the egotistical… If he thinks he can make me call him by his first name, he's got a disappointment coming. I refuse to give the gossips of this town one more reason to discuss me. I will not give them the satisfaction!

She ruthlessly quashed the little thrill of longing

that accompanied the thought of having her name coupled with his.

The only reason he's interested in you, Meri McIsaac, is because Faither was involved in the holdup and because—she groaned, remembering—*because you probably pricked at his ego with your refusal to use his name.*

It wasn't that she didn't like his name. She did—there, she'd admitted it—but using his name felt too informal, too…intimate, as if she was letting him get too close. She needed to keep him at arm's length, so when he lost his interest in her and moved on to someone prettier and more feminine, it wouldn't matter.

Before long someone would kindly inform him that Miss McIsaac was more interested in working cattle and riding her horse, Sandy, than in sewing a fine stitch and filling her hope chest. They'd shake their heads in laughing pity and observe that at the ripe old age of nearly thirty, she had never entertained any serious suitors and likely never would.

All of which was true, but anytime Meri overheard such comments, they made her feel like the local oddity. She could only imagine how those remarks, coming from a smiling, eyelash-batting, oh-so-willing-to-please female, would sound to the handsome marshal. Meri shook her head. No. She *wouldn't* imagine it.

Besides, the only *interest I have in him is whether he finds the man that tried to kill my father or not. And I hope Faither heals quickly so we can go home. Once we're back on the ranch, life will get back to normal, and I'll stop worrying about what everyone else thinks.*

"That's a fierce look. Do you not like roses?" Mrs. Kilburn's amused tone interrupted Meri's mental rant.

She turned away from the glossy bush just erupting in tiny buds she'd apparently been glaring at. "I *do* like roses, but I'm afraid I was quite lost in my thoughts."

"From the look on your face, they weren't pleasant. Are you worried about your father? He's doing remarkably well today, and Doc says he doesn't see any reason he won't have a full recovery."

"I think the week is just catching up to me." Meri evaded the question.

Mrs. Kilburn laced her arm through Meri's and led her through the back door into the kitchen. "What you need is some food. Come on in, I have lunch ready."

Inside Meri found a tray prepared for herself and her father. Mr. McIsaac was less than impressed, however, when he realized his lunch consisted of a light broth, toast and glass of milk.

"Dr. Kilburn says you can have something a little more substantial tomorrow if your stomach handles this okay. It has been empty for several days, and it'll be best not to overwhelm it just when you're starting to feel better. Now, do you want me to feed you?"

"Allow me the dignity of feeding meself, even if it is a paltry excuse of a meal," Ian said scornfully, carefully spooning broth into his mouth. "Oh, what I wouldn't give for a thick steak!" he moaned, eyeing Meri's thick sandwich.

Meri grinned at his antics but quickly sobered. "Did we lose an awful lot in the robbery, Faither?"

"We lost some, but ye know I never trusted all me money to the bank. I only kept a small amount there to stay on good terms with Mr. Samuels. I've never let anyone except yer mither know how much we managed to save back and that includes the banker. I'm sorry the bank was robbed at all, but it didn't surprise our Heavenly Father. Savings or no savings, He's always taken care of us and always will, so don't worry over what we did or didn't lose. Our treasure is in Heaven, not some safe or bank down here."

They discussed the ranch and what had happened while he was unconscious as they ate. Gathering up the dishes when they'd finished, Meri noticed her father was drooping a little. "Why don't you close your eyes and rest so you'll be ready when Jonah drops in. I think I'll go check on Sandy."

He argued, but there wasn't much effort in the argument, and she left the room carrying the tray of dishes. After washing up the lunch things, she went into her room and changed from the blue skirt she'd donned earlier into her tan split riding skirt. Slipping a dark, buttery-soft leather vest over the yellow calico blouse, she grabbed her hat and hurried to Franks's Livery.

As she neared the stables, she heard Franks's rich, deep voice raised in song, the sound rumbling pleasingly through the air.

His singing halted as he greeted her warmly. "Miss Meri! I hear de Lawd has answered our prayers!" Sitting down on a bench against the wall, Meri filled him in on the doctor's prognosis and Franks's wide grin split his face. "It be a day ta praise de Lawd for his mah'vlous goodness ta man!"

A weak smile and nod was Meri's only reply.

"You is mighty quiet for someone who should be rejoicin'. Is yo thankful bone broke?"

"I am very thankful God heard the prayers of you and the men who prayed for my father and that he's doing so much better." Meri squirmed under Franks's penetrating gaze.

"What 'bout yo prayers?"

Meri shrugged her shoulders. "It feels like my prayers aren't heard anymore, like there's something in the way."

"Honey chil'! Yo Heavenly Father promised never ta leave or fo'sake you! If dere's sumpin' in de way, it ain't on his end!"

Meri felt the familiar ache in her throat return. "I feel like I've been forsaken."

"Mmm-hmm, evah since yo momma died, I reckon. You put on a good show and mos' likely fooled ever'one, but I'se noticed the joy and peace in yo eyes been missin' fo' some time now."

Meri fired up at the gentle rebuke. "How am I supposed to have joy and peace when Mither died so suddenly, and then I almost lose Faither?"

Franks shook his head sadly. "Joy and peace ain't foun' in yo circumstances, they is foun' in God's promises." Franks bowed his head all of a sudden, leaving Meri staring at him. "Lawd, You know dis chil' is hurtin'. Open her eyes ta what needs fixin' so You can heal de hurt. Amen." He stood abruptly. "Now go see dat spoiled pony. He been a hollerin' for you all day."

Meri frowned as he returned to his forge and stirred the coals. She loved the man dearly, but she was a little miffed at his scolding. *I'm hurting and somehow it's my fault?*

She drew a deep breath to calm herself. She'd never been angry with Franks before. *You do have a problem if you're getting upset with Franks!*

She stood and went outside to Sandy. The palomino

saw her coming, whinnied deeply and ran for the gate.
At least someone was glad to see her. She slid through
the fence and wrapped her arms around his neck, burying her face in his mane and breathing deeply of his
horsey scent, of fresh air, sweet grass and hay. After several moments she led him to the barn and saddled him,
feeling some of the tension leave her shoulders. Scolding herself for her poor attitude, she mounted Sandy and
called over her shoulder to Franks, "We'll be back later."

"Be careful."

With a short nod she rode out of the barn. Detour-
ing to Doc's place and finding her father still asleep,
she retrieved her guns. Sheathing the carbine in the
saddle scabbard, she strapped the cartridge belt and
pistol she'd brought back from the ranch around her
slim waist. She'd lived in the West long enough to
know it was wise to have protection from four-legged
and two-legged varmints even if she was only going
to be on the outskirts of town.

Her father had long ago ensured she was proficient
with firearms, giving her the .44-40 Winchester carbine, sometimes called the Saddle carbine, several years
ago for her birthday. It was four inches shorter than the
regular .44-40 Winchester rifle and made for a lighter,
more compact gun for her to handle. The rifle and the
pistol Meri carried on her hip were chambered for the
same rounds, therefore the extra cartridges she carried
in her belt would fit either gun. Altogether, Meri felt
very capable of protecting herself from any threat.

Swinging up aboard the pretty palomino, she took
the long way to the cemetery, circling the outside edge
of town. Maybe by the time she reached it she would
have worked up the nerve to go in. Meri kept Sandy at

a sedate walk, waving at a few townsfolk who called out as she passed. All too soon, she reached the waist-high wrought-iron gate in the fence that lined the front edge of the burial grounds. Dismounting, she reached for the latch then let her hand fall back to her side.

She'd put this off so long it had become a monster she couldn't face. She should've made herself come with Faither when the headstone was set, but at the time, her cold was too convenient an excuse.

Sandy shoved his nose against her back, giving her a hard nudge. "I just can't do it, Sandy." The horse snorted and shook his head, setting his bridle to jingling. "I know. I'm a coward, but let's get out of here."

Remounting, she escaped into the hills behind the cemetery. There was a place nearby conducive to a full-out gallop without danger of running over someone on the road or running her horse into a hole and Meri took full advantage it. After an hour of riding, though, she felt only marginally better. A long, solitary ride, the joy of a smooth-moving horse, the wind in her hair and the beautiful countryside had always been the cure-all for anything bothering her, but the remedy was sorely lacking today.

Meri berated herself. She should be feeling at least a small portion of the joy and peace Franks mentioned earlier, if only for the fact that her father was now on the mend. Why was she still feeling completely out of sorts? And why did her thoughts keep straying to a certain star-toting man? Maybe when she got out of town and back to normal ranch life, her unsettled emotions would straighten out. For now she'd just have to live with them.

Reluctantly she turned Sandy toward town. They'd

ridden east through the foothills bordering the north-
ern edge of Little Creek and were only a couple of
miles from town if they dropped down and took the
road in. Riding through the thickly forested area that
lined the road, Sandy slowed, pricked his ears and
lifted his nose, scenting the air.

"Someone else around, fella?" Meri asked quietly,
letting him have his head. She hadn't expected to be
followed like she always was on her ranch, but her
horse had heard something. Maybe Franks had sent
someone after her.

Sandy slowly stepped to the edge of the trees, pausing to peer intently down the road away from town.

Two men were standing between their horses in the
bend of the road about one hundred and fifty yards away
from Meri. Both men had their hats pulled low, shading
their faces, and from their body language they seemed
to be arguing. Meri could hear their raised voices but
was unable to understand what they were saying.

"So that's what you heard. I wonder what their problem is?" As Meri whispered this to Sandy, the taller
of the two men grabbed the other man by the collar,
yanking him off his feet and shaking him as he yelled
and shook his other fist in the poor man's face.

"Hey!" Meri shouted, simultaneously pulling her
rifle and nudging Sandy toward the men.

The smaller man, his back to Meri, nearly fell as the
larger man dropped him and shoved him away roughly.
He recovered his balance, and both men ducked their
heads and scrambled onto their horses. Wheeling their
mounts away, the smaller man glanced over his shoulder as he spurred his horse.

Meri saw a flash and something whistled past her ear.

Chapter Eight

Crack!

Sandy flinched at the loud report and sidestepped, saving them from the second bullet that whizzed past. Meri dropped the reins and jerked her own rifle to her shoulder, snapping off a quick shot before the men disappeared around the bend.

"Get 'em, Sandy!"

Scooping up the reins in one hand, she held her rifle ready in the other as Sandy leaped forward into a full run after the men. They had a good head start on her, and as she rounded the bend, they were already rounding the next curve in the road. Meri knew a straight stretch was around that corner and thought she could gain on them by then for a better look, but when she reached it, they were nowhere in sight. Sandy slid to a halt at Meri's signal, snorting impatiently.

"I know, I wanted to catch them, too, but they must have left the road and could be lying in wait for us now. I'll be in plenty of hot water if Faither finds out I followed them at all!"

Suddenly uneasy over the whereabouts of the two

men, Meri turned Sandy and they flew back toward town. They were within a half mile of the edge of town when Meri saw two riders racing toward her. Wheeling the palomino sharply, she dived off the edge of the road into the trees. Flinging herself out of the saddle almost before Sandy had stopped moving, Meri flipped his reins over a limb and ducked down behind a tree. Heart racing, she steadied her rifle, waiting as the two riders neared the spot where she'd flown off the road.

She heard the horses slide to a halt and a familiar voice spoke. "Miss Meri, is that you?"

Meri closed her eyes, resting her forehead against the tree trunk as she drew a much-needed breath into grateful lungs. *Jonah.* Her pulse began to slow its frantic pounding.

A second voice commanded, "Come out where we can see you, but be careful about it!"

Wyatt.

Meri groaned quietly as her pulse surged into panic mode again. *No! He's the marshal.* She corrected herself. *I will not call him Wyatt.*

Willing her racing heart to cease with the acrobatics, she retrieved Sandy. Mounting, she gulped another steadying breath then ducked back through the brush to the road.

Two guns were hastily reholstered as Jonah spoke. "I thought that looked like you an' Sandy. Are you all right?"

"I'm fine." Something brushed Meri's ear, and she flinched at the unexpected sensation. Trying to recover a facade of unconcern, she felt around her ear and discovered a twig snagged in her hair.

"If you're fine, would you care to explain why we

heard gunshots, and why you're running and hiding?" All warmth had disappeared from the marshal's hazel eyes, leaving only cold steel behind.

"I am not running and hiding!" Steely eyes bored into her as she untangled the stubborn twig and tossed it aside. "Okay, fine! I was hiding. Now, will you quit glaring at me?"

"I'll decide whether to quit glaring when you finish answering my question." His eyes never wavered from hers.

"I was headed back to town when I saw two men on the road having an argument. When they started fighting, I yelled at them. When they saw me, they took off. One, or both of them, fired a couple of shots."

Both men inhaled sharply.

"I fired back and chased them…"

"You *chased* them! After they *shot* at you? Have you lost what little sense you may have ever had?" The marshal's glare sizzled as he growled in her face.

Meri blinked. When had he gotten so close? And how was it possible for him to be so close when they were both still on horseback? She fought the impulse to move Sandy away from the growling marshal and instead leaned toward him. "Yes, I *chased* them!"

He copied her movement, leaning in until she felt his breath on her face. He held her eyes for several breaths without blinking. In a low dangerous tone, he asked gently, "Why?"

Meri barely heard him over the pulse thudding in her ears. "Because…"

Her brain stuttered to a stop. Why *had* she chased them? At the moment she couldn't remember. His nearness was making it nearly impossible to think.

"Because they made me mad?" she finished lamely, feeling as foolish as she no doubt sounded.

He blinked and warmer hazel softened the steeliness. Settling back in his saddle, he looked at her. "You chased them because they made you…mad?" He sounded as if he were choking.

A strangled sound turned Meri's attention to Jonah. The red-faced man coughed out another funny sound before breaking into belly-deep laughs. What in the world was wrong with him? A similar noise from the marshal swiveled Meri's head back to look at him. His lips were clenched, but at the look of perplexed confusion on her face, his own laugh escaped.

Meri's gaze bounced between the two men, a frown creasing her forehead. After half a minute the laughter subsided, leaving grins in its wake. "What is so funny?"

Wyatt shook his head. "I'm not sure, exactly. Just remind me never to make you mad."

"Unless, of course, you *want* her to chase you!" Jonah chuckled.

Meri felt the color flare in her cheeks as the marshal grinned at her. "I might not mind her chasing me, so long as she wasn't shooting at the time."

"If you think for one minute, Marshal, that I'd chase you—"

He interrupted her. "My name is Wyatt, not Marshal, and back to the issue at hand—show us where you found those men and recount what happened from the beginning, please?" Grabbing the offered distraction, Meri led them back in the direction she'd come, explaining what had happened. "When I saw you two, I thought they had circled around and were coming back. I got off the road and under cover." Meri pointed out where she'd first seen the two men.

When they arrived at the spot in the road where the men had stood, Jonah dismounted and studied the ground. "Why don't you take Miss Meri back to town, Captain? I'll follow these tracks and see where they lead."

Meri caught a look that passed between the two men and wondered what it meant. "I'm riding with you two. Three pairs of eyes will see more than one pair."

Jonah swung onto the back of his horse. "I was tracking before you were born, Miss Meri, and although the captain here is pretty good, I've still got him beat. Besides, it's time for you to get back to town. Your pa is gonna be wonderin' where you are. He won't be happy with me if he finds out I let you ride back alone after this little excursion."

"He doesn't need to know about this. He's got enough on his mind right now."

Jonah gave her a stern look. "I'm not keeping this a secret, Miss Meri. The men need to know to keep an eye out for these two."

"I'll take you up on your offer, Jonah, but be careful. Fire a couple of shots if you get into trouble, and I'll come running. Otherwise come see me when you get back to town, and let me know what you find. Coming, Miss McIsaac?"

Meri reluctantly turned her horse toward town, thinking about the unspoken signal that had passed between the two men. "How long have you and Jonah known each other?"

He frowned, thinking. "Almost eleven years, now. He was stationed at the first fort I was transferred to after graduating from West Point." A slight grin quirked his lips. "I was a freshly minted second lieutenant full of book learning and no real knowledge of anything west of the Mississippi. The major over the fort had dealt with know-it-all West Point graduates before. He had a habit of quietly assigning Master Sergeant Jonah Chacksfield the job of keeping an eye on those brash, overeager officers. They outranked him, but Jonah had a way of subtly reining in bad judgment and pointing out a better way without appearing to question an officer's authority, all the while making the idea seem like their own."

"Did he do that to you?"

"More than once. I thought I knew all about Indians after growing up playing with my Cherokee cousins in the wilds of Rocky Gap, Virginia. I could sneak through those woods with the best of them and was more than a fair tracker." A grimace crossed his face. "My first encounter with a band of Apaches taught me how much I *didn't* know. I came close to getting my men killed that day. It was due to Jonah's guidance and God's mercy we survived that encounter."

They rode in silence for a several minutes. Meri could envision a fresh-faced young army officer decked out in crisp uniform with shiny buttons and a cavalry saber swinging from his hip. She wondered how many female hearts he had conquered. Something he'd said snagged her attention. "You don't look Indian." The words were out before she could catch them.

Narrowed hazel eyes turned toward her. "What is an Indian supposed to look like?"

Meri blushed and shrugged. "I just meant you don't have dark eyes or black hair."

"My grandmother was full-blood Cherokee, but I take after the Scottish side of the family." He grinned at her. "And I can see you have another question. What is it?"

Meri felt relieved that she hadn't upset him with her impulsive question and then wondered why she cared. "You said you grew up with your Cherokee cousins in Virginia. Weren't the Cherokee Indians removed west?"

"Most of them were, but a few escaped into the Appalachian Mountains. My family owned their own property farther north. Indians that actually owned their own land instead of living on communal grounds were by law allowed to stay."

Meri thought about her parents and the boatload of others evicted from their homes in Scotland, and the Indians evicted from their lands and homes in America. Two different nations and cultures, both forever changed because of greed coupled with power.

"You're awfully quiet. Does my being part Cherokee bother you?"

Meri thought she detected a hint of worry. "No." He eyed her for a second, and she looked him square in the eyes. "It doesn't bother me."

The answer seemed to satisfy him, because he smiled slightly. "Good."

Something shifted in the air between them and, growing uncomfortable, Meri turned her focus back to the ride. She was thankful he seemed content to let the silence continue.

They reached the saloon at the edge of town and turned down the street to the livery stable.

"Thank you for coming out to check on me." She didn't understand why a simple thank-you should make her feel so nervous—vulnerable.

He touched the brim of his hat in a snappy salute. "Just doin' my job, ma'am."

Franks greeted them at the door of the livery stable and asked about the gunshots. He listened soberly as the marshal recounted the details while Meri unsaddled Sandy. Turning to her afterward, Franks scolded, "I shore is glad de good Lawd was watchin' out for you, but you might'a stretched his protection a bit far when you chased after dem fellas! Don' you go doin' a fool stunt like da' again, you hear?"

Wyatt turned his horse into a stall beside Sandy. "Don't go riding alone out of town until we figure out what this was all about and catch those men, either."

The thought of being cooped up in town unable to ride when and where she pleased was smothering. "I shouldn't have chased after those two men, but I'm not going to stop riding just because of them."

"While you're in this town, you'll do what *I* say." His eyes were turning stormy again, she noticed.

Meri opened her mouth to reply and remembered the last time she'd argued with him in this barn. Biting back the words that sprang to her tongue, she spun on her heel and stomped out of the barn. She heard him follow and ignored him hoping he'd go away, but he stayed on her heels all the way to the doctor's house. Reaching the bottom step, she could take it no longer and faced him. "Why are you still following me?"

He took her by the arm, marched her up the steps and opened the door for her. "Since you refuse to abide by my authority in this matter, we're going to take it up with a higher authority."

Meri yanked her arm away from the sparks his touch caused. "What higher authority? God?"

"No. Your father." Leaving her standing at the front door, he stalked toward her father's room.

Wyatt found McIsaac awake and, much to Miss Meri's annoyance, relayed the happenings of the afternoon. He then retreated from the field of battle, more than happy to leave her father to engage her in this particular skirmish. Pulling the bedroom door shut behind him to cut off the glare she aimed in his direction, he shook his head ruefully. One slender female had just caused him to fall back faster than any band of attacking Apache warriors ever had.

His stomach growled, reminding him it was near supper time, and he pointed his steps toward the café. A savory, tantalizing odor greeted him as he entered the dining establishment, and he requested a plate of whatever smelled so good. He chatted with the other diners, feeling the weight of their concern over the missing money, until the hearty stew and hot, buttered bread arrived then he dived into his meal while pondering the events of the past week. Were the bank holdup and today's events random coincidences or did they somehow tie in together?

When he finished his meal, he decided to have a talk with Franks. Meri had described the men's horses, and Wyatt wondered if Franks would know anything about them.

The blacksmith was finishing his own meal in his small living quarters off the back corner of the livery stable, but he warmly invited Wyatt in. Wyatt explained his errand and repeated Meri's description of the men and their horses.

Franks rubbed his head and thought for a minute

before replying. "A bay hoss and a gray hoss… Dere's a lot a bay hosses 'roun' here. Dat could describe any a dem. I has sev'ral myself, but I ain't rented any a dem out today. Now de gray…dere's only two a dem in dis area dat I know of—Rufus Bascom's matched carriage hosses and his prize possessions. He's a rancher on past de McIsaac place, and he keeps dem s'clusively to pull his carriage." He paused thoughtfully. "Dey *was* a gray hoss I ain't never seen afore tied in front a de saloon, couple nights ago. It were a big, han'some geldin', but I ain't seen it since."

The only description Meri had given of the men themselves was their clothing and the height difference between the two men. She'd been too far away to distinguish facial features under the brims of their hats. Franks and Wyatt both agreed the clothing description could fit a dozen men in town on any given day.

Wyatt thanked the man for his help and stood to take his leave. Franks followed him to the door. "You be careful wid Miss Meri, she's a han'ful, and she's hurtin', but she's sumpin' special! I don' wanna see her hurt!"

Stepping outside, Wyatt settled his hat on his head. "I'll do my best, but I'm beginning to believe keeping her out of trouble will be the hardest part of my job as marshal!"

Wyatt's next stop was the saloon. The bartender remembered a man who rode a gray horse and gave Wyatt a rough description of the man: tall with shaggy black hair and a mustache, a man who asked too many questions. The bartender said he recognized his type as a troublemaker and was glad to see him leave. Wyatt thanked him and asked him to let him know if he saw the man again or remembered anything else about him.

Leaving the foul-smelling, smoky saloon behind, Wyatt glanced down at the pocket watch his parents had given him upon his graduation from West Point. It was only a little after six in the evening, plenty of time to talk to a couple more people before calling it a day. He walked to the boardinghouse. The bank teller had roomed there before leaving to be closer to his widowed mother, according to Mr. Samuels. At the large two-story house Wyatt asked the proprietress if she knew where the teller had gone.

"Mr. Dunn was such a nice young man, one of my best boarders. I so hated to lose him, and I'm glad he found another job so soon after Mr. Samuels fired him." She offered Wyatt a cup of tea, which he declined.

"He told you Mr. Samuels fired him?"

"Yes. He was naturally upset about it, but I think it almost came as a relief after the way he was treated."

"How was that?"

"In the past few months, he would come in from work with such a sad, tired slump to his shoulders, but I finally got out of him what the trouble was. Mr. Samuels was constantly finding fault with the way he did anything and made the poor boy's life miserable. Then he fired poor Mr. Dunn—said he was just too incompetent. Grouchy old man lost me one of the tidiest boarders I had," she said indignantly.

Wyatt asked her where Mr. Dunn had gone, and she named a town in the next county. He thanked her for her time and left, jotting a note to contact that town's marshal to verify Dunn's whereabouts. Wyatt wondered why Mr. Samuels hadn't mentioned any of this and added it to the growing list of questions he had for the man. However, when he arrived at the banker's house, the housekeeper informed him that as the bank was closed, Mr. Samuels had left town on business and wouldn't return until sometime the following day.

Wyatt turned over the fragmented bits and pieces of information he'd gathered as he walked through the south side of town back toward First Street. When he reached it, he saw Jonah walking toward him in the dim light of evening.

"I just got back in and was coming to find you."

"Let's go to my office and talk."

"You're the marshal, but Mr. McIsaac is my boss, and I think he needs to hear what I found, too."

"I'll take your word for it. Do you want to get something to eat before we head over there?"

"No. Let's get there before it gets any later. I can rustle up some grub afterward."

They hurried to Doc's house and found McIsaac still awake and eager to talk to them. Dr. Kilburn advised them to keep it short.

"I know that look. What's up, Jonah?" McIsaac propped himself higher against the headboard.

"The tracks out on the road, I'd seen 'em before." Jonah's face was grim.

"I figured that's what your look meant earlier," Wyatt replied. "You didn't want Miss McIsaac to know it."

Jonah shook his head. "The tracks of one of those men and his horse matched the ones I found on the ranch after our horse was stolen and returned. The same man I tracked and lost in the cattle drive, and I believe, the same man you were tracking, Cap'n."

"Och! Are ye telling me one of the men me daughter ran into on the road today was that de'il who held up the bank?" McIsaac nearly shouted the question, his brogue thickening noticeably.

"Yes, sir. I believe so. And from the tracks today and some tail hairs I found snagged in the brush, I'd say the gray horse Meri described to us is the one we tracked out on the ranch."

Wyatt quickly recounted what he'd learned from Franks and the bartender about the gray horse.

"The man who came through our ranch was riding a gray horse and had black hair and a mustache." McIsaac's voice was grim.

Wyatt felt his own pulse quicken. "If it is the same man, between the barkeep and yourself, we have a description of our thief. It also means he's been in the area for a while."

"Why would he still be hanging around? Why hasn't he hightailed it out of the area?" Jonah wondered aloud.

"And who was he meeting on the road today?" Wyatt added. "Where did you trail them to?"

"After they left the road, they didn't take time to hide their tracks. They rode as fast as they could to the next town. I lost their tracks once they hit town, but the boy at the livery stable hadn't seen a bay or a gray all day, and the marshal and saloon keeper hadn't, either. I figure they rode on out of there as quick as they rode in, but I couldn't find where."

The three men hashed over this information for several more minutes but were unable to come up with any solid conclusions.

"Did you remember anything else about the bank job?" Wyatt asked McIsaac.

"No, but there's sure something bothering me about it. If I can figure out what it is, I'll let ye know."

"Okay. I'll bring some wanted posters for you to look through, and I'll write up a description of the man you and the barkeep saw and wire it to surrounding towns, see if anyone's seen our thief. I need to talk to Mr. Samuels again and clear a few things up, and I'd like to talk to that bank teller and hear his side of the story." Wyatt eyed both men thoughtfully before he continued. "Mr. McIsaac, I need a deputy, at least 'til we get this trouble solved. The town council gave me authority to hire whomever I wanted. I know Jonah, but more importantly, I trust him. I wonder if you'd be willing to let me hire him away from you, if he's willing."

Mr. McIsaac nodded. "Jonah's his own man. Yer business is with him, not me."

"Jonah?" Wyatt offered his hand.

"I'd be honored to be of service as long as you want me." Jonah grasped the outstretched hand and gave it a firm clasp.

A tap alerted them to a visitor, and they turned to see Meri poke her head around the door. "Oh. I didn't know you had company. I'll be back later to say good-night." She withdrew hurriedly.

"I don't think she's forgiven ye for ordering her not to ride out alone or for tattling to me." McIsaac laughed as they heard her footsteps retreating.

"I was glad to leave that fight in your hands." Jonah and McIsaac laughed at his feigned shudder.

"She's an independent lass, that's for sure. Just like her dear mither was." McIsaac looked at Wyatt thoughtfully. "There are only two men she's ever taken orders from and even then she kicked up occasionally."

"I assume you were one?" Wyatt guessed.

"Aye, and God. Ye just might make the third."

Wyatt felt his pulse jump and a sudden burn in his cheeks. He cleared his throat. "She has spunk, but she's going to give me gray hair if she pulls any more stunts like the one today." Just thinking about the potential consequences of her actions still sent chills down his spine. He'd wanted to shake her earlier for putting herself at such a risk.

McIsaac chuckled, tugging at his own gray locks. "Where do ye think I acquired these? Some things are worth it, though."

Wyatt stood and shook hands with McIsaac, changing the direction of the conversation. He already had Mrs. Van Deusen after him. He didn't need any other potential matchmakers trying to outflank him. "I'd better find my new deputy some food and get him sworn in, or I'll lose him before I've officially hired him."

Bidding their farewells, Wyatt and Jonah departed the house for Wyatt's office.

"Little Creek is a solid little town, recent trouble notwithstanding. It's growing, but there is a lot of good land still available."

Wyatt looked at the ex-sergeant. "Your point?"

"No point. Just got to thinking about your dream to settle down and raise horses. This is as good a place as any."

"Hard to do that when I'm trying to catch a bank robber."

"That won't last forever. Besides, it's high time you started thinking about finding a wife."

"You, too, Jonah? You, too?"

Chapter Nine

Meri stepped outside and felt the warmth of the sunshine bathe her face as she inhaled the heady perfume of fresh spring air. She'd planned to stay with her father instead of attending church, but he'd put his foot down, insisting he didn't need her hovering all day. She smoothed her hands down the glossy purple fabric of her dress. As much as she preferred the freedom of her less cumbersome riding skirts, it was Sunday morning, and according to her upbringing, that meant wearing her best to church.

At least that's what she'd told herself this morning when she'd given in to a fit of vanity and applied her favorite lilac scent, which she'd tucked into her bag on a whim at the ranch. She'd also taken time to twist her hair into a smooth chignon, but a sudden attack of nerves had butterflies fluttering in her stomach as a tiny voice inquired if she were trying to impress anyone in particular.

Ruthlessly squashing the mocking imp, she threw up her head and walked briskly toward the church building. *There's no reason to dither about how you look* or *smell, Meri McIsaac! As long as you're clean and neat, no one will care either way.*

"Mmm…lilacs, I believe."

The masculine voice so unexpectedly close to her ear caused her to trip, but firm hands gently snared her waist, steadying her and sending the butterflies into frenzied acrobatics.

"Steady there. You don't always have to fall at my feet. Besides, I'd hate to see you muss your lovely dress." Mirth danced through the marshal's words.

Meri pulled away from him and walked on, trying to untangle her tongue and ignore the disturbing sensations left by the feel of his hands at her waist. That became impossible, however, when he grasped her hand and folded it around his arm as he fell into step with her. A tingling sensation raced up her arm at the contact, and she jerked her hand back as if she'd been burned.

When the sensation faded somewhat, she found her tongue. "If you would quit sneaking up on me, I wouldn't *be* in danger of falling for you." A huge grin spread over his face, and Meri wished she could bite her unruly tongue off. "That's not what I mean! I meant… Oh, you know what I meant."

"Do I?" His eyes twinkled merrily at her.

Meri tried to concentrate on where she was walking instead of the man beside her. "Don't you have marshal duties to take care of or something?"

"I'm attending one right now."

"What? Pestering innocent law-abiding citizens?" Sparring with him was safer than noticing how sharp he looked in his starched black trousers, white shirt and string tie.

"I'm ensuring that the citizens of Little Creek arrive at church safely," he corrected patiently.

"So you walk everyone to service on Sunday mornings?" Meri couldn't resist a sideways glance at him when he touched her elbow to steady her as they stepped off the boardwalk to cross the street. She could almost imagine her suitor was walking her to church.

"Oh, no, I only accompany the most dangerous. That way everyone else stays safe."

Suitor indeed! Meri corralled the nonsensical thought and searched for a suitable rebuttal.

"Yoo hoo, Marshal." A fog of perfumes enveloped them as three pretty females floated toward them.

Cold reality slapped Meri. Imagining she could compete with such visions of feminine loveliness as these lacy, beribboned, graceful specimens was as foolish as it was dangerous. No man was going to look at a straggly wildflower when such hothouse roses were on display.

She stiffened her shoulders and shored up her sagging defenses. *Who said I was competing against them?*

She quickened her steps to escape, but the marshal stayed with her as did the three young ladies. Their bubbly conversation filled the air, but Meri focused on the little white church building coming ever closer.

When they arrived, she slipped away to speak to Pastor Willis, thanking him for his prayers and asking him to pass along her gratitude to the church family. Squeezing into the end of a pew as the opening hymn was announced, she thought she'd been successful in putting some distance between herself and the marshal, but the rustle of cloth against the wooden pew behind her warned her as someone leaned close and whispered.

"My plan worked. Everyone arrived safely."

The pastor asked the congregation to rise and join in song, and Meri gratefully sprang to her feet, hiding her face behind the hymnbook. As she filled her lungs to join the congregational hymn, the fresh piney scent of shaving lotion filled her nostrils and, distracted, she forgot to sing. Her eyes were on the hymnbook, but her attention focused on the man behind her, his fine baritone voice lifted in joyful praise.

In her perplexity, she nearly missed the pastor thanking the congregation on her behalf, but the smattering of applause when he announced Mr. McIsaac was well on the way to recovery recalled her wandering attention. Other prayer requests were voiced and, after he prayed, Pastor Willis reminded the congregation that the church social was coming up the following Saturday. He then began his message.

Meri opened her Bible to follow along, but her mind drifted over the events of the week until her father's name grabbed her notice.

"We had a pretty big answer to prayer this week in the recovery of Mr. McIsaac. But what about those times when it seems our prayers don't reach any higher than the top of our head?"

Meri looked up expectantly. She'd felt that way many times recently.

He continued, "God hasn't moved, and His grace hasn't failed, but maybe we've let something come between and hinder our relationship with Him. Look at this list in Ephesians 4:31. 'Let all bitterness, and wrath, and anger, and clamour, and evil speaking, be

put away from you, with all malice…' Have you allowed one or more of these to fester in your heart and
damage your walk with God? The good news is, it
doesn't have to be permanent. Put it away from you.
He's waiting to forgive and restore sweet fellowship.
All you have to do is ask Him. Let's pray."

Meri bowed her head with the rest of the congregation, her thoughts in turmoil. Convicted spirit warred
with proud flesh as the pastor's words rattled around
her head. A hand touched her shoulder.

"You're coming to lunch with us, dear."

Mrs. Van Deusen's statement startled Meri, and she
jerked her head up in surprise. She'd missed the end
of service, and her mind scrambled to register what
the woman had said.

"Don't worry about your father. Doc announced
that anyone who wanted to visit him could come today
after lunch, and I've already overheard several people
planning to stop in and say hello. He'll have all the
company he can stand." She chuckled.

Meri's brow furrowed; she'd missed that particular
announcement, too.

Mrs. Van Deusen continued speaking, leaning
closer in a conspiratorial manner. "Marshal Cameron
is joining us for lunch. It will give you two a chance
to get acquainted before the picnic."

Meri surged to her feet, pulse racing. She was not
going to get caught in the woman's matchmaking plot.
Just the thought of lunch with Wy—that man…made
her feel…what? Excited?

"What's wrong, dear?"

Meri hadn't realized she was shaking her head.
Reaching for her Bible, she scraped together some

much-needed poise. "Thank you for the offer, but I'm… I'm not feeling very well. I'm sorry."

"That's all right. You can rest in the parlor and chat with the marshal while I finish lunch. You just need a good meal and some time to relax." Mrs. Van Deusen patted Meri on the arm.

"No. I'm not hungry. I—I should go lie down. I'm sorry." Meri edged away from the woman as she spoke, heading for the nearby side door.

"Well, okay. Maybe I can have both of you over for lunch later this week before you and your father go home." Stepping closer to Meri, she leaned in and whispered none too quietly, "The marshal is a wonderful man, and all the single girls have been trying to get their hooks in him already. I know you've been busy with your father's injury, but if you don't hurry and fix his attention, some scheming female will lure him away, and you'll lose your chance."

A muffled sound made Meri look over her shoulder straight into the eyes of Marshal Cameron. He stood a couple of pews away, but from the look on his face, he'd overheard every word Mrs. Van Deusen had said. Meri's cheeks heated, but she squared her shoulders and looked back at the matchmaking woman.

Raising her voice slightly and speaking firmly, she spoke to Mrs. Van Deusen but addressed the marshal. "They can have him." Meri left the woman sputtering and escaped out the side door, feeling two pairs of eyes on her back until the door closed behind her.

Midafternoon Wyatt strode toward the livery stable to check on his horse after a cutthroat game of checkers with Mr. Van Deusen. Lunch had been delicious—

Mrs. Van Deusen was nothing if not a good cook—but by the time the meal was over, Wyatt's ears were tired from the woman's constant chatter. Most of her conversation had been reserved for singing Miss McIsaac's praises, but he had a sneaking suspicion Miss McIsaac would not appreciate being described as a "poor, motherless lamb." He'd nearly choked on his food at that remark. The last time he'd checked, lambs didn't carry firearms and pursue fleeing gunmen.

Or wear Sunday-go-to-meeting dresses that made their skin luminous.

He'd welcomed the distraction of the three women joining them on their way to church this morning because he had been having trouble remembering his reasons for not pursuing Meri. Unfortunately those overdecorated females had only succeeded in making Miss McIsaac shine like a rare gem amid a pile of imitations.

Wyatt shook his head to dislodge the fanciful thought and entered the barn, pausing to let his eyes adjust to the shadowed dimness.

"Oomph!" His arms instinctively closed around the slight figure that plowed into him, saving them both from hitting the dirt.

A startled squeak reached his ears the same time that it registered he was holding a decidedly feminine form. Firm hands shoved at his chest, and wide eyes blinked up at him from a smudged face.

Meri McIsaac. Except a much-disheveled version of the one he'd escorted to services.

Reluctantly he let his arms fall away, and she stepped back. *Did she have to pull away quite so fast?* He wouldn't think about the empty feeling she left behind. She swiped at a strand of hair that had worked its way loose from her fancy twist, leaving another smudge on her cheek. In the shadowed light of the barn, the wet smear looked like blood.

Wyatt snagged her arm, ignoring her protest. "Where are you hurt?"

She tried to tug away, but he turned her where the light from the open barn door fell across her. He couldn't see the source of any blood, but something smudged her hands, arms and clothing. His heart pounded painfully as he demanded an answer. "Are you hurt?"

"No." She pried her arm out of his grasp and started for the barn door.

Wyatt stepped in front of her. "Then what's wrong?"

Her voice was frantic as she tried to sidestep him. "I have to get Franks. One of his mares is foaling, but she's having trouble, and I can't get the foal turned."

He grasped her shoulders and peered into her face; she vibrated with worried energy. "Show me. I can help."

"But…" She glanced toward the door as if deciding whether to go for Franks.

"We're wasting time." Wyatt pulled his hands away, unbuttoned his shirt cuffs and began to roll up his sleeves.

His calm actions seemed to refocus her attention, and she nodded abruptly. "Over here."

She led him to a large corner stall in the back of the barn where a chestnut mare lay in a thick bed of straw. Stepping inside the stall, she quietly crooned to the sweating, groaning horse and knelt to stroke its head. "I think the foal is in a breech position, but I couldn't get it turned."

Wyatt knelt beside the horse and stroked it softly before reaching to feel for the foal. "I think you're right." He held still as a contraction tightened around his arm. When the contraction eased, the mare struggled to rise to her feet. "Hold her still. I'll try to work with her contractions and turn the baby."

Meri murmured soothing words and stroked the distressed mare, preventing her from rising.

Wyatt worked as quickly as possible and finally maneuvered the foal into a better position. Wiping his arm on the straw, he sat back on his heels to let the mare finish her job. "Where is Franks?"

"He went to play checkers with Faither. I said I would keep an eye on her, but we didn't think the foal would come this early. They usually wait 'til late at night to foal." She moved away from the mare to watch. "I was outside with the other horses, so I don't know how long she's been pushing, but when I checked on her, I knew she was in trouble." She drew in a quick breath. "Oh. Here it comes."

Wyatt and Meri watched as a tiny horse quietly entered the world. The tired mare didn't immediately notice her newly arrived offspring, so Wyatt cleared the sac away from the foal's face and head. "Come on, momma. This is your job."

The foal began to struggle, and one little hoof kicked the mare, bringing her head up and around. Meri sank down in the straw with her back against the stall and watched as the mare began to lick her baby.

Wyatt sat down beside her. "It never gets old, does it?"

She shook her head, wonder and excitement filling her face as she brushed back the loose strand of hair again.

Wyatt turned slightly, resting his shoulder against the stall, and studied her. She'd changed from this morning's pretty dress into a simpler skirt and blouse. She had smudges on her face, arms and clothes; her hair was falling out of its fancy twist and bits of straw clung to her, but she didn't notice them. She'd seen a problem and dived in to fix it, heedless of the damage to her clothes and the rather unpleasant task.

Her attention focused squarely on the foal struggling to get to its feet. "Is it a colt or a filly?"

"A good-looking colt." Wyatt's attention never wavered from her. He didn't have to look, he'd checked earlier.

A pleased smile stretched across her face. "Franks will be happy." She rested her head against the stall and let it roll to one side until she was looking at him.

Wyatt grinned back at her, but he was finding it a bit hard to think straight. Or breathe for that matter. She was a tousled mess, and she'd never looked more beautiful. When she smiled at him the way she was doing now, her eyes warm and shiny, it was downright dangerous. A man could get addicted to seeing it. He leaned in closer, not stopping to second-guess himself.

Her eyes flickered, and her breath hitched. She straightened away from the wall and looked down at her hands. "Thank you."

Would he have kissed her if she hadn't pulled away? He settled back against the boards of the stall and took a much-needed lungful of air. "For what?"

"For helping her." She motioned to the mare now on her feet grooming her baby. "I was scared we would lose them both." Her voice dropped to a whisper. "And I'm tired of things dying on me."

The despair in her voice made Wyatt's heart ache. He gently reached over and tucked the wayward strand of hair behind her ear as he spoke softly. "I'm glad I could help."

Raw, open vulnerability filled the brown eyes that turned to look at him, and Wyatt forcibly restrained his hand from touching her face. If her smile was dangerous, this look was downright deadly.

To his plans.

He forced a grin onto his face. "The would-be horse thief and the marshal. We make a pretty good team of nurses."

She blinked, and that fast, the look was gone. Replaced with a shielded wariness that made Wyatt regret the teasing comment.

"Miss Meri, where is you at?" Franks's deep voice rattled the silence.

Meri sprang to her feet. "In here." Her voice broke, and she cleared her throat. "You have a new colt."

The moment was gone. Wyatt had the cold comfort that his plan to remain unattached until he had a safer profession and a place of his own was still intact. Which was exactly what he wanted.

Wasn't it?

Chapter Ten

Monday morning after her father again ordered her to quit hovering about him, Meri wandered over to the mercantile. Bored and feeling a little guilty about missing lunch with the Van Deusen's the previous day, she volunteered to help around the store for a spell. Mr. Van Deusen took her up on her offer since his wife was at her weekly quilting circle, and Meri worked off some energy wielding a dust rag over the many items in the store. But the quiet morning and even quieter storekeeper left her mind free to brood over Pastor Willis's nagging sermon.

The message and scriptures resonated in her spirit even as her mind argued against the conviction that had settled in since yesterday. Bitterness wasn't her problem. Yes, she had lost her mother, but she'd had her far longer than some people had their mothers. She'd had a relatively easy life: wonderful parents, wonderful place to grow up, a life she loved. The knot in her chest was grief not bitterness, she reasoned, but her spirit wouldn't accept that answer, and the argument continued.

She was carefully dusting some delicate china dishes displayed in the front window when a tap on the glass pulled her out of her thoughts. Marshal Cameron smiled as he tipped his Stetson, and Meri's heart skipped a beat before hastily correcting its lapse and inserting a few extra. He resettled his hat, and Meri forced her eyes back to her task as she replaced the dusted dishes. It was time to get back to the ranch. Being in town this long was affecting her thinking! She was *not* going to become one of those silly females who got all flustered and—and *silly* whenever a good-looking man happened to glance their way.

And a good look at herself in the mirror upon returning to her room yesterday showed she was nothing a man, good-looking or otherwise, would do more than glance at. What a scruffy mess she'd been. Dirt and dried blood all over her face and clothes, hair in a tangle with straw in it.

There had been a camaraderie between them as they'd helped deliver the foal. She'd actually been comfortable with him, but then she'd made a fool of herself when he'd tucked her hair behind her ear. For a moment she'd thought he was going to kiss her.

She shook her head and rubbed fiercely at a smudge on the shelf. How wrong she'd been. He was simply being kind when he could have laughed at her grimy, disheveled condition. He'd certainly retreated fast enough when she'd looked at him like…like a moon-eyed calf.

Meri felt her cheeks heat. She'd obviously forgotten to stick in her good sense when she'd packed her bag at the ranch. The man drove her crazy with his know-it-all grin and bossy attitude!

Didn't he?

Spinning on her heel, she stepped away from the window and her chaotic thoughts. She slammed into a solid immovable object. "Oomph!"

Warm hands steadied her. Meri closed her eyes and breathed in his scent. The feel of powerful hands gently encasing her shoulders and the fresh cleanness of his aftershave swirling around her were...

Pulling away, she frowned, irritated at her illogical reaction. "Do you enjoy sneaking up on everyone, or is it just me?"

His eyes twinkled at her from a straight face. "It must be you since I don't get this reaction from anyone else. I thought you saw me coming this time."

"You were outside. I didn't realize you were going to be right behind me." Meri pointed toward the front window, the forgotten dust rag waving from her outstretched hand like a flag. Jerking her hand down, she gripped the offending rag in both hands. His eyes were laughing at her, but her own eyes didn't seem to care. The traitors kept straying upward to catch another peek.

"So I noticed."

"Noticed what?" Meri's eyes entangled in the hazel trap.

"I noticed you didn't realize I was behind you." He tucked his hands into his back pockets as the laughter moved south and quirked the corner of his mouth.

"Oh." She really did need to pay more attention to this conversation, but she was a little busy avoiding those all-seeing eyes. She focused on the rag in her hands.

"Then again, maybe you ran into me intentionally."

"What!" Meri's eyes widened; her gaze slammed into his.

"I thought that'd get your attention." The satisfied smirk was back. "Now, the reason I came in was to see if you wanted to walk with me. I'm headed to see your father."

"No! I mean…" She glanced around hastily before remembering the dust cloth in her clenched fists. She lifted it triumphantly. "I'm not finished here. You go on." Meri stepped around the well-built form blocking her path and industriously attacked a shelf she'd dusted earlier.

"I'm in no rush. Take your time. I'll be outside taking advantage of that new bench."

Meri watched him walk away out of the corner of her eye and heard the bell chime over the door as he exited. How had she missed that when he'd entered? Peering over her shoulder, she was in time to see him glance at her on his way to the bench located just past the big window. He smiled again, and she whipped back around to scrub at an invisible spot. She was not walking back to Doc's with that man. She'd lose what little sense she still possessed at this rate. She'd already proved she had the conversational ability of a goose today. She needed some space to get her head, and her heart, working intelligently and normal again.

Mr. Van Deusen came out of the storeroom from straightening stock. "You've got things looking spick-and-span. Run along and enjoy the rest of the morning."

"I think I will. I'll wash up before I head out."

Meri tossed a quick glance toward the window. No one was visible. Heading into the storeroom, she rinsed out the dust rag, washed her hands, hung up her apron and slipped out the back door.

Wyatt chuckled under his breath, stretching out his long legs and leaning back against the bench. He had smiled and laughed more since meeting Miss America McIsaac than he had since his parents had died and maybe even longer.

He had excelled in army life, but losing friends in battle and taking the life of another human being tended to sober a man very quickly. Killing was occasionally a necessary part of protecting people's lives and property, but only a callous, heartless individual was unaffected by it. Wyatt was neither callous nor heartless, but his naturally sunny, cheerful disposition had grown graver, and he laughed much less easily. The deaths of his parents had further dampened his ability to smile or laugh easily.

Until a shapely spitfire of a lass had landed at his feet.

Wyatt didn't try to contain a grin. Had she been just a tad reluctant to pull away after she'd run into him? And that poor dust cloth. It had been wrung within an inch of its life before she'd remembered its presence. Her spitfire attitude reminded him of a scared, hissing kitten, yet the confused shyness blanketing her brown eyes had belied the indignant tone.

Winning her trust and…friendship would outweigh the risk of a few scratches along the way. Her relationship with her father and Franks showed a character that was deeply loyal and loving. Her spunky independence might clash with Wyatt's desire to protect

her, but beneath the pretty exterior and prickly attitude, there was a heart worth winning.

Wyatt snapped his reckless thoughts back to attention. He should have continued on his way after
catching a glimpse of Meri fetchingly framed in the
mercantile window instead of stopping to see if she
wanted to accompany him back to Doc's. He wasn't
in a position to win *anyone's* heart. Asking someone
else to bear the burden and hardship of his job wasn't
fair. He couldn't even come close to providing the kind
of place and life Miss McIsaac was used to, so it was
no use daydreaming about it. She deserved someone
who could give her a safe, comfortable life.

Wyatt surged to his feet. The thought of another
man winning her heart was as abhorrent as facing an
angry skunk.

"Somethin' I can help you with, Marshal?" Thomas
Van Deusen interrupted Wyatt's thoughts.

"No, just stopped to see if Miss McIsaac was ready
to head back to Doc's."

The storekeeper leaned against the door frame. Sly
amusement on his face. "Might be a while."

Wyatt's brow furrowed. "Oh? I thought she was
close to finishing. Hasn't she been here awhile?"

"Yep."

The man certainly was the opposite of his voluble
wife. If two words were needed, Thomas made do with
one. Suspicion bloomed in Wyatt's mind. "She went
out the back door, didn't she?"

"Yep."

"How long ago?"

"Couple minutes, maybe."

A little more information would have been helpful,

Wyatt thought ruefully. "Did you happen to see which way she went?"

"Nope."

The man's eyes twinkled in a bland face, and he slowly, deliberately looked up the street. Wyatt followed his gaze in time to see a familiar yellow blouse and tan skirt step nimbly around a passing wagon and disappear between the buildings on the other side of the street a couple of blocks away.

"Thanks!" Wyatt tossed the word over his shoulder, his feet already moving in her direction.

"If you ever catch that girl, you'll have your hands full." A chortle punctuated the storekeeper's words.

Wyatt's eyes narrowed. Oh, he fully intended to catch this particular handful! She'd find it wasn't so easy to escape from a soldier-turned-marshal.

Concerned citizens stopping to inquire about his progress in catching the thief impeded his chase, however. Swallowing his frustration, Wyatt kindly put them off, saying he was waiting for reports to come back from area towns, which he was. He didn't tell them that at the moment he was on the trail of more important quarry!

He was passing the small community park, thinking she might have succeeded in eluding him after all, when he heard a shout that sounded like the woman he was pursuing. Taking off at a run, he raced toward the sounds of a fight issuing from behind a house at the edge of the park.

Rounding the corner, he skidded to a halt. A relieved puff of air left his lips. Meri was unhurt.

Two half-grown boys rolled around the ground, throwing punches and kicks that were mostly ineffectual. Meri was unsuccessfully trying to grab the closest combatant, and Wyatt threw up a prayer thanking the Lord she wasn't injured.

As the prayer crossed his heart, a booted foot found a target in the shape of Meri's shin, and she stumbled. Her gasp moved Wyatt forward to put a stop to the fight, but the sound of a fierce growl brought him to standstill after only two steps.

"That's it!" Meri grumbled as she limped toward the well and hauled up a dripping bucket. "If you want to play dirty, then you're going to get a bath!"

Wyatt leaned against the side of the house curious to see what would happen. Neither Meri nor the continuing-to-tussle boys had caught sight of him, as yet.

Meri emptied the bucket of water into a washtub that had been propped up against the well. Dropping the bucket back down to the water with a splash, she refilled it and poured a second bucketful of water into the tub. She repeated the procedure a third time then leaned down, hefted the full washtub to her hip and limped slowly toward the boys who were still rolling around the ground. Wyatt was impressed. That tub of water had to be as heavy as it was bulky, but she toted it with seeming ease. She neared the boys and paused, waiting.

A grin cocked the corner of his mouth; this was going to be downright entertaining.

The boys rolled toward Meri, fists and feet still flying. Calmly upending the tub of water on the unsuspecting victims when they came within range, Meri drowned the boys in the resulting waterfall.

The fight came to an abrupt end when the boys found they were unable to fight or breathe underwater. Gasping coughs replaced furious grunts, and they struggled to untangle themselves. Wyatt smothered a groaning laugh at the boys' howls when Meri reached down, grabbed each waterlogged boy by an ear and dragged them over to a low woodpile.

"Sit!"

They wilted onto the stacked wood, staring wide-eyed at the woman towering over them, muddy rivulets running down their faces.

"I would like to know why two boys, who claim to be best friends, are suddenly trying to kill each other?" The disarmingly quiet question was met with silence as the two boys glanced nervously toward one another before dropping their gazes to the ground. The silence stretched thin as Meri waited, arms crossed.

Wyatt wondered who would break first and saw the toe of Meri's shoe begin to tap the ground. Both boys glanced nervously at it. Wyatt almost felt sorry for them.

The shorter of the two boys broke the silence with a rush. "Sue Ann said Danny told her he was taking her to the picnic Saturday, and that I couldn't go with them!"

The second boy shot to his feet. "That's a lie! I never did no such thing!"

The first boy shot up, too, and faced him. "Quit calling me a liar!"

"Danny! Billy! Sit down!" The snapped order cowed the boys back to sitting positions.

"Danny, did you ask Sue Ann to the picnic?"

Danny's "No!" was vehement.

Billy scowled at his friend. "Then why would Sue Ann say you did?"

Meri interrupted before Danny could reply. "Hmm…sounds like a Proverbs problem."

"Huh?" Both boys glanced at her curiously. Wyatt was just as curious to hear her explanation.

"Proverbs says, 'A forward man,' or in this case girl, 'soweth strife: and a whisperer separateth chief friends.'"

"What do you mean?" Billy frowned.

"It sounds like someone is trying to break up your friendship by 'whispering' things that aren't quite true, and you fell into the trap of suspecting your best friend instead of her."

"Why would she do that?" asked Danny.

"Proverbs says, 'a lying tongue hateth those that are afflicted by it…'"

"Sue Ann hates us?" Billy asked.

"Well, I think she might be jealous of your friendship and saw this as a way to break it up."

"Why?" This came from Danny.

"Maybe because she likes you and wanted to get your attention."

"But lying is wrong!"

"Yes, and you should pray for her, but I'm more concerned with your friendship at the moment. Proverbs also says, 'Thine own friend…forsake not…' and 'It is an honor…to cease from strife.' Do you want to be honorable friends?"

Both boys nodded, squaring their shoulders.

"Then there's one more piece of advice from Proverbs. Shake hands and apologize."

"Where does it say that in Proverbs?" Danny's brow furrowed skeptically.

"Proverbs 6:3. 'Make sure thy friend.' I want to make sure you're friends again, so shake hands."

A bubble of laughter swelled Wyatt's throat at the sight of the bedraggled, dripping boys solemnly shaking hands and giving shamefaced apologies. Both were developing shiners, but their sheepish grins showed the incident was well on its way to being forgiven and forgotten.

"I know another way to make sure you're friends," Meri added.

"What?"

"I hear there's a three-legged race at the church picnic. Since you're both already dirty, this would be a good time to find a piece of rope and practice working with each other. By the end of the week, you should be able to beat all the competition." Wyatt could hear the grin in Meri's voice and wished he could see her face.

Excitedly discussing where a suitable length of rope could be found, the boys wrapped their arms around each other's shoulders and began to practice, hopping away from Meri.

When they disappeared from view, Meri turned and caught sight of Wyatt, a grin lingering on her face.

Wyatt shook his head and shivered theatrically. "I'm glad you're not my mother."

Her grin faded. "Why?"

"I've never heard so many Proverbs thrown into a tongue-lashing in all my life!"

Reluctant amusement crept back over her face. "My mother used Proverbs on me all the time. She said they were more effective than anything she could come up with since God promised *His* word wouldn't return void, but He never promised the same thing about her words!" A short laugh punctuated her statement.

"You were pretty thorough, but I think you missed a couple that apply."

"Oh?" It was amazing how quickly her suspicion returned.

"Proverbs 27:6 and 17." He waited.

Her eyes narrowed as she sifted through her memory. Shaking her head, she said ruefully, "I don't recall what those verses say."

"'Faithful are the *wounds* of a friend…' and 'Iron sharpeneth iron; so a man sharpeneth the countenance of his friend.' Danny and Billy certainly had the wounds to show for their sharpening session today!"

Meri snickered, and Wyatt grinned, pleased with himself.

"You are terrible, Marshal!" Laughter wove itself through her voice.

He grinned, pleased with the sound. "Just following your example, Mac."

Lingering humor ruined the effect of her scowl. "My name is not Mac."

"And mine's not Marshal. It's Wyatt, or Cameron, if you prefer."

Meri edged around him. "On that note, I think I'll say good day."

"Not so fast." Wyatt touched her arm to stop her, unsuccessfully ignoring the spark that jumped between them. "I've not forgotten that you snuck out on me."

The way she looked at her arm made him wonder if she had felt that spark, too. "I never said I was going with you."

Was there a hint, just a hint, of coyness in her reply?

He assumed a serious expression. "I've always tried to be an 'honorable' man, so I'm going to 'cease from strife' and not argue the point—"

Meri rolled her eyes.

"—but since my job is protecting the citizens of Little Creek and danger seems to be just around the corner lately, I wouldn't be doing my job if I allowed you to walk the streets alone and unarmed." Reaching for her hand, he tucked it around his arm and guided her steps toward Dr. Kilburn's house.

Meri was remarkably quiet, and surprisingly, she left her hand on his arm. After several moments she spoke. "I'm not exactly unarmed, you know."

Wyatt heard a trace of amusement. "Are you carrying a hideout gun?"

"I'm talking about a different kind of weapon," she hedged. He noticed she didn't say no. "It's called the '...sword of the Spirit, which is the word of God...'"

"Ah. In that case, I'll escort you to protect the town from *you!*"

A snicker escaped her, and Wyatt laughed. She cast furtive glances in his direction as they continued to walk along in silence until they reached the doctor's house. Stopping, he nudged her around until she was facing him. "If the town council hears about this, I may lose my job."

There was a slightly dazed look in Meri's eyes as she wrinkled her brow in confusion. "What do you mean?"

"If they hear how you keep charging in and facing down danger on your own, they'll decide they don't need me and hire you because you're cheaper."

She waited, eyes narrowed expectantly.

"The town has to buy the ammunition for my gun, but the last time I checked, swords don't need bullets!"

Warm brown eyes rolled again, and he saw her bite the inside of her lip to hide a smile. "Don't worry, Marshal. Your job is safe from me. I do *not* want to deal with the nuisances of town life."

Wyatt nodded sadly in agreement. "There *are* some nuisances, like people who don't listen to the marshal—" he looked pointedly at her before continuing "—but I must admit that there is some compensation."

"Like what?"

"Some nuisances are prettier than others... Mac."

Her eyes sparked, and he removed his hat with a flourish, sweeping her a low, courtly bow. Then he turned and walked swiftly back toward his office, whistling retreat as he went.

Chapter Eleven

The initial replies to the telegrams Wyatt sent out had been disappointing; there were no reports of anyone matching the description of the suspect. Tuesday morning, however, Wyatt received some much-needed information. A marshal in an adjoining county wired that the bank teller was living and working there, and a man matching the thief's description had been seen.

Leaving his new deputy in charge, Wyatt saddled his stallion, Charger, and rode out to gather further information on the identity or whereabouts of the bank bandit. He spent part of the long ride in prayer over the case, asking the Lord to guide his steps and open his eyes to the truth about the theft. When he wasn't praying, his thoughts ranged between mulling over the case and picturing Meri's smile the previous day.

It felt good to be astride his own horse again. Charger had developed a troublesome limp on the last of their journey from Texas to Little Creek, and Wyatt had given him ample time to recover. Now fresh and raring to go, Charger eagerly covered the long distance as fast as Wyatt would allow him and listened willingly whenever Wyatt shared his thoughts aloud.

Midafternoon, they arrived at the office of the marshal who'd sent him the telegram. After a discussion of all the particulars of the bank robbery, the two men walked over to the saloon. However, upon talking with the bartender and several of the regulars, Wyatt learned little he didn't already know.

The man in question had come in for a meal and a drink, but hadn't spoken beyond giving his order. His clothing matched what the thief had worn, but the description of his physical appearance was vague enough to have been anybody. And the horse he'd ridden was sorrel, not gray. A quick stop at the livery stable confirmed there was a gray horse in town, but as she had just presented her proud owner with a lovely filly a couple of days previous, she couldn't have been the horse Meri had seen Saturday. The livery stable owner didn't know of any other gray horses in the area.

At this dead end Wyatt turned his attention to the bank teller Mr. Dunn. Like Wyatt, the marshal was newly hired and knew little about Mr. Dunn. He did know Dunn was the newest employee of the bank and resided at a local boardinghouse. He pointed toward the bank and said although it was near closing time, Wyatt might be able to catch Mr. Dunn there.

Mr. Dunn had already gone for the day, but the manager invited Wyatt into his office, curious about the holdup. Wyatt filled him in on a few details and asked what he knew or thought about Mr. Dunn. The man informed Wyatt that in the time Mr. Dunn had worked for him, he had found him a hardworking, conscientious employee. In addition Mr. Dunn's family lived in the area, and the bank manager had known them for years. They were well respected in the community, and he was glad to have been able to hire their son. He also confirmed that Mr. Dunn had been at work the day of the holdup in Little Creek. Wyatt thanked him for his time and upon receiving directions to Mr. Dunn's lodgings, departed.

At the boardinghouse he was informed Mr. Dunn had a room there but ate his meals at his folks' place and was probably still there. Wyatt was feeling hungry himself when he finally located the Dunns' residence. An older gentleman answered his knock, and after introducing himself and explaining his errand, Wyatt accepted the offer of a meal while they talked and was ushered into the kitchen of the small home.

The older man introduced himself as Mr. Dunn, the local schoolteacher. He then presented his wife, his youngest daughter and his son George. Requesting everyone to be seated, he spoke the blessing over the food. "Enjoy the meal while it's hot. We'll discuss your business after we've eaten."

With a minimum of conversation, everyone dug into the simple but tasty fare. When Mrs. Dunn served a delicious dried-apple pie, Mr. Dunn turned to Wyatt. "We heard about the robbery, but how can we be of help?"

"I've been unsuccessful in tracking down the culprit, and since your son was employed at the bank, I'm hoping he can shed some light on a few inconsistencies I've run across in my investigation." Turning to George, he continued, "I've heard a couple of different reasons why you left Little Creek. Would you tell me your side of the story?"

George, a bookish-looking young man wearing wire-rimmed spectacles, set down his fork and wiped his mouth before responding succinctly. "Because I was fired."

"Your former landlady said as much. The banker had a slightly different story."

The young man scowled. "I can only guess what that old skinflint told you."

"George!" Mrs. Dunn's shocked reply softened her son's face, and he shot her a look of apology.

"I'm sorry, Ma, but he was a hard man to work for."

"Would you elaborate, please?" Wyatt asked.

"I went to Little Creek to work in the bank because I wanted to try and make it on my own. I knew I could get a job in this town because everyone respects my father, but I wanted to make it on my own name. Mr. Samuels was okay to work for the first couple of years, but after his wife died, I couldn't seem to do anything to please him. It was as if he no longer trusted me."

"What do you mean?"

"I had more responsibilities when I started working for him. The longer I was there, the less he let me do. He wouldn't let me near the safe, and the only money I handled was what he placed in the teller's drawer. He got so suspicious that if he needed to leave the bank, he'd send me home early and lock up 'til he got back. He frequently accused me of accounting mistakes and finally outright accused me of stealing before he fired me. He didn't even give me a chance to defend myself. By that time I was so tired of it all, I just let it go and moved back home."

"Why didn't you quit sooner?"

"He didn't used to be that bad. I was going to tough

it out 'til he got better, but then he fired me. I thought I could make it on my own. Guess I was wrong."

"Maybe the grief over his wife's death was more than he could handle." Mrs. Dunn patted her son's arm soothingly.

"Maybe—" his voice was doubtful "—although he sure was more attentive to her after her death then he ever was before."

"What a thing to say!" Mrs. Dunn chastised again.

"I'm sorry, Ma, but he was. When he did talk about his wife, which wasn't often before she died, he wasn't very complimentary, and he spent all hours at the bank. After she died, he was constantly talking about how he missed her, and he'd send me home so he could lock up and visit her grave. I think he spent more time with her after she died than before." Addressing Wyatt, he asked, "How much did the bank robber get?"

"Mr. Samuels said the man cleaned out the safe, but he won't divulge the amount taken until the culprit is apprehended. I was hoping you could tell me how much was normally kept in the safe."

"Like I said, Mr. Samuels wouldn't allow me near the safe, and he certainly didn't tell me that information. The only money I ever saw was what was in my drawer for the day. Mr. Samuels put it in the drawer each morning and took it out each afternoon. For all I know, that was the only money in the bank!" George Dunn said sarcastically.

Wyatt changed the subject and gave the description of the thief. "Did you ever see anyone that matched that description or acted suspiciously?"

George thought for a minute before replying. "No.

I rarely dealt with anyone I didn't already know. Mr. Samuels made me send any newcomer directly to him."

"Were there any 'newcomers' recently?"

"No. Wait. Somebody came in one day when I was coming back inside from dumping the wastebasket. Mr. Samuels hustled him into his office and sent me home. I heard him lock the door behind me when I left."

"Did you get a good look at him?"

"I didn't see anything but his back before he entered Mr. Samuels's office. Anyway, he hurried me out of there and didn't say anything about who it was. I didn't ask, either, as he didn't take kindly to questions. About a week later, I was out of a job."

Wyatt had been scratching notes as George talked and now returned the little book and pencil to his pocket. Thanking the family for the meal, he asked George to send word if he remembered anything else that might be of use and stood to take his leave. "One more question. I know you were here at work the day of the holdup, but did you have anything to do with the robbery? Revenge on Mr. Samuels perhaps?" He watched George closely.

"No! I don't like the man, but I'm not a thief!"

The man's shock seemed genuine, and Wyatt didn't press him further, taking his leave of the family.

Deciding against riding back home in the dark, he stabled his horse at the livery and bedded down in an empty stall at the invitation of the stable owner. Crossing his hands behind his head as he lay on his bedroll, he sifted through the information he'd learned.

There were so many odds and ends that didn't seem to fit anywhere. Was George Dunn telling the truth or was it a case of sour grapes over losing his job? Then again, the banker had said George left to be near his widowed mother, and there was clearly no widowed mother. Why would the banker lie? Or had George lied to the banker and about the banker?

Wyatt had seen the empty safe in the minutes after the holdup; he'd seen the bandit riding away; he'd seen the wound on the banker's head from his fall; he'd seen Mr. McIsaac bleeding on the floor. A robbery had occurred, but every clue led to dead ends and conflicting testimony. If only he could get some solid answers.

He fell into a fitful sleep, dreaming he was in pursuit of the bank robber. Every time he neared the elusive thief and reached to grab him, the man melted away leaving only questions in Wyatt's hands. Before daylight he rolled his bedroll, saddled Charger and hit the trail for Little Creek. A little before noon he reached town, his first stop, the bank to speak to Mr. Samuels.

But its doors were locked, and his knock brought no response. At the man's house the housekeeper informed him Mr. Samuels was out of town visiting investors in the hopes of replacing the bank's capital, since the marshal couldn't seem to find the stolen money. Ignoring the not-so-subtle dig, Wyatt politely inquired about the banker's return, but was informed condescendingly that Mr. Samuels would come home when he'd finished his business and not before.

Again Wyatt was left with unanswered questions as he rode Charger to the livery where he was met by the blacksmith and Jonah.

"I saw you ride up to the bank and figured I might catch you here," Jonah said.

Recounting what he'd learned, Wyatt unsaddled and rubbed Charger down before turning the animal out with Franks's geldings to graze. Franks and Jonah confirmed that the banker had frequently complained in public about his "worthless bank help" although the young man had been unfailingly polite to customers.

No new pieces of the puzzle appeared as the three men discussed the findings but agreed Wyatt needed to pin down the banker when he returned. "The town's been real quiet since you and Miss Meri left," Jonah said dryly.

"Meri left? Where? When? She wasn't supposed to ride out on her own," Wyatt snapped.

Franks chuckled, his hammer clanging a horseshoe into shape as Jonah replied to the question. "McIsaac talked Doc into letting him go home. Between Miss Meri and Mrs. Van Deusen, they filled a wagon bed full of quilts and bullied McIsaac into lying down in the back for the ride. They headed home yesterday afternoon."

Wyatt resumed breathing. "Anything else I need to know about?"

"Nope, like I said. It's been quiet without you two to stir up trouble."

"Then let's go get some food. After that I need to catch up on some reports. See ya later, Franks."

Meri straightened and stretched her aching back. The sun was warm, but the breeze cooled her sweat-dampened skin as she leaned on her hoe and checked her progress. The garden was coming along well and looked as if it would deliver an abundant harvest this year. It was also weed free, thanks to her hard work.

It was good to be home and back in the thick of ranch life. Faither was anxious to be back out on the range he loved, and Meri didn't know how long she could keep him off a horse, but at least for now he'd agreed to work in his office for a few days. She'd worried the trip home would tax his strength and set his recovery back, but he appeared invigorated by the fact that he was home, and she was pleased with how well he seemed to be doing. He tired quicker than normal, but that was fading a little more each day. Before long, he'd be back to full strength.

Meri, on the other hand, had about worn herself out making sure he took it easy while trying to outwork her own disordered thoughts. Coming home was supposed to restore life to normal, but normal had packed its bags and departed for parts unknown. Pastor Willis's sermon continued to nag her heart, and Wyatt Cameron seemed to have taken up permanent residence in her thoughts. When ignoring them didn't work, Meri tried to keep herself too busy to think, and evidence of her frenzy lay all around her.

They had arrived home Tuesday afternoon; it was now Friday. In that time she'd cleaned the chicken coop and horse stalls before progressing to every corner of the barn. She'd cleaned and oiled every saddle and bridle she could lay her hands on, and Barnaby good-humoredly accused her of trying to put his men out of a job. She would have tackled the inside of the house if Ms. Maggie and her father hadn't shooed her out from under their feet, so she tackled cobwebs on porches and weeds in flower beds instead.

Looking over her latest endeavor, Meri viewed the weed-free garden with satisfaction.

Now what? a little voice asked mockingly. *You can't run forever.*

Hoofbeats caught her ear, and welcoming the interruption, she turned, shading her eyes to see the oncoming rider. Meri's heart gave an odd little skip as she recognized the figure on the beautiful bay. She groaned. Just when she'd managed to stop thinking about the man, he had to show up!

Sure you stopped thinking about him...for all of five minutes!

Wyatt lifted his hand in greeting.

Meri glanced down at herself. She was a mess! Sweat dripping, dirt smudges everywhere and her hair probably a wild tangle from the wind teasing it all morning. She couldn't meet him looking like this! Dropping the hoe along with any attempt at dignity, Meri raced for the back door.

The kitchen door slammed in her wake, and Ms. Maggie jumped away from her bread dough, slapping her hand to her chest. "Good grief, girl. What's wrong?"

Meri slid to a halt and attempted to retrieve the composure she'd left in the garden dirt. "Um, the marshal. He's here. I'm going to my room."

The housekeeper shook her head in exasperation, and Meri ran up the back stairs as a knock rattled the front door. Reaching the sanctuary of her room, she frantically washed up, donned a clean pink blouse and fresh skirt and with trembling fingers rebraided her windblown hair. Finally she plopped down in her rocking chair, hands shaking and nerves fluttering.

Why was she so worried about her appearance? She wasn't vain about her looks, at least not much. They'd had visitors to the ranch when she wore the stains of hard work, but never before had she raced away to clean up, then remained hidden in her room.

Meri rocked the chair vigorously. *I am not hiding! Besides, he didn't come to see me. He came to check on Faither.*

"Meri? Are ye coming down, lass? Ye have a visitor." Meri jumped as her father's voice echoed up the stairs.

Taking a deep breath and checking her appearance in the mirror once more, she noticed she was visibly shaking. Meri uttered a quick, desperate plea.

"Lord, help!"

The prayer had been instinctive, and a sudden thought froze her in her tracks. Maybe it wasn't that the Lord wasn't hearing her prayers, maybe it was that she'd actually stopped praying except for an occasional desperate yelp. Had she prayed at all since she'd gotten home?

"Meri?"

Shelving the thought, she called, "Coming, Faither."

Feigning courage, she opened the door and hurried to the stairs. She'd fully expected to see both men waiting at the bottom and breathed a sigh of relief when they weren't. Descending the stairs slowly, she heard voices coming from her father's study and headed that direction.

"Ah. There she is." Both men stood from overstuffed chairs as she entered the book-lined room where her father's desk stood. Most of the books had been collected by her mother and lived undisturbed until long winter evenings. "I've invited Cameron to stay to lunch. Ms. Maggie said it would be ready shortly."

"It's ready now. Come and get it." The housekeeper spoke behind her.

Meri followed the woman back to the kitchen. "I'll help you put it on the table."

"It's already on the table." The woman waved Meri toward the door.

"Where?" Meri looked at the bare kitchen table.

"We have company. It's time that big dining table was used again, and this is as good a time as any. Now shoo, you have a guest."

Entering the little-used dining room, Meri was surprised to see the housekeeper had set the table with a linen cloth, napkins and Catriona McIsaac's good china. When had she had time to do it all? Surely Meri hadn't spent that much time in her room?

Marshal Cameron held a chair for her to the right of her father, and she slid into it while avoiding his eyes. His hand brushed her shoulder, and Meri nearly jumped out of her skin at the reaction the simple touch caused. Glancing at him as he took his seat across the table from her, she intercepted a penetrating look and dropped her eyes to her plate, wondering why he was here.

After McIsaac asked the blessing and their plates were filled, Wyatt and her father continued a discussion that must have started in the study before she'd come down. It seemed that once again there were more dead ends concerning the bank robbery.

Meri chewed and swallowed automatically, losing track of the conversation. He wasn't here to see her. He was only here to keep her father informed. So why did her heart pound just a little faster every time she caught his eyes on her?

Because you've allowed yourself to imagine something that isn't there. The man is simply doing his job. Once it's done, he'll move on. Meri fought to keep her wandering gaze on her plate and off their handsome guest.

The interminable meal ended, and McIsaac leaned back in his chair, propping his elbows atop the armrests and crossing his hands over his stomach. "I believe ye had something ye wanted to ask me daughter, Cameron."

Meri stiffened, waiting, but neither man spoke. She darted a look at her father, but he merely pointed toward Wyatt. She steeled herself to brave the hazelgreen eyes watching her.

"Ah. There you are. You've been very quiet." His smile was gentle instead of teasing.

Meri felt her cheeks color. When had he gone from the most annoying man she'd ever met, to the most handsome? Taking a deep breath, she forced a composure into her voice that she was nowhere close to feeling. "What is your question?"

His gaze shifted to the table, and Meri felt like she'd lost something—which was nonsense. How could you lose something you didn't have in the first place?

He looked back, determination gleaming in his gaze. "May I escort you to the church picnic tomorrow?"

Chapter Twelve

Meri's breath froze in her throat. Had he really come to ask her to accompany him to the picnic? Her—Meri McIsaac? The old maid of Little Creek?

Hope sparked then an appalling question doused it. After those two men had shot at her, Marshal Cameron had said she wasn't to go riding outside of town alone. Had he simply decided it was part of his job to escort her to the picnic—a way to keep an eye on the troublemaker? Had her father asked him to take her since he was staying home?

Her father cleared his throat, reminding her Marshal Cameron was still waiting for an answer. She swallowed the lump of mortification that stuck in her throat, and it hit her stomach like a cannonball. "Thank you, but I'm not going to the picnic. I don't want to leave Faither alone." At least her voice didn't sound as embarrassed as she felt.

"Ach. I don't need a babysitter, lassie. Frankly, I could use a break from yer frantic cleaning, and so could ye. Ye've worked yerself to a frazzle this week.

Now it's time for a little fun." He looked at Wyatt. "When will ye be here to pick her up?"

"But…" Her feeble protest was lost in the continuing conversation.

"I'll be here about ten o'clock in the morning. That should give us plenty of time to get there before the meal at noon. When do you want your daughter home, sir?"

"Have the lass home before dark."

"Yes, sir."

They stood and shook hands as if they'd completed a business transaction. Apparently, her suspicions weren't far from the mark. Dazed, she watched them walk out of the room toward the front door. "Wait! Don't I have some say in this?" she demanded, scurrying to catch up.

Both men replied in unison, "No."

"Why do I get the feeling I've been ambushed?" She sounded peeved, but it was better than melting into a puddle of humiliation.

Wyatt laughed as he stepped outside and off the porch. "See you in the morning."

As he loped his horse away, Meri turned to her father and took a deep breath. "Why—"

He held up his hand. "Ye need a break, and ye wouldn't have gone on yer own. Don't forget, ye'll need to make something for the dessert auction." McIsaac turned to go in the house.

She stopped him. "Did you ask him to take me?"

The surprise in his eyes was genuine. "Wheesht, lass. Why would I need to ask the man to escort me beautiful daughter to the picnic? He's smart enough to have the idea for himself. Now, if ye'll excuse me, I'm wee bit tired. I think I need to lie down." The twinkle in his eye belied his plea of fatigue as he left her standing on the porch.

Meri threw the third dress across her bed in frustration. She was working herself into a dither over what to wear to the picnic.

You're being ridiculous, Meri!

Running downstairs, she found Barnaby exiting her father's study.

"Can I do something for you, miss?"

"Would you have someone saddle Sandy and bring him around, please?"

Faither followed him out of the room. "Lass, a gentleman brings a buggy when he's taking his girl to a picnic. Ye don't need yer horse."

"I am *not* his girl. I'm riding Sandy in." She smiled winningly at the foreman. "Will you do it, Barnaby? Please?"

Looking at McIsaac, who only shrugged in exasperation, he sighed. "Yes, if that's what you want."

"Thank you." Planting a quick kiss on the cheek of each man, she turned and ran back up the stairs to her room.

"This is gonna be interesting," Barnaby muttered.

Determination filled her as she headed back to her wardrobe and grabbed an outfit. It wasn't what most females would wear to a picnic, especially when they were escorted by a handsome gentleman, but then again, she wasn't most females. When Wyatt Cameron arrived at her doorstep with a buggy, she would meet him on horseback. As Meri McIsaac, the content-to-be-single cowgirl. Not a delicately dressed husband-hunting female.

Donning the outfit, Meri scoffed at herself. Obviously her rebellion only stretched so far. She'd pulled out her newest, fanciest riding habit. The long and full divided skirt was a buttery-soft fawn-colored leather, paired with a crisp white blouse and belted at the waist with a black leather belt. A black velvet ribbon circled the collar of the blouse in a feminine bow. A matching fawn-colored leather vest with shiny black jet buttons topped the blouse, and a tan flat-brimmed hat and black boots completed the ensemble.

Meri studied herself in the mirror. She'd smoothed her hair into a neat braid, coiled and pinned at the base of her neck and neatly tucked beneath the brim of her hat. A flush warmed her cheeks, and the color of the skirt and vest mimicked the color of her hair and the light tan on her skin. She'd always thought the outfit was pretty and polished, but all at once, she saw the contrast she'd make against the backdrop of dressed-up females.

"Well, if your aim was to stand out like a sore thumb, America McIsaac, you're going to accomplish it in rare form." Looking at the little clock on her nightstand, she muttered, "And it's too late to change your mind now. He'll be here soon."

Giving in to a last-minute impulse, she opened her jewelry box, pulled out a pair of jet earbobs and fastened them to her ears. Tucking a handkerchief in her pocket, Meri avoided the mirror again and left the room.

The clock was chiming ten as she stepped onto the porch. Sandy was standing patiently at the hitching rail, groomed and saddled, and a distant horse and rider were approaching the house.

Meri blinked, surprised. He wasn't driving a buggy?

Swallowing past a bundle of nerves, she focused on the horse he was riding. It was the tall bay with the white star she'd seen in Franks's pasture the day she'd first met the marshal. The same horse he'd ridden yesterday, come to think of it, but in her haste to get to the house and change, she'd not spared the animal any attention.

Wyatt rode up beside Sandy and leaned his arm against the saddle horn, tilting his hat brim up with one finger. He wore his holster and star, but a black string tie adorned the collar of the spotless gray cavalry-style bib shirt that stretched across firm shoulders. Dark blue pressed trousers and polished boots covered the muscular legs that draped around the horse. "Great minds think alike."

"They do?" Meri asked guardedly.

Wyatt pointed to Sandy. "I didn't figure you'd want to ride in a buggy on this pretty day, so I took a chance you'd be ready to ride."

This man seemed able to read her like a book. It was a bit disconcerting to say the least.

Wyatt swung his leg over the front of the saddle and slid lightly to his feet. Sweeping off his hat and holding it against his chest, he bowed deeply. Meri had originally thought the gesture was his way of mocking her, but today it felt…courtly.

"You look fetching." His eyes swept over her, frankly admiring as he straightened to his full height.

Meri dropped her own eyes in confusion. This didn't feel like an escort simply to keep her safe. "Thank you."

Stepping off the porch, she walked over to the magnificently tall bay and held out the back of her hand for him to smell. "Who is this handsome fellow?"

She felt Wyatt move up behind her, and his arm reached around to stroke the horse's neck. "Meet Charger. He came with me all the way from my folks' place in Virginia. I haven't been able to ride him until this week because he developed a limp on our way up from Texas. It's good to be back on him."

Meri withdrew from the disturbing awareness the man was causing and walked around the sleek animal, stroking him as she circled. "Is he a thoroughbred?"

"Yep, from old Virginia bloodlines. I hope to have a place someday where I can run a few head of good horseflesh. He's my start. He's also a good friend. We've been through a few scrapes together, and unlike some people, he's never let me down."

"He looks like he could cover some ground." Meri swung up on Sandy.

"He can, and he's raring to go today." Wyatt stayed on the ground.

"Then let's not keep him waiting, Marshal."

He glanced at the house. "Do we need to take anything with us for the picnic?"

"No. The housekeeper and some of the hands are bringing food in the wagon. They'll leave here shortly." Meri's nerves were beginning to make Sandy antsy, but the marshal didn't seem in any hurry to leave.

"Who's staying with your father?"

"The bunkhouse cook. He and Faither are having a chess rematch. They're evenly matched right now, and each one swears he's going to be the winner of the tiebreaker."

The man finally swung up on his horse. "Well, then, Miss Mac. Let's go, shall we?"

Meri's father stepped out the front door. "Have a nice time. I trust ye'll take care of me daughter?"

"Yes, sir! I won't take my eyes off of her."

Meri caught her breath sharply. His eyes were dangerous when they sparkled like that.

"What's that, Meri-lass?"

She cleared her throat with a cough ignoring Wyatt's grin. "We're going to be late."

"Well, who's stoppin' ye? Get goin'."

Meri and Wyatt turned their horses and rode out of the ranch yard. Silence stretched between them for several minutes before Meri broke it. "You know, I never knew our town was so compassionate."

"How so?" Wyatt's tone indicated he knew something was coming.

"They took pity and hired such a forgetful person for so important a position."

"Meaning me, I suppose."

Meri nodded, looking appropriately sad but hiding a grin.

Wyatt made a show of looking all around and down at himself. "What did I forget?"

Meri shook her head gloomily. "See? You can't even remember to remember that my name is *not* Mac!"

Wyatt's hangdog, mournful demeanor was comical, but she smothered the impulse to laugh. The man didn't need any further encouragement. "Yes. Unfortunately it's a highly contagious condition. I contracted it from a certain young lady who can't seem to remember that *my* name is not *Marshal!*"

She was regretting her choice of subjects. *Hoist on your own petard, Meri.*

"There is a cure, however." Wyatt paused, catching her eye before continuing quietly, "When you can remember to call me Wyatt or even Cameron, I believe my memory will improve, and I'll be able to remember *your* name." Earnestness peered through the teasing expression.

Meri searched for a reply that would rescue her from the hole she'd entrapped herself in. "But you *are* the marshal. It's…it's a term of respect," she finally managed weakly.

A laugh burst from Wyatt's lips. "If the way you obey orders is any indication of the level of your respect, I'd much rather you just call me by my name!"

Meri didn't know whether to laugh or search for a witty rebuttal, so she did neither. She ran.

Touching Sandy with her heels, the horse sprang into a full gallop, taking advantage of the long open stretch of road and leaving the marshal behind in two jumps.

Charger strained to follow Sandy, but Wyatt held him in check, taking a few moments to admire the slim figure that moved as one with her horse. The color of Meri's apparel matched the coloring of the flashy palomino, and highlighted the golden glints in her hair. Horse and rider presented a striking image as they flew down the road. He had wrestled with himself about asking her to the picnic and in the end had decided to do it, trying not to examine his motives too closely. It was a day to enjoy the burgeoning spring, not worry about the future.

The distance between them widened, and Wyatt stroked Charger's sleek neck. "Okay, fella, let's show those two what Virginia boys can do." Charger leaped into action, long legs stretching easily to eat up the distance.

Meri glanced over her shoulder, and her eyes widened when she realized they were gaining. Turning back, she leaned low over Sandy's neck and urged him to greater speed. The sturdy palomino surged forward with renewed effort, but Charger's longer legs relentlessly narrowed the gap between them. In minutes they were alongside Meri and Sandy.

While Wyatt was momentarily checking Charger's speed to match Sandy's, Meri's eyes flashed at him, gleaming with competitive excitement. He tapped the brim of his hat in a salute. Charger tossed his head impatiently at the delay, and Wyatt let him go. Surging forward in a renewed burst of speed, they quickly left Meri and Sandy behind.

Wyatt allowed him to run several more strides before guiding him down to a smooth lope. Flashing a look over his shoulder, he saw Meri racing to close the distance Charger had put between them. As they came alongside, Wyatt slowed Charger's pace again, but Meri ignored the gesture, tapping her own hat as she and Sandy raced past.

Wyatt growled, half amused, half irritated. The stubborn woman didn't know when she was beaten because she refused to quit! He allowed Charger to leap after the palomino immediately this time, and they were alongside the pair almost instantly. Nudging Charger in close to Sandy, Wyatt snaked an arm around Meri's waist and pulled her off her horse and across the front of his saddle in one fluid movement.

Shock widened her eyes and one hand convulsively

clenched Sandy's reins as Wyatt slowed Charger to a walk. Sandy quietly followed alongside, eyeing his unseated mistress curiously.

Wyatt looked down into her surprised face and grinned at the traces of dirt Charger had kicked up on her when they'd passed. Right arm cradling her back, right hand holding Charger's reins, he used his left to pull out his handkerchief and gently wipe her face. "You've got a little dirt here…and here…" Wyatt heard her sharp intake of breath as he wiped the dust off.

She was a frozen bundle of tension for half a second longer before she snapped into frantic motion. "Put me down…" she squeaked as she struggled to slide off his lap.

Wyatt tightened his arm around her, pinning her into place. "Nope. You haven't asked me nicely, yet." Her stubbornness was no hardship; he could hold her all day. He refused to lose this battle of wills.

"Would you put me down…please?" Meri tried again to pull away and slide down.

"Uh-uh. You still haven't asked correctly." He could feel her trembling. The horses had continued traveling at a brisk walk, and they would soon be in view of town. Wyatt wondered how long the stubborn woman would hold out before realizing she was in danger of being seen…sitting on the marshal's lap!

They were at the final turn toward town before she gave in. The ramrod-straight spine was as stiff as a poker, but her voice was wobbly as she spoke. "Please put me down, *Mr. Cameron*."

Wyatt looked into nervous brown eyes before she cast a quick look down the road toward town. Wyatt brought Charger to a stop. Sandy kept his nose even with Meri's feet.

"That's not exactly what I had in mind, but I guess it'll do. For now." He tugged the reins out of her hand and moved Sandy into position before smoothly, regretfully, swinging Meri back into her saddle. His arms immediately missed the feel of her.

She fastidiously straightened her skirt and vest and adjusted her hat, before reaching to take the reins from his hand.

He moved them out of range and cocked an eyebrow at her.

She exhaled noisily. "*Thank you.* Now would you *please* give my reins back, Mar...?" She bit off the last word but not quickly enough.

She was persistent, but she had met her match. Wyatt grinned and reached to pick her off her horse again. "Ah, ah, ah, Miss Mac. That's not my name."

Meri nudged Sandy with her heel, and he swung his hindquarters away, placing the horses in a T position and putting Meri temporarily out of reach. She lifted her chin regally and focused somewhere over his shoulder. "As I was saying, Mr. Cameron, thank you. Now I suggest we get a move on if we plan on attending the picnic."

Wyatt wondered what she'd do if he hauled her off her horse again and kissed her senseless.

Probably slap your fool head off!

Wyatt chuckled before handing over the reins. It might just be worth it, but he'd back off and accept the unspoken truce for now. He waved toward town. "After you, Miss *Mac...* Isaac."

Chapter Thirteen

Meri stood outside the marshal's office and contemplated the abnormally quiet street. The townsfolk must already be at the picnic grounds. She would have been there, too, but for the fact she had wanted to leave Sandy in Franks's pasture for the afternoon. That detour had given her a few extra moments to recover her composure after being held by... Mr. Cameron, as well as giving her a chance to duck into Franks's living quarters and wash the remaining dirt off her face.

Walking back toward the picnic grounds, Wyatt had stopped at his office to check in with Jonah who would be keeping an eye on the nearly deserted town while everyone was at the picnic. Meri had waved hello through the open door and now waited on the porch while the two men talked.

Letting her idle gaze linger on the bank, she relived the terrifying moment when she'd seen her father lying bleeding on the floor. A shudder rippled through her at how close death had come to robbing her again.

Something flashed inside the bank.

That was odd. She had assumed the bank would

still be closed and the banker at the picnic with the rest of the town.

She walked down the boardwalk toward the bank, staying on the opposite side of the street. She'd just take a quick look-see and make sure everything was okay, although from what she'd heard, there was nothing left to steal. Meri stopped across from the bank, in the shadow of the dressmaker's shop. The bank's large front window shed light into the dim recesses of the building, and a figure stood just on the edge of the pool of sunlight.

Meri let out a breath she didn't know she'd been holding. It was only the banker. After being shot at, she was imagining trouble behind every bush.

Another silhouette moved into view. Whoever was in there was certainly having an animated conversation with the banker. Their body language shouted irritation. Someone unhappy with the bank's closure, maybe?

The two figures moved out of sight, and Meri walked back to the office, arriving as Wyatt stepped out with Jonah.

"Best not keep the lady waitin' any longer, Cap'n. I know where to find you if I need you."

"I'll send someone with food so you won't miss out on the good cookin'." Wyatt tucked Meri's hand under his arm, covering it with his free hand, and stepped off briskly toward the church grounds.

Meri allowed her fingers to curl lightly around Wyatt's arm. She should pull away, but it felt good, hand nestled in the crook of his arm, hidden under his own. She had a sudden wish that her entire person could hide. The whole town was about to see her walk in on the marshal's arm.

Her. Meri McIsaac. The I'd-rather-be-riding-the-range-than-going-to-a-party spinster was being escorted to the spring picnic by the most eligible bachelor in town. She could hear the catty tongues now. They'd say he felt sorry for her or something along those lines.

Maybe he did feel sorry for her, or maybe he still wasn't sure she and Faither were merely victims of the bank robbery. Maybe he was trying to get close enough to find out if they were somehow more deeply involved.

He definitely had you close enough when you were on his lap!

Heat flooded her face as she remembered the feel of his arms around her. She hadn't wanted to leave them, and that realization had made her desperate to get out of them. Besides, why would she want to be held by someone she wasn't even sure liked her; someone who only did it to prove a point? She had to get her unruly emotions under control. When she'd let them peek out after they'd helped the foaling mare, he'd backed off as if she'd stuck a gun in his face.

"I've heard one of the highlights of the picnic is the dessert auction. What's it all about?"

Meri grabbed the distraction from her disconcerting thoughts. "The women bake special desserts, and the highest bidder gets to enjoy it with the lady who made it. The proceeds go to something the church or school needs. Originally the women were supposed to keep their dessert a secret, and the buyer found out only after he'd purchased the dessert. But we've been doing it so long that everyone pretty much knows who made what before the meal is even served."

"Did you make a dessert for the auction?"

There was no way she was answering that question truthfully. "I didn't even know I was coming until yesterday, and I rode in on horseback, in case you forgot, not a good way to carry a dessert."

"That was an evasive answer. A simple yes or no would have sufficed."

"You have a very suspicious nature, Mars…sir."

"Hazards of the profession, Mac…ma'am."

The man was as dogged as she was. She bit back an unexpected grin as she looked up at him. Her gaze tangled with his, and she caught her breath as his laughing hazel-green eyes sobered and darkened. Meri ducked her head and concentrated on something safer. Like breathing.

Reaching the picnic grounds behind the church building, they paused to survey the scene before them. Women in brightly colored frocks mingled around tables covered in various sizes of dishes, and the sounds of cheery chatter filled the air as they assembled the upcoming meal. Deeper voices and more muted clothing identified the male portion of the gathering, and happy shrieks marked children busily at play.

"There's Marshal Cameron, now," a high-pitched voice squealed.

Meri jerked her hand away from Wyatt's arm as a group of young women headed toward them, maneuvering for Wyatt's attention. She gave ground as the women talked over each other, giving broad hints regarding the choicest dessert on which to bid. The fluttering eyelashes and simpering voices were enough to give her a headache. Retreating from the field without firing a shot, she left the victors to their spoil.

She spent the next hour helping with setup and food preparation as families continued to arrive and contribute their food dishes, but Meri unconsciously kept track of Wyatt as he moved around the picnic grounds. Sometimes he was talking with a group of men; sometimes a young lady and her mother would be smiling and chatting with him. Finally the women called Pastor Willis over to ask the blessing on the food, and afterward, Meri busily dished up food for little ones or those with full hands.

Ms. Maggie tried to shoo her away several times, but she stubbornly continued serving. When the last straggler headed for a place to sit, she filled her own plate and planted herself next to Ms. Maggie. She took a long-awaited drink of cool, tart lemonade.

"Mind if I share your blanket?"

Her head snapped up to see Wyatt holding a plate full of food. She'd thought he would have finished eating already. There had certainly been plenty of invitations for him to join certain picnic blankets. Not that she'd counted.

"Go right ahead, young man." Ms. Maggie grinned.

The blanket had seemed roomy until he sprawled his large frame across one side. Now it felt entirely too small. Meri watched him attack his food while she picked at her own, appetite lost in a stomach full of busy butterflies.

"The ladies of Little Creek have certainly outdone themselves today." Wyatt wiped his mouth in satisfaction.

Meri noted he had the manners to use one of the

cloth napkins Ms. Maggie had provided instead of his sleeve, unlike some of the other men on nearby blankets.

"So you came west from Virginia?" Ms. Maggie asked.

"That's where I grew up, yes. My parents are gone now, but my brother and three sisters still live there. They're all married, and my brother lives on the home place."

"You don't plan on going back?" Meri asked, mangling a piece of chicken with her fork.

"Not to live. I've been out West too long. It's my home now."

"What was it like growing up in Virginia?" Ms. Maggie set her empty plate aside.

Meri nibbled on her food and watched Wyatt's face light up as he answered Ms. Maggie's question and regaled them with stories of growing up in the wilds of Virginia with his Cherokee cousins.

"I learned to read the woods before I learned to read. In fact, I didn't want to learn to read at all, told Ma I'd never need it." He chuckled ruefully. "She sure reminded me of that when I was taking the exams to enter West Point, but she'd made sure I had a sound education, and it stood me in good stead. After graduating West Point, I was shipped west as a shavetail second lieutenant."

Meri voiced a question she'd been wondering about. "Why did you leave the army?"

For a second she wondered if he was going to answer, but then he took a deep breath and began, "I got word about two years ago that my father was gravely ill, and I obtained a leave of absence to go home. He rallied for a few weeks after I arrived, and we had a wonderful visit, but it didn't last long enough. He started failing again, and within a month of my arrival, he slipped away in the night." His voice grew rough. "Mother took it so hard." He paused to clear his throat. "I resigned my commission so I could stay with her. I thought if I was home for good and she had all her children back around her she'd eventually come through the grief."

He slowly shook his head. "We didn't realize how deeply she felt the loss of her other half. Cy and Hanna Cameron were two sides of one coin, and she just lost the will to go on without him. Within a year of Father's death, we buried Mother beside him. My oldest brother had the family farm well in hand, and after all these years of working it and staying by the stuff, he deserves it. My sisters are all married and live nearby, but I just didn't feel like it was home after Ma passed. I started itching to be back out West but didn't have a desire to return to the army, so I said my goodbyes and started drifting. I was down in Texas working as a deputy when I heard about Little Creek looking for a marshal. The sheriff down there was kind enough to send a recommendation, and here I am."

Meri was stunned. He'd recounted his tale so calmly, it had taken a moment for her to grasp the fact he'd recently lost *both* of his parents. He knew better than she the pain of loss.

She was on the verge of apologizing for bringing up sad memories when Mr. Hubert's voice rang out across the picnic grounds. "Graaaab your partners, and let the games begin." The town barber loved being the master of ceremonies and brought a certain flair to the festivities.

Wyatt sprang to his feet, pulling her up with him. "Let's go. I signed us up as partners in the three-legged race."

"Uh-uh." She shook her head and dug in her heels, but she was no match against his gentle, persuasive strength. "We're going to fall flat on our faces."

Ms. Maggie made a shooing motion with her hand. "Oh, go on. Have some fun."

Wyatt tugged her, protesting, toward the gathering competitors. "I think you'll be surprised what we can do if you'll work with me instead of against me."

"I'd rather not," she blurted, heart racing.

"Scared?" he challenged.

Meri glared at him. She was, but she'd never admit it. "Okay, fine. But don't say I didn't warn you."

Reaching the starting line, Wyatt took one of the long strips of cloth the barber handed out to contestants. "Tell you what. If we win this race, I won't call you Mac any more—"

"Deal!"

"—today." The impish smirk reappeared on his face.

"You can't change the rules just like that."

"I didn't change the rules, you interrupted before I finished." Wyatt knelt beside her and tied their booted ankles together, her right to his left, leaving the holstered pistol on his right hip free of obstruction.

She was immediately grateful for the shorter riding skirt instead of a frilly dress as he looped the cloth around her ankle. "Has anyone ever told you how vexing you are?" She shouldn't be able to feel his touch tingle through her leather boot.

Wyatt looked up at her. "I think you just did."

Standing, he wrapped his arm around her waist, and Meri tried to hide the shiver that ran down her spine. Why did a simple touch from him cause her to react like a wild horse, flinching and shying at the slightest thing?

"Are you cold?"

Apparently she hadn't been successful. "No."

"Have you ever done this before?"

"It's a little late to be askin' that." Her insides might be a quivering mass, but her tongue apparently still worked.

The children's portion of the race ended, and Billy and Danny ran up to Meri, blue ribbons fluttering from their hands. "Thanks for tellin' us to practice, Miss Meri. We won!"

"Good for you." The boys ran on almost before Meri got the words out.

"All right, ladies and gents. Line up. Let's see if you can do as good as those youngsters."

It took a second to figure out which foot should move first, and she stumbled, but Wyatt's arm around her waist kept her upright.

"If you'll wrap your arm around my waist, I think you'll find it a tad easier," Wyatt instructed casually. As if his arm around her waist was the most natural thing in the world.

Meri tentatively complied, trying to ignore the feeling of his broad back against her arm. Other young ladies seemed to have no qualms about wrapping their arms about their partners, and apparently it wasn't a big deal to anyone except her. Well, if those giggling females could do it, then Meri McIsaac should certainly be able to do it. She concentrated on her feet as they stumble-hopped toward the starting line.

"Con...tes...tants! At the sound of the bell, make your way to the big oak down by the creek, circle the tree and head back to the finish line. If you fall, you're disqualified. First team across the line wins the blue ribbon. On your mark..."

"This is gonna hurt," Meri muttered under her breath.

"Get set..."

"Have a little faith, and remember, start with your right foot."

The bell rang, and all the teams shuffled, hopped and tripped their way toward the oak tree as fast as three legs could carry them. The field of contestants was swiftly whittled down as couples lost their balance and fell, laughing good-naturedly. Meri nearly followed their example several times, but Wyatt's strong arm kept her safe.

"Work *with* me," he whispered near her ear each time she stumbled.

She was having more than a little trouble concentrating on anything but the distracting sensations caused by his arm around her waist, but eventually they were circling the oak tree and heading back the way they'd come. Meri looked up to see there were only two teams ahead of them.

"Stay with me, Mac, we're almost home free."

As he spoke, a young man and his pretty partner fell and landed in front of them. Meri braced herself for the inevitable tumble, but Wyatt pulled her up short, and they sidestepped the fallen, laughing couple. Reaching clear ground again, Meri caught the exhilaration of the competition and the rhythm of the race, and a giggle bubbled up.

"You ready to make a run for it? I think we can catch them."

"Let's do it!" She tightened her arm around his trim, muscled waist.

She regretted the words as soon as they left her mouth, for Wyatt surged headlong, and Meri realized how much longer his legs were. He'd been holding back, and now she struggled to match his longer stride and faster pace.

The onlookers were cheering on their favorites, yelling out encouragements as Meri and Wyatt gained on the last team. She felt his arm tighten, and he lifted her slightly. Her feet were barely touching the ground. She might look like she was helping, but he was doing all the work himself.

She wasn't going to complain because his move paid off. They swept across the finish line, mere inches ahead of the other team, to the cheers and applause of the picnickers.

Meri untangled her arm, leaning over to catch her breath from the last mad dash. "You did it," she panted happily, reaching to untie the scrap of cloth that bound their ankles.

"*We* did it."

"Congratulations on a race well run." Mr. Hubert thrust a scrap of blue silk at them before hurrying to announce the next contest.

Wyatt handed the ribbon to Meri. "I told you we could do it if you worked with me."

"And since we won, you have a deal to keep." She cocked her head and grinned triumphantly.

"I'm a man of my word. I won't call you Mac again. Today." He placed his hand over his heart.

"Laaaadies and gentlemen! The potato-sack race!" Mr. Hubert's voice boomed again.

"Come on." Wyatt grabbed her hand. "I signed us up for this."

Meri noticed a few females shooting daggers at her, and others that had their heads together whispering as they watched. She was the subject of gossip once more. "You go ahead, I'll watch from the sidelines." And fade back into the woodwork.

"But I was the 'Champeen' potato-sack racer of my county," Wyatt pleaded boyishly.

"Then by all means, go. Have fun." Why did her mouth say one thing when she really wanted something else?

"I see." He shook his head morosely. "You're afraid to be beaten by a Virginia boy."

"We'll see about that," Meri growled. Let the biddies talk. They always did, anyway. No matter what she did or didn't do.

She stalked over to the pile of potato sacks, grabbed one and marched to the starting line, Wyatt beside her all the way. She stepped into the sack and pulled it up around her waist. "It's time to put up or shut up, Marshal." Meri watched him start to speak and cut him off, grinning. "And you can't call me Mac, remember?"

The starting bell sounded, and Meri gripped the top of the rough burlap, hopping frantically in the direction of the finish line.

Don't fall. Don't fall. Don't fall! The words accompanied the beat of her frenzied jumps.

Wyatt's long legs carried him past her, but Meri kept hopping, trying to avoid those that fell and took others down with them.

The finish line grew closer. Wyatt was hot on the heels of the young man in the lead, and Meri was behind Wyatt. She would have laughed at the sight of the marshal leaping like a gigantic jackrabbit, but she needed all her breath to catch up.

Suddenly the young man slipped and went down right across Wyatt's path. This time Wyatt was unable to avoid the fallen contestant and toppled to the ground over the poor fellow. Meri hopped as swiftly as she could, crossing the finish line a mere breath ahead of the remaining contestants.

A familiar arm snaked around her shoulders as she accepted her ribbon, and Wyatt pulled her into quick side hug. "I knew you could do it." Wyatt's flushed face beamed at her as he released her.

"Champeen potato-sack racer, huh?" Meri felt another giggle bubble up. Good grief. She sounded like those silly females earlier.

He shrugged, unperturbed. "Did I mention I was only ten at the time?"

"Laaaadies and gentlemen! The egg race!"

Wyatt grabbed Meri's hand and led her to a table holding spoons and eggs.

"Don't tell me. You signed us up for that one, too," Meri groaned dramatically.

"Yep."

"I don't want egg on me." A protesting laugh accompanied the words.

"O ye of little faith. They're hard-boiled."

Mr. Hubert explained the rules and handed each team a spoon and an egg. "This is a relay race. The team that crosses the finish line first without dropping their egg will win the blue ribbon. There are several flags between the starting line and the finish line. One team member will go to the first flag. When the bell sounds the team member at the starting line will place the spoon in their mouth and their egg on the spoon. They will then carry the egg to their partner at the first flag and pass the egg to them, without dropping it and without using their hands. The new egg holder will head to the next flag, where their partner will meet them to pass the egg off again. And so on and so forth until they reach the finish line. First team across with an undamaged egg still on the spoon wins. Drop the egg, and you're disqualified. Touch the egg with your hands, and you're disqualified. Take your places!"

Wyatt thrust the egg at Meri and jogged to the first flag. Accepting the inevitable, Meri put the spoon between her teeth and laid the egg in the bowl of it. When the bell sounded she carefully made her way toward Wyatt. She reached him with little trouble, and by concentrating on the spoons instead of the nearness of his face, she was able to exchange the egg smoothly. Racing to the next flag, she watched as Wyatt carried the egg toward her on the next leg of the relay. He moved quickly, but the journey and the exchange again went smoothly.

This was easier than she'd thought it would be! She set off for the next flag, balancing the egg easily and moving quicker. Just as she reached Wyatt, her toe connected painfully with a rock hidden in the grass. She pitched forward.

"Mmph!" Her teeth clamped hard around the spoon handle as her hands flew out. She closed her eyes tight, bracing for the impact.

Solid hands caught her shoulders and stopped her descent toward the ground.

The egg wasn't so fortunate.

She heard a dull smack, and the sulfurous odor of rotten egg filled the air. Wyatt looked down, nose wrinkling at the smell emanating from the slimy mess dripping off his shirtfront. He gingerly pulled the fabric away from his body, leaning over to swipe the worst of it off into the grass.

Meri was helpless to stop the laughter that erupted at the look of disgust on his face. He pulled out his handkerchief to wipe his hands free of the odiferous slime. "I appreciate your concern."

"I thought you said they were hard-boiled." She gasped breathlessly.

"Apparently I was wrong," Wyatt replied dryly.

A fresh round of giggles choked her. "Looks like the yolk's on you."

Wyatt rolled his eyes and groaned. "I think now would be a good time to take Jonah some food and change into a fresh shirt."

"If I'd known all it took was a little egg to get out of all these games, I'd have tossed it a little sooner."

"You little imp. I think you did this on purpose."

Meri escaped the yolk-soaked handkerchief that threatened retaliation, and hurriedly retrieved the basket of food Ms. Maggie had put together for Jonah.

"Hurry back, Marshal," Mrs. Van Deusen called

out. "The dessert auction starts as soon as the horse-shoe tournament ends."

"I wouldn't miss it. I can almost taste those desserts I've been hearing about all day."

Wyatt took the basket of food from Meri. "I'll return shortly."

"Watch out for bad eggs, Marshal," she warned, tongue in cheek. It was absolutely ridiculous that a man covered in rotten egg should look so attractive.

"Next time, warn me a little sooner." With a wink, he spun on his heel and jogged away.

Wyatt whistled as he changed into a fresh shirt. He was dangerously close to becoming attached to Miss McIsaac, but he didn't care when he remembered her slender arm around his ribs, her delight when she'd won and her spontaneous laughter at the egg mishap.

He tucked his shirt in and swung his holster back around his hips. He might have let his guard down around Meri—that only had the potential to damage his heart—but he refused to let his guard down when it came to protecting the town. He was keeping his eyes open and his gun handy to ensure everyone had a memorable, safe picnic.

"Someone sounds awfully chipper today. Might it be due to a certain young lady?" Jonah looked up from his plate of food as Wyatt came out of the back room.

"Evidently you weren't as hungry as you professed, if you have time to talk instead of enjoying that pile of food the ladies sent you."

Jonah grinned and changed the subject. "I took a turn around town a while ago. Looks like ever livin' soul is at the picnic. I didn't find a thing stirrin'."

Wyatt opened the front door and settled his hat on his head. "Thanks. I think I'll take a quick look around myself before I head back."

"Glad to do it. Don't take too long. Miss McIsaac'll get tired of waitin' around and find some other good-lookin' fella to share dessert with."

"Go back to your food, you old coot, before I regret making you my deputy." He grinned, removing any sting from the words.

Jonah's laugh followed him down the boardwalk.

Wyatt strolled around the different businesses lining the main thoroughfare through town before heading back to the picnic grounds. Jonah was right. Little Creek was as quiet as a graveyard.

The games were over and picnic goers were slowly gathering around the table that held the decorated dessert baskets, but Wyatt didn't see Meri. He glanced around, searching for her. Had she left?

A waving figure caught his eye. Naoma Van Deusen grinned widely and pointed to the tree-lined stream bordering the picnic grounds. Maybe he should have made her the town deputy, the way she managed to keep track of everyone's movements. Tipping his hat toward her, he followed the sounds of voices and splashing coming from the creek. Quietly slipping through trees, he paused to watch, unnoticed.

A barefoot Meri was wading in the creek alongside Danny and Billy. He grinned, appreciating the glimpse of slim ankles as she held her skirts above the water. The woman wasn't afraid to get dirty, and when she relaxed, she wasn't afraid to have fun. She'd make a good mother.

The thought startled him. Thoughts like that were

dangerous territory for a man who had nothing but dreams on which to build a future. A family needed more than dreams to survive. A family needed a home, security.

Then maybe it's time you take that money you've been squirreling away and stop planning and start doing.

He shoved aside the frighteningly intriguing thought. He was simply enjoying a picnic with a pretty girl while keeping an eye out for trouble.

He stepped onto the creek bank toward the slender woman who was bent over intently watching something in the water flowing around her ankles. She sure made a fetching picture.

Stop it, he commanded himself. Even if she *was* the first woman that made him want to, he wasn't ready to plan a future around her.

So why was it impossible to walk away from her?

Chapter Fourteen

The day wasn't overly warm, but the exertion of the games made the cool shade and running water of Little Creek look especially inviting. Plopping down on the bank, Meri watched Danny and Billy try to capture a school of minnows with their pails while her thoughts wandered to the dessert auction.

She'd evaded Wyatt's question earlier because she *had* prepared a dessert last night but was now regretting it. She only had herself to blame. In trying not to compete with the town girls, she'd gone totally in the opposite direction. Take her outfit today, for example. It was neat and functional, but painfully plain compared to the bows, ruffles and frills on the bright colorful dresses the other young women wore.

Her dessert was another attempt at self-sabotage. Not that her dessert would taste bad, she'd made it plenty of times and father and Franks liked it, she'd just never prepared a dessert for the auction before. The desserts on display today would be fancy pies, luscious cakes and other dressed-up treats designed to make an impression, but what did she bring? A pan of plain-and-simple boring old gingerbread.

Oh, it would make an impression all right. She could hear the snickers and see the looks of pity now. She dropped her head into her hands. *Ugh!* She'd never particularly cared before what people thought of her. Why was she so worried about it now?

Because you're not worried about what people *think. You're worried about what* Wyatt Cameron *will think.*

"I am not!" Meri's head flew up as she uttered the words aloud.

"Aren't what, Miss Meri?" Danny asked from the edge of the creek.

"Nothing, Danny. Just arguing with myself, I guess."

"Miss Meri, you told *us* it was an honor to cease from strife. Isn't arguing with yourself strife?" Billy spoke up, a rascally look on his face.

Meri grimaced as her words returned to haunt her. Mother had always said to season your words with a little salt because you might have to eat them someday.

"Yes, it is. So I'm going to cease right now." Discreetly removing her boots and socks, she stepped into the icy stream, holding the hem of her riding skirt clear of the running water as she waded.

So she was different from most of the young women in town. They weren't enjoying the cold water flowing around their ankles or seeing silvery flashes of tiny fish dart over their feet. She was glad she'd given in to the urge to join the children in the water. It was relaxing and relatively peaceful as Billy and Danny moved upstream to investigate the tadpoles the other children had found.

Standing motionless in the ankle-deep water, Meri bent over to watch little creatures swim out of hiding. A variety of aquatic life, that had found it advantageous to hide from inquisitive little boys, now returned to their various underwater tasks around Meri's bare feet.

"I was beginning to think you'd run off and left me again."

Meri straightened and spun around, but the slick stones under her feet shifted at her sudden commotion, and she lost her balance. With a startled cry she sat down hard—chilly ankle-deep creek water splashing upward as she landed.

Drops were still falling from the splash when she surged to her feet, streams of water pouring off the soft leather skirt. A hand reached to assist her to the creek bank, but Meri's hands were busy shaking the water out of her clothing as she waded out of the streambed. A quick glance showed Wyatt biting his lip and struggling not to laugh. "For the luv' a— Is this gonna' be a habit?"

"What, you falling for me?" He cocked his head innocently.

"No!" Embarrassment scorched its way across her face.

"Me sweeping a beautiful woman off her feet?"

Meri couldn't have looked at the man if her life depended on it, and she retreated into silence. She was digging herself deeper every time she spoke. She dripped her way over to her boots and stockings. Sitting down with her back to Wyatt, she quickly pulled on the dry footwear. A hand cradled her elbow as she stood, and Meri pulled away from the disconcertingly welcome contact, heading downstream away from the picnic.

"Where are you going? The dessert auction is just starting."

"I'm going to get Sandy and go home. I'm all wet, in case you forgot." Falling into the creek might not be such a bad thing after all. It gave her an excuse to leave before her dessert came up for auction.

Hands halted her escape and turned her back toward the picnic. "You'll dry quickly in this warm sun, and everyone will be too busy with the auction to notice a little damp clothing."

"I want to go home." Meri hated the whine she heard in her voice.

"Come on. I've got my mouth all set for dessert," he coaxed as he inexorably drew her along with him up the creek bank into the sunshine to a blanket just on the edge of the picnic area.

It was the blanket they'd sat on for lunch, but it had been moved to a new location farther away from the other scattered picnic blankets. Meri sat reluctantly. At least no one seemed to have noticed her dripping emergence from the trees. Everyone was already gathered around the dessert table where Mr. Hubert was explaining the rules of the auction.

Wyatt dropped down alongside her, leaning back on his elbows, legs outstretched.

"Aren't you going to go bid?" And leave her to her embarrassed misery, free to slip away when he purchased a fancy dessert and the baker claimed her good-looking prize?

"Since I'm new to this, I'm going to study how this all works for a minute."

Bidding started on a plump canned-peach pie with Mr. Hubert reminding bidders that the money raised would go toward a new church piano. The pie sold for fifty cents to the husband of the proud baker. The next items up were a cherry pie, an apple pie and a dried-berry cobbler. Wyatt commented on each item but didn't bid, laughing when a bidding war started over the cobbler.

"Mrs. Van Deusen makes the best cobbler in town. Sometimes Mr. Van Deusen wins it, sometimes he doesn't," Meri informed him.

The bidding went to two dollars before Mr. Van Deusen triumphantly carried away the cobbler, magnanimously offering to share with the loser but only after he'd had the first piece. An angel food cake, another pie and delicate cookies were the following items, but still Wyatt sat and watched.

Nerves were nearly strangling her. Why hadn't she escaped when Wyatt had gone to change his shirt or persisted in leaving after her fall in the creek? Then she wouldn't be sitting here agonizing over which girl would claim Wyatt with her dessert. At least she'd found another reason to be glad she'd chosen this particular outfit. The leather skirt hadn't absorbed the creek water, and she was drying faster than a regular dress would have allowed.

"I thought you wanted dessert."

"I do, but my mouth's all set for something specific, and I haven't seen it yet."

Meri looked at the girls standing close to the dessert

table. She'd seen a couple of them talking to Wyatt earlier; maybe he was waiting on one of their confections.

Another cobbler passed without a bid from Wyatt.

"You're going to run out of choices." Maybe biting her tongue would silence it.

"Nope, they're just saving the best for last." He smiled, unconcerned.

They were down to the last three desserts, and Meri's heart thudded painfully as tension built inside her. She smothered a groan as a thought occurred to her.

You could have at least brought some cream to garnish the top of your gingerbread, but you can't even get that right! You are your own worst enemy!

Wyatt stood abruptly and walked toward the dessert table. This was it. This must have been what he was waiting on. Which girl would walk away on his arm?

"Dig deep, fellas. This one will make your mouth water." Mr. Hubert carefully reached into a ribbon-frilled hamper and pulled out a tall, beautifully frosted chocolate cake.

A murmur of excitement rippled across the assembled crowd. Mr. Hubert started the bidding at fifty cents, and bids flew fast and loud. A pretty blonde stood by the dessert table beaming proudly. Finally Mr. Hubert closed the bidding at four dollars.

Meri strained upward to see who'd won.

It…*wasn't* Wyatt.

She sat back with a squishy thud. One of her father's ranch hands smugly accepted the basket of cake and escorted the attractive girl to a picnic blanket.

"Next up, folks…" Mr. Hubert reached into a basket and pulled out a small square pan.

Meri's heart stopped. It looked even plainer than she'd remembered.

He sniffed the pan. "Gingerbread, and it smells wonderful. I don't know who the baker is, but if it tastes as good as it smells, it'll be a real treat. Who'll start the bidding?" The words had hardly left Mr. Hubert's mouth before a firm, ringing voice spoke.

"Five dollars."

Meri's heart started again with a painful bound.

"Did you say...*five*...*dollars?*" Mr. Hubert stuttered.

She strained to hear the answer through the roaring silence.

"Yes. I bid five dollars."

Meri's heart and lungs had functioned automatically for nearly thirty years, but they seemed to have forgotten how to perform their most basic functions. Her eyes and ears, on the other hand, were capturing every detail in agonizing clarity.

"Our new marshal must like gingerbread, folks. Anyone want to give him a run for his money?" The crowd laughed, but no one bid. "Come on, folks, who'll give the marshal some competition?"

"Five twenty-five." Franks walked toward Wyatt, a big grin showcasing pearly teeth.

"Five fifty," Wyatt countered.

"Five seventy-five," Franks shouted.

The bidding war continued, and Mr. Hubert's gaze bounced between the two men. When the bidding neared eight dollars, Wyatt leaned over to Franks and whispered something. Turning back to Mr. Hubert, he bid again. "Eight dollars!"

Mr. Hubert looked at Franks, but that gentleman only shook his head, grinning.

Mr. Hubert slammed his hand down on the table. "Sold!"

Wyatt walked to the table and handed some bills to the auctioneer.

"Now that the marshal's won his dessert, will the baker step forward to claim her dessert partner?"

Meri was frozen to the blanket. She couldn't even stand up, much less walk up there.

Mr. Hubert called again for the lady to come claim her dessert partner, and the assembled picnickers glanced around curiously. Wyatt leaned over the table and said something. Mr. Hubert smiled, nodded, then carefully picked up the next dessert and called for bids, recalling everyone's attention to the last item of the auction.

Meri's eyes were glued to Wyatt as he returned and carefully set down his burden before seating himself.

"Ahh, good things come to those who wait." He winked at her and reached into the basket, pulling out the pan of gingerbread and inhaling deeply. "Smells delicious."

Meri watched in a daze as he carefully cut two large pieces of thick, dark gingerbread and slid them onto plates. Opening a small crock that he'd pulled out of the basket along with the plates, he spooned something over the top of the fragrant cake.

Whipped cream!

"Just the thing to top it off," Wyatt said satisfactorily, handing her one of the plates

Thank you, Ms. Maggie. She must have brought it along with the rest of the food the ranch had supplied today and tucked it in the basket when Meri wasn't watching.

He forked a generous piece into his mouth and chewed. "Umm…good." A second bite quickly followed the first.

Meri found a voice that sounded nothing like her own. "This is what you had your mouth set for?"

"Yep!"

His smirk wasn't nearly so intimidating or irritating when surrounded by smudges of frothy whipped cream.

"You *knew* there'd be gingerbread?' He nodded, his mouth full. "How?"

He stuck another piece into his mouth and pointed at her untouched plate with his fork. "I have my sources, and you're not eating your gingerbread."

Meri took a small bite, too distracted to enjoy it. "What did you say to the auctioneer?"

"I just told him I knew who the lady was and to go on with the auction." His eyes twinkled merrily.

"How did you know there would be gingerbread here?"

He slowly chewed and swallowed before speaking. "I have to protect the identity of my sources, or I'd have people afraid to bring me information."

Meri's eyes narrowed. "You knew I brought gingerbread—" she pointed to her plate "—all this time?"

Wyatt popped another forkful into his mouth and nodded, grinning roguishly. "It was kind of fun watching you squirm."

"Why would you wait around for my gingerbread when you could have had your pick of much fancier desserts…"

…and fancier girls?

Wyatt cut another serving for himself and slathered

it with cream. "First off, I haven't had gingerbread since my mom made it for me as a boy, and I really like it." Wyatt carefully forked a cream-covered piece into his mouth, chewed slowly and swallowed before continuing. "Second, I really didn't want to sit with any of those man-eating females!" He shivered theatrically.

Meri looked down at her forgotten piece of expensive dessert. Putting a piece into her own mouth, she chewed without tasting. He didn't see her as a threat? Was that good or bad? Finally she could resist no longer. "You're not afraid *I'm* a 'man-eating female'?"

Hazel eyes twinkled. "Nope."

Meri took another bite to give her mouth something to do besides ask foolish questions. The last one had left her confused as to whether she was relieved or offended. If she kept opening her mouth, she was going to drown in these dangerous waters.

She hurriedly finished her dessert as Wyatt set his plate down and leaned back with a full groan. "That was delicious. My compliments to the cook."

She gathered up the used plates and utensils and restored them to the basket.

"What's your hurry?"

"I'm uncomfortably damp, and it's time I headed home." She reached to set the pan of gingerbread in the basket.

"You're not taking all that gingerbread, are you?"

Meri had to smile at the pitiful puppy-dog expression Wyatt assumed. "No. I'll send it home with you."

Wyatt immediately resumed a cheerful smile. "Good. I told Franks I'd share it with him if he'd stop driving up the price. I wouldn't want him to come after me when I don't bring him any of it. He said it'd be delicious, and he was right." Wyatt rubbed his stomach in appreciation.

"Did everyone know what you were up to?" she whispered in a mortified tone.

Wyatt chuckled ruefully. "No. Franks knew the gingerbread was yours and wanted to make me work for it."

Meri ducked her head in bewilderment and shooed Wyatt off the blanket so she could pick it up, avoiding his eyes as he helped her fold it neatly. Taking the blanket and basket from her, he walked her toward the ranch wagon.

Nearing the accumulated variety of wheeled vehicles, she saw the banker climbing into his buggy. "Hello, Mr. Samuels."

He nodded shortly. "Miss McIsaac. Marshal."

"I'm glad you were able to make it to the picnic. I saw you were busy with someone at the bank earlier."

Mr. Samuels picked up the reins and slapped the back of the horse, and the buggy moved away at a quick clip.

Meri turned to watch him go. "That was abrupt. I wonder what his problem is."

"I was just about to ask you the same thing," Wyatt said.

"What do you mean?"

"You didn't try to run off with *his* horse or something, did you?" There was a teasing glint in his eye.

"Very funny. No, I didn't take his horse or something. I haven't done anything to him except be polite."

Wyatt chuckled at her sarcasm. "Then why worry about it?"

"I don't know. He's never been overly friendly, but

he's never been outright rude, either. First he ignores me at the cemetery, and today he acts like he can't get away from me fast enough."

"He's probably just distracted by the bank robbery."

"I guess." Meri shrugged her shoulders, dismissing the subject.

Setting the basket and blanket in the bed of the wagon, Meri transferred the dirty plates and utensils to another container and handed the basket containing the gingerbread to Wyatt.

"We can pick up the basket and pan next time someone comes into town." She ducked her head. What did one say at the close of an occasion like this? "Thank you for bringing me and for buying my dessert." Spinning away from him, she set off in a brisk walk for the livery stable. She hadn't taken two steps when she felt him beside her.

"You're not getting rid of me that easy. This day's not over until I've escorted you home."

Meri sighed resignedly as she continued walking, but didn't argue. At least she told herself it was a resigned sigh. She ignored the fact it had sounded happy.

The ride back to the ranch was slower and less competitive than the ride in, and Meri was very quiet, responding to Wyatt's attempts at conversation with monosyllabic replies. When he failed to get a rise out of her by teasing her about her dip in the creek, he allowed silence to accompany them the rest of the journey, contenting himself with stolen glances at his fellow traveler.

After they reached the ranch house, Mr. McIsaac invited Wyatt into his study, and Meri disappeared after shyly thanking him again. Mr. McIsaac quizzed him about the picnic, laughing heartily at the account of the games and creek incidents. "Did ye snag her gingerbread?"

"I did. It was as good as you said it'd be." He nodded his appreciation to the older man.

McIsaac rocked back in his chair with a satisfied grin. "Most folks think the fancier the package, the better the dessert will be, but there's a wealth of flavor waiting to be discovered in that unassuming little cake. And like that gingerbread, the boys in town never looked past the fancier-dressed females to see the treasure underneath her intimidating independence. Until now I thought that was unfortunate, but ye might hold a different opinion."

Wyatt did. But he wasn't ready to admit it out loud. "Did you ever figure out what was bothering you about the bank robbery?"

Ian McIsaac's eyes measured him for a moment before nodding. "I finally remembered this afternoon, but I don't think it means anything."

Wyatt sat down, pulling the little notebook from his pocket. "Tell me anyway."

"After I hit the floor, something was said before I passed out. That brigand shouted, 'Where's the rest of it?'"

Wyatt looked up from his notes when McIsaac didn't continue. "Anything else?"

"No, that's it. 'Where's the rest of it?' I was hoping I'd heard something important. Maybe that's why it took this long to remember. It wasn't anything big." Ian McIsaac's voice was regretful.

"I'm beginning to think the pieces that don't look

relevant to the case are the ones that are going to solve it," Wyatt said thoughtfully as he tucked away the little notebook. "I need to get back to town and give Jonah a break. Tell your daughter I enjoyed her company today."

McIsaac followed him to the front door, bidding him good afternoon.

Wyatt shelved thoughts of Meri and her reaction to the dessert auction and pulled out his little notebook as he rode toward town. Splitting his attention between his surroundings and his notes, he mulled over the pieces of the frustrating case. The only conclusion he'd come to by the time he reached town was that he needed to talk to the banker.

He pointed his horse toward the man's house. It was time he pinned Mr. Samuels down on a few unanswered questions.

Chapter Fifteen

This time when he knocked on the banker's door, the housekeeper admitted him into a dark stuffy parlor.

"Can I help you, Marshal?" The banker's tone belied his offer of helpfulness.

"I have one or two more questions."

"That seems to be all you have."

Wyatt ignored the verbal jab. "I talked to your former employee. He has a slightly different account of why he left." He watched the man's face closely, but the lack of light in the room made it difficult to read his expression.

"I can only imagine what George Dunn told you." He sniffed.

"He said you fired him. Did you?"

"Yes."

"Why didn't you tell me that in the first place?"

"Because it had nothing to do with the robbery, and I dislike casting aspersions on a man who isn't around to defend himself." The little man puffed out his chest pompously.

"Why did you fire him?"

"He was unreliable, and I could handle the business until I found someone more competent."

"He said you accused him of stealing."

"I told him his incompetence was as bad as stealing. As usual, he misunderstood."

"The townsfolk seemed to think highly of him."

"They didn't have to work with the young jackanapes. I fail to see how this has anything to do with the holdup, Marshal," Samuels said impatiently.

"Why did you shout at McIsaac when he was trying to stop the thief?" Wyatt changed course abruptly.

"What?" The man startled as if struck.

"McIsaac said you yelled something when you saw him start to pull the gun and that's what caused him to be shot."

"No. I was trying to *keep* him from being shot."

"And yet you neglected to tell me this when I first questioned you."

"I fail to see how yelling at someone during the confusion of a robbery has any bearing on catching the culprit." Mr. Samuels stood to walk out of the room.

"I have one more question before you leave." The man was pricklier than a cactus and sourer then a barrel of pickles.

"What, pray tell, can it be this time?" The banker sighed sarcastically.

"What happened to Mr. McIsaac's gun?"

"His gun?"

"Yes. Mr. McIsaac would like it back, but I didn't see it at the bank that day, and no one else seems to know what happened to it."

"I assume it was taken along with the bank's money. Are we done here?"

"You didn't see if the bank robber picked it up?"

"I was dealing with my own injury at the time!"

"You've been out of town a lot lately. Have you made any progress toward getting the bank reopened?"

"It's been difficult, but I think I've talked a few investors into lending capital to reopen the bank. I should hear word in the next week or so. I'm sure they would be much more amenable should they hear that the perpetrator has been caught. And that was *three* questions, Marshal. Are you quite finished?"

"For now. Thank you for your time."

The housekeeper ushered him out the door, and he was glad to exit and feel the evening sun on his face. That gloomy house would make anybody cranky. He unwrapped Charger's reins from the hitching post and led him down the street.

Who was telling the truth? An employee who'd been fired, one everyone else seemed to like, including his new boss, or the banker everyone seemed to find difficult?

One of the more blunt citizens he'd questioned had commented, "He runs a mortuary, not a bank. When he undertakes your money, you never see it again!" Another had said, "He doesn't run a bank, he runs a natural history museum. Naturally, when he loans you money, you're history!"

He'd been tempted to laugh at the tongue in cheek answers. Mr. Samuels might not be popular, but didn't most people fear bankers to some extent, especially if they held the mortgage on your land?

"Howdy, Marshal."

"Hello, Billy. Danny. Aren't you tired from the picnic?" The two boys ran up to Wyatt as he led Charger down the rutted street.

"Nah. We're workin'. We're private eyes, like Mr. Pinkerton. You need any help with anything?" Billy asked hopefully.

Wyatt had an impulsive idea. "As a matter of fact, I could use your help. Danny, don't you live near here?"

"Yep. Right over there." Danny pointed proudly to a two-story home a short distance away.

"I need some information, but it has to be kept strictly between us or it will be useless. I'll pay for this information." Wyatt jingled a few coins in his pocket for emphasis.

"We know how to keep secrets," Billy said defensively. "We didn't tell anyone you made Miss Meri fall in the creek. Besides, private eyes don't go around spilling the beans about their cases."

Wyatt eyed them thoughtfully. They were such a familiar sight around town people paid them little attention unless they wanted an errand run or some small task done. The boys might prove valuable eyes and ears at times when sight of the marshal would put people on their guard.

"Good. Here's what I want you to do." Wyatt leaned close to the boys and spoke quietly. "I want you to watch Mr. Samuels's house. Let me know if you see anyone visit him or if you see him leave with a bag like he's going out of town. Can you handle that?"

"Sure."

"Don't try to follow him or sneak up on him. Go about as you normally do, and just keep your eyes peeled for anything out of the ordinary. Can you follow that to the letter?"

Billy and Danny nodded, taking his instructions very seriously. Wyatt pulled out two half-dollar coins and handed one to each boy.

"Our first paying case." Billy clutched the coin proudly, awe filling his voice.

"We won't let you down, Marshal." Danny solemnly shook Wyatt's hand, and Billy followed suit. Both boys hurried off, talking to each other in low guarded voices, and Wyatt returned to his office to relieve Jonah, wondering if he would regret his impulsive decision.

It stormed hard that night, and the McIsaacs didn't show up at church the following day, but Pastor Willis reminded the congregation to pray for them: the anniversary of Mrs. McIsaac's death was coming up later in the week.

As the week progressed, Wyatt missed seeing Meri every day but resisted riding out to the ranch to see her. Instead he kept his hands busy with his duties and his mind and heart busy in prayer. He prayed that God would help him bring the bank robber to justice, and that He would heal Meri from her mother's loss.

When Billy and Danny breathlessly showed up on his doorstep early one morning, Wyatt began to believe the first prayer was close to an answer. Little did he guess both prayers were about to be answered almost simultaneously.

Meri was grooming the fourth horse of the morning when her father stalked into the barn. She could tell by the way he walked he had something on his mind but ducked her head and pretended not to see him, continuing to comb snarls out of the horse's tail. But the comb was plucked from her hand.

Her father calmly untethered the horse and turned him into the paddock.

"I wasn't done with him," she protested.

"Yes, ye are." McIsaac led her over to a wooden bench. "Sit."

Since his order was reinforced with a gentle, irresistible push, Meri sat.

He turned, folded his hands behind his back and paced a few steps before coming back to stand in front of her, planting his feet determinedly. "It's high time ye dealt with whatever's bothering ye." He spoke kindly but firmly.

"Nothing's bothering me." She tried to speak convincingly, but her father's eyes bored into hers, and she glanced away uneasily.

"Do not lie to me, lass. Ye've nearly driven everyone crazy this week. If ye're not bossing the hands around on some new project ye've thought up, ye're hovering 'til I trip over ye, or ye're pacing back and forth sighing up a windstorm."

"I am not."

"The fences on this ranch have never been in as good a shape as they are now, thanks to the men trying to get away from the next crazy scheme ye've cooked up. Ms. Maggie is upset because ye've rearranged every cupboard on the place, and even though Dr. Kilburn cleared me to return to riding, ye nearly panic every time I even think about going farther then the front porch."

McIsaac sat down beside her, wrapped an arm around her shoulders and pulled her stiff body into a hug as he continued talking. "I don't know why we lost Catriona so soon, and there will always be a hole left by her passing, but, lassie, it is okay to move on. It's okay to be happy again. Mither would be the first to tell ye she's happier and healthier with her Savior than she could ever be down here. I'm not saying the grief over her loss will ever be completely gone, and that's okay. But yer anger is not okay. It's an infection that keeps eating away at yer insides, and until it's dealt with, ye won't get better." McIsaac stood and gave a short whistle.

Barnaby entered the barn leading a saddled Sandy. How had they managed that without her noticing?

"Ye always seem to think better on the back of a horse, and I think part of yer problem is that ye haven't had a good ride in a week or more. Sandy's ready, and yer hat, canteen and rifle are on the saddle. Go, take Sandy for a run, and don't come back 'til ye've had a heart-to-heart talk with yer Heavenly Father."

McIsaac pulled Meri up from the bench and laid the reins in her hands, looking into her eyes for a couple of heartbeats. "Be careful, and pay attention to yer surroundings—"

The familiar warning was one she'd heard since childhood.

"—but it's time to face whatever ye're running from." He kissed her on the forehead, turned and walked out of the barn.

Meri looked at Sandy who shook his head up and down as if to say "Hurry up, let's go."

"All right," she muttered grudgingly. She swung into the saddle and guided the horse outside.

Sandy hit their favorite trail at a smooth lope, but

the familiar thrill of the horse's smooth rhythm and the sense of freedom were missing.

The anniversary of Mither's death was only two days ago. How can Faither tell me to get over it? How can he be okay when I feel so stuck, so rotten?

Her father had been sad on the anniversary of her mother's death, but it was not the despairing anger she felt. Anger?

Yes. She'd been angry. A lot. She'd tried to tell herself it was grief, but if she were completely honest with herself, it looked and acted a lot more like bitter resentful anger.

She turned Sandy off the trail, and the horse snorted his surprised displeasure at the sudden change of plans. "Sorry, boy." Meri patted his shiny blond neck. "I think it's time I faced something."

A half hour later Meri dismounted, flipping the palomino's reins around a decorative spike atop the cemetery fence. The wrought-iron railing didn't enclose the entire grounds; it extended partway up the slope, ending just past the ornate marble crypt near the tree line. Taking a deep breath, she pushed open the gate, cringing as it protested with a metal-on-metal squeak, and entered the burial ground. She slowly walked past each gravestone, reading the names as she passed, delaying the inevitable. All too soon she reached her mother's headstone.

Catriona McIsaac
1825-1882
Beloved Wife
Beloved Mother
Beloved Child of God

The cold gray stone could never communicate the true meaning of the life it represented.

Meri felt a tear run down her cheek, and wiped it away in surprise. She hadn't shed tears since the funeral. Even when her burning eyes and aching throat had begged for the cathartic release, her eyes had remained stubbornly dry. She sank to her knees in the soft grass.

"Oh, Mither. I miss you so much it hurts." Another tear slid down, and all the grief and anger of the past year boiled up with it, refusing to be contained any longer. "God, why did you take her? You could so easily have healed her! Why did You let her die?"

The sound of the vicious words rocked her back on her heels. She'd never spoken the questions aloud, but they had festered just below the surface slowly infecting her whole being.

Meri finally accepted the truth that had been gnawing at her spirit since Pastor Willis's sermon. "I have been so angry with You, Lord. You could have healed Mither of pnuemonia, but You didn't and I couldn't accept that. I've blamed You for her death. I've been angry and bitter that You allowed that to happen to us, to me, and that anger has become a barrier pushing me away from You."

As confession cleared the windows of Meri's soul, the tears began to flow in earnest. "Father, You say that all things work together for good to them that love You. I don't understand how Mither's death is good, but she was Your child, and I know You love her more than I ever could. Forgive me for being angry at You, for acting like a spoiled child who gets mad when things don't go my way. I'm tired of fighting You. I'm tired of being angry and hurting all the time. Please forgive me."

Sobs shook her shoulders and tears poured, but as she cried out to a loving Heavenly Father, long-lost peace began to seep through the cracks in her heart, softening the hardness and restoring what bitterness had choked out. Long minutes passed before her tears began to dry, and snatches of Scripture watered peace deep into her soul.

A few more tears leaked out as she pictured her mother in Heaven at Jesus's feet. She had focused entirely on what she had lost when she should have been focusing on what her mother had gained. Her father was right. Mither was happier with her Savior than she could ever have been here on earth.

Meri shifted to pull a handkerchief from her pocket and realized she'd sat on her legs so long she'd lost feeling in them. Gingerly stretching them out, she leaned against the headstone, wiping her face and wincing as sleeping limbs awakened with a rush of fiery prickles. But in spite of aching legs and tear-soaked eyes, Meri felt better than she had in months. The oppressive weight was gone, and her heart felt light and clean. She would always miss her mother, her friend and confidante, but sweet peace had replaced aching sadness, and Meri basked in the calm that followed the long storm.

Fatigue washed over her, and she leaned her head back against the cool stone, letting her eyes drift shut. She had almost dozed off when a soft nicker made her jump. Sitting up, she saw Sandy was not looking at her. He was watching the high end of the graveyard, ears pricked intently.

Meri rose to her knees to follow his gaze. What had caught his attention? The only thing up there was that silly marble tomb, imposing in its haughty grandeur and looking down on lowly rank-and-file headstones.

She froze, heart pounding. Had the door on the crypt...*moved*?

Shivers raced up her spine, and she jumped to her feet and sprinted to Sandy's side, unsheathing her carbine and spinning back to scan the area in one quick move. Nothing stirred. She would have doubted she'd seen anything except Sandy was still cautiously looking toward the top of the cemetery between quick bites of grass.

A thought caused Meri to take a deep breath and laugh at herself as her racing heart slowed. Boys had probably found a way into the crypt and thought to scare her.

Let's see who scares whom!

Meri reentered the burial ground, thankful she'd thought to leave the gate open thus avoiding its noisy squeak, and walked toward the two imposing lions flanking the door of the marble monstrosity.

"I know you're in there. You can come out now," Meri called out sternly.

Silence fell and she heard nothing but the swish of her own footsteps through the grass as she reached the last row of gravestones and stopped. Darting a glance around, she saw nothing but her own horse calmly grazing.

"I said, come out," she ordered again, but nothing moved.

She thought she'd only *started* to doze off, but

maybe she'd actually been asleep and dreamed this whole thing up.

No. Sandy saw something, too.

Another shiver raced up her spine as she squinted at the latch on the door. It was undone and the door stood slightly ajar. It had never been used, but who would want to hide in there? That seemed terribly unnerving, even for a bunch of mischievous boys.

"I have a Winchester carbine aimed straight at this door. Come out with your hands up. Now!" The words sounded braver in Meri's mind then they did when they hit the air.

She held her breath as she waited, but still nothing happened. She argued with herself before slowly stepping within reach of the cold marble edifice and touching the toe of her boot to the metal door. She swallowed hard as the door moved smoothly and silently inward.

You're crazy! You could have gotten on Sandy and ridden home, but no, you have to go investigate!

Meri stepped back hastily, bringing the rifle up as sunshine illuminated the shadowed crypt. It was too late to turn and run now. Something—no, someone was in there. Meri backed farther away, voice squeaking when she ordered, "Hands up! Come out where I can see you."

Her heart beat furiously in her ears as the shadows in the crypt shifted toward her.

Chapter Sixteen

Daylight washed over the shadows, and they melted, leaving behind two men. One wore an amused expression on his face and a star on his shirt; the other wore a similar star but a sheepish expression. Both men raised their hands placatingly as they exited the marble structure, Jonah pulling the door shut behind him with one hand.

"You!" Meri's knees suddenly threatened to buckle, and the barrel of her carbine drooped toward the ground.

"May we put our hands down, or are you going to use that on us?" Wyatt grinned and motioned toward her gun.

She kept the barrel pointed toward the ground but shifted it toward Wyatt. "That depends on how you answer my question. What were you and Jonah doing in there?" It took some effort, but she kept the tremor out of her voice.

But then dismayed realization dawned. "How long have you been up here?" She cringed, thinking how she'd blubbered over her mother's grave.

"Long enough to realize you wouldn't appreciate an audience," Wyatt said softly.

She almost dropped the carbine. Of all the people to witness her tears... She didn't know whether to melt in mortification or... She tightened her grip on the gun and took a step toward Wyatt and Jonah. Jonah stepped back.

Wyatt stood his ground with a crooked grin. "You just figure out if you shoot us there won't be any witnesses?"

How does he always *know what I'm thinking?* "Would you quit changing the subject?" she huffed. "How did you two get up here? Where are your horses?" She moved another half step closer, but Wyatt still didn't budge. It was hard to intimidate a man who didn't scare.

"Which question would you like answered first?" Wyatt scratched his forehead with a knuckle, nudging his hat up.

The man was impossible. He had no right to look so devastatingly attractive when she was upset with him. "How 'bout all of them?"

"Well, let's see..." In one swift move Wyatt's hand came away from the brim of his hat and swiped the barrel of the carbine to one side. Stepping in close, he pulled the gun from her abruptly nerveless hands.

Meri stiffened as he leaned down, hat brim nearly touching hers, forcing her to look up at him. He held her gaze for several breathless heartbeats. "You were saying?"

Meri blinked and scuttled backward trying to collect her scattered wits. What had she been saying? Glinting green-gold eyes had short-circuited her brain.

Crack! Crack! Ping!

She jerked, feeling the sounds like a physical blow.

"Get *down!*" Wyatt roared, and lunged at her, wrapping her in his arms. The ground rose up to meet them with a thump, and he used their momentum to roll down to a row of headstones for cover. Pain radiated through her as they slammed to an abrupt halt against a wide stone marker. She groaned. Her arms were pinioned to her sides by Wyatt's arms, and she couldn't breathe against his weight pinning her to the ground. "Stay down! You okay, Jonah?" Wyatt shifted Meri out of his arms, tucking her tightly against the base of the marker.

Jonah hollered he was unhurt, and Meri decided to argue with the bossy marshal when she'd recovered enough breath to speak more forcibly. Her back loudly protested the sudden contact with the ground, and her lungs ached with the effort to refill them.

"Can you see anything?" Wyatt removed his hat before peering cautiously around the bottom edge of the headstone.

"No, but those shots sounded like they came from farther down the slope. Maybe those cedars left of the road," Jonah barked.

"We're pinned down pretty bad," Wyatt gritted out. "Let's see if we can shake something out of those trees." He levered Meri's carbine open—he'd managed to hold on to it in their tumble for cover—and jacked a shell into the empty chamber. He left his own pistol securely in its holster and aimed for the clump of trees about a hundred and fifty yards down the slope. Firing two quick shots, he paused and repeated the action. "See anything move, Jonah?"

"No. Wait! You hear that?"

"Yeah, sounds like a horse leaving fast—with or without the rider I can't tell. He's using his cover too well." He sounded disgusted.

"There haven't been any more shots fired at us since those first two. Maybe he's hightailing it out of there."

"Let's see if we get any bites." Wyatt grabbed his hat, slowly raised it above the top of the headstone and held it there a second. The deafening silence was broken only by the return of tentative birdsong.

"Try your hat, Jonah, maybe he's playin' 'possum."

Jonah repeated Wyatt's actions, but no further gunshots sounded. "You think he's gone?"

"If he's not, he soon will be." Wyatt peered around the base of the stone. "Look at that dust coming. Someone must have heard the shots and decided to come investigate. All we have to do is lay low 'til they get here." He turned and sat, tucking his back against the stone. He swiped his arm over his damp forehead and looked at Meri. "You shock me, Miss McIsaac. I figured you'd be trying to take that gunman down all by yourself. Instead you followed my order to stay down. I'm surprised and proud of you!" He grinned.

"You had my rifle. What was I supposed to use?" Meri had to force the words through her tight throat. She was feeling completely useless and nearly crosseyed with dizziness. "I think you broke my shoulder when you threw me down and landed on me, you big ox." It hurt to breathe.

"Now, now, Mac, don't call names. It isn't ladylike. And I didn't land on you, I cushioned your fall."

"If that's what you call cushioning a fall…"

"Drop your weapons and come out with your hands where we can see them!" The command rang out below them.

"Where have I heard this before?" groaned Jonah.

"Take it easy, fellas. It's just us," Wyatt shouted before he and Jonah got cautiously to their feet.

"Marshal? What's all the shootin' about?" The man sounded closer, but Meri was having trouble recognizing the voice through the pulse hammering in her ears.

"Some polecat started throwin' lead at us. You can see where one of 'em hit the top of that tombstone over there." Jonah motioned toward a marker near where they'd been standing when the shots had been fired.

"Where's Miss McIsaac? Her horse is down here," another voice asked.

"She's right here." Wyatt looked down at Meri as he spoke. "You're taking the order to stay down a bit too seriously, Mac."

"Don't call me Mac. I'm still trying to catch my breath." Meri struggled to push herself up, but a bolt of pain streaked through her, and the bright afternoon spun wildly, colors dimming and blurring together. She slumped back as Wyatt whispered her name, and the world went black.

Wyatt fell to his knees beside Meri, yelling her name. She didn't respond. He reached under her motionless body to lift her into his arms and something warmly wet and sticky met his touch. Heartsick, he withdrew a hand covered in thick red blood.

He should have known something was wrong. She just didn't lie around taking orders. "Somebody go get Doc! Now!"

Pastor Willis ran to his horse, leaving Mr. Van Deusen and Mr. Hubert standing by helplessly. Wyatt gently shifted Meri. Torn blood-soaked fabric met his eyes.

Mr. Hubert hissed sharply as he peered over Wyatt's shoulder. "That looks pretty bad."

Wyatt grunted acknowledgment as he finished turning her over carefully. "There wasn't blood on the front of her shoulder. Did it go in or just cut her up?" He reached for his knife, and slit the torn edges of the fabric, pulling it away from the wound to look.

"Looks like she caught a ricochet." Mr. Van Deusen knelt beside Wyatt. "They make wounds like that."

A jagged furrow plowed up her back, ending in a ragged hole just below the top of the shoulder. Wyatt yanked off his neckerchief and pressed it onto the wound. "Hold that in place, and put some pressure on it!" he barked.

Mr. Van Deusen complied, and Wyatt lifted the hem of Meri's riding skirt and ripped a wide strip off her cotton petticoat. Tearing the strip lengthwise, he knotted the two ends together to make a longer strip and wrapped it around her shoulder, holding the improvised bandage in place. With infinite care he rolled her onto her back and into his arms. Standing, cradling her limp form, he saw Jonah leading his own horse and Charger down from the trees where they'd been hidden.

"Figured you'd want to get her into town quick—looks like she's still losing quite a bit of blood. I'll go after the shooter and leave a trail for you to follow after you get her to Doc's." Jonah's tone was brusque, but his hands were gentle as he took Wyatt's fragile armful.

Wyatt leaped into the saddle and wrapped the reins around the saddle horn. Reaching down, he tenderly retrieved his precious burden and cradled her once more. He looked toward Mr. Van Deusen and Mr. Hubert. "You men stay here and make sure no one enters that crypt. If anyone tries, you hold them prisoner 'til I get back."

"What? Why?" Matching looks of confusion covered their faces as they glanced from the mausoleum back to him.

"I'll explain later. Until then, make sure no one goes anywhere near it. Your word on it?"

"Our word, Marshal." Both men nodded solemnly, still bewildered.

With a nod of thanks, Wyatt used his legs to guide Charger out of the gate and toward town. The big horse stepped carefully but quickly as if he understood the gravity of the situation.

Wyatt struggled to pray beyond one-word syllables, and his heart ached at the pale face cradled against his chest. "Lord, help her. Help me. Hang in there, Mac. Stay with me."

Meri groaned and mumbled something.

"What is it?" He lowered his head to catch her words.

"...not... Mac," she breathed.

Wyatt's chest rose and sank on a relieved sigh. "You just keep fighting, sweetheart, and I'll call you any name you want." But she was beyond hearing.

He shifted a hand until he could feel the pulse at her wrist. Weak, but steady. He hugged her a little closer and resumed praying. "Father, please, stop the bleeding and heal her body."

The ride was interminable. He prayed and wondered why the doctor hadn't already met him. He was at the edge of town before he saw Franks riding toward him. "Where's Doc?"

"Deliverin' a baby. Brotha' Willis rode ta git 'im.

Doc's wife is waitin'." Franks turned to ride along-side Wyatt, glancing worriedly at Wyatt's limp bundle.

When they arrived at the Doc's, Franks dismounted and reached for Meri. Wyatt reluctantly relinquished her so he could dismount but quickly reclaimed her as soon as his feet touched the ground.

"Bring her in." Mrs. Kilburn waved them through to the examination room. "Lay her there." She pointed to the exam table, and Wyatt tenderly lowered Meri onto her uninjured side.

Mrs. Kilburn immediately set about removing the bandage he had hastily fashioned and examined the wound critically. "You two step out of the room, but don't go far."

Wyatt and Franks retreated to the office. Wyatt slumped into a chair, suddenly aware of his weak knees.

"How bad…?" Franks's deep bass trembled a little.

"She caught a ricochet that tore up her shoulder. Looks like one of the first shots glanced upward off a headstone, slicing up her back before angling into her shoulder. She's lost some blood. She woke up on the ride in, but almost immediately lost consciousness again." Wyatt sketched the details of the ambush then dragged in a deep breath before continuing. "Can you round up someone to go get her father?"

Franks didn't waste time answering. He just turned on his heel and ran out the door.

"Marshal, can I have your assistance?" Wyatt reen-tered the exam room at Mrs. Kilburn's call.

"Pastor Willis went after my husband, but he's all the way out past the Bascom place, and if he's in the middle of delivering that baby, it'll be a while before he can get here. The bullet stopped just under the skin on the top of her shoulder. I can get it out. I've assisted my husband enough to be able to handle it, but an extra pair of hands will make the job easier. Once it's out, I can get the wound cleaned and bandaged until Doc gets back."

Wyatt looked at the fragile creature lying facedown on the table, a heavy sheet pulled discreetly over her. All her spunk and fire extinguished, she looked tiny and helpless.

"Have you ever done anything like this before?" Mrs. Kilburn questioned gently.

Wyatt gritted his teeth and nodded. "Yes. Many times after a skirmish with the Indians I'd assist the army surgeon, even dug out a few bullets on my own when he wasn't around."

"Good. Wash up," the efficient nurse directed. She carefully folded back a corner of the sheet and bared Meri's bloody shoulder.

Wyatt ached all the way to his soul at the sight of the ugly, seeping wound marring pearly skin.

Mrs. Kilburn pointed out a small bluish lump that bulged the skin along the top of her shoulder. "There's the bullet, just under the skin. This shouldn't take long. Hold that lamp for me and be ready to apply pressure after I cut it out." She handed him a bright reflecting lamp and thick cloth then leaned over Meri with a sharp scalpel.

In seconds she had removed a small deformed piece of lead and dropped it with a clatter into the bowl beside her. Wyatt pressed the cloth firmly over the oozing hole, while the woman briskly rewashed her hands. Then she returned and thoroughly cleansed the wound before applying a thick layer of ointment.

"Doc will check this over when he returns. Now, you wait in the office while I bandage her up. If my husband still hasn't returned, I'll have you carry her to a bed where she'll be more comfortable."

Wyatt collapsed onto the chair outside the door and dropped his face into his hands. He was a trembling bundle of limp bones. All he'd done was hold a lamp and press a bandage over the wound, and he was a mess. What had happened to the coolheaded lieutenant who calmly cut arrows and bullets out of the flesh of his comrades?

Dragging his head out of his hands, he stared at the quivering members. He'd more than likely cut off his own hand if he had to do anything like that right now.

Time dragged until Mrs. Kilburn summoned him again. "Help me move her to the room her father was in."

Wyatt cradled the delicate woman in his arms. The torn bloodstained blouse and riding skirt had been replaced with a long loose gown. He could feel the bulky bandages swathing her shoulder as he followed the doctor's wife down the short hallway. Laying Meri on her side, he stepped back, and Mrs. Kilburn tucked pillows behind her back and gently laid a quilt over her.

"I'll stay right here with her 'til Doc gets back. You go get the coyote who did this to her."

The woman's fierce expression would have made Wyatt smile on any other day but this one. He nodded grimly and exited the house. Leaping onto Charger, he raced back to pick up Jonah's trail.

If it took the rest of his life, he would not rest until he had caught the man who'd shot Meri.

Chapter Seventeen

Wyatt was halfway between town and the cemetery when he recognized Jonah and Barnaby riding toward him, their rifles trained on a man astride a gray horse riding slightly in front of them, hands bound securely behind his back.

"How's Miss Meri?" Barnaby asked anxiously, keeping the barrel of his rifle aimed unswervingly at the battered-looking man as their horses came to a halt.

"Doc's out of town on another call, but Mrs. Kilburn got the bullet out of her shoulder. She was still unconscious when I left." He gestured toward their prisoner. "Looks like you caught him."

"Yep." Grim satisfaction surrounded the single word.

"He looks a little worse for the wear." Wyatt eyed the man's bloody, bruised face and dirt-smeared torn clothing.

"He got off easy." Barnaby's eyes glinted dangerously. "I came real close to shootin' him off his horse and leavin' him for the buzzards."

"Where did you come from, by the way?" Wyatt asked the foreman.

"I was shadowing Miss Meri on her ride today. I knew you two were somewhere around 'cause I found your horses, and then I spotted you in the doorway of the crypt about the same time Miss Meri's horse did. When I heard the shots and saw you take her down and get her behind cover, I started working my way closer to him." Barnaby jerked his thumb toward the bound prisoner. "When this skunk lit out, I rode cross-country to cut him off."

"I caught up to them about the time Barnaby was explainin' the finer points of the consequences of shootin' a woman." Jonah's chuckle held no humor. "From the tracks his pretty gray horse is leavin', this is the same rat that stole McIsaac's horse and shot at Meri the first time."

"I don't know what they're talking about, Marshal," the man broke in belligerently. "I was just drifting through and suddenly this crazy fool jumps out of no-where and knocks me off my horse."

Barnaby patted the stock of a second rifle resting in the saddle scabbard. "His rifle's been fired recently."

"I shot at a rabbit."

"His tracks lead straight back to those cedars he shot at us from. I found these before I trailed him to where Barnaby had him cornered." Jonah pulled two brass cartridges from his pocket. "I'll also wager he's our bank robber."

"Why did you shoot at us?" The man turned his head away and refused to answer Wyatt's query. "Do you know anything about the bank robbery?" Again he vouchsafed no answer. "All right then, before we take him to jail, I need to make a quick stop at the cemetery."

"You want us to take him on in and lock him up?" Jonah stuffed the cartridges back into his pocket.

"No. I want him to see what we found this morning."

The four men rode toward the cemetery, Jonah and Barnaby vigilantly keeping their guns on the prisoner. Mr. Van Deusen and Mr. Hubert heard them coming and walked out from the tree line where they'd been keeping watch. They lowered their guns when they recognized the riders.

"You gonna explain why we've been keeping guard over a bunch of dead people and an empty tomb, Marshal?" Mr. Hubert peered at Wyatt quizzically, chuckling ruefully as he added, "I'm beginning to feel like those Roman soldiers in the Bible."

"This tomb isn't as empty as it appears." Wyatt dismounted, walked between the two marble lions and swung open the metal door.

He disappeared inside and scraping sounds were heard before he reappeared carrying several canvas bags. Dropping them on the ground, he untied the top of one and displayed its contents, keeping his eyes on the face of the suspected robber.

There were gasps from everyone except Jonah and bitterness spewed from the lips of the bound man. "That scheming double-crossing little weasel! I knew there was more money than what I…" He clamped his lips tight.

"I assume this is what you've been roaming the countryside looking for?" Wyatt retied the bag of money.

Mr. Hubert stared wide-eyed at the loot. "What is all that?"

"I believe that's the money from the bank," Jonah replied sardonically.

"How did it get here?" queried Mr. Van Deusen.

"I think our prisoner has a pretty good idea." Wyatt motioned toward the man on the gray horse. All eyes turned toward him, but he only glared sullenly.

"Maybe a little time cooling your heels in jail will loosen your tongue." Wyatt removed the rolled slicker from the back of his saddle and tied the three money-bags in its place. Flipping open the slicker, he draped it over the bags, concealing them from view.

"You gonna' drop that off at the bank on our way to the jail?" Mr. Van Deusen asked.

"No. It's going into the safe in my office. It's evidence. And I need all of you to keep quiet about it." Wyatt swung atop Charger.

"Why? Looks like we got the man who took it." Mr. Hubert waved his hand toward the sullen prisoner.

"He may have been the one to hold up the bank, but he didn't take this money." Wyatt cut off further questions by riding out of the cemetery toward town.

The next few hours flew swiftly. Wyatt locked the money in the office safe and secured the prisoner behind bars. He provided the man with a bucket of cool water and some rags to clean up with, but the man refused to talk.

Jonah returned from the banker's house with news that the man had packed a bag and departed an hour or so previous. The housekeeper had no idea when he would return.

Barnaby rode to the doctor's house for word on

Meri and returned to inform Wyatt that Doc and Ian McIsaac had arrived. Although Meri was still unconscious, Doc said she was simply weak from loss of blood and the shock to her system and should make a full recovery barring infection.

Leaving Franks in charge of the jail and the prisoner, Wyatt and Jonah snuck away from town in opposite directions. Slowly and silently they worked their way into the woods behind the graveyard, hiding themselves and their horses. Then they sat down to wait.

The last light faded from the sky. Wyatt strained his ears for any sound, his senses on full alert. Was he trying to close the trap on an already-escaped prey? The squeak of the gate at the lower end of the cemetery broke the heavy stillness.

Motionless, he and Jonah watched a shadowy figure sneak up the slope through the silent gravestones. When it disappeared into the crypt, they glided soundlessly from their hiding places. A muffled oath echoed from the interior of the pale mausoleum, and the sinister shape hurtled out the door.

"Put your hands up. You're under arrest," Wyatt ordered, gun held ready.

Crack! Crack!

Flame stabbed the darkness, and Wyatt felt a tug on his sleeve as the bullet tore past. His own gun fired simultaneously with Jonah's, and the indistinguishable figure slumped to the ground. They cautiously neared the man, and Jonah kicked the gun away from his hand. Wyatt knelt and rolled the groaning man over. Mr. Samuels's pasty face shone in the dim moonlight.

"You were right, Cap'n."

"Regrettably." Wyatt hauled the man none-too-gently to his feet. "Let's get him into town, see what shape he's in and hear what he has to say for himself."

Bright sunlight streamed in the window when Meri forced her eyes open. Why was she in Doc's house? Had she only dreamed her father was back home? No. It couldn't have been a dream. She was in the same room her father had occupied all those terrible days.

She sat up, gasped and fell back against the pillows as a wall of pain collided with her shoulder. Blackness threatened to swamp her, and her breath hissed between clenched teeth. What was wrong with her?

The sharp teeth of agony gnawed interminably, but when it began to ease, the events of the previous day flooded back. In spite of the physical pain, the weight of sadness and anger she'd carried so long was gone. Her spirit was light, and the world looked brighter in spite of the torment in her shoulder.

Thank You, Lord, for not giving up on me.

As the prayer filled her heart, a little smile turned up the corners of her mouth. She felt better and hurt worse than at any other time in her life. *Why* am *I hurting so badly?*

Meri gingerly fingered her shoulder, feeling the bandages under the fabric of the gown. The image of Wyatt taking her to the ground replayed in her memory, and a sudden blush heated her face. She'd made an idiot of herself in front of him. *Again.*

She groaned. Why was she so quick to lose her composure with him? So much for getting things right between herself and the Lord. It lasted mere seconds before she promptly flared up at the marshal, forgetting all about her newfound peace.

Footsteps warned her of someone's approach, and she looked toward the open door. Dr. Kilburn walked in followed by her very-worried-looking father.

"And how is our patient?" Doc moved to her side, lifting her wrist and looking at his pocket watch.

"Why am I here?"

"You were shot yesterday. Don't you remember?" Her father looked concerned

"I remember hearing gunshots and Wy... Marshal Cameron throwing me to the ground. My shoulder hurt, but I thought it was because he landed on me."

"No. One of those bullets ricocheted off the top of a headstone and ripped upward along your back to your left shoulder. You lost quite a bit of blood before Wyatt got you here and helped get the bullet out."

At Meri's questioning frown, Doc explained, "I was at the Adams place delivering a baby boy. Mother and baby are doing fine, incidentally. Anyway, that ricochet spent the last of its energy cutting up your back before burying itself in your shoulder just below the skin. My wife cut the bullet out. Marshal Cameron was her extra pair of hands before leaving to round up the gunman."

Doc stirred something into a glass of water and gently raised her head to allow her to sip it. Meri grimaced at the taste of the liquid and the ensuing pain when her shoulder protested even that slight movement.

"What is that stuff?" she gasped.

"Laudanum. I'll need to change those bandages soon, and this will take the edge off the worst of the pain."

"They caught him, in case ye were wonderin'," Mc-

Isaac announced, grimly pleased. He seated himself by the bed.

"Who was it?"

"The same eejit who shot me." The burr in McIsaac's voice intensified.

"The bank robber?"

"Aye, and he better be thankful he's surrounded by iron bars, or..." McIsaac's jaw clenched; his hands knotted into fists.

"Why would he shoot at us? I thought he was long gone." Meri blinked slowly, heavy drowsiness creeping in.

"It's a long story. I'll let Marshal Cameron tell it. He's the one who figured it out."

Her father's voice faded as she struggled to stay awake, but her eyelids had grown too heavy.

A piercing cry filled her ears when someone rolled her over, and the burn ravaging her shoulder blazed into an inferno. Hands were a million teeth gnawing her flesh, and another cry stabbed her ears. She dimly recognized her own voice before gratefully surrendering to unconsciousness.

Time ceased to exist. Meri was vaguely aware of a damp cloth on her face or a cool trickle of water down her throat, but these blurred and floated together in a crazy pain-racked dream.

It was dark when her eyes opened, and the memory of intense pain kept her motionless. The burning ache in her shoulder was still very much present, but Meri marveled at the restored peace warming her soul. She thanked the Lord for his gracious love, and asked forgiveness as she recalled again the events at the graveyard. *Lord, why do I lose my cool around Marshal*

Cameron? I really have been quite unpleasant, and I'm sorry. Why can't I just ignore him and go on?

A quiet little voice whispered in her heart, stopping her thoughts in their tracks.

Maybe you can't ignore him because he's dangerous to your heart.

No! she argued silently.

Maybe you're in love with him. Maybe that's what you're fighting.

I am not in love with him!

But in spite of her denial the words dug into her heart, and Meri was wide-awake as slow realization dawned.

How can I be in love with him? He drives me crazy. He's bossy. He laughs at me. He... He... His horse is faster than mine. The thought was petty, and she knew it. Laughing hazel eyes peered through her memories coaxing her to join in their merriment. *They are rather pretty eyes,* she admitted with a sigh.

Another memory lit up the dark room. A handsome man placing an outrageous bid and sitting across from her to indulge in his hard-won gingerbread. More images paraded past. An arm supporting her during the three-legged race; his chagrin at losing the sack race, but his delight in her win; the look on his face when rotten egg dripped down his shirtfront.

Meri grinned. Since when did a man look good in rotten egg? She sighed again. At the very least the man fascinated her. She was beginning to believe it went much deeper than simple fascination.

"Are ye awake, lass?" McIsaac's whisper broke the silence, and she jerked at the sound. Biting back a moan, she breathed past the pain. "Yes."

The strike of a match warned her, and she closed her eyes as the lamp flamed to life. Squinting against the sudden brightness, she watched her father pour a glass of water. Bringing it to her, he carefully raised her head to allow her a drink. The cool liquid tasted wonderful, and Meri drank the entire glass before resting her head back on the pillow. "Thank you. That tasted so good."

"How do ye feel?" He placed a hand on her forehead.

"Sore."

"I heartily sympathize."

"Now I know why you were unconscious so long. You didn't want to deal with the pain." Meri grinned at him.

"Me secret comes to light at last." He shook his head in mock shame.

Silence fell for a moment, and Meri swallowed hard before she spoke. "Faither?"

"Aye, lass?"

"Will you forgive me for my terrible attitude the past few months? I know I've been a pain to be around, but the Lord finally got my attention. I was angry and blaming Him for Mither's death, thinking He wasn't hearing my prayers. I kept telling myself I was sad, but I was taking out my hurt and anger on those around me." Meri choked on the sudden rush of tears.

Arms surrounded her in a gentle hug. "Wheesht, lass. I knew ye were hurting, and I prayed ye'd let the Lord heal ye as He has me. Of course I forgive ye. I love ye more than me own life. I'm so grateful the Lord spared ye."

He pulled away, tears glistening on his cheeks. Pulling a handkerchief from his pocket, he dried her tears before wiping away his own. "Yer mither would be laughing at the both of us. She always said she was the only stoic Scot in the family."

Meri grinned at him. For the first time since her mother's death, the mention of her didn't send a shaft of pain through her heart. Instead the memory of her mother's teasing statement whenever father got emotional was heartwarmingly pleasant. They softly reminisced until Meri's eyelids drooped again, and her father turned the lamp down low.

Leaning over, he softly kissed her forehead, his Scottish brogue rumbling softly against her ears. "Sleep well, lass. Yer Faither will be watching over ye. And so will I."

The day passed in a confusing blur, laudanum keeping the worst of the pain at bay, but making Meri's brain so foggy, wakefulness and sleep swirled together in a surreal tangle. She wasn't sure if she dreamed Wyatt's voice, but the word *sweetheart* spoken in a rich baritone brought a drowsy smile to her lips.

The sun was high in the sky the following day when she finally woke with a clear head and ravenous hunger. Her father was busily scanning the newspaper, but at the sound of her growling stomach, he lowered the paper to his lap. "Ye're awake. And hungry from the sound of it." A relieved smile lit his face.

"I'm starving."

The door swung open, admitting Dr. Kilburn. "How's our patient feeling today?" Meri's stomach rumbled in answer. "Sounds like your appetite is in good working order." Doc laughed as he felt her head and reached for her wrist. "We'll get it quieted down in a few minutes. Until then, how are you feeling?"

"Still trying to figure out which end is up." Meri shifted slightly, regretting it instantly as the pain reminded her why she was flat on her back, or rather, propped up on pillows.

Dr. Kilburn smiled. "Your wound is looking good, no sign of infection, and you haven't had any laudanum for several hours. How's the pain?"

"Bearable, as long as I don't move."

"Then don't move. It's going to take some time to heal, and you'll be sore even after that. Now, how about some food?"

"Yes, please."

He left the room, and soon Mrs. Kilburn breezed in with a fragrant-smelling tray. Setting it down on the bedside table, she turned to Meri. "Do you want to try sitting up?"

"Yes, I'm tired of lying down."

Meri thought better of the idea when Mrs. Kilburn helped ease her into an upright position, but she gritted her teeth and refused to let a whimper escape. Mrs. Kilburn artfully arranged the pillows to support her while keeping pressure off the damaged shoulder, and Meri gratefully sank against their softness. Pain had effectively quieted the noisy rumbling of her stomach, leaving her nauseous instead.

"I don't think I'm hungry anymore." A bead of sweat trickled down her back.

"I brought some nice broth to start with. Why don't you try a few sips and see if it doesn't calm your stomach?"

Meri felt very weak and helpless as the woman

spooned broth into her mouth, but after a few swallows, Mrs. Kilburn proved she knew what she was talking about.

Meri's appetite returned with a vengeance. The broth disappeared quickly, and she gratefully accepted the soft, buttered bread. "Thank you. That tasted wonderful."

"We'll give you something a little more substantial for supper, but Doc wanted to make sure you handled this okay before trying anything heavier." She gathered up the dishes. "I'll be back in a few minutes to help you freshen up. You'll have guests before long. You're quite our most popular patient." Mrs. Kilburn grinned and winked before bustling out of the room.

"What did she mean?"

McIsaac lowered the paper he'd been quietly reading. "I'm not sure who's left to run the ranch since most of the hands rode in at various times yesterday to 'check on you' and carry news back there. Half the town has stopped by to check on 'Miss Meri.' Franks is more worried than I've ever seen him."

She was humbled so many people cared about her, but had Wyatt not stopped in? Was that why her father hadn't mentioned him? Maybe she *had* only dreamed the sweetheart endearment.

Mrs. Kilburn returned, interrupting her musings. Hustling McIsaac out of the room and closing the door behind him, she helped Meri with a personal urgent need. When she was settled back in bed, exhausted, Mrs. Kilburn brushed Meri's hair smooth and tamed it into a neat braid. Then she bathed Meri's hands and face in refreshing warm water before arranging a pretty little crocheted bed jacket about her shoulders and straightening the colorful quilt around her waist.

"There," she said, stepping back to admire her work. "Don't you make a lovely picture?"

"If you happen to like looking at what the cat dragged in."

"Absolutely not!" the woman argued stoutly. "You look fashionably pale, and I know a certain lawman who won't be able to take his eyes off you." A distant knock sounded, and Mrs. Kilburn smiled knowingly. "I suspect that's him now." She eyed Meri's blooming cheeks. "Ah, you're not quite so pale now. Feel up to a little company?"

Meri's heart was in her throat, so she could only nod. First she was disappointed when she thought he hadn't dropped by, and now she feared seeing him again.

Fickle female! You don't know your own mind.

"I'll show him in then." Mrs. Kilburn pulled the door closed behind her.

Meri barely breathed, straining to hear identifiable voices. When she heard steps approaching, her heart shuddered to a stop.

You don't even know if it's him.

But she did. She recognized his steps on the wood flooring. Her stomach lurched as they came to a stop outside the door, and a light tap caused her heart to explode back into action.

"Come in." It was more croak than voice, but it did the job because the door swung inward.

Chapter Eighteen

Wyatt stepped into the room and stood looking at her for a long moment, his eyes seeming to absorb every inch of her. His powerful presence shrank the space until it felt too small to hold two people comfortably, and Meri felt he could see all the way through her. She wanted to lower her gaze, but it tangled irretrievably in his.

He exhaled a noisy sigh. "You look so much better today. You had me worried, Mac."

Meri opened her mouth to protest the name then shut it abruptly. She might actually be starting to like it.

"Uh-oh. I thought you were doing better, but maybe I ought to call Doc."

"Why?"

"You're not arguing with me. You must be feeling worse than I thought." The sparkle in his eyes belied the concern in his voice, and Meri felt an answering grin struggle for freedom.

She sobered quickly, however, and dropped her eyes to the quilt. "I need to apologize for that."

"Apologize for what?"

"Apologize for always arguing with you."

"You don't *always* argue with me. I seem to recall we worked pretty good together at the picnic."

Meri ignored the heat in her cheeks and forced herself to continue. "I've been fighting the Lord on some things, and I allowed it to affect my attitude and how I treated those around me, you especially. I've been rude to you, lost my temper..." Meri felt tears sting her eyes but refused to release them. "I've asked the Lord to forgive me, now I'm asking you to forgive me." The apology was hard enough without blubbering all over the man.

"Forgiveness granted, and I have a confession of my own."

Her eyes flew to his.

"You're not completely at fault here."

"I'm not?"

"No." He chuckled. "I did my fair share of provoking you."

"Why?"

"Unlike most females of my acquaintance, instead of fussing about a ruined dress, a mussed hairdo or even acting helpless when you landed at my feet that day at Franks's, you came up fighting. I liked your spunk and wanted to see it again. You mind if I sit down?"

The question caught Meri off guard. "Of course."

"You want me to leave?"

"No! I mean... Yes, you can sit down."

"You had me worried for a minute there. I was afraid you were going to throw me out on my ear,"

Wyatt said good-naturedly, seating himself in the chair by the bedside.

If the room had shrunk when he'd walked in, it now felt positively minuscule. Meri looked down at her fingers mindlessly twirling a bed jacket ribbon. She folded her hands, forcing her gaze back toward Wyatt. He was watching her with a look she couldn't decipher, but it made her stomach quiver. She rallied her retreating courage; just because she was more accustomed to arguing with him didn't mean she was incapable of carrying on a normal, civil conversation, despite evidence to the contrary.

Lifting her chin slightly, she broke the silence. "Thank you."

Those intense eyes never left hers. "For?"

"For saving my life."

A breathtaking smile curved his lips. "The Lord saved your life, but it was absolutely my pleasure to be of some assistance. You scared a few years off my life when I realized you were bleeding. I'd rather not experience that again, if you don't mind."

"I'd rather not repeat it myself. It's painful. Would you tell me what happened after I was shot? Faither said the bank robber and the man who shot at us were the same person and you had him in jail. And you never did tell me why you and Jonah were out there in the first place."

Wyatt leaned back in the chair and crossed one ankle over his knee. "There were a lot of pieces that didn't add up about all that, and I couldn't figure out why the bank robber was still hanging around."

"Why did you think he was still around?"

"Jonah matched the tracks where he stole your ranch horse to the ones on the road where you…"

Meri interrupted. "The two men I saw on the road—I knew you and Jonah were acting funny. One of those men was the bank robber?"

"Yes. His name is Ernie Mullins."

"Who was the other man?"

"Mr. Phineas Samuels."

Meri's eyes grew large, and her mouth dropped opened in surprise. "Mr. Samuels?"

Wyatt nodded grimly.

"But—I don't understand."

Wyatt related what he'd learned from the bank clerk. "I'd already figured out someone else was involved in the bank job, and when every inconsistency kept leading back to Mr. Samuels, I began to have my suspicions. I could never pin him down on any explanations, and then you mentioned seeing him at the cemetery and his strange behavior. It just added to all the things pointing his direction. I put a couple pairs of eyes to watching him and sure enough it led back to the cemetery."

"I still don't understand why you were there."

"Mullins was hanging around because he didn't find a safe full of money like he was expecting. The majority of the money was gone long before he arrived. Mr. Samuels had been embezzling a little at a time and engineered the robbery to cover his tracks. He didn't expect Mullins to realize there had to be more money somewhere and want more than his share of what he cleaned out of the safe. Mullins was trying to scare Mr. Samuels into giving him a bigger cut. That's what you saw on the road that day and what you saw through the bank window the day of the picnic." He shook his head. "There is absolutely no honor between thieves."

"I can hardly believe it." Meri was stunned.

"You were the other wrinkle in Mr. Samuels's plot."

"Me? What did I do?"

"You'd seen too much. Or so Mr. Samuels thought."

"I didn't see anything. I wasn't anywhere around when the bank robbery occurred."

"You saw Mr. Samuels in the cemetery, you saw him out on the road with Mullins and you saw the two of them in the bank. When you mentioned that at the picnic, he thought you were putting it all together and panicked. He told Mullins if he got rid of you, he'd give him a larger cut. You were too hard to get to at the ranch, but Mullins got his chance when you rode into the graveyard. He wasn't shooting randomly that day. He was aiming for you."

Meri shivered at how close he'd come to being successful. She decided not to dwell on that thought. "What were you doing there?"

Wyatt shifted in the chair and leaned forward, elbows on his knees. "Jonah and I were following a hunch—one that played out. Mr. Samuels had been 'depositing' money in that ridiculous crypt. He buried it under a loose stone in the floor, believing no one would ever think to look in there. We'd just uncovered it when we saw you. We didn't want you asking questions and were waiting 'til you left, but Sandy caught us peeking out."

Wyatt threw his head back suddenly and laughed. "I wish you could have seen your face when we walked out. You looked like you were expecting a ghost, but you got me instead."

"I came close to shooting you just for scaring me." Meri couldn't hide an embarrassed grin.

"I thought for a moment you *were* upset enough to pull that trigger." He grinned back at her to show there were no hard feelings and continued his story. "Word got to Samuels that you were shot, and he went to retrieve the money before hightailing it out of the country. He got quite a surprise when he found an empty hole in the ground instead of his money. We were waiting when he burst back out the door."

"You got him."

"And found your father's missing gun, too. Samuels had it and used it. Ruined a good shirt, too." He scowled.

"He shot you?" Meri jerked forward and yelped as the injured shoulder objected to the sudden move.

Wyatt was gently easing her back against the pillows before she realized he'd moved from his chair. "Easy does it. Give it a minute, the pain will pass." He gently rubbed her arm. "Breathe, sweetheart. Want me to get Doc?"

"No," Meri bit out, eyes closed and teeth clenched against the searing burn. Maybe she hadn't dreamed up the sweetheart endearment in her drugged stupor after all.

A cool cloth touched her skin. She opened her eyes, surprised to see Wyatt tenderly dabbing her forehead. Concern radiated from him. "Is it easing up any?"

"Yes." It wasn't great, but it was bearable, given the distraction of his fingers against her forehead. "Go on with your story."

He studied her closely before folding the cloth. Laying it over the edge of the basin, he reseated himself.

"Okay, but no more sudden movements," he cautioned anxiously.

"I think I'll take you up on that advice." She breathed shallowly as the pain began to ebb.

"Following orders? That would be a first for you, wouldn't it?" Wyatt asked seriously.

"Funny. I can understand why you're a lawman. Your career as a jester was so short-lived." Meri grinned dryly.

Wyatt swiped his hand across his brow. "Pshew! Now that's the Miss McIsaac I know and... I was beginning to worry that I didn't have the right room."

She rolled her eyes with a grin. "You didn't say if Mr. Samuels hit you or Jonah."

"He missed on both counts and only tore up the sleeve on my shirt. We didn't miss."

"Is he dead?"

"No. Jonah and I winged him, one on each side. He's sitting in jail with two very sore arms awaiting the U.S. Marshal to transport him to the county seat for trial."

"Sounds like you both nearly missed."

His eyes narrowed playfully. "No, Miss Doubting Thomas, we hit exactly what we were aiming at. We didn't want to kill him. We wanted him to stand trial."

"What will happen to him?"

"That'll be up to a judge, but he'll be tried for the attempted murder of you and your father as well as the theft of the bank's money."

Meri shook her head in unbelief. It was bewildering that the man who'd attended church with them year after year had tried to have her killed! "But he was hurt in the holdup, too."

"I've not been able to get out of either of them whether Mullins hit him or if Samuels did it to himself, but either way, it was done to make the holdup look real."

"Why would he do it—rob the bank?"

Wyatt shook his head, thoughtfully quiet for a moment before answering. "I asked him that myself, and a lot of pent-up anger spewed out. Says he deserved to have the money because God never did anything for him. He's raved about his poor childhood, the loss of a baby son, a wife that withdrew after the baby's death, every little slight anyone's ever done to him and on and on. Bitterness poured out of him like a festered sore. He doesn't even sound rational half the time. I guess he let all his disappointments weigh on him until he snapped."

"So the money's all back?"

"Every penny according to the records we found at Samuels's house. We even got back most of what Mullins took. He'll stand trial for attempted murder, as well."

"What will happen to the bank?"

"That's up to the bank's investors. Apparently, they were part of Samuels's problem. Several of them wanted him replaced as bank president and had been working toward that end. Samuels knew about it and decided to get revenge along with what he thought he deserved."

She leaned her head back against the pillow. Just hearing the whole sordid story tired her out. "What a mess."

"I can't help but think about Pastor Willis's message a couple weeks ago. Samuels is a prime example of letting anger and bitterness fester until it ruined him. I suppose he's had a hard life, but so has everyone to some extent, and he'd made something out of himself. But instead of letting the Lord help him through his difficulties, he allowed every little problem to grow out of proportion until he was willing to kill to get what he wanted."

Meri blushed to think how close she'd been to starting down the same path. She didn't realize her eyes had drifted closed until they flew open when she heard Wyatt stand up from his chair.

"I can see I've bored you to sleep," he teased gently. "I'll let you get some rest before Doc comes in and runs me out." He pulled out his watch. "He gave me a time limit, and it's almost up."

"Thank you for explaining what happened." She swallowed the yawn that threatened.

"You are most welcome." Wyatt bowed. "May I drop in to see you again?"

"Could I keep you away, Marshal?" she teased.

"If you really don't want to see me, Mac, I won't come, but I'm hoping that's not the case." Wyatt was completely serious.

"I..." She cleared her throat in nervous confusion. "I don't mind if you come by."

Wyatt grinned hugely. "Good." In the blink of an eye he picked her hand up from the quilt and, leaning over, kissed it gallantly. Straightening, he squeezed her fingers before releasing them, gave her a jaunty grin and headed out the door.

Meri was speechless. Her eyes followed the broad shoulders until they disappeared. She was still staring, pondering his actions, when Dr. Kilburn stepped into the room and after a quick look at her, ordered her to get some rest. She had no desire to sleep; her mind was too busy ordering her heart not to indulge in foolish dreams, but the kiss on her hand accompanied her into dreamland where chivalrous knights wore shiny badges instead of rusty armor and rode beautiful bay stallions instead of washed-out white horses.

When Wyatt arrived back at his office Friday afternoon, a U.S. Marshal was waiting to escort the prisoners to the county seat. He also requested Wyatt's assistance in delivering the two men. Wyatt thought the trip would be a quick there-and-back, but he had to stay long enough to testify in a preliminary hearing Monday morning.

The time away gave him plenty of time to think. Almost losing Meri to a gunman's bullet brought a new perspective to his belief that he needed to wait until life was safe before thinking about a wife and family. Seeing the hardship military life placed on wives and families, he'd erected a barrier to keep himself from being hurt or hurting someone else. The loss of his parents had shown him he couldn't control circumstances around him, only his response, but still, he'd tried to protect himself with a wall around his heart.

Then Miss McIsaac had sailed a rangy black horse over his carefully fortified barriers as if they were no more substantial than a cobweb fence.

Although she had struggled for a while, she'd proved she was resilient enough to deal with the loss of her mother. Was her self-sufficient independence strong enough to deal with the uncertainty of his job and an unknown future? He hoped so, because the thought of not having her in his life was as scary as almost losing her to that bullet.

Whether he was an officer of the law or a simple horse breeder, it was impossible to guard completely himself or those around him from loss. He could, however, stop waiting for life to be perfect and go after the woman who made him laugh and his heart beat faster. After years of trying to control his future, it was time to trust the One who held the future in His hands.

Equal parts excitement and fear accompanied him on his return to Little Creek. Her reaction to him, whether it was a fiery retort, an all-out retreat or the shy softness she'd worn the last time he'd seen her, suggested she wasn't completely indifferent to him. He clung to that hope as he let Charger pick his own pace—fast—toward home.

Chapter Nineteen

Meri caught herself glancing up nervously every time the door rattled, but the longed-for sight of a particular star-toting individual did not appear. The pain in her shoulder was less severe, but she was achy and chafed at the unaccustomed inactivity of the past several days. She had slept a great deal due to the laudanum, and when she was awake, she'd had a steady stream of visitors. It felt like she'd seen everyone in town. Everyone except the one person who she most wanted to see.

Not too many days ago you were convinced you couldn't abide the man, yet here you are working yourself into a dither wondering why he hasn't come by to see you again. Just because you've decided you lo—like him after all, doesn't mean he's of the same opinion.

But he called you sweetheart and kissed your hand, the little voice argued.

He was merely being a gentleman.

She couldn't bring herself to ask his whereabouts, but when Jonah casually mentioned Wyatt had escorted the prisoners to the county seat, her internal argument ceased.

For all of ten minutes.

In spite of her unsettled emotions, however, her soul rested in the peace of restored fellowship with her Heavenly Father.

Meri had been injured Thursday, and by Tuesday morning, she had developed a case of cabin fever. By keeping her arm quiet in the sling Dr. Kilburn had fashioned, pain was kept to a dull ache, and he allowed her to be up and about as she had energy. He also gave her the welcome news she could return home the next morning if she promised to curtail any riding or lifting for another week.

Mrs. Kilburn assisted her into real clothes, a pale yellow blouse and simple blue skirt, and pulled her hair up and away from her face in a soft twist. Meri then celebrated her impending release by escaping the enclosing walls of the house for Mrs. Kilburn's shady garden.

After exploring every nook and cranny of the verdant bower, Meri made her way to the pretty bench tucked under the rose arbor. A few buds were just beginning to peek open, subtly perfuming the air, and some thoughtful soul had padded the bench with a thick quilt and several soft pillows. She gratefully tucked her uninjured side into the pillowed corner and lifted her legs to rest on the seat, more drained than she would have admitted. It was good to be outside in the fresh breeze, but getting shot definitely took the starch out of a person.

Leaning her head against the high-backed seat, she allowed her mind to wander as she listened to a chipper little sparrow singing his heart out as he hopped to and fro on his bird duties.

She was drifting on a drowsy daydream somewhere between sleep and wakefulness and didn't immediately notice when floral-scented air changed to spicy bay rum. She enjoyed the new aroma for several breaths before the contrast dawned on her. Her eyes flew open, and her gaze riveted to the shadow lying across her lap. A wave of shyness washed over her, and she hesitantly turned lowered eyes toward her visitor.

Shiny black boots, firmly anchored to the ground and tucked beneath spotless black trousers, stood inches outside the rose arbor. Her eyes slowly traveled up the sleek, solid form. A holster circled narrow hips, and a crisp red shirt with silver buttons was belted into the pants. One hand dangled a black Stetson by the brim; the other hand was tucked into a back pocket.

The spick-and-span, too-handsome-for-his-own-good marshal appeared as if he'd just stepped out of a bandbox. He didn't move nor speak during Meri's scrutiny and, swallowing past the lump in her throat, she forced her eyes to his face. There was no smirking grin or teasing eyes as there had been the first time she'd met this man. There was only a soft gaze and a hint of upturned lips.

Intense hazel eyes snagged hesitant brown eyes as the thick silence continued. Meri felt his piercing gaze read her every thought. She tried to read him, but unfamiliar with this new language, she remained unsure of what she saw in his eyes and on his face. Her gaze dropped, breaking the connection, and a sense of loss registered.

"Excuse me, ma'am."

The husky sound drew Meri's eyes back to the tall shadow-casting figure who bowed slightly, still keeping one hand tucked behind him.

"I don't think we've been properly introduced. Allow me to present myself. I am Wyatt Cameron from Virginia by way of Texas."

A smile dawned in Meri's heart in delight of the pretentious tone he assumed and the haughty tilt of his head.

"Some might know me better by my job description here in Little Creek—Marshal Cameron."

She resisted the laugh that bubbled at his continued air of superiority but a little burble escaped her.

Wyatt lifted an eyebrow at the outburst. "Please do not interrupt my introduction, ma'am."

She pulled her face into some semblance of matching dignity while the impish twinkle in his eyes made her heart do an undignified jig.

"Now where was I?" He pretended to ponder a second. "Ah, yes. I was raised in the fine state of Virginia by my parents, Recyrus, better known as Cy, and Hanna Cameron. I graduated from West Point a second lieutenant in the United States Army. I served for over ten years and attained the rank of captain but resigned my commission after the death of my father."

Wyatt's voice had taken on a serious note as he mentioned his parents, and he paused a moment before continuing. "Might I ask whom I have the honor of addressing?" The condescending tone had returned.

She held out her hand in feigned hauteur. "*Miss* America McIsaac, sir."

He stepped toward her. Setting his hat on a nearby

table, he cradled the offered hand in his own and saluted it with a kiss.

Delightful tingles raced up her arm, and she admired the lustrous head of hair bent over her fingers. "But my friends call me Meri," she added with the barest whisper, "or Mac."

Wyatt watched her for a long breath before straightening. The hand she had assumed to be in his back pocket emerged from hiding holding a small bouquet of deep purple violets. He bowed low again as he offered them to her. "With my compliments, Miss McIsaac."

His fingers brushed hers when she accepted the pretty flowers. She was beginning to look forward to the thrill that raced through her whenever he touched her. Burying her nose in the delicate blooms, she hid her face a moment and inhaled their faint sweet scent as he resumed speaking in his newly acquired supercilious manner.

"I was hired to be the marshal of Little Creek, and soon found the town was plagued with a rash of burglaries." He paused dramatically and rocked back on his heels, tucking his thumbs into his belt loops and gazing at the top of the arbor. "However, I was brilliantly able to resolve all but one of the thefts."

Meri grinned at his impudence. "You surprise me, sir."

"The horse theft was solved immediately by my quick action. I had the thief rounded up before she knew what hit her."

She rolled her eyes as he glanced down to check her reaction to this statement but refused to rise to the bait. "Next...?"

"It took a wee bit longer, due to a slight cleverness on the part of the next thief, but I soon solved the mystery of the bank robbery with my usual dazzling detective skills."

This time she laughed outright at his unmitigated arrogance.

A satisfied grin marred the haughty upturned face, until a look of abject despondence replaced the smirk, and his head fell forward abashedly. "But alas, I have been unable to resolve the most grievous theft."

Meri had never seen puppy-dog-sad eyes retain such a deep, mischievous gleam. "So even your brilliance has its limits?"

"Repeat offenders are sly, hardened characters and more difficult to apprehend. Especially when they don't even realize they've committed a theft." His head shook remorsefully.

"How can a thief not realize they've stolen something?"

"This particular thief happens to be rather forgetful."

"So an absentminded thief has outwitted our brilliant marshal? How can that be?"

"Shocking, I know. It has been a rather severe blow." Again, his glossy head bowed in contrite shame. "This thief cannot seem to remember my name even though she has stolen my most valuable possession."

Too late, she realized the clever trap she'd blindly walked into. She crossed her arms as best as possible, considering one arm was in a sling, and narrowed her eyes at the merry hazel ones that peeked at her through thick lashes. "And what, pray tell, am I supposed to have stolen this time?"

All traces of humor fled, and his eyes glowed with a fierce look that took Meri by surprise. Her own eyes widened, and her heart stuttered.

He scrutinized her with a long, measuring look before responding in a low voice. "My heart, fair lady. You've stolen my heart. And I don't know how to function without it."

Meri searched him for any trace of teasing or humor but found only resolute earnestness. "I've never heard of anyone living without a heart," she said tentatively. She had to clear her throat of a sudden lump. "Would it help if I gave it back?"

"No. It wouldn't fit anymore. Someone has taken up residence in it."

Silence fell again. Meri forgot to breathe. She had two choices, fearful retreat or bold advance. After a short but hard-fought internal struggle, she chose boldness. "Would it help if I offered a replacement?" She'd forgotten to notify her mouth that she was being bold. It barely broke a whisper, and Wyatt had to step closer in order to hear. His closeness very nearly destroyed her hard-won bravery.

"What do you mean by a replacement?" he asked cautiously.

"Would you take mine in exchange for yours?" Fear swamped her heart, and she ducked her head as she made the request, unable to look at him. Silence fell and was almost unbearable, but she dreaded looking up to find rejection on his face.

Gentle, calloused fingers touched the tender skin under her chin, and lightning raced through her at the unexpected contact. Like velvet steel, they softly, inexorably forced her face up out of hiding. The second she saw his expression, she understood he'd been wait-ing for her to look at him before replying.

Expectation filled his eyes as he searched her face. She timidly allowed him to look his fill. "Do you mean what I hope you mean?"

She'd never heard that tone of anxious longing from him before, and a surge of confidence replaced shyness. She'd discovered the key to a new language. What had been undecipherable before was beginning to make sense. "You called me a forgetful thief, but the charge can just as easily be leveled at you. You said I didn't know I'd stolen your heart, yet *you* didn't realize you had stolen *my* heart. So you see, Marshal Wyatt Cameron, I'm in good company. It takes a thief to catch a thief."

Hope birthed a huge smile, and Wyatt moved to the bench. "Do you mind if I sit down? I find my knees are suddenly in need of support." Meri started to move her legs off the seat, but Wyatt stopped her with a hand gently laid atop her slippered feet. "Let me."

Ever so carefully he tucked her skirt modestly around her legs, lifting them and sliding under to sit on the bench and lowering them again to rest across his lap. He kept one hand on her ankles and rested the other arm along the back of the bench as he admired the pretty, rich color that sprang to her cheeks.

She was absolutely beautiful, and he longed to kiss her, but he didn't want to scare her away. Besides, he'd seen the curtain move in the kitchen window and figured they had an audience. "Since we seemed to have exchanged hearts unknowingly, might I have the honor of calling on you, Miss Meri? I miss my heart, you know."

Her eyes twinkled before her lashes veiled his view. "I'd like that, but I do have one request, Marshal."

He narrowed his eyes in mock sternness. "And what might that be, Mac?"

Her lashes swept up. "Yes. That's it."

Wyatt cocked his head in confusion and felt his brows knit. "Huh?" Not exactly the most eloquent speech he'd ever uttered.

Laughter spilled unhindered from her lips and danced along the fragrant air.

"It's not healthy to mock the marshal, young lady. Please explain yourself!" He jostled her ankles lightly in emphasis and felt heat race up his arm.

"I was going to request that you call me Mac occasionally, but you beat me to it." She grinned, blushing slightly.

He grinned right back and shook his head. "Women! My father said I'd never understand them."

Two pairs of laughing eyes met and held and awareness sizzled the air between them. Wyatt found himself leaning toward her.

"How 'bout something to eat?" Mr. McIsaac stood by the arbor holding a tray.

Wyatt straightened and glanced at Meri. Another blush deepened the pink of her cheeks, and she tried to twist her legs off his lap. He quietly stilled her movements, holding her in place. "I don't know about Meri, but I'm hungry. I think we misplaced lunchtime somewhere along the way."

"Meri still has a little trouble handling food one-handed. Could I impose on ye to help her since ye're already so nicely situated?"

"You make me sound helpless," Meri protested.

They ignored her as Wyatt took possession of the tray while McIsaac pulled the little table within Wyatt's reach.

"I'll take yer hat into the house out of the way. Holler if ye need anything." He gave Wyatt an approving nod and wink, and Wyatt released the breath he'd unconsciously held.

"Would you care for a sandwich, Mac?" He offered her one of the small plates from the tray.

She blinked in charming confusion, looking from the closing screen door back to him. "Why do I get the impression someone is being hustled?"

She must have seen her father's wink. "Maybe you just have a suspicious nature, dear. Sandwich?"

Her frown held no heat, and Wyatt could see her searching for a comeback. He distracted her by asking a blessing on the food and filling her plate. There was little conversation as they ate, Wyatt keeping her supplied with food, drink and napkins as needed, but there were plenty of tentative smiles on her part and not so tentative on his.

When they'd finished, and Wyatt had replaced the dishes on the tray, Meri suddenly blurted, "I won't be here."

"Hmm?" He glanced at her, idly fingering the bow decorating the soft kid slippers on her slender feet.

"We're going home tomorrow. I won't be here." Panic colored her words.

Wyatt stretched his arm along the back of the bench again and allowed his fingers to rest against her shoulder. "I think I remember the way to your ranch. And if not I'll refresh my memory when I escort you home tomorrow."

"But what about your job?"

"What's the use of having a deputy if the marshal can't take an evening now and then to court his girl?"

The shock in her eyes would have been funny if it wasn't so sadly genuine. "You're courting me?" she squeaked just like a mouse.

"Does it mean something else out here when a fella asks to call?" Wyatt watched confusion cross her face again and waited patiently for her response. When it came, it was halting and muffled.

"I… I'm not sure. I've never had anyone ask me before."

The men who had overlooked her were idiots. And he was extremely grateful. "Leave it to a Virginia boy to be the only one to recognize a true gem in this land of fool's gold." He assumed a haughty tone again, and she grinned nervously in answer.

"What happened with Mr. Samuels?" She changed the subject so abruptly, it took him a full second to catch up.

"We delivered the prisoners to the county jail without any problems, and after the hearing, the judge ordered them held for trial, which has been scheduled for next month. Your father will probably get a notice to go testify along with Jonah and myself. I figure Samuels and Mullins will go away for a long time afterward."

She asked a couple more questions, and they chatted for several minutes before Wyatt regretfully announced he needed to return to his office. "May I walk you to the house, or do you want to stay out here?"

"I'm ready to go inside."

Wyatt lowered her feet to the ground, and offered her his arm. His heart swelled as her hand curled around it.

Arriving too soon at the kitchen door, he again brushed his lips across the back of her slim, firm hand. "Until tomorrow."

She nodded, the hand resting in the sling caressing the hand he'd touched with his lips.

Knowing he'd see her tomorrow didn't soothe the ache of having to leave, but he forced himself to turn and start back toward the office.

He heard the kitchen door open before Meri spoke. "Oh! Your hat!"

Walking back, he took it from her hand and swept her a gallant bow before settling the hat on his head. "Good afternoon, my fair lady."

A completely un-Meri-like dreamy sigh whispered past his ears as he left, and a jaunty whistle sprang to his lips. Turnabout was fair play. She'd sailed over the barriers around his heart altogether too easily, but it looked as if he'd knocked down a few of her own today.

Chapter Twenty

Meri's departure from the Kilburns' home was accomplished only after much to-do and many hugs the next day.

Franks delivered a freshly groomed, gleaming Sandy who nickered eagerly at sight of his mistress. Tying him to the back of the wagon, Franks hugged Meri, careful of her injured shoulder. "They be a lot a answered prayers 'roun' here lately, Miss Meri. I's shore grateful He healed you."

"He did, Franks—in more ways than one. Thank you for praying and for taking such good care of Sandy."

"Anytime, Miss Meri, anytime."

Naoma Van Deusen was next in line, and after an admonition to take it easy, she whispered loudly, "I hear a certain marshal can't stay away from the doctor's house lately. I knew you would catch his eye if you put your mind to it."

Her exuberant hug left Meri wincing, and as she disentangled herself from the self-satisfied matchmaker, she looked into the eyes of Wyatt. He'd ridden up on Charger, and from the grin on his face, it was clear he'd heard the not-so-quiet statement. He dropped one eye in a lazy wink. Meri's reproving look failed miserably due to a grin that impeded its progress.

The Kilburns took care to avoid her sore shoulder, and Meri was warmed by their gentle hugs. The time spent in their home had given her a new love and appreciation for this couple who'd dedicated their lives to caring for those around them, and she was profuse in her gratitude. Dr. Kilburn promised to ride out later in the week to check on her, cautioning her to allow herself time to heal before she went riding around the countryside like a wild Indian.

McIsaac grinned, vowing to keep his daughter quiet. "I believe it's me own turn to hover tiresomely." He and Doc assisted a grumbling Meri into the back of the wagon padded with thick quilts and pillows. "If I had to ride home in the back of the wagon, lass, so do ye."

"You're enjoying this entirely too much," she groused.

"Aye, that I am."

Meri propped a pillow against the side of the wagon and leaned in to it, primly folding her hands across her lap. She borrowed Wyatt's look of hauteur. "Home, driver."

Laughing goodbyes filled the air as McIsaac climbed onto the wagon seat and clucked to the horses. Wyatt turned Charger to ride alongside where Meri had a bird's-eye view of him.

As McIsaac threaded the wagon through town, several people waved and called out cheery greetings. Danny and Billy ran out of the mercantile and hopped onto the back of the wagon as it passed to hand Meri a slightly sticky peppermint stick to "help make the trip more comfortable." Meri thanked them, smiling at Mr. Van Deusen who waved from the doorway.

The boys amused her, jabbering of their new status as Little Creek's detectives and bragging how the town would be safer now that they were on the job. When they reached the bridge over Little Creek, they promptly forgot their detective status and ran down the creek bank to terrify the local crawfish population.

McIsaac commenced singing a fine old Scottish ballad in a not-too-rusty tenor, and Wyatt quickly added his baritone. One song became two, and when the second one ended, Wyatt suggested a third that drew a nod of approval from McIsaac.

O, my luve is like a red, red rose,
That's newly sprung in June.
O, my luve is like a melodie,
That's sweetly played in tune.
As fair art thou, my bonnie lass,
So deep in luve am I;
And I will luve thee still, my dear,
Till a' the seas gang dry.
And I will luve thee still, my dear,
Till a' the seas gang dry.
Till a' the seas gang dry, my dear,
And the rocks melt wi' the sun;
And I will luve thee still, my dear,
While the sands o' life shall run.
But fare-thee-weel, my only luve!
O, fare thee weel, awhile!
And I will come again, my luve,

Tho' 'twere ten thousand mile!
Tho' 'twere ten thousand mile, my luve,
Tho' 'twere ten thousand mile,
And I will come again, my luve,
Tho 'twere ten thousand mile!

Meri had sung along many times when her father had crooned the familiar ballad to her mother, but never before had the song stirred her so deeply. Never before had the words *my bonnie lass,* or *my only luve* been directed at her in a lovely baritone; emphasized by a pair of luminous hazel eyes.

She was trembling by the time the song ended and closed her eyes to hide the sheen of tears. She'd always chuckled when some old book hero serenaded the heroine beneath a balcony, but it wasn't a laughing matter. It was one of the most heart-touching moments of her life, and her emotions were about to leak all over the wagon bed.

Meri swallowed past the lump in her throat and joined the singing when they switched to the lively old "Will Ye Go Lassie?" tucking the experience deep in her heart. There would be plenty of time to examine the moment in detail in the quiet of her room.

"Ye huv a fine singing voice, laddie, and a knowledge of the auld songs, I would be able to tell ye were a Scotsman even if I didn't ken ye carried a guid Scottish name." Faither's brogue was in full force as he spoke over his shoulder.

Wyatt was riding abreast of Meri in the wagon, putting him slightly behind McIsaac. "Aye, me granfaither spoke the Gaelic and taught all the wee bairns the auld songs." Wyatt mimicked McIsaac's brogue perfectly, and Meri laughed as he grinned at her, obviously proud of himself.

The remainder of the ride flew by and, all too soon, they slowed to a stop at the front porch of the ranch house. Their arrival acted as a signal. Ms. Maggie, Barnaby and the rest of the ranch hands swarmed the wagon.

"Is anybody left to watch after the cattle?" McIsaac's voice was gruff, but his eyes twinkled brightly.

"Boss man, when they heard she was coming home today, I had a near mutiny on my hands. All of a sudden nobody wanted to be a cowboy anymore; they were too busy taking baths and stinking up the bunkhouse with their hair tonics and smelly potions. This bunch of dandies would start a stampede if the cattle caught sight or smell of them. I figured it was safer to keep 'em home today. Maybe you can do something with them."

It was the longest speech Meri had ever heard from Barnaby, and she swallowed a giggle at the sight of the cleanest, reddest-faced ranch hands she'd ever seen. Wyatt, still mounted on Charger, reached to give her a hand up as she rose to her feet to address them. "Thank you for the warm welcome. I've missed each of you, and I'm very glad to be home."

Rough voices called out greetings as they jostled each other for the best position at the back of the wagon to help her down. Meri hesitated, wondering how to handle the situation. Whom did she allow to help her descend? Wars had started with less provocation.

Her quandary resolved itself when a strong forearm circled her waist and lifted her easily out of the wagon to sit across muscular thighs.

Wyatt reined Charger around the wagon, circling until they stood at the porch's edge, and Meri heard a muttered, "So that's how the land lies…" as Wyatt lowered her gently to her feet on the porch.

Wyatt tipped the brim of his hat slightly. "Thank you for allowing me to escort you home, Miss Mc-Isaac."

"Are you leaving so soon?" She couldn't keep the disappointment from her voice.

"I need to get back, but with your permission, I'd like to call on you Saturday afternoon." He spoke firmly and clearly as if some of the assembled men might have trouble hearing, but their eyes and ears were firmly glued to the little tableau playing out before them. They weren't missing a single word.

"I would be honored, Marshal Cameron." Meri tilted her head like a queen bestowing a favor.

A roguish grin twinkled through hazel eyes and promised retribution, but the onlookers saw only the matching nod. "Until Saturday then."

All eyes followed Wyatt as he departed and disappeared over the rise. When they turned back to the porch, they found Meri regally ensconced in one of the rockers. She rested her aching shoulder and reigned as queen while her humble subjects paid tribute with little carvings, pretty rocks, new leather reins and additional small trinkets.

After a Ms. Maggie–enforced rest in her room, a welcome-home feast finished the day in grand style. When she tumbled into bed that evening, tired and sore but not quite sleepy, she replayed the events of the day, smiling as the strains of a Scottish ballad filtered through her thoughts. Excitement and apprehension concerning Saturday threatened to keep her awake, but a weary body prevailed and worry surrendered to dreams of a handsome, singing lawman.

Wyatt had to force himself to wait until Saturday to return to the McIsaac ranch. After all, he did have a job to do, but the three days felt like a month. At times a vague fear that Meri's soft smiles were simply gratitude for catching the men responsible for her and McIsaac's injuries would trouble him. At other times, a memory, like the heart-in-her-eyes look she'd worn when he'd sung the Scottish ballad to her, would leave him grinning like a simpleton.

Friday afternoon he was passing the front window of the Van Deusen mercantile, and the new window display caught his eye. A delicate parasol sat unfurled next to a handsome picnic basket. The image of Meri twirling the parasol over her shoulder as they sat together on a picnic blanket halted his steps and turned his feet toward the mercantile door. Before he could change his mind, he entered the store, plucked the parasol and picnic basket from the window and carried them to the counter where Mr. Van Deusen carefully wrapped the parasol in brown paper.

Wyatt was counting his blessings for the quiet, reserved Thomas and the absence of the voluble Naoma as he picked up his parcels and thanked the storekeeper.

Thomas nodded, waiting until Wyatt was at the door before speaking. "Happy courtin', Marshal."

The bell over the door jingled a jolly laugh as Wyatt exited, feeling an unaccustomed heat in his cheeks. Hurrying to his room at the back of the marshal's office, he tucked the items out of sight underneath his bed. He was guardedly eager to court Miss McIsaac; he wasn't quite so enthusiastic to be teased for his previously unknown romantic streak. He'd never seen Meri carry a parasol, but he had a hunch she might like it. After all, she had worn that fancy purple dress to church with her hair swept up so pretty. The parasol would just complete the picture.

Saturday morning he painstakingly tied the slender brown package to his saddle and rode toward the ranch. Keeping Charger to a fairly sedate canter, he tried to bring his attack of nerves under control. For the first time in years, he'd cut himself shaving this morning because of unsteady hands. When Jonah arrived after breakfast to watch the office, he had simply shaken his head and laughed at Wyatt's bloody face.

He topped the rise above the ranch and gingerly felt his cheek. Good. The bleeding had stopped.

A slender figure stood from the porch rocker and walked to the edge of the porch.

Wyatt took off his hat and gave a short wave. Meri lifted a hand in acknowledgment, and his nervousness vanished.

For the first time since he'd met her, she wasn't turning and running when she saw him. The times he'd seen her after she'd been shot didn't count; she'd been too injured to run away if she'd wanted to. This time she was not only waiting on his arrival, she actually came forward to greet him.

Wyatt gave a whoop and jammed his hat farther onto his head. Charger lived up to his name, flying down the lane to the house. They came to a sliding halt at the porch, and Wyatt leaped off the horse and onto the porch in an effortless dismount.

Meri hadn't batted an eye as the horse had raced toward her and slid to a snorting halt nearly at her feet. Nor had she flinched when Wyatt had landed in front of her on the porch. That was his girl. Fearless almost to a fault.

Wyatt reached for her hand and kissed it. "You are looking remarkably pretty today, Mac." She was, too. Her eyes sparkled, and her pink blouse brought out the glow in her cheeks.

A smile accompanied her thank-you as the porch door opened, and Ian McIsaac stepped out. He greeted Wyatt and waved them toward the rocking chairs before picking up Charger's reins and leading him toward the barn.

Wyatt started to sit, but upon remembering the package he'd brought, sprang to his feet and off the porch. Running toward his horse, he brought a startled Ian to a stop and untied the paper-wrapped parasol. "Sorry. I forgot something."

Meri was chuckling and shaking her head when he landed back on the porch. "Should you see a doctor for those fits?"

"Keep it up, Mac, and I won't give you your surprise."

Eager curiosity filled her face as she looked at the slender object in his hand, but the question she asked wasn't what he was expecting. "Would you like a glass of lemonade after your long ride?"

He nodded. She filled a glass from the pitcher on the table and handed it to him before filling the second glass and sitting carefully.

He sat down in the other rocker before draining his glass. "How are you feeling? I notice you're not wearing your sling."

"I'm fine, and I don't need the sling as long as I keep my arm quiet." She eyed the package across his lap.

He grinned. "Getting curious?"

Her eyes flew back to his innocently. "No."

He laid the parcel across her lap. "Go ahead. See what's inside."

Her hand shook a little as she untied the string and slowly unwrapped his gift. A smile bloomed across her face, and she fingered the parasol's lace. "It's so pretty."

"I'm glad you like it. I thought we'd go for a stroll. I'd like to see your home, and this will keep the sun off your pretty face." His mother's romantic streak was apparently alive and well in her son.

A soft blush suffused her face. "I'd like that."

She stood, and he offered her his arm, taking the parasol from her as they stepped off the porch. Opening it, he held the sunshade over her head.

"I'm perfectly capable of carrying a parasol," she protested without force.

"I would hate it if you strained your poor shoulder carrying my gift." Wyatt grinned and tugged her a bit closer as they walked away from the house, pleased when she didn't argue further.

Ms. Maggie was ringing the bell for the noon meal the minute Meri finished giving him the grand tour of the ranch grounds. When the meal was over, Ian McIsaac excused himself to talk with Barnaby, and Ms. Maggie shooed Wyatt and Meri to the front porch.

The ranch lay silent and drowsy under the afternoon sun as they settled into the rocking chairs. Wyatt toed the porch and set the rocker in motion, listening to its faint creak for a moment. "Would you tell me about your mother?"

She was quiet for so long, he was afraid he'd upset her. "I, uh…" She blinked rapidly and a tear slid down her cheek. "Fiddlesticks! I don't cry the whole year after her death, and now I cry at the slightest thing."

"I didn't mean to upset you. You don't have to tell me anything, if you don't want to." Wyatt regretted his stupidity, cringing as another tear followed the first.

She shook her head. "No. I want to tell you about her. Just ignore my leaky face, please." She leaned her head against the back of the rocker. "Growing up, it was Faither, Mither and me against the world. There weren't a lot of children around when I was small, and my whole world was my folks and then our ranch. We had so much fun together, even in those early hardscrabble days." She smiled a little. "Faither is the dreamer and planner. Mither was our rock." She laughed deprecatingly. "She was very even-tempered, not like me at all. When Faither or I got too excited, she'd calm us down. On the other hand, she had the driest sense of humor and could raise our spirits whenever either of us got down. And then, out of the blue, she became sick."

She broke off on a sobbed breath and another tear wet her cheek. Wyatt dug out his handkerchief. He leaned over and ever so gently blotted her cheeks.

Watery brown eyes met and clung to his. "Thank you." The words were so quiet he saw rather than heard them. He nodded and pressed the handkerchief into her hand.

She sniffed. "When we realized just how ill she was, I starting praying like I'd never prayed before, but one night, she slipped away. Faither was beside himself. I stayed strong for him even though the only world I'd ever known was shattered. When he started healing, he wanted to talk about her, but the only way I could cope was not to think about her. The better Faither got, the angrier I became. The morning before he was shot, he simply mentioned her on the way into town, and I nearly snapped his head off." She ducked her head. "I was feeling guilty about that and running away from another of Mrs. Van Deusen's matchmaking attempts when I ran into you. I'm sorry I took it out on you."

Wyatt covered the hand that was gripping the arm of the rocker with his own. Her eyes flew up and met his. "I'm tough. You didn't hurt me. You just very effectively grabbed my attention."

"I didn't mean to." Her cheeks went pink, and her eyes widened. "I mean…"

He smiled and squeezed her hand. "I know what you mean. You caught me by surprise, too. I had a plan, I had a dream and I wasn't going to pursue a woman until I had those accomplished."

He heard her quick intake of breath before she spoke. "Are…are you pursuing me?"

Chapter Twenty-One

W_{yatt} grinned. "Yes, ma'am, but if you have to ask, I must be going about it all wrong."

Her hand had been curled over the arm of the rocker when his own had covered it. Now, however, she turned her hand until it was actually holding his, and he felt the pulse in her wrist racing madly. She cleared her throat. "No. You're not."

Wyatt's heart swelled at her shy glance, and for a moment, there was no need for any words to fill the silence.

"What is your dream?" She shifted slightly in the chair to face him better and grimaced a little.

"Are you hurting?" He was a cad for keeping her out here so long. She was injured.

"Sit down. I'm fine. I just rubbed against the back of the chair a little too hard."

He hadn't realized he'd stood, but he hovered over her for a long minute to make sure she was really okay before he sat back down. "Wouldn't you be more comfortable inside?"

"No. Now quit dodging the question. What is your dream?" A smile softened the order.

He grinned right back. Did she have any idea how

much she'd changed his dream? "I've long wanted a place of my own to raise good-quality horses—mix Charger's speed and bloodlines with some of these tough Western horses like your Sandy to produce a line that has both speed and endurance." It seemed so small compared to what he wanted now. He scooted his rocking chair closer to hers and reached for her hand again. "And maybe raise a family of my own."

She looked out across the front yard, her fingers tightening around his. "That's a nice dream. Do you have a particular place picked out yet?" A slight tinge to her cheeks belied the casual-sounding question.

Wyatt rubbed his thumb over the back of her hand. "No. I'm still looking." His eyes traced her profile. He could easily look at her all day.

She took a deep breath. "There's good horse land around here." She glanced toward him and just as quickly glanced away again. "And Franks could get you started with a couple of good mares." She paused slightly. "If you're interested." Her shy uncertainty was endearing and encouraging.

"I'm very interested." In everything about her.

Meri twisted to face him, her eyes bright with cautious hope. "You are?"

Wyatt smiled and nodded. "Any place you'd recommend?"

Her face lit up, and she immediately began to list the good and bad points of various pieces of land, growing more animated the longer she talked. She attempted once to pull her hand away to emphasize a point, but he kept his grasp until it nestled back down.

His heart busy with plans, Wyatt relaxed into his chair, content for the moment to enjoy the expressive face of his new dream.

* * *

Meri twirled in front of the mirror for a final inspection, the skirt of the new dress flaring softly around her slim high-button shoes. Mother-of-pearl combs held her hair off her face, the length falling in soft waves down the back of a green calico dress sprinkled with tiny yellow flowers. She'd picked the fabric because the colors reminded her of the green-and-gold flecks in Wyatt's eyes while making her own hair gleam with golden highlights, and the cut flattered her figure with its slim bodice and full skirt.

"Hurry up, lass. We'll be late if ye don't quit fussin'."

Meri quickly pinned on a little straw confection of a hat, barely acknowledging the small twinge when her shoulder protested the movement. Picking up her Bible, reticule and lace parasol, she hurried from the room and down the stairs to her father and the awaiting buggy.

It had been a month since Meri had returned home, and Wyatt had ridden out to the ranch every subsequent Saturday afternoon. They would play checkers, stroll around the ranch, or as Meri healed, venture farther afield on horseback. On Sundays Wyatt would meet them at the church door, and he'd become an expected fixture in the McIsaac pew.

Meri smiled, admiring the lace-patterned shade the parasol cast over her skirt as the buggy rolled toward town and Sunday services. It was all frills and femininity, and she loved it. Because every time she went for a stroll with Wyatt, he insisted on carrying it. Which meant she had to walk very close to him.

The days stretched long during the week after seeing Wyatt on Saturday and Sunday, and she quickly found that absence truly did make her heart grow fonder. Occasionally Wyatt would make it out for supper during the week, but as she had resumed riding Sandy, her path somehow always wound up heading into Little Creek and the marshal's office.

Meri fingered the fabric of her dress. The mercantile and dressmaker had certainly benefited from her frequent trips to town, and she had the new dresses to show for it. Her feminine vanity had come to life with a belated vengeance.

Wyatt was waiting to assist her from the buggy, and he escorted her inside the church building. The service flew by with Meri endeavoring to pay attention to the music and sermon instead of Wyatt's nearness. Closing her eyes, she focused her wandering attention on the verses the pastor had read instead of the arm laid casually along the back of the pew, just brushing her shoulders.

Thank You, Lord, that You defend us and that Your joy is our strength. Thank You for defending me against the evil intentions of Mr. Samuels, for showing me that I am not strong when I try to stand on my own, but I am strong when You are my strength. Help me to remember joy isn't found in my circumstances, it's found only in You. Wyatt shifted, turning her attention back to him. *Father, I'm in love with this man, and I think he loves me. Would You give us wisdom, and if he does love me, would You remind him that he hasn't told me?*

"Amen."

Meri's eyes flew open in surprise as Wyatt's voice uttered the single word. Had she spoken aloud? No. The congregation was standing, gathering their belongings and chatting with one another. Service was over.

Wyatt grabbed her hand and hustled her toward the back door. After greeting the pastor, he hurried her outside to the buggy. Hands spanning her waist, he lifted her onto the seat.

"Where's the fire?" Meri asked, amused as he loosed the horses from the hitching rail before climbing into the buggy. "Wait, this isn't Faither's buggy."

"Nope." Reaching behind him, he pulled out Meri's parasol, opened it and handed it to her.

She took it and glanced curiously at the uncommunicative man beside her, but he ignored her silent question. She'd left the parasol under the seat of her father's buggy before services started and hadn't seen him or Faither move it.

Wyatt guided the horses around the other conveyances parked about the churchyard, clucking to them as they turned onto the road. Meri looked back at the church building as the horses broke into a quick-stepping trot. They'd departed the building so quickly no one else had exited the doors yet; everyone was still inside visiting.

"This could be considered kidnapping, you know," she said seriously, hoping to get an explanation out of him.

"It would be, if your father didn't know my plans."

"Aha. So you had a conspirator in your nefarious schemes." She twisted on the seat to see him better, her back brushing the armrest.

"Yup."

The man made Mr. Van Deusen look like a blabbermouth. "May I know what your plans are?"

"Nope."

"I must warn you, I get very hungry when I'm kidnapped. I hope you brought food." She twirled her parasol and watched it spin over her head.

"Been kidnapped often?"

"Dozens of times, but they always brought me back and told Faither I ate too much."

Wyatt had kept both hands on the reins, looking steadily down the road and keeping a straight face at her foolishness, but now he shifted the reins to one hand. His free hand snaked around her waist and pulled her up against him on the bouncing buggy seat.

"That's better. Can't have you so far away you think you can escape."

Meri loved riding Sandy alongside Wyatt and Charger, racing each other or merely exploring together the past few weeks, but a buggy ride had its own distinct charm. Especially when a handsome lawman had his arm wrapped around you.

Silence surrounded them as the scenery rolled by, but she was more absorbed in the delightful sensations caused by her traveling companion than the passing landscape. They headed in the direction of the ranch, but before they reached the rise that allowed them to see the ranch buildings, Wyatt turned the horses off onto a trail that climbed gradually to a high meadow. The sun was shining brightly and butterflies were busily flitting around the wildflowers dotting the large expanse of open ground.

Wyatt pulled the team to a stop under the trees that fringed the edge alongside a cool, clear stream. Hopping down, he turned and reached for Meri, swinging her to the ground easily. "Would you care to have a picnic with me?" He reached into the back of the buggy and held up a large picnic basket.

Meri looked around slowly and grinned. "Well… since I'm hungry and since you seem to be the only other person around… I suppose I'll have a picnic with you."

Wyatt's eyes danced. "I appreciate your kindness. If you'll give me a couple of minutes to tend to the horses, we'll eat."

He set the basket down and moved to the horses. Unhitching them, he led them to the water for a long drink, hobbled them and turned them out on the grass to graze. Retrieving the basket, along with a thick quilt, he offered his arm to Meri and led her farther up the sloped meadow to a large, shady tree that stood magnificently alone in the center of the field.

Meri helped him spread the quilt and sat down, legs curled to the side. "I've always loved this spot."

"That's what your father said."

"He knows we're here?"

"I didn't tell him specifically, but he probably guessed."

He busied himself filling two plates with delicious-looking pieces of fried chicken, sliced cheese, fresh tomatoes, pickles, biscuits and cold baked beans. She accepted the food and cup of lemonade he handed her, closing her eyes when he offered a quick blessing. They hungrily dug into their food; comfortable silence high-lighted by the sounds of trickling water in the distance and birds flitting back and forth over their heads.

Meri thought back to her prayer in church; at the rate they were going, there would be no confession of feelings today. In all the times they'd been together re-cently, she'd never seen him this quiet and enigmatic. She finished her food and set the plate aside.

"Dessert?"

"Not right now, thank you." She watched, fascinated, as Wyatt refilled his plate and continued eating. Where did he find room for it all? There wasn't an ounce of spare flesh anywhere on the man.

When he finished, he set his plate aside and flopped back, head cradled on his crossed arms. He closed his eyes and let out a satisfied groan. "That tasted good."

"It did. You're a man of many skills, Marshal," Meri teased, standing to her feet to put some distance between herself and the man who overloaded her senses just by his very presence.

One eye slid open lazily. "I thought we settled this."

"Settled what?" Meri feigned innocence and didn't wait for an answer but turned to stroll across the meadow.

A growl sounded. She looked over her shoulder to see him surge to his feet quicker than she thought should have been possible. She was running before she realized what she was doing, pulse racing harder than her feet when she heard him drawing closer. Changing directions unexpectedly, she managed to evade him, lifting the hem of her skirt to keep it from tangling around her ankles and wishing she were wearing her much more practical split skirt.

Feeling him behind her, she darted to the side again, but he was anticipating it, and muscular arms closed like steel bands around her. She emitted a surprised squeak and stumbled to a rather ungraceful halt. She tried to step away but the arms refused to yield their captive. He turned her to face him.

Heart racing and breath coming in quick little gasps, she looked up into his face.

"I can't have you running away with my heart if

you can't remember my name. You just might forget you even have it, and then where would I be?" He held her loosely, but there was no escaping the arms that enfolded her, or the eyes that devoured hers.

"Do I still have it?" she whispered. Her eyes fastened on an eye-level shirt button.

The sinewy bands around her tightened, drawing her inexorably closer, and she braced her hands against an expanse of rock-hard chest.

"Ah, Meri," he crooned. "Don't you *know* I love you? You irretrievably have my heart whether you want it or not. I'm just hoping you do." One hand came up to lift her head, knuckles lightly grazing her chin as his thumb caressed her jawline.

"You love me?" She thought she uttered the words, but his hand on her face was causing her heart to do all sorts of acrobatics, and she wasn't at all sure her tongue was still in proper working order.

"Didn't you realize I love you? I said you had my heart." One hand caressed the wavy hair hanging down her back.

"I wasn't sure… I mean… I hoped so, but you didn't say it…specifically… I don't know. I guess I'm pretty naive when it comes to things like this." Meri ducked her burning face and leaned her head into his chest to hide from his keen eyes.

Both arms enveloped her and held her close, the silence allowing her to hear the steady thump of his heart. "Well?"

Meri felt the vibration of the low question rumble through his chest. Captivated, she waited for it to happen again.

He shook her a little. "I'm waiting."

"Hmm?" She wanted to place her ear to his chest and hear that interesting rumble again.

His hands shifted to her arms, and he nudged her back a step, leaning down slightly to peer into her eyes. "Do *you?*"

She smiled into his eyes. "Yes. I love you." It felt as wonderful to say the words as to hear them.

They were barely out of her mouth when he hauled her back to his chest. She fully anticipated a kiss, but he only tucked her head under his chin and held her tight as a gusty sigh of relief escaped him. "Thank You, Lord!"

Meri's heart mirrored his prayer of thanksgiving. *He loved her.* Her arms tightened around his waist as she smiled and inhaled the scent that was Wyatt Cameron.

She was abruptly pushed back, and hazel eyes peered intently into hers. "I have a solution."

"For what?"

"For remembering my name. Permanently."

Her breath froze. He sank to one knee and gathered her hands in his. "Miss America Catriona McIsaac, would you change your name to mine?"

Tears sprang to her eyes, and she hastily blinked them away so she could see his face clearly. She wanted to remember this moment. "Yes." The answer barely whispered past her lips.

He looked at her with hopeful uncertainty. "You'll marry me?"

"Yes." She nodded. "I'll marry you." That came out a little stronger.

A huge smile lit his face, and he stood, gathering her tenderly in his arms. Her hands slipped up to his shoulders. "Wait." He leaned back slightly. "Yes, I'll marry you, what?"

She smiled a bit mistily. "Yes, I'll marry you. Thank you for asking."

"That's not quite what I had in mind." He leaned in and placed a tiny kiss on her nose.

Breathing was highly overrated. "Did you not want me to say yes?"

"You little minx. Of course I wanted you to say yes. But who are you saying yes to?"

She circled his neck with her hands, sliding her fingers into his closely cropped hair. "Yes, I'll marry you, Wyatt Cameron."

A huge smile bloomed across his face and took what little breath Meri had left. "That's what I wanted to hear."

His eyes caressed her face, and she rose up on tip-toes to meet him halfway. He leaned down and settled his lips against hers in a first kiss. The world rocked and then stood still and silent except for the sound of each other's heartbeats. Wyatt tightened his grip and straightened, lifting Meri off her feet as he continued kissing her.

The kiss lasted a lifetime and was entirely too short. He twirled her around, throwing his head back and laughing joyously. She was dizzy when he set her down, leaning in for a second kiss that trailed over her eyes, cheeks and nose before landing hungrily on her lips.

She could get used to this.

When they finally pulled apart, breathless, he tucked her head under his chin and snuggled her close. They stood that way for several minutes, simply enjoying the moment. Finally he snuggled her under his arm, and they walked back to the forgotten picnic blanket.

"Do you want dessert now?"

"Yes. I'm suddenly hungry again," Meri admitted, surprised.

"Good." He helped her sit down and knelt by the basket. "Close your eyes."

She did and listened to the sounds of his rummaging around.

"Okay. You can open them." A plate holding a large piece of a dark-colored cake topped with cream balanced on his outstretched hand.

Meri shot him a puzzled grin. "Gingerbread?"

"Yep. It will forever remind me of you, our first picnic together and the spice you bring to my life. I had Ms. Maggie bake it for me when I asked your father's permission to marry you yesterday. I thought it'd be the perfect way to finish our picnic today."

Meri blinked, stunned. Her father had known and hadn't said anything? A smile blossomed slowly; God had answered her prayer this morning before she'd ever even prayed it. "You were certain I'd say yes?"

"No. But I had a backup plan in case you said no."

"What?"

"I didn't intend to let you go until you said yes." He winked and laughed when her attempted scowl shattered into a pleased grin.

Taking the plate, fork and quick kiss he offered her, she dug into the gingerbread. Never before had it tasted quite so delicious.

Epilogue

Summer flew by in a flurry of preparations for a late-September wedding.

Wyatt purchased the meadow and surrounding acreage from Meri's father, and the town threw a house-and barn-raising social. The house was small but cozy with plenty of space to build on as needed, and the barn had ample capacity for Charger and Sandy and the other horses they intended to raise.

Meri would be near her father, Wyatt was close enough to town to continue in his capacity of marshal, and Jonah had decided to remain permanently as deputy. Moreover the town council voted that in view of the recent bank robbery and expanding population they would hire a second deputy as soon as Wyatt found a suitable candidate.

The trial of Mr. Samuels and Mr. Mullins had ended; their fates decided by a judge and jury. Mr. Samuels would spend the rest of his life in prison, but Mullins was sentenced to death for his role in multiple shootings and robberies.

The townsfolk continued to shake their heads over

the fact that one of their own deceived everyone so completely. There were a few, however, that argued they'd been suspicious of him from the start.

The bank reopened its doors for business, but the new manager was finding it slow going to rebuild the trust that had been broken concerning the credibility of the bank. Meanwhile Mr. Van Deusen had picked up business since he had a good-size safe in his store, and for now, many people preferred to trust him with any savings they had.

Meri and Wyatt continued to fall deeper in love as the days passed. There were serious discussions and occasional arguments, lighthearted moments and of course, the inevitable teasing. One such moment transpired a couple of weeks after their engagement while they were planning the layout of their new home.

Meri was admiring her handsome husband-to-be as he stepped off the layout of house and barn when a thought occurred to her. "You know my middle name, but I don't know your full name." He continued pacing off measurements as if he hadn't heard her, so she trotted over to him. "Are you named after your father?" Again he didn't answer. "Are you ignoring me?"

"No, just the question." He continued his careful measuring steps.

"Why?" She matched his stride.

"Because it isn't important."

Meri stepped into his path and slammed her fists onto her hips, eyes narrowed. "You pestered me for weeks to use your name and now you won't tell me what it is?"

"You're a pest, and you know my name." He reached to move her out of his path, but she dodged his hand.

"Not all of it."

He sidestepped, but she stuck like a bur in front of him, ignoring his attempt to bait her and intrigued by the faint pink tinge just above his shirt collar.

"Are you blushing?"

He closed his eyes and sighed heavily. "Why are you making a big deal over this?"

"You *are* blushing," she crowed. "And it wasn't a big deal until you started evading the question. Now I'm curious, and I'm not letting you go until you tell me." She wrapped her arms around his waist and grinned up at him.

His own arms draped loosely around her shoulders, and he leaned in to brush his lips lightly over hers. Meri stretched up to deepen the kiss and forgot everything but the feel of his mouth on hers for the next few blissful moments. When he pulled back, she sighed happily and leaned her head on his chest. They remained in that position for a full minute before she recalled her mission.

"I haven't forgotten that you haven't answered my question, and I'll keep after you until you tell me."

"Of that I have no doubt, so… I'll tell you after we're married."

"But that's not 'til September."

"Uh-huh, it'll give you something to fuss over 'til then." He laughed when she growled at him and kissed her forehead, but he refused to give in.

She eventually changed the subject, a little miffed that he was having fun at her expense. After a couple more tries over the next few weeks, she put the question aside and focused on other things. The man was quite possibly more obstinate then she was, and she was head over heels in love with him. Best of all, she was fully loved in return. In spite of his refusal to share his full name.

At long last the day of the wedding rolled around. McIsaac walked his daughter down the aisle to the accompaniment of the newly arrived piano purchased with dessert auction proceeds, presenting Meri's hand to the marshal who'd captured her heart. The service was sweetly solemn, and when they exchanged their vows, Mrs. Van Deusen employed her handkerchief to dab teary eyes.

When Pastor Willis directed, "You may now kiss your bride," Wyatt eagerly obeyed. Meri emerged from the assault on her lips, breathless, blushing and beaming. The congregation broke into cheers and applause, and Pastor Willis presented them as Mr. and Mrs. Wyatt Cameron.

Following the ceremony everyone moved to the shade of the trees and feasted on a bountiful wedding luncheon. There was plenty of food and gifts for the bride and groom, as well as congratulations, well wishes and lots of good-natured advice. When the cake had been cut and served, Wyatt and Meri made their way to a shiny new buggy decorated with white ribbons and left the festivities to wind down without them.

Once out of sight and sound of the gathered wedding guests, Meri wrapped her arms around Wyatt and snuggled into his side. She peeked up at him through her lashes. "We're married, Mr. Cameron."

"I do believe that's what the preacher said, Mrs. Cameron." He squeezed her close and kissed her slowly, quite forgetting the animals attached to the other end of the reins.

In time the absence of motion alerted them to the fact the horses had taken advantage of their freedom to graze along the roadside, and Wyatt tightened up the sagging reins. Meri looped her arms around Wyatt's arm as he gently reminded the horses of their responsibility to carry them home, and a comfortable silence fell as they reveled in each other's presence and quick stolen kisses.

They were within sight of their home when Meri spoke. "Now that we're married, I believe you have something to tell me."

"I do?" He dropped a kiss on her upturned lips.

"You do. Now quit distracting me and 'fess up. Why wouldn't you tell me your name?"

He laughed. "Because wives can't testify against their husbands, and you weren't my wife yet."

Meri gently slapped his arm. "Be serious. What's so bad about your name?"

"It's a sad story." He sighed so tragically that Meri giggled at the affectation. "A month or two before I was born, mother was reading Shakespeare's *Twelfth Night*. She fell in love with one of the names in the book, and when I was born, she decided to burden me with it. Mother was the only one who ever used it, but I finally convinced her to stop about the time I was ten. I was tired of having to fight the boys who laughed at me when they heard her use my full name. And I think Mother was tired of patching me up."

Meri had read *Twelfth Night* years ago, but couldn't recall any names that would explain Wyatt's reluctance to share his full name.

He took a deep breath; released it. "My full name is Wyatt Valentine Cameron."

Meri kept a straight face with much difficulty, but her eyes were sparkling with glee. "I don't remember a Valentine in the book." She loved his name, and he looked absolutely disgusted.

"He was a minor character—Duke Orsino's attendant. Do you see why I dislike it?"

"No, I'm like your mother, I love the name Valentine."

"Thank you," he said dryly, "but you didn't have to grow up with it. Please don't use it in public, or I will have to resort to drastic measures."

Meri shrieked as his fingers tickled her ribs, and the horses flinched at the sudden outburst. Her giggles filled the air as the horses pulled the buggy up to the barn and stopped, looking back as if exasperated at the foolishness behind them.

Wyatt swung down from the buggy and reached for his new wife. He cuddled her close, ignoring her wiggling, and walked to the shady side of the barn to set her on her feet. "Stay there." His twinkling eyes softened the command.

He unhitched the horses and turned them into the grassy paddock, making quick work of hanging up the harness. Then he returned, swept her into his arms again and walked toward the sparkling new little house. Stepping onto the porch, he opened the door and carried his bride over the threshold, kicking the door closed behind them.

"Have I told you today that I love you, Mrs. Cameron?"

Meri sighed happily. "If you did, I've forgotten. Say it again, please."

Her arms wound snugly around his neck, her fingers luxuriating in the feel of his hair. She was content to stay in the safe haven of his strong arms forever.

"I love you, Mrs. Cameron." His nose touched hers.

"*I* love *you,* Wyatt Valentine." There was a twinkle in her eyes as she spoke.

He groaned, resting his forehead against hers. "Why do I get the feeling I'm going to regret wanting you to use my name, Mac?"

"That's Mrs. Cameron to you, and you asked me to call you by your name. I'm going to be a good, dutiful wife and obey you." It was hard to be prim and innocent when you were giggling.

He pulled his head back and gave her an incredulous look. "I'll believe *that* when I see it."

"Oh!" Meri's eyes widened as a thought suddenly occurred to her.

"What?" His eyes narrowed suspiciously.

"We should have waited to be married until February 14!"

"And that's exactly why I didn't tell you my full name, Mrs. Cameron." He plopped down onto the lovely new divan and started pulling pins from her elegant chignon.

"But it would have been perfect! On Valentine's Day, I would marry my very own Valentine!"

Wyatt snarled menacingly and tickled her ribs until helpless giggles pealed forth, filling the room with the happy sound.

"Stop, Wyatt Valentine Cameron!" she gasped breathlessly, futilely trying to escape.

"Hmm...if that doesn't work, maybe this will shut

you up." He nestled her close, imprisoning her lips with his own in a bone-melting kiss.

Meri began to giggle again, and Wyatt pulled back, puzzled. "What's so funny?"

"If this is the consequence of using your full name, I'll never call you anything else, Wyatt Valentine!"

Wyatt Valentine Cameron was more than happy to mete out her punishment swiftly and thoroughly.

* * * * *